NO ACCIDENT

NO ACCIDENT

BY

ROBERT CROUCH

www.penmorepress.com

No Accident by Robert Crouch
Copyright © 2016 Robert Crouch

ISBN-13: 978-1-942756-66-8(Paperback)
ISBN :-978-1-942756-67-5 (e-book)

BISAC Subject Headings:
FIC022090FICTION / Mystery & Detective / Private Investigators
FIC022000FICTION / Mystery & Detective / General
FIC022100FICTION / Mystery & Detective / Amateur Sleuth

Editing: Chris Wozney
Cover Illustration by Christine Horner

Address all correspondence to:

Penmore Press LLC
920 N Javelina Pl
Tucson AZ 85748

DEDICATION

DEDICATION

Dedicated to Carol, my wife, best friend and inspiration.

ACKNOWLEDGEMENTS

I'd like to thank Tamara McKinley for her help, support and inspiration over the years; to Jim Bond for his encouragement and the introduction that started it all, and to Michael James for believing in me.

REVIEWS OF NO ACCIDENT

With a lead character who is so much more than "just another copper", Robert Crouch has brought both a fresh voice and a new twist to conventional crime drama.

—**Alaric Bond**, author of *True Colours* and *The Scent of Corruption* in the Fighting Sail series.

In the quirky tradition of the English whodunnit, Robert Crouch has produced a murder mystery which will keep you reading through the night. Agatha Christie fans will love it!

—**Tamara McKinley**, author of *Undercurrents* and *Firestorm*.

This is a traditional English murder mystery, and at its heart is Kent Fisher—a man with a troubled past, an aptitude for witty one-liners and the fashion sense of Detective Columbo on a bad day! When Kent attends what looks like an industrial accident, his inquiring mind and natural suspicion leads him into an investigation that will ultimately challenge all he's ever believed in. A most enjoyable read.

—**Ellie Dean**, author of *While We're Apart* and *Sweet Memories of You.*

THURSDAY

CHAPTER ONE

I'm the best officer to investigate this accident, and probably the worst. But let's focus on the positive—Miles Birchill could be dead.

It's a long shot, I admit. Downland's wealthiest resident is more likely to be entertaining celebrity friends in his London casino than dying in a remote corner of East Sussex. But you never know.

Only 40 minutes ago, after a night in a hide with ten badger enthusiasts, I'd arrived home, longing for my bed. The phone call from my boss put paid to that. After a quick shower, I pulled on the only ironed shirt from the wardrobe. Electric blue may be more suited to clubbing than accident investigation, but I could soon be dancing on someone's grave.

It feels strange to be back in the only stretch of woodland ignored by the bulldozers that plundered 500 acres of England's countryside to create Tombstone Adventure Park. Surrounded by oak, ash and sycamore, I listen to wood pigeons struggling to be heard above the coarse cries of crows that have overwhelmed the area. In the grass alongside the barn, a green woodpecker searches for insects.

When it sees me climb out of my Ford Fusion, it laughs and flies away, obviously amused by my shirt.

Despite the early hour, the air is hot and humid for the third week of September. A few shards of sunlight pierce the foliage and bounce off the windscreens of the patrol car and the silver Peugeot 206 convertible beside it. Ahead, a charcoal grey hearse waits with its hatch open, ready to swallow a coffin.

My fingers skim along the black weatherboarding that cloaks the barn. It's low grade softwood, riddled with knots and blemishes, unlike the large sliding doors, clasped together by a hefty padlock. A healthy strip of grass and weeds run along the base, telling me the doors have remained closed for some time. I stretch up to peer through a small glass panel, but a film of dust and bird droppings obscures the view inside.

"Machinery, Mr. Fisher. It's full of machinery."

The reek of cigar smoke tells me it's Alasdair Davenport, long before his lazy drawl reaches my ears. Tollingdon's most successful independent undertaker—as he describes himself in his brochure—has a sympathetic, effortless manner that reassures grieving relatives. But I can't take to a man who's passionate about embalming.

Everything about him is pale, from the thinning blond hair beneath his Stetson to a complexion the colour of bone. Eyes the colour of dirty washing-up water look me over.

"The machines have never been used," he says, staring at my shirt. "I find that unusual, don't you?"

Not as unusual as an undertaker in a lumberjack shirt tucked into old jeans. All he needs are spurs and he'd be at home in the Wild West theme park. Or maybe he listens to Dolly Parton while he pumps formaldehyde into corpses. Thankfully, he makes no effort to shake my hand.

"Some say it's haunted." His colleague, who also looks ready for line dancing, strolls up, eyes wide with intrigue. "Trevor Maynard and his missus died here in a fire about five years ago. Some say their troubled souls remain."

Davenport takes an impassive last draw on the stub of his cigar and blows the smoke into the air. "They're waiting for you in the clearing, Mr. Fisher."

"Is it as bad as it sounds?"

He grinds the cigar into the dirt. "All violent deaths are bad."

It could be a social comment or a criticism of anything that hampers embalming.

"Not if you're an undertaker," I say, slipping past.

The clearing seems unusually quiet and peaceful. After a steady diet of cop shows on TV, I suppose I'd expected to see crime scene officers in white coveralls, crawling over the grass. There's no barrier tape to cordon off the Massey Ferguson tractor and bench mounted circular saw. The two uniformed constables are in no position to stop me trotting down the slope to the fibreglass coffin, resting with its lid to one side.

And who's in charge?

The sound of retching disturbs the stillness. At the far edge of the clearing, a man in jogging pants is bent over some bushes. The nearest constable looks up briefly and then examines his fingernails once more. The second constable, who looks like he spends too much time in the staff canteen, calls out to me.

"Stay where you are. This area's out of bounds."

He hurries over, his cheeks reddening with each step. When he pulls up in front of me, I hold up my ID card. He takes a look and calls over his shoulder. "Miss Montague? Environmental health officer's arrived."

A woman in a white coverall emerges from the vinyl tractor cab and thuds to the ground. Short and stocky, she has a bullish face, dominated by a thick nose, flattened at the tip. I can't help wondering if she spent her youth with her face pressed against a window, wishing she were inside. She swings her arms as she powers up the slope, ploughing through the fan of blood and flesh on the grass. Her cheap perfume reaches me seconds before she does.

"You come straight from a nightclub, Mr. Fisher?" she asks, pointing a short finger at my shirt. "Is that why you're late?"

"I'd demand a refund from the charm school, if I were you," I reply.

Her steel grey eyes fix me with a piercing stare as she puffs out her chest. "You're not what I expected, Mr. Fisher. You don't talk posh, and you're nothing like your father. So why do they call you Lord Snooty?"

They don't. Seven years ago, during an interview, the Lifestyle Editor of the *Tollingdon Tribune* asked me why I'd never married. "I prefer animals to people," I'd told her. "Animals never let you down."

If I sounded aloof, it was unintentional, but it coloured the whole article. My father, the Conservative MP for Downland, owned a vast country estate, so she dubbed me Lord Snooty.

"Maybe you should tell me who you are in case I misjudge you," I say.

She takes a few moments to smile and then thrusts out her hand, still covered with a disposable glove. "I'm Carolyn Montague, the new Coroner's Officer. I think we'll get along fine."

"You're not the inspector in charge?"

4

"DI Briggs is probably on his second round of toast by now. Soon as he realised we had a work accident he left me in charge. I called your governor, Daniella Frost, over an hour ago."

I say nothing, wondering why Danni took half an hour to ring me.

"I have three fatalities back at the ranch, so I'd like to get on," she says. "You wanted to check the body."

"I didn't want the scene disturbed."

She turns toward the tractor and points. "You got any idea what a power takeoff can do? It's the shaft in the middle that powers the bench saw."

"It spins at a lethal speed," I say, aware the guard is missing. "Catch a loose sleeve or cuff and it can rip your arm off."

"Imagine what it can do if you're wearing a tie." She smacks a fist into the palm of her hand. "There wasn't much of his face left. Most of it's strewn across the grass, as you can see. We couldn't leave him like that."

It's a fair point, well made. "Is DI Briggs coming back?"

"For a simple work accident?"

In my experience, few work accidents are simple. Companies are quick to blame employees for ignorance, breaking rules or horseplay, but employers can be negligent, either intentionally or by omission.

"Don't the police take the lead in case it's corporate manslaughter?" I ask, wishing I could remember the protocol.

"Corporate manslaughter? Come on! The guy got careless. End of." She heads over to the coffin. "I saw plenty when I was in uniform and Scenes of Crime. That's why DI Briggs left me in charge. You can ring him if you want."

I ignore the phone she holds out. "I'm not questioning your competence. We've never had a fatal work accident in Downland."

"I thought you were the council's most experienced officer."

"That doesn't mean I've investigated a fatality. I'd appreciate your help."

"I'll send you copies of my photographs," she says, bending to unzip the body bag. "I reckon he dropped his cigarette and bent to pick it up."

I point to the man in jogging pants. "Did he see it happen?"

"Mr. Cheung was out running. He came past shortly after the incident." She wrinkles her nose when she pulls the body bag open. "You can have a copy of my interview notes too— unless you want to talk to him."

Jogging Man, who looks about 19 or 20, seems to have had the life sucked out of him. Pale and shaken, he won't forget this morning in a hurry. Me neither, I suspect.

"I hope you have a strong stomach, Mr. Fisher."

I've seen the suffering and injuries people inflict on animals. And as much as I want to hurt those people, I've learned to suspend my emotions, to work calmly and effectively to save the poor animals.

After a deep breath to prepare myself, I look into the coffin.

Ouch! I wasn't expecting that.

The victim's face is a mess of red raw flesh and torn muscle, clinging to the bone beneath. Blood, congealed into dark syrup, leaks over the shirt and boiler suit he's wearing. The odour of death reminds me of a slaughterhouse.

"Doesn't look like he could face the day," I hear myself saying.

Carolyn nods. "Gallows humour. I like it."

I take a closer look at the victim. He has grey hair, cut military style, and a deep scar that bisects his right eyebrow. That's all I can determine with any certainty.

"You mentioned a tie, Carolyn."

"I cut what was left away to release him. It's bagged if you want to look."

I glance up the slope, wishing Lucy would hurry up with our Grab Bag. It contains everything we need for emergencies, including digital camera, blank notices and witness statement forms, tape measure, flashlight, and our emergency procedures. While I wait, I take some photographs with my Blackberry. If the guard had not been removed from the takeoff the victim would be alive. Had he buttoned his boiler suit, or not worn a tie, I'd be asleep in bed.

I step aside to let the undertakers remove the coffin. While I make some notes, Carolyn peels off her coverall and shoe protectors and balls them into a polythene bag. Her black blouse and jeans are a little too tight and her old trainers are practical rather than fashionable. After a mouthful of mineral water, she strides over.

"The first one's always the worst. How do you feel?"

"Puzzled," I reply, looking up. "Why was he wearing a tie?"

"My dad wore a shirt and tie when he mowed the lawn."

Mine too, but lawn mowers don't kill. "What time did the accident happen?"

"Mr. Cheung ran past around six twenty."

"Two hours ago? That's a bit early to start work, isn't it?"

She gestures at my shirt. "Or a bit late to go to bed."

I glance at the machinery, set in an isolated clearing in the middle of woodland at least a mile from the main park. What's it doing here, adjacent a barn that's never used?

"Have you identified him?" I ask.

She reaches into a flight case and pulls out an evidence bag, containing credit cards and a driving licence. "Sydney Collins with two 'Y's. Why, I don't know." Her self-conscious laugh doesn't make the joke any better. "Have you heard of him?"

"No."

"You know Miles Birchill, though."

He would be my specialist subject on Mastermind. He worked for my father in the stables for years and then tack, and valuables began to go missing. While he was never charged with theft, he disappeared from the scene. He emerged a few years later, buying rundown rented properties in Brighton and Hove during the 80s and 90s.

"He evicted tenants from their flats and sold the properties with vacant possession," I say. "He made a killing."

Carolyn nods. "Collins did the evicting. Men or women— he didn't discriminate. He threw them out of windows, dumped them naked on the South Downs in winter, you name it. People were too scared to complain," she says, sensing my question. "He knew their families, where their children went to school. Well, he can't intimidate anyone now, can he? Not that anyone's going to miss him."

His family might. "I'll check the tractor now."

Collins kept the Massey Ferguson clean and polished on the outside, repairing the splits in the vinyl cabin with clear waterproof tape. I step onto the footplate and peer inside. Everything is coated in dust, except the stack of Nuts magazines in the foot well. The few editions I check feature models with impossibly black hair, fake tans, and oversized boobs.

Carolyn jumps up beside me. "They're in date order, in case you're interested."

I step down and head to the rear of the tractor. The power takeoff and three-point linkage that connects the bench saw to the tractor are splattered with blood and tissue. Even though the takeoff isn't spinning, I don't want to get too close. I'm more concerned with what brought Collins out here early. I walk over to a small enclosure crammed with fence posts. They're sharpened to points and stand in rows like giant pencils. The timber has greyed in the months, maybe years, since they were made. There's no timber waiting to be cut, so he didn't come out here to make fence posts.

Back at the tractor, I drop to my knees. Cigarette butts, all filter tipped, pepper the ground. If the power takeoff hadn't killed him, lung cancer would have. I'm about to get to my feet when I spot a rollup cigarette, speckled with blood, directly below the takeoff.

"Carolyn, do you have an evidence bag?"

She retrieves one from her flight case. "What have you found?"

"A rollup among the filter tips. Someone else was here."

"Mr. Cheung rolls his own. He could have dropped it when he found Collins."

I glance across at Jogging Man. "Runners don't usually smoke."

"He does. Maybe he dropped it after he spotted Collins."

"Then it wouldn't be covered with blood."

"Good point. Maybe it belonged to Collins and when he bent to retrieve it, his tie became entangled."

A diet of Lieutenant Columbo films has made me curious about anything that's out of place or unusual. I doubt if the rollup will play any part in the investigation, but at least it looks like I know what I'm doing. I stretch my arms between the lower linkage and takeoff, careful to avoid any contact, and nudge the rollup into the evidence bag with my pen.

"Why did Collins come here this morning?" I ask when I'm back on my feet. "He didn't need any fence posts."

Carolyn shrugs. "I gave up trying to guess why people do what they do a long time ago. Stick to the facts, Kent. Collins wouldn't be the first worker to take a short cut, would he?"

"Tombstone wouldn't be the first employer to default in its duty to provide and maintain safe equipment."

"That's why we're here." She pauses, distracted by something behind me. "Is this your glamorous assistant?"

Lucy would laugh all the way to the Doc Marten shop if anyone described her as glamorous. It can only mean Danni has sent Gemma, the Chief Executive's niece. She joined the team a few months ago to give her something worthwhile to do. Apparently, waiting tables and beauty therapy are not worthy career choices.

She's dressed more for the beach than for work in a sleeveless white dress and matching sandals with diamante trims. Her glossy brown hair tumbles in thick waves around her slim face, half hidden by Audrey Hepburn sunglasses.

Though petite, her muscles are toned and supple, giving her the strength to grapple with the Grab Bag. She hoists the strap over her shoulder and brushes past the young constable, who looks desperate to help her. Gravity and the weight of the bag threaten to overbalance her as she careers down the slope, stumbling to a halt in front of me.

She looks back and gasps. "I nearly went ass over tit there. Just think, Kent, you nearly had the pleasure of me on the grass."

Her cheeky brown eyes, sparkling with confidence and humour, dare me to cast caution aside, but I'm too sensible for that. Gemma might be the most attractive woman I've met, but I daren't think of her in that way.

We met seven years ago when I called at La Floret, Tollingdon's most exclusive restaurant. Armed with my white coat, I went inside to carry out a food hygiene inspection. I wasn't expecting to find a young waitress on a chair, reaching up to change a light bulb. There's something about a white blouse, stretched to transparency over a well filled bra, which fires my imagination. Add a short black skirt, a mischievous smile, and remarks like, 'If anything takes your fancy, just ask,' and you'll understand my weakness for waitresses.

"Be careful," I said, as she stretched on tiptoes. "You might fall."

She looked down and smiled. "Then you'd better catch me."

By the time she jumped down and stumbled into my arms, I was in love.

The thud of the Grab Bag on the ground brings me back to the present. "I'm so pleased you chose me, Kent. I won't let you down."

"Even though I asked for Lucy?"

She pushes the hair from her eyes and looks up through long lashes. "Am I not good enough for you?"

I introduce her to Carolyn. While she explains her role, I check the Grab Bag.

"What do you want me to do?" Gemma asks.

I point to the ground. "Watch where you put your feet."

"Ugh, gross!" She places a hot hand on my shoulder and raises her foot to check the underside of her shoe. "You could have warned me."

Her face is inches from mine, radiating heat from her lightly-toasted skin. The subtle scent of soap wafts towards me. "That was close," she says, checking the other shoe. "I paid a fortune for these."

"An old pair of trainers would have been more sensible."

"You know I don't do sensible."

"Then it's time you did."

I lead her to the tractor and set the bag down on the footplate. She pulls out the camera and points it at me. "Didn't you wear a shirt like that the day we met?"

I can't tell her it's the same shirt. "You know blue's my favourite colour."

The arrival of a text message distracts her. She puts down the camera and fishes her phone out of a small flap in the bag. "It's Uncle Frank, wishing me luck. He's delighted you asked me to help."

"You called him? No wonder you took an eternity to get here."

She folds her arms and stares at me. "And how else was I supposed to get the office key so I could collect the Grab Bag?"

I should apologise, but she still took her time getting here. I take her round the machinery and tell her what I want photographed. I ask for scene setting shots of the clearing, the barn, the tractor and the fence post enclosure.

"Take plenty at the back here, and zoom in on the power takeoff," I say. "Give each photograph a unique code—date, initials and consecutive reference numbers. Record them in your notebook so we can use them as evidence later. Can you manage that, Gemma?"

"I can if you promise not to patronise me."

I return to Carolyn, who's grinning. "I wish she looked at me the way she looks at you."

"I wish she'd dress for an accident investigation. I mean, look at those shoes. No protection, no arch support."

"I'm only saying she likes you, Kent. And she's very pretty."

"She's engaged and I'm almost twice her age."

She smirks. "And your father's much older than your mother."

I bite back a retort, fed up with people comparing me to my father. "Actually, she's my stepmother."

"And here's your favourite cowboy."

I follow her gaze to the top of the clearing, where a black Mercedes glides to a halt. The last time I saw Miles Birchill, I'd just emptied the contents of a muck spreader into his convertible.

CHAPTER TWO

Miles Birchill owns casinos, clubs and a Wild West theme park in Sussex, but none of them are household brands. He mixes with politicians, footballers and pop stars, all past their prime. Photographs of him with bleached blondes make the inside pages of the tabloids, but not the covers of the gossip magazines. He's Downland's richest resident, but every year the local golf club turns down his application to join.

Close but no cigar, as my father would say.

Too close for my liking. I was banking on a day, maybe two, before Birchill crossed my path. By then the investigation would be too advanced for him to interfere. No hope of that now. He's raced down from London to take charge, I suspect, and I'm his first challenge.

Maybe his second if you count the young constable who intercepts him.

Thanks to cosmetic surgery, Birchill can no longer smile or frown, leaving him with a frozen, almost startled expression. While the tucks have removed lines and wrinkles from his face, they can't erase the cold stare of contempt from his eyes. Gold rings glint like knuckledusters in the sun as he pushes his wiry black hair behind his ears.

"I'll take it from here," I tell the constable.

He steps back but continues to stare at Birchill, who unbuttons a designer jacket that costs more than I earn in a month. He hooks his thumbs behind the belt of his jeans. "I thought you'd rather die than set foot in my adventure park, Fisher."

"I would, but someone beat me to it."

He looks skywards and shakes his head. "Still trying to be the comedian instead of the joke, I see. Go on, amuse me. Tell me why you're here."

I point to the tractor. "One of your employees lost a fight with an unguarded power takeoff. That makes it a work accident."

He moves to one side to get a better view. "Nice try, but no one works here."

"Apart from Sydney Collins, you mean?"

"Syd never rises before ten." He pulls out his mobile phone. "I'll call him."

"That won't be necessary." Carolyn steps up beside me. She holds up the evidence bag with his credit card and driving licence. "Syd Collins is the victim."

Birchill takes a closer look. "And you are?"

She introduces herself. "I believe the two of you go way back, Mr. Birchill. If it's any consolation, he died instantly."

Birchill puts his phone away. "He's been dying for years. That's why he didn't work. He could hardly lift a fence post, let alone sharpen it."

"Then who made them?"

"He did, years ago. He bought the machinery from the Maynards. They lived in the farmhouse that was here before

I constructed the barn." He takes a cigarette from a gold case inside his jacket. He tamps the cigarette on the back of his hand. "The tractor broke down after a few months so he retired."

"It was working this morning," Carolyn says.

He lights the cigarette and exhales smoke through his nostrils. "Evidently, if it killed him."

She ignores the sneer in his voice. "Did you have it repaired?"

When he doesn't answer, I say, "Maybe Tombstone repaired it. You must have a maintenance contract."

"The machinery belonged to Syd. He was too ill to work. Without any work activity, you have no authority to be here, Fisher, and even less to question me."

I'm tempted to point out you can't get less than no activity, but resist. "If Tombstone serviced the tractor and bench saw that makes you liable. Do you want me to cordon off the area?"

"Tombstone is out of bounds to you. Or have you forgotten the court order?"

I wondered how long it would take him to mention that.

Carolyn looks at me for an explanation. "Court order?"

"It was only an injunction."

"A restraining order," Birchill says. "Fisher and his cronies chained themselves to trees. They dug tunnels and trenches to stop my contractors clearing the site. I had no choice."

I love the way developers play the injured party. They destroy habitats and wildlife to create hundreds of new jobs on zero hour contracts, and plead poverty. This time, I'm ready for him.

"The order applied while you were building Tombstone," I say. "Now the park's open it no longer applies."

"My lawyers will soon correct you on that."

"Your lawyers will be too busy dealing with a health and safety prosecution to worry about an injunction."

He extinguishes his cigarette between thumb and forefinger. "I'm sure my lawyers will be delighted to learn you've found me guilty of an offence before you've even started your investigation."

"Then you've nothing to fear from my investigation," I say, ignoring the reprimand in Carolyn's eyes. She's right—I should be careful what I say. I should ignore his arrogance and goading, but I'll never beat him playing by the rules.

Birchill stands there, arms folded as he considers his response. He knows he'll look bad if he tries to stop the investigation. His lawyers will soon advise him not to obstruct an official. Far better to claim persecution if things go against him. But if I prove he's broken the law, he's stuffed.

Like me, he knows the risks, but will he take a chance?

He puffs out his chest as he draws himself to his full height. "Have it your way, Fisher. Go where you like, talk to who you like, it won't make any difference. This is not a work accident."

He saunters back to his car, already on his phone, instructing his managers, no doubt. They'll be friendly to my face, but the records I want to examine will be on a computer at head office. They won't have access to them because the server's not working. I'm assuming the people I want to talk will be available, of course. But I have a chance to build a case. If I fail, I'll be looking for a new job.

Carolyn signals the constables over. "Do you want the lads to stay?"

I shake my head, certain they're bored out of their heads. "Thanks for the offer, but I'll be fine."

She lowers her voice. "You're taking a chance if he has a restraining order against you. Is there anything I can do to support you, Kent?"

"Do you have somewhere free and safe where I can impound machinery?"

"No, don't you?"

Since Danni took over I'm not sure we have a budget. No doubt there's a policy and procedure somewhere in her matrix management system. Maybe I could develop a strategy to understand these changes. Maybe not.

I thank Carolyn for her help and watch her stride away with her constables. When she turns the corner and disappears behind the barn, I'm on my own in charge of a fatal accident investigation. At least Gemma appreciates the enormity of the situation.

"Miles look great for his age, doesn't he?"

"Oh, come on, Gemma. Don't tell me you fancy him. He prefers bleached blondes with boobs bigger than their brains."

"Then you have something in common." She stares at me for a few moments and then breaks into a smile. "Lighten up, Kent. You might hate him, but he is Downland's only celebrity."

Now there's a word stretched beyond its intention. "I'll get you his autograph," I say as we make our way back to the tractor. "First, we need to impound the tractor. I'll need a Seizure Notice from the Grab Bag, which you can serve on our celebrity. Then you ask him to autograph your notebook to say he's accepted it."

While she searches for the notice, I join Jogging Man. Of mixed European and oriental descent, he's trying to look cool and aloof, giving me the merest glance as I approach. Close up, he looks like a frightened teenager, his complexion pale, his eyes avoiding mine. His fingers tremble as they cling to a tobacco pouch. He looks surprisingly dry for someone who was running not that long ago.

"Cool hair," I say, admiring his thick black hair, gelled into orange spikes that glisten in the sun. "Did you style it?"

He makes a grunting noise that sounds like confirmation.

"I know you've had a tough time, but I need to ask you a few questions."

His dark eyes glare at me. "I told the woman I saw nothing. Why don't you people listen?"

Normally, I wouldn't press someone in shock, but I can't afford to let Birchill intimidate Cheung. "I'll only take a few minutes."

"Yeah, but I've been here hours, man. I got work to do."

"You're going to work after what you saw?"

He glances across the clearing at Birchill. "I don't work I don't get paid."

"Okay, give me five minutes to clear the area while you collect your thoughts. Don't go away."

I return to Gemma, who's sitting on the tractor's footplate. I point to the blank space on the notice she's holding. "We're impounding a Massey Ferguson tractor with a bench mounted rip saw and power takeoff shaft. When you're done, I'll sign and date both copies."

"Don't you need Danni's permission?"

"The inspector takes action under health and safety law, not the council."

"I was thinking about the cost. The police charge, don't they?"

I nod. Low loaders don't come cheap. Neither does storage in a secure compound, but I'll worry about that after I've checked and served the notice. It takes me a few seconds to skim through the details.

"Let's serve your first notice," I say, heading for Birchill.

He watches us approach, or more specifically he watches Gemma. She flicks back her thick chestnut hair and deliberately avoids meeting his eyes, but her slight smile tells me she's enjoying his interest. When we draw close, he slips his phone into his jacket and leans against his Mercedes.

"I see we share an interest in beautiful women," he says, looking past me. "Delighted to meet you, Miss..."

"Gemma Dean." Her cheeks flush a little as she steps forward, holding up the notice. "I have something to give you, I'm afraid."

"Don't be afraid. I'm not an ogre. But let's set aside the formalities for a few moments, Gemma. Is this your first time at Tombstone?"

She nods. "I haven't seen the main park yet."

"I'd give you the guided tour, but I fancy Fisher would prefer to do that. Not that he'll pay much attention to you or the park while he thinks he can shut me down." He steps forward and holds out his hand. "Best give me that."

"Sorry, but we've got to impound the tractor and machinery."

"The notes on the reverse detail your rights," I say.

"I have lawyers for that." His hand brushes hers as he takes the notice. "They will demonstrate it's not my machinery."

"I'm still impounding it."

"Where are you taking it?"

"If it's not your machinery, what do you care?"

20

His eyes grow dark with anger. "A loyal friend and associate, who worked with me for over 30 years, is dead. I want to know what happened."

"Then let me do my job."

He turns, opens the door to his Mercedes, and slides inside. The engine purrs into life and he's moving. As he draws level, he stops. "Okay, Fisher, do your job, but step out of line and it'll be your last."

He accelerates away before I can say anything. Not that there's anything to say. "Still interested in our only celebrity?" I ask Gemma.

"You're like two bulls, ready to lock horns. Honestly, Kent, they must have smelt the testosterone at the main gates." She puts a hand on my arm. "Don't make this personal."

I walk into the shade by the barn and ring Tollingdon Agricultural Services. The company maintained the equipment on my father's estate for decades. It also has the grounds maintenance contract for Downland District Council. About 18 months ago, it won the contract for maintaining the equipment at Tombstone Adventure Park.

The owner, Tom Gibson, believes in old fashioned values like answering the phone himself, even though he has a receptionist and PA. His practised tone soon deteriorates after he hears my voice.

"Tell me you don't want the shirt off my back. You've had everything else."

He likes to exaggerate. "This is official, Tom. I need you to collect and store a tractor involved in a work accident."

"Official? Then you have a purchase order number?"

"The moment I return to the office. I can't leave the site until the machinery's safe. I'll ask an HSE expert to give it a thorough examination."

"I'm not having the Health and Safety Executive crawling around my depot. Last time they were here it cost me thousands."

"We're talking a tractor expert, not an inspector."

"That means you're thinking about prosecution," he says. "My compound could be out of action for months. Will you reimburse me for that?"

Not a hope. "Of course we will," I reply. "We can't win without your help."

"Okay, where's the tractor?"

"Tombstone. I'm just north of the park, by a barn."

"Can't do it. Not for you, not for your father, not for anyone," he says, unable to mask the relief in his voice. "I service their machinery."

"You're also a preferred contractor for Downland District Council."

"Yes, and the contract's for three years. You can't squeeze me that way."

I draw a breath. "I can. We've had complaints."

"What complaints?"

"You know how it is, Tom. Some people take photographs when parks and playing fields are cut. They don't understand the pressures your men are under or how small the margins are. They just email us photographs, demanding action. I can't keep ignoring them, Tom."

"You're a bastard, Kent—just like your father. Only he has finesse."

I should feel bad, forcing Tom to do my bidding, but his compound's big enough for five or six tractors. His company grew thanks to my father. "You can't afford to lose the Council contract," I say.

"I can't afford to lose the Tombstone contract either. Miles Birchill won't be pleased when he finds out."

"Then don't tell him."

"Sorry, I had to duck to avoid the pigs that flew past. Someone will be with you inside the hour."

I lean back against the wall, relieved Tom gave way. Had he held his ground I wouldn't have a refuge for the tractor. Now all I have to do is convince Danni. She picks up on the third ring. "How's it going, Kent?"

My brief overview omits Birchill's visit. "I'll be happier when the tractor and bench saw are impounded," I say.

"Aren't our partners in the police letting us use their compound?"

"Only if we pay," I reply, sounding suitably unenthusiastic. "As custodians of the public purse, we must use our money wisely, you said. So, I engaged a local company at a fraction of the cost."

"You obtained three quotes, did you?"

Three quotes? Is she on another planet? "We need to impound the tractor now, not in three days, Danni. I don't want anyone tampering with it."

"Read the expedited procedure in the Grab Bag," she says, as if we're conducting different conversations. "Three verbal estimates, confirmed in writing within 48 hours will do."

I push a hand through my hair, trying to remain calm. "When did this come in?"

"I brought the procedure from Surrey."

Obviously she hasn't had time in the four months since she took over to update us. "Someone's already on their way," I say.

"Then stop them until Gemma can ring round and get more quotes. You may even knock their price down if they know there's competition. That's value for money." I can almost hear her ticking another box on her procedure. "While she takes care of that, you're free to concentrate on the investigation."

I'm pacing now, wondering how I can prevent my boss from turning the investigation into a paper trail. My response is so feeble, I'm almost embarrassed. "How can I do that when I have to check quotes?"

"I think Gemma can work out which is the most competitive quote, don't you? And she's so enthusiastic and willing. Does that sound like Lucy? Can you imagine her striking a deal?"

Striking a deal? Who the hell does she think we are—double glazing sales people?

"Tollingdon Agricultural Services won't charge to impound the machinery," I say, turning away from Gemma. "They have capacity in their compound."

"But Tom Gibson is a family friend," Danni says. "That sounds like nepotism. Even a lame barrister will see through that."

"Then give me an order number and I'll pay." I dread to think what else she knows about me and my family. "Tom will be the cheapest quote, I'm sure. Fortunately, the HSE expert won't charge for his report."

"Why do we need an expert? You took photos, didn't you?"

"We need an expert because they'll employ one. We have to fight like with like in court."

"Shouldn't you finish the investigation before you decide we're off to court?"

"Danni, someone removed a guard which would have prevented the accident."

The silence lasts for almost ten seconds, which allows me to cool off a little.

"If we're prosecuting," Danni says, "then the last thing you need are accusations of nepotism. Tollingdon Agricultural Services must not be used, even if they provide the cheapest quote. Is that clear?"

She ends the call before I can protest. It looks like justice is now in the hands of the accountants.

Gemma strolls over, an amused smile on her lips. "From the number of faces you pulled, I'm guessing you didn't get what you wanted."

"No, I got you." I push the Blackberry back into its holster and head towards the clearing. "Let's interview Cheung while we wait for Tollingdon Agricultural Services."

The moment we turn the corner, I spot the empty log where Cheung was sitting a few minutes ago. He's gone.

CHAPTER THREE

Gemma breaks into a run. "Cheung can't have got far."

"Agreed," I call. "The Grab Bag will slow him down."

Fortunately, she finds the Grab Bag behind the log. "Everything's here," she says, plunging inside the bag.

"Is Cheung in there by any chance?"

"There's no room, the bag's full."

Her humour softens my sarcasm, but not my mood. We shouldn't have left him alone. He could have walked off with the camera and our photographs. I dread to think what Danni would have said if that happened. "You'll need to get three quotes for a new camera," no doubt.

I walk around the log and head for a path that leads into the trees. The undergrowth's trampled flat, suggesting regular use.

"Let's try this way," I say, waiting while Gemma zips up the Grab Bag and hoists it over her shoulder.

"I bet Lucy never carries this," she says.

"No, she's never carried it."

Gemma looks at me in disbelief. "So, why are you making me carry it—because you wanted Lucy on the case, not me?"

"No, we only got the Grab Bag a month ago. You're the first person to use it."

The path heads through stinging nettles, bramble and bindweed, all wrestling for supremacy. The white flowers of the bindweed trumpet a narrow victory. A few yards into the tangle the path divides. The left branch turns back towards the barn. The right disappears into the woods. Like the detectives in TV dramas, I search for a snag of jogging pants on a bramble to give me a clue which way Cheung went. I'm about to give up when something in the undergrowth catches the light. I slide a cautious hand between the brambles and extract an empty vodka bottle. I recognise the label from a recent Food Standards Agency alert.

"It's illicit," I say, handing it to Gemma. "Trading Standards caught one of the local off licences selling the stuff. What do you think?"

She turns the bottle in her hands. "The label isn't faded or wrinkled, so it's not been there long. Who dropped it there? Teenagers?"

"In the middle of nowhere? I doubt it. My money's on Collins."

"Do you think it has something to do with the accident?"

I shrug. "If he was drunk this morning, it might explain the accident. Bag it until we know more."

She drops the bottle into an evidence bag, seals it with a tag and labels it. While she does this, I rummage through the brambles, looking for the bottle cap. It should be close by, but Collins could have discarded it half a mile away.

"What makes you think he was drunk?"

I think about this as I straighten. "Don't you think it's an odd place to find an empty bottle? Who comes here, apart from Collins and Cheung?"

"Are you always this suspicious?"

My best friend, Mike Turner, calls me Konspiracy Kent. I'm intrigued by things that are out of place or unexplained. I love unsolved mysteries. If I could go on a cruise, it would be aboard the *Mary Celeste*. I don't care if conspiracy theories are true or false. They allow me to speculate.

"I think Cheung went right into the woods," I say. "If he was running, he must have come from that direction."

We're about to set off when I hear a man clear his throat and noisily despatch phlegm into the bushes. Cheung ambles into view from the opposite direction, hoisting his jogging pants over his faded Nirvana tee shirt. Something tells me he's unlikely to have a sunny outlook.

He stops and stares at me, pushing his hands into the pockets of his pants. "I needed a piss, alright? I don't know nothing," he adds when I remain silent. "Syd was dead when I found him. Lying there. Blood everywhere."

His hand covers his mouth for a few moments as the horror plays in his eyes.

"Why did you come this way?" I ask, keen to distract him.

"For a piss, like I told you."

I can't help wondering why he's not wearing shorts, which would make much more sense in the hot weather. I step closer, hoping to smell the odour of exertion, or alcohol, but I detect neither.

"Does the path lead to the barn?" I ask.

He mutters something unintelligible and turns. There are no sweat stains on his back, though his neck glistens. He saunters along the meandering path, taking his time, until we reach the barn. The bushes and undergrowth recede a couple of yards to reveal a concrete block extension with a flat roof. The door and adjacent window are locked, but inside I can make out kitchen cupboards, sink, refrigerator, and a wooden table and chairs. An empty ashtray lies abandoned on the window sill.

"Do you use this place?" I ask.

"I don't have a key."

The scuff marks around the keyhole tell a different story. He has no keys on him, as far as I can tell. I can make out the shape of his lighter and tobacco pouch in his pockets, but nothing else. I'd like to feel along the top of the doorframe for a key, as he must use the toilet at the rear of the kitchen. It looks like there might also be a shower, judging by the waste pipes feeding into the soil stack. In such a remote location the facilities would make sense.

"Did Collins have a key?"

"Don't know. He surfaced long after I went to work."

"But not today."

He swallows and looks down. Trembling fingers pull out the tobacco pouch from his pocket. He extracts a thread of tobacco and trickles it into a cigarette paper, pinched between thumb and forefinger.

"How can you smoke and run?" I ask, unable to stop myself.

He struggles to roll the cigarette, almost dropping it as I speak. Gemma steps forward and takes the paper and tobacco from him. With a couple of neat movements, she rolls a cigarette that's not much thicker than a match. A dreamy smile spreads over his face as he watches her, his eyes full of wonder. I think he's in love.

I can understand that.

"You have it," he says when she offers it to him. "I'll roll another."

"I don't smoke. It's not good for my chest."

He glances down, eyes on stalks. "No, you mustn't smoke," he says. "Do you run? There are so many lovely trails round here."

"I prefer the gym," she says before he can suggest they run together.

"Me too. The nearest one's in Uckfield. Syd used to go there, but he stopped about a year ago. I don't know why; he was in good shape for his age."

I gesture to Gemma to start walking. *Talk to him,* I mouth.

"What was Syd like?" she asks.

"Scary. He had eyes like a shark. Dark and empty, they were."

"I thought you said you didn't see him because he overslept," I say.

He snatches a nervous lungful of smoke. "I never thought I'd see him like that. Man, I've never seen so much blood. And his face. I can't shift it from my head."

He closes his eyes and turns away.

"Take it easy," I say gently. "You've had a shock."

I'll never forget seeing a fox torn apart by hounds in a frenzy of bloody muzzles. It was the way the fox, exhausted and trapped, just relented to its fate. One moment it ran for its life. The next it stopped, a look of resignation in its eyes. It took all my willpower to keep filming when I wanted to maim the hunt people, who got such enjoyment from the suffering of a defenceless animal. I've never watched the film. I don't need to—it's lodged in my head.

While we walk, Gemma talks and asks questions, coaxing answers from him. I can't decide whether he's in shock or simply defensive. His answers are short, usually loaded with accusations. Every few seconds, his cigarette goes out, interrupting the flow, but she's more patient than me. I'd probably pin him to a tree.

"David, you should talk to someone about what you saw." She stops and looks straight into his eyes. "You need help."

"Like therapy? Mr. B won't give me time off for that."

I don't often agree with Birchill, but talking about problems rarely solves them. You end up sharing your misery and baring your soul. It's not long before everyone knows your secrets. No, books are much better at solving life's mysteries. Conan Doyle's master detective, Sherlock Holmes, solved puzzles that baffled others with cunning and reason. He taught me to embrace being different. In *To Kill A Mocking Bird*, Atticus Finch stood firm against ignorance and prejudice. He gave me values and idealism. Ian Fleming gave me a role model.

"It's a shit job," Cheung's saying as I tune back in to the conversation. "But it's better than doing nothing."

"What do you do?" I ask.

"I have the most important job in the park, according to Mr. B."

"You mean, you clean the toilets, right?"

"And I pick litter and empty bins. I'm so important I get a special spade for horse poo."

"Were you running when you discovered Collins?" I ask, trying to move things along.

"Sure."

"Do you always run that early?"

"Yeah, before work."

"Do you follow the same route?"

"Varies, but this one's the easiest to follow."

"So, you must have known Collins was working this morning."

"No." He throws the remains of his cigarette into the bushes. "I told you, I saw nothing. You make it sound like I had something to do with it."

Gemma sighs when he marches off. "I was getting somewhere then."

"He was telling you nothing. Look, if I started the tractor you'd hear it from here. So would Cheung. Why's he lying?"

She adjusts the Grab Bag. "I see what you mean. We'd better go after him."

In less than a minute the trees thin and the path dissolves into a grassed area with wild flowers. A tired brick cottage with dormer windows like sleepy eyes lies beyond, weighed down by a wisteria drape. It can't quite hide the blistered paint, peeling away from the rotten wood beneath. Even the chimneys, like bookends on either side of the cottage, can't stop the roof from sagging with neglect. Cheung sits on the flint garden wall, his shoulders slumped in sympathy.

"Welcome to my hovel," he says, pushing another cigarette between his lips. "In summer it's cold and miserable. In winter it sweats."

I can't make out whether he wants to talk to us or not. "Let's go inside and chat over a cup of tea," I say.

He shakes his head. "I'd rather not. You might catch something."

So much for getting a drink to ease my thirst. I point to a path to my left that leads back into the woods. "Where does that go?"

"Syd's house. It's warm and dry all year round."

"Did you see him go past this morning?"

"I was in the kitchen at the back, eating breakfast."

In my experience, runners don't eat just before a run. Though tempted to perch on the flint wall beside him, I keep my distance. "You must have been surprised to hear the tractor when you left this morning."

"I never heard the tractor."

"Really?"

"I listen to music while I run."

"Then where are your headphones? Where's your music player?"

"I keep my music on my phone."

"Where's your phone?"

He taps his pocket as if he expects it to be there. "No, I left it on the kitchen table."

"Really?"

He shifts on the wall, avoiding eye contact. "What do you mean?"

Gemma glances at me. She's realised that if he left his phone in the kitchen he must have heard the tractor.

"I thought you took your phone with you when you went running."

He nods. "I did."

"Then why's it not in your pocket?"

"I came back here."

I want to snatch the unlit cigarette that wags in his mouth as he speaks. "When?"

"After I rang for an ambulance. I needed a piss so I came back here. I left the phone on the table."

I'm wondering if he has a weak bladder. "Then you went back to the barn, right?"

He stares at me as if I'm nuts. "You wouldn't have found me there if I hadn't."

My fingers grip my notebook a little tighter. "Did you return to the barn straight away?"

"The police came quickly."

I open my notebook and glance at my notes. "Did you speak to Detective Inspector Briggs?"

"Was that the woman in charge, the one you spoke to?"

"That was the Coroner's Officer."

Finally, he lights the cigarette. "She was definitely in charge, man, bossing everyone around. Everything was kicking off, with ambulances and coppers everywhere. And Syd was just lying there, wrapped around that shaft."

He swallows and looks down, his face turning pale. He's had a tough morning. The shock's affecting his recollection. Either that or I'm missing something. I could be looking for something that isn't there. It wouldn't be the first time.

"Thanks for your help," I say. "I'll take a statement from you when you're feeling better, maybe tomorrow."

He jumps to the ground and pushes through the rusty gate, leaving it open in his determination to get away. He's halfway down the path when I call out. "David, do you like vodka?"

"Doesn't everyone?" he calls, heading out of sight around the corner.

"What do you make of that?" I ask Gemma. "He didn't ask me why I wanted to know about vodka."

"Maybe he didn't care."

In my youth I was fed too many lies to take anything at face value. "Being inquisitive is good," I say, checking my watch. It's nearly ten, so the low loader should be on its way. I hoist the Grab Bag over my shoulder. "Let's make sure Collins isn't asleep in his bed."

Once in the woodland we pass through a chestnut grove where the trees are planted in regimented rows. The branches swoop down with leaves that look like hands with large extended fingers. I run my hand over the rough bark, soft yet strong, as I peer up through the ripening chestnut clusters, searching for a scampering squirrel.

"Why didn't you ask David when the guard went missing?"

I should admit it never occurred to me. "Do you think he'd notice?"

"He might. I'm no expert, but if Tombstone provides the machinery then they're to blame. If Collins provides the machinery, he's to blame."

She's right, of course, but I don't understand why Collins was out here. "He hadn't used the tractor in years. He didn't need any fence posts. What was he doing here at six in the morning?"

She sighs. "If the guard had been fitted he would be alive."

"If he'd stayed in bed he would be alive."

We continue in silence through the trees, reaching Collins' house five minutes later. Though similar to Cheung's hovel in build and style, this cottage is pristine, wearing its Sussex hanging tiles with pride. The straight roof holds the chimneys erect, allowing the sun to illuminate the intricate corbelling. But even the chimneys have to pay homage to the oak framed porch, garlanded with the most stunning pink roses I've seen. Their fragrance tempts me into the garden when I open the wooden gate.

This image should be on a jigsaw box.

The small front garden is smothered with drifts of marigolds, petunias and geraniums, their bright colours at odds with the mellow bricks of the Victorian building. Alpines scramble over the gravel path, scampering up the rope edge tiles to the garden beyond. Chunky earthenware pots spill over with herbs and hostas, forcing their purple spikes of flowers through the deeply veined leaves.

I'd like to lift the pot with the variegated hosta and find a front door key beneath, but I pound the door with the brass knocker, shaped like a fist.

"Are the curtains drawn upstairs?"

Gemma steps back to look up. She shakes her head.

I peer through the letterbox into a spotless hall with a cream carpet, and a hat stand and dresser. Moving across to the adjacent window, I notice the same carpet and cream Art Deco furniture in the living room. The monster flat screen TV on the wall makes up for the lack of photographs, paintings, ornaments and trinkets.

The gravel path leads around the corner into a homemade carport, which covers a dull green Land Rover, coated with a lingering smear of dust and dirt. It has four flat tyres, locked doors, and an interior littered with empty sandwich cartons and crisp packets. Cigarette stubs overflow from the ashtray.

"Collins preferred his Land Rover to the living room," I say.

A single-storey kitchen extension eats into the small rear garden. A lifeless concrete drive connects the carport with the lane beyond, leaving half the garden for vegetables. Not a weed in sight.

Gemma heads straight for the glazed back door, trying the handle. She raps delicate knuckles on the glass before peering through the kitchen window. Like the first floor, the curtains are open but the windows are closed, despite the heat. I'm more interested in the oil stains on the concrete. Another car regularly parks here.

I glance at my watch. "Tollingdon Agricultural should be here soon. Once they've finished we can visit the main park and interview management."

Back at the clearing, Gemma sits in the shade. She draws up her slender legs and rests her notebook on her knees to write up her notes. I sit on the footplate of the tractor, watching her when I should be making sense of what happened this morning. Every few minutes I have to stop my thoughts drifting back seven years to the week we shared a cramped bedsit.

At 10:23, the low loader rumbles into view at the top of the clearing. The driver, a short man with a shiny bald head and a neck like a bull, jumps down from the cab. He's wearing the standard issue Tollingdon Agricultural Services black tee shirt and shorts, which look comical above his steel toe cap boots. He saunters down the slope, hands in pockets, studying the machinery.

"Can't move the saw without a forklift," he says, staring at me as if I've wasted his time. "Can't use a forklift on this surface."

"So tell me what you can do."

He examines the power takeoff, glances at the spray of blood, and tuts. "Mate of mine had an arm ripped off when his sleeve got caught. Only takes a second, you know." He clambers onto the footplate and peers inside the cab. "Can't move this without a key."

I can't believe I didn't notice the key was missing. Cheung switched off the engine, but why remove the key? Carolyn must have taken it.

"As I said, tell me what you can do."

"I can take the magazines," he replies, eyes glinting as he spots Gemma strolling over. "How would you like to help me turn this old girl on?" he asks her.

"This old girl just killed a man," she replies.

"Now that could be a country and western song." He sings the line as he walks back to his truck. He returns with an assortment of keys on rings. He selects one of the rings and chuckles. "I'll have to take off the takeoff."

I retreat back to the log and watch. Moments later, the rumble of the diesel engine echoes off the barn wall. "There's no way Cheung didn't hear that," I say in a loud voice. With the Grab Bag hoisted over my shoulder, I call out as we pass by the tractor. "Can you ask Tom to ring me when you get back?"

The driver nods, but he's busy staring at a Nuts magazine.

Back at the barn, Gemma and I reach her mother's battered old Volvo Estate. An angry ram crumpled the rear driver's side door, which has refused to open since, not that there's any room in the back with the dog cages. Like the car, they've seen better days, but they're good at keeping shopping bags upright.

"No point taking both cars," I say, heading for my Fusion.

"I'm not going with you if you're still listening to that dreary music."

We've had this discussion before, but I can't help feeling defensive. "Barclay James Harvest is the best band this country produced. Their songs have depth, drama and emotion."

"But nobody's heard of them. Haven't you got something cheerful like Kylie Minogue?"

"Kylie Minogue?"

"Sure," she replies, opening the Estate's driver's door. "You'd like her in your car, wouldn't you?"

"I should be so lucky."

I wrench open the passenger door. The stale odour of dog permeates the interior, clinging to the worn upholstery. The smell brings back memories of the cats, injured badgers, fox cubs, and occasional lambs we used to rescue, and the hours it took to clean up after them. Most of them recuperated at my animal sanctuary.

I scoop the copies of *Veterinary Practice* magazine from the seat and slide them onto the parcel shelf. It takes me several wrenches to pull out enough seatbelt to click it home. Gemma has no such problems, sliding it across her slim waist with ease.

"To the park?" she asks, starting the car.

"We'll track down the general manager. I doubt if he'll tell us anything. Birchill will see to that." I wind down the window to let the breeze blow over my face. "Not that it matters. There's always someone who will talk. All we have to do is find that person."

"How? There must be hundreds of people working here. We can't interview them all."

"No, but we can antagonise a few."

CHAPTER FOUR

The road back to the park takes us through fields and pastures, partitioned by ranch style fencing for that authentic Wild West look. Thankfully, small clusters of trees escaped the pillage, providing sanctuary for some local wildlife and shade for the horses and cattle. Most of the hedgerows that provided arteries for insects and small mammals are gone, torn out to allow buffalo, ostrich, and horses to roam unhindered. Fodder crops for the winter, like sugar beet, grow in some of the smaller fields.

"I'd love to ride on the railway," Gemma says as we cross the tracks. "They have an authentic Western train—like the one in *Back to the Future*."

Not on a narrow gauge line they don't.

The main park is laid out like a Wild West town with a mixture of timber and brick buildings, corrals and boardwalks. There's no doubting the quality of the reproduction, but I can't help feeling it's diminished by names like, Billy the Kid's Kebabs and OK Corral Cream Teas, which probably serves Earp Grey. At the back of these buildings, concrete dominates. It covers the service areas where industrial scale refuse bins and compactors huddle together at the side of loading bays. It amplifies the hum of compressors, working overtime to keep refrigerators cool. It provides a flat, impervious surface that allows pigeons and gulls to pick through the food waste that spills from the bins. The concrete absorbs the sun like a storage heater, fermenting much of the rotten food.

Gemma screws her face and closes the window, but she's too late to stop the stench permeating the car. "Haven't they heard of disinfectant?"

The workers and catering staff on the slip road seem oblivious to the smell as they make their way from a staff car park adjacent the substation. Many of them smoke, even more have tattoos, and nearly all are engrossed in their mobile phones. I wonder how they'd react if I texted the word 'smell' to them.

"Pull over, Gemma," I say, pointing to a burnt out portacabin on the left. The roof has collapsed and the windows have gone, leaving gaping holes in the charred walls. The blackened remains of desks, cupboards and chairs are strewn about, abandoned on the grass verge. Computers and monitors, distorted by melting plastic cases, are piled in a small heap, enclosed by emergency tape. The smell of burnt portacabin suggests the fire was recent.

I signal to a cowboy in chaps and spurred boots. He looks hot in his waistcoat, and the sweat stains on the brim of his hat confirm it. He places a hand on his gun as if he expects trouble. As long as he doesn't say, 'Howdy', we'll be okay.

"Can I help?" he asks in finest middle class English. He notices Gemma and taps the brim of his hat with a forefinger.

"Environmental health," I say. "What day was the fire?"

He pushes the hat back to reveal damp hair, flattened against his scalp. "Sunday night through Monday morning. It had burnt out by the time we arrived for work. The guys salvaged what they could, but there wasn't much."

"Did the fire officer say what caused the fire?"

He gives me a blank look. "It happened overnight. Ben Foley might know. He's the Operations Manager. That was his office."

"Where can I find him?"

"He's moved to the jail on Main Street."

"That's one way to get a captive audience," I say, unable to stop myself. At least I didn't offer to call his cell phone.

"Wait a minute," the cowboy says, turning. "I heard someone say he went to the front gate to sort out a tricky customer."

I climb back into the Volvo. "They like fires here. First the farmhouse burns down, now the manager's office. When we get to the car park, keep going out through the main gate. I didn't get a proper look at the entrance earlier," I say in response to her puzzled look. "I want to see what all the fuss is about."

"Why?"

"We spent two years trying to stop Tombstone getting planning approval. When that failed, we spent the best part of another year chaining ourselves to trees, lying in front of bulldozers, doing our best to stop the development."

"Who's we?"

"People who think the environment is as important as profit. You can develop in harmony with the environment, if you try. It's not impossible."

"You sound like my mother."

"She was one of us."

She flashes me a look of surprise. "My mother chained herself to trees? She never told me that."

"You were in London at the time."

"And I never rang home, I know." She makes the last two words sound like a bored yawn. Then she accelerates out of the park onto the long slip road, flanked by lime trees. About 100 yards from the gates I spot a layby and farm gate.

"Turn here."

Gemma swings into the bumpy layby and stops. With a nifty piece of reversing into the farm entrance, we're facing the park. The sun pierces the front windscreen, almost blinding me as we dip in and out of a hollow. We lurch onto the road and head back.

"Slow down," I say.

An arched sign, riddled with bullet holes, straddles the opening between two log watch towers. Beneath the words Tombstone Adventure Park the slogan says, '*We'll bring out the cowboy in you.*'

Does it refer to Birchill or his builders, I wonder.

"Awesome!" Gemma says, stopping behind a people carrier.

"Niagara Falls is awesome. The Grand Canyon is awesome. This is timber cladding, pretending to look like a fort."

"It's still awesome."

Once through the gates, we return to the prairie of a car park. It's divided into themed sections, bounded by billboards with murals of locomotives, American Indians on horseback, and Monument Valley, interspersed with hoardings from local companies, eager to use anything western to promote their products. I can 'beat the stampede to Billy's Burger Bar', or get an insurance quote from the company that likes to 'shoot from the hip'. It's a shame I can't join a posse to lynch the slogan writers.

Ranch-style fencing divides each section into zones, flanked by footpaths. Litter bins, hidden inside yellow fibreglass cacti, mark every intersection. On a busy summer weekend over 2000 cars can be accommodated, according to a fact board. On a Thursday morning in September about 100 cars are herded close to the ticket office.

"Awesome!"

Breath-taking would be more apt—like the decision by the government inspector to overrule the council and grant planning permission. "Have you any idea how many hedgerows and trees Birchill ripped out to create this?"

"What about the jobs he created?"

"Short term contracts on the minimum wage? Casual staff on zero rated hours?"

"You're such a cynic, Kent. Lots of people are happy with that. Lots of locals work here. Don't you read the economic development reports? Tombstone's the largest employer in Downland."

As all the shops are independent small businesses, that's rubbish, but I keep that to myself.

We follow yellow hoof prints to the ticket office, shunted into a small timber railway station. Tombstone Halt has a platform with trolleys, a water hopper on wooden stilts, staff in period costume, and an ice cream freezer by the turnstile. A young girl is throwing a tantrum, which won't stop until her mother buys her an ice cream.

Gemma raises a finger. "Don't you dare say a word."

"I was only going to say the girl's performance is awesome."

We soon reach the counter, where a teenager with pierced eyebrows and a spider's web neck tattoo examines my ID card. "Is Mr. Foley about?" I ask. "I heard he was here."

"No, he's in jail." The teenager grins and hands me a leaflet with a plan of the park. "It's on Main Street. I can radio through and tell him you're coming."

"It's all right. He's expecting us."

I push through the turnstile and walk into a room lined with stills from Hollywood's finest Wild West films. Actors like John Wayne, James Stewart, Alan Ladd, Gary Cooper, Burt Lancaster, Henry Fonda, and Audie Murphy cover the first wall, which details the zenith of the Western in the forties and fifties. Further along, the sixties are represented by Paul Newman and Robert Redford, along with the Spaghetti Westerns that starred Lee Van Cleef, James Coburn, and my personal favourite, Clint Eastwood as the 'man with no name'.

"I love the idea that one man can make a difference," I tell Gemma as we stop at the huge photograph of Eastwood. "Think how much better the world would be if every person made one small difference."

"These two made a big difference to me." Her shoes slap on the wooden floor as she saunters over to Kurt Russell and Val Kilmer as Wyatt Earp and Doc Holliday.

"What about Kevin Costner?" I ask, pushing open the saloon doors to exit. "Isn't *Dances with Wolves* a great western?"

"Don't know," she replies. "I fell asleep halfway through."

A path of authentic concrete paving weaves between flowerbeds of geraniums, petunias and begonias, native to Arizona, I imagine. On either side long murals depict a cattle drive across dusty plains. The murals change to arid desert and rocky outcrops as we pass islands of cacti. At the end, two wooden doors proclaim Tombstone. It's Wednesday, 26th of October, 1881. There's going to be a gunfight at the OK Corral, on the hour every hour.

We push through the doors and step into the past.

"Awesome!"

It's not quite the Wild West, but the timber buildings that flank either side of the street look impressive. I count two saloons, a hardware store, and enough fast food outlets to induce a heart attack. Raised timber boardwalks run on either side, ending in the disabled ramps the Building Inspectors demanded. In the distance there are brick buildings, housing a bank and a hotel. While there are quite a number of people milling around, the whole scene is slightly muted.

"What do you think?" Gemma asks, her eyes wide with excitement. "Go on, admit it. You're impressed."

"I want to smell and hear horses," I say, looking about me. "I'd like to hear the sound of a piano, drowned out by the raucous laughter from the saloon. A gunshot or two would be nice."

The waft of fried onions, chilli and greasy extract vents doesn't quite do it for me.

There's no escaping the quality of detail and workmanship that's gone into recreating Tombstone. It must have cost some serious money. That's why the place is full of shops and food outlets, all paying a premium for the crowds that flock here during the summer and at weekends. But it's those shops that trivialise the experience, exchanging history for amusement arcades, trinket shops, and an-all-you-can-eat-for-a-tenner Chinese restaurant. The side streets are full of arcades emitting brash electronic music.

At the end of Main Street, the town gives way to barns and corrals, houses and log cabins. I point to a sign and cringe. "You can spend all your silver and pan for gold."

"Maybe I'll come back with Richard," she says. "He won't walk round criticising everything."

"In case you'd forgotten, Gemma, we're investigating a fatal accident."

Her sour look suggests I was a little harsh, but it won't hurt her to remember she's not my first choice for assistant.

"You need a second mortgage to spend a day here," I remark, raising my hand to deter the employee in traditional costume. I don't want my face on a 'Wanted' poster. I don't want to ride in a buggy. And I most certainly don't want a second pizza at half price. "The only thing that's free is the weather."

"And the stunt show." Gemma points to the sign. The twice-daily stunt show in the corral allows unlucky visitors to be roped into lasso demonstrations before experiencing shooting displays, bucking broncos and stunt riding. Every hour, on the hour, a gunfight starts in the saloon and spills into the street. Visitors can become deputies and join the sheriff's posse, while the less energetic can dress up as cowboys and cowgirls for the day.

"This is how they should teach history," she says, dodging a party of oriental visitors, who are experiencing the Wild West through mobile phones and tablet PCs. "Tombstone brings it to life."

"Indeed. Nike trainers and combat trousers were all the rage in 1881."

Across the street, in a gap between the buildings, parents sit at picnic tables provided by the Hole in the Wall Tea Room. Their children will be in the soft play area beyond, hurling themselves around the bouncy fort until their ice creams make a return visit.

I turn towards the jail, sandwiched between two eateries. There's a narrow passageway to the right, leading to the service area behind, I imagine. Built of stone with a slate roof, the jail's barred windows are flanked with wooden shutters. Sepia 'Wanted' posters (only five pounds to have your face and name added) warn people of dangerous outlaws. A sign on the doors tells us the jail's closed.

"The manager's escaped for a cigarette," I say with a smile.

I raise the latch and the door creaks open into a small, dimly lit room, dominated by a large desk. The woman behind it must be a filing clerk, if her manicured fingernails are anything to go by. Like so many of her peers, she has thick black hair, false eyelashes, and a render of make-up that neutralises her expression. Her face is small and thin with a delicate nose and mouth. She rests her chin on her hands as she studies me with striking blue eyes that suggest interest beneath the indifference.

"You can't come in here," she says in a soft Scouse accent that has me in raptures. "We're not open to the public."

"We've spoken before," I say, striding in. "You rang to see if an accident had to be reported." I bend to check the name badge, pinned to her blue silk blouse. "Hi, Rebecca, you're much lovelier than I imagined."

Somewhere behind me, I hear a groan.

Recognition raises a smile. "You're Kent Fisher from environmental health. You wore that shirt when you came to our school to talk about your job. Must be about ten years ago."

"Did you enjoy the talk?"

"Not really. I wanted to be a singer."

I ignore Gemma's smirk. "What went wrong?"

She smiles, revealing even white teeth. "I can't sing."

The phone rings. Her tone is polite, but detached, suggesting previous employment in a call centre. I wander across the room and join Gemma by the rifle cabinet, where she's checking the padlock. Several posters detail the work and conditions of sheriffs in the frontier towns.

"I thought we were investigating a fatal accident, not chatting up the receptionists."

"Can I help it if her voice paints pictures in my mind?"

"You were picturing her tits. You know they're as false as her nails?"

Like that's going to put me off. "So?"

"You're so shallow, Kent. Maybe this will change your mind."

She hands me a leaflet on the Wild West weddings Tombstone offers. I resist a joke about shotguns, distracted by Rebecca's soft laughter. Why would I get married when the next day I could meet someone like her?

"You and Richard could get married here," I tell Gemma. "It would be awesome."

For some reason she ignores me. Then Rebecca cuts in. "Ben Foley, our Operations Manager, wants to know why you're here."

"One of your employees died a couple of hours ago."

She relays the details, nods as he responds, and then looks up. "If you mean Mr. Collins, he's nothing to do with Tombstone."

"He lives in a house on the park." I haul a wooden chair across and straddle it, cowboy style. "Tell Mr. Foley I'm here to interview him and check his health and safety systems and records."

"I can make you an appointment," she says

"No problem. Let's say five minutes." I wink and get to my feet. "We'll wait in his office."

"A boy's gone missing. I don't know how long he'll be."

"I'll wait, but I'm not known for my patience."

"His office is through the door," she says. "It's the first cell."

The door opens into a bare corridor that leads to two identical cells, constructed in concrete blocks. There are no bars across the front, only on the small windows in the rear walls. Each cell has a bunk bed, piled high with cardboard boxes. The first cell has a desk with an old PC and monitor on top, wedged between more boxes. I head inside and stop at the end of the bunk. "Gemma, there's an en suite toilet here."

She shuffles past me to look. "It's a bucket."

"What did you expect—a bidet?"

I cross to the desk and pick up a mug proclaiming 'World's Best Boss'. Inside, it has enough stains to hide undiscovered strains of bacteria. I notice an amplifier and microphone connected to the rear of the computer. Speaker cable runs up the wall and through the window to the outside.

Gemma calls from next door. "There's a coffee machine in this one."

The adjoining cell is crammed with spare furniture, including chairs and desks, bookcases, a couple of filing cabinets, and a vending machine that's not plugged in. The filing cabinets are locked, and there's no sign of any paperwork or folders that might contain the systems the business should have. Sensing they're on the computer, I return to the desk and tap the space bar on the keyboard. A blue crash screen appears. The sound of Rebecca's heels on the floorboards makes me step back.

"What are you doing?"

"Nothing—it's crashed."

"Not again." She brushes past me, leaving the subtle, musky scent of perfume in her wake. She taps the ESC key several times, and when nothing happens she depresses the power button. "Ben needs to make a public announcement. Are you sure you can't come back later when he's not so busy?"

"Is the announcement about the missing child?"

She nods as she switches the PC on. "After our office burnt down, this was the only PC we could find. It works, but it can't read the memory stick where I keep the holiday calendar."

"I could pop round with my laptop."

"When you came to the school, you couldn't get the projector to work. Let me know when it's booted," she calls over her shoulder.

Gemma smirks. "She's got the measure of you."

I return to the bunk bed and nose through some of the boxes, finding masses of promotional leaflets. I want to explore the files on the PC or the locked filing cabinets next door. As a child, I couldn't resist closed cupboards and locked drawers. They held secrets. Sometimes I'd spend hours, trying paperclips and penknife blades to open the locks. Today, I'd look it up on Google.

The noise of people gathering outside draws me to the window. The trickle of people has swelled to a noisy throng, thudding along the boardwalks like cattle. Heads turn to look up the street as a cowboy on a horse rears into view. If this is Foley, it's one hell of an entrance.

"That's Gregor," Rebecca says, returning to the computer. "He a dead ringer for Clint Eastwood, if you don't get too close. He rides up and down before confronting the outlaws. It's much better if you watch from the street."

It's almost eleven and it's time I stopped waiting. "Stay here," I tell Gemma. Outside, I slip along the passageway to the back of the jail. The courtyard smells of rotten food, probably emanating from the thick black ooze that trickles through the drain hole under one of the wheeled bins.

I head into the shade and ring Tollingdon Agricultural Services. As expected, Tom Gibson picks up. He doesn't sound too pleased to hear from me.

"Miracles I perform on Friday," he says in his slightly peeved tone. "Your tractor hasn't arrived yet."

"I'm ringing about your maintenance contract with Tombstone. Does it include the Massey Ferguson you're collecting for me?"

"How would I know when I haven't seen it?"

"You keep records of what you service, Tom."

"Kent, I'm a low loader down. Don't push your luck."

"A man is dead thanks to that tractor. I want the date you serviced it."

"*If* we serviced it. The tractor won't be specified in the agreement. It only stipulates that we maintain their equipment."

Despite his prevarication, I can hear the click of his keyboard as he speaks. He'll have invoices, details of any repairs carried out on each machine that's serviced. How else can he justify his bill? But he's not going to give me the information, especially if it could harm his contract.

"Tom, that's not what Tombstone's records show."

His voice is sharp, tinged with suspicion. "What are you talking about?"

I learned how to lie like a pro from my mother. You need to sound credible, which means using just enough detail. Say too much and you can be caught out. Say too little and you might not fool anyone. Best of all, tell a half truth that misleads people, and let them assume something different.

I've no idea what records Tombstone get from Tom, so I need to be careful. I lower my voice. "Tom, I think someone's altered your invoice."

"How? What have they altered?"

I try to remember what he puts on his invoices when he services my mowers. "I don't know. That's why I'm calling. Can we compare records?"

"I've pulled up the job sheet for the tractor you mentioned. We've only carried out the one service on the 5th June this year. Does that tally?"

"That's correct, Tom."

"The engine was knackered. We had to replace a lot of parts and it took us the best part of a day to get it going."

"What about the power takeoff?" I ask.

"Lubrication and a new guard."

"So, that's what it says," I say, sounding relieved. "Someone's tried to white it out. The guard was missing when I examined the takeoff."

His tone is forceful. "I assure you we fitted a new one."

"If it was the first time you'd worked on the tractor, was it added to the contract?"

"I doubt it. The request probably came by email. Have you got a copy?"

"Why don't you forward the email to me? I'll compare it to the ones on their computer. You might want to print some copies of your work sheets, because I think they're covering their backs."

I hang up, not sure he'll print the records for me. If he talks to Birchill about someone altering invoices, I could be in trouble, but at least I know someone wanted to get the tractor working after years of neglect.

And now Collins is dead.

CHAPTER FIVE

I take an instant dislike to Ben Foley. It's not because he uses the word 'dude', though that would be cause enough. It's not the way he swaggers about the office like he's being filmed. It's the way he blanks Rebecca to focus on Gemma.

He's lean, muscular, and tanned from working outdoors. His untamed hair makes him look more like a surfer than a sheriff, despite the black suit, frilled shirt, and bootlace tie. In his mid-twenties, with hazel eyes, a square jaw, and a mouth that's as loose as it is wide, he likes the sound of his own voice so much he slips into a Yankee drawl from time to time. Like his fingernails, which are bitten so far back they're almost non-existent, the effect is hardly flattering.

"There's nothing like the feel of all that muscle between your thighs," he says. "Do you ride, Gemma?"

I've heard enough. "Mr. Foley, I'm Kent Fisher. Judging from your banter it sounds like you've found the missing boy."

"Indeed I have, dude. Wouldn't be here if he was still missing, would I?"

"Let's talk about Syd Collins. How long did he work for you?"

Foley drops into the chair and leans back, clasping his hands behind his head. "Syd never worked for Tombstone. He's nothing to do with me."

"Then why did you service his tractor?" I ask, trying not to look at the sweat stains below his armpits.

"I didn't."

"Are you sure?"

He rolls his eyes. "Dude, I'm the Operations Manager."

"Then why did Tollingdon Agricultural service it on 5th June this year? They got the tractor running and replaced the missing guard to the power takeoff."

He yawns and lets the chair drop back onto four legs. "Nothing to do with me, dude. Same with Collins."

"You have a record of the service on your computer."

He stares at me for a moment and shakes his head. In a slow, almost lazy way, he gets to his feet and saunters past me, winking at Gemma. "All our servers went up in smoke last weekend. We had a fire."

"Luckily, Tollingdon Agricultural didn't. They emailed the records." I pull out my Blackberry to demonstrate. "Collins' tractor was serviced under your maintenance contract. That makes you liable."

He stops in the doorway. "No way."

"You emailed them to service the tractor."

He shakes his head once more, but without his earlier conviction. I suspect he's the kind of manager who has no idea what's going on. Fresh out of university, he's overworked and underpaid, lurching from one problem to the next. "You wait till I tell Mr. Birchill about this," he says.

"Call him. I'll be happy to show him the email you sent."

Foley hesitates. Whatever his shortcomings, he knows what Birchill might do to him.

"I didn't send an email. I have nothing to do with maintenance."

"You're the Operations Manager. You said so."

His fingers go to his mouth, but he's got no nails left to chew. After a few seconds pacing, he looks up. "Rebecca must have sent it."

I watch with amusement, glad to see how loyal he is to his secretary. "Are you saying she added the tractor to the service list for the first time in five years?"

He manages a feeble shrug of the shoulders.

"Maybe we should ask her? Gemma, could you call her in?"

He raises a hand. "There's been a mistake, dude."

I walk across, forcing him back until his shoulders hit the bars. He crosses his hands as I step even closer. "Maybe she was following your instructions, Foley."

Though pressed against the bars, he manages to shake his head with plenty of vigour. "It had nothing to do with me, honest."

"If it wasn't you and it wasn't Rebecca, who could it be? Could someone else add the tractor to the maintenance list?"

He swallows and glances at Gemma, maybe hoping she'll take pity on him. "People wander in and out of here all day," he tells her, "but they know nothing about maintenance contracts."

"Someone did," I say. "Who knew about the tractor?"

"Syd Collins?" His hopeful expression melts as quickly as it formed. "We'll never prove it without a Ouija board."

I back away and raise a finger to my lips to tell Gemma to keep quiet. I'm hoping the silence will encourage Foley to redeem himself and give me some names. Only he doesn't. He just stands there, shoulders sagging, expression blank.

He shows no desire to fill the silence. Outside, the cheering reaches a crescendo as Gregor gallops past.

"Was he friendly with anyone?" I ask. "The young kid, Cheung, maybe?"

"Syd was a loner. I think he drank in a pub up the road from his house."

"The Game Cock," Rebecca says, walking in. Her cheeky grin fades as she looks at Foley. "It didn't live up to its name, did it?"

"Was Syd friendly with anyone?" he asks her.

She turns to face me. "Artie Tompkins gave him a ride on the train sometimes. It passes close to Syd's house."

"Then I'll talk to Artie," I say, heading for the door. "I'll be back to take a written statement from you later, Mr. Foley."

The crack of gunshots in the street makes him start. He wipes the sweat from his forehead with his sleeve and almost falls into his chair. "Artie doesn't break for lunch till one," he calls.

Outside, the boardwalk's packed with spectators. We follow the signs for the train and weave our way through till we reach the intersection with Terminus Street. The spectators thin out here, probably tempted to eat by the aroma of various fast foods, all served with a salad garnish and fries. I want a bacon sandwich, dripping with brown sauce.

"You're quiet," I remark to Gemma.

"It's difficult to get a word in when you're antagonising people."

"That was hardly antagonistic. Anyway, it worked, didn't it? We got a name."

"You got the name of a train driver. Awesome!"

Her sarcasm cuts deeper than I expect. "What if Collins confided in Artie? He might have said he removed the guard from the power takeoff."

"What if he didn't?"

The distinctive sound of Enrico Morricone spills out of speakers above the window of Tombstone Tacos, the last restaurant before the level crossing. The tables with their red check tablecloths and miniature cacti menu holders are empty. A couple of waiters with olive complexions and black hair chatter at the bar, pausing only to admire Gemma.

"Someone removed the guard," I tell her. "And I think I know where it is."

"The barn?"

"No one uses it, but Cheung slipped round the back. Why?"

Orange lights on either side of the crossing begin to flash. The barriers come down and people gather to watch the train come through. A couple of toots on the whistle direct my gaze to the station, where the train eases away from the platform.

The diesel locomotive rumbles past, pulling five open carriages packed with parents and children, all waving to us. Artie is sitting sideways, with his back to us. He toots the whistle again, encouraging more frantic waving. In a little over a minute the train has passed. The barriers rise and we cross the track towards Tombstone Central.

The timber clad building looks just like the ticket office at the entrance, but with a few additions to offer latte and cappuccino, and ice cream for children. They have plenty of time to enjoy their refreshments as the queue snakes through a rope maze until it finally reaches a barrier at the ticket office. Adjacent is a bright yellow exit gate and path. No snaking for them as they walk past all those frustrated and impatient parents waiting to ride the train.

Gemma stares at the queue. "You've got proof that Tombstone serviced the machinery. Why do we need to talk to Artie?"

"It's not that simple."

"Why not?"

"Why did someone suddenly decide to repair the tractor? Why didn't they do it years ago? Why three months ago? Why did Collins want fence posts today?"

"Who cares, Kent? We check compliance with the law, don't we?"

"Don't you want to know why a man went to a tractor he hadn't used for years?" I stop, realising people are listening. I draw her to one side. "Those questions cast doubt."

"Doubt on what?"

"All the arguments and lies Birchill will use against us. If Foley didn't arrange the service, then Collins is a good bet. So, why did he remove the guard he had fitted? I'd say that was a valid line of investigation, wouldn't you?"

"How can you be sure Foley didn't arrange the service?"

"You saw his face. He didn't know about the email. That's why we talk to Artie about Collins." I head down the exit path towards the platform. "I'm not waiting till lunchtime. What's the point of having powers if you don't use them?"

"What's your game, mate?" A man with a shaven head and biceps the size of my thighs leans over the rope to stop me. "I've been waiting nearly an hour."

I hold up my ID card. "Someone said the train wasn't safe. I'll be as quick as I can."

He pulls back and we continue to the gate, which opens towards me, triggered by a sensor on the other side. I vault over, activating the sensor as I land. The gate swings open. The platform is short and clean, spoilt only by the sandwich board which promotes refreshments. Discarded cans and bottles, confectionery wrappers, and various juice cartons fill the gaps between the sleepers. I check the notice board, which tells me the next trip starts in 15 minutes. Allowing for passengers to disembark and the next ones to get on board, I should have five minutes to question Artie.

In the meantime, there's a lanky teenager with a spotty complexion and gelled hair to deal with. His ticket collector's shirt, which is soaking up sweat like blotting paper, looks three sizes too big. His trousers seem to be held up by willpower, hanging low on his hips. Thanks to a lack of punctuation, his badge identifies him as Tommy Ticket Supervisor. With a name like that, he's a natural.

"Someone's complained about the train. I need to speak to Artie." I show him my ID and stroll into the shade before he can ask any questions.

Gemma follows. "Why did you lie and say we'd had a complaint?"

"It doesn't matter to Tommy why we're here."

"You mean it doesn't matter to you."

I pull her close to the wall so Tommy can't hear or see us. "I'm not going to discover anything by pursuing Birchill or his company," I say, a little too sharply. "Don't you understand that? He's too smart. He can use our quarrels against me. How do you think Danni will react when she finds out about the injunction?"

"She'll want to know why you didn't tell her." Gemma's tone remains defiant, reminding me why I'm the worst officer for the investigation. "If you carry on like this, Kent, she'll suspend you. She won't have a choice."

There are always choices. Danni could sack me.

CHAPTER SIX

The Tombstone Express judders to a halt. There's a moment of calm before excited children fling open the carriage doors with a crescendo of bangs. Like a tidal wave the children spill onto the platform and swarm past, shouting at the tops of their voices while their parents scoop up toys and fizzy drinks.

I'm on my feet, eager to use those minutes to talk to Artie Tomkins.

He's short, stout, and well past retirement age if the creases in his ruddy face are anything to go by. With his silky white hair and beard, he looks like a favourite grandfather, ready to hand out toffees. Only there's no jolly smile, just a weariness that drags down the corners of his mouth and his hooded eyelids. In fact, his whole posture makes him look like he's wilting, accentuating the sag of his shoulders.

He stares at my shirt and frowns. "Who are you?"

"Kent Fisher, environmental health. This is Gemma Dean."

He waves away my ID card. "You tried to stop this place being built. Lucky you failed, or I wouldn't have a job." He looks in the mood for another fight, despite the weariness in his eyes. "What do you want?"

"You knew Syd Collins," I say. "He died this morning."

He walks past me. "I heard. Look, I have five minutes to clean the carriages and check everything's safe before the next circuit of fun and adventure."

"You can talk while you work, can't you?"

"Who says I want to talk?"

He climbs into the first carriage and works his way down the side of five rows of slatted wooden seats, varnished to a shine, picking up potato crisp packets and Coke cans, which he drops into a black plastic bag. As he turns to exit, I block his escape.

"Tell me about Syd Collins."

He stares at me for a few moments and then holds out the bag. "If I'm going to talk then you can help me clean up."

I take the bag and step aside. We reach the second carriage before he speaks. "It's no secret. The doctors gave him six months to live two years ago. I'm surprised it took him so long to shuffle off this mortal coil."

"It's more of a bludgeon than a shuffle."

"What are you talking about?"

"He didn't die of natural causes. He had a tussle with an unguarded power takeoff, which pulverised his skull."

Artie shrugs and then bends to retrieve more litter. "He only got the tractor working again a few months ago. Why are you interested?"

"It's a work accident."

"Syd never did a day's work in his life." He laughs, sounding like a donkey. "I shouldn't speak ill of the dead, I know, but he was the most miserable sod on God's earth, especially after a couple of pints."

"You drank at the Game Cock, right?"

He sits on a bench and strokes his beard as he speaks. "Syd drank too much. He smoked too much. He gambled too much. He fed more money into the machines in a night than I earned in a month."

"Where did he get the money if he didn't work?" Gemma asks.

"Birchill has deep pockets. He and Syd go back a long way."

"Tell me about it."

"Syd never stopped talking about the old days. Birchill and him were like Butch Cassidy and the Sundance Kid, the way he told it. They evicted scum, cleaning up the housing market. They had politicians who did their bidding. Not to mention the celebrities they rubbed shoulders with."

He raises his eyebrows and shakes his head. "It was all rubbish, of course, so I asked him to name a few. He gave me a look that sent a chill through me, I can tell you. Then he tells me I can read it in his autobiography."

"He wrote an autobiography?"

Artie laughs. "He could hardly sign his name, let alone write. He said he'd sold it to a newspaper, but he wouldn't say which one."

"You didn't believe him?"

"You think Birchill's going to let him spill the beans? No, it was the beer talking. Syd liked to feel important because he was only the hired help. I told him so. Then, a couple of weeks later, he hands me an email from a journalist."

"Can you remember which newspaper?"

Artie shrugs. "Anyone could have sent the email. Syd was an old man, dying from cancer. He looked like a tramp, dressed like one and smelt like one."

"Not one for shirts and ties then?"

"What do you think?" He glances at his watch and then over to the platform. "Actually, he did wear a suit and tie once. It was a Wednesday evening back in March. European Cup football on the telly, I remember. He came in smelling of cheap aftershave. He'd met a woman on the Internet or something and wanted a bottle of wine. We never saw him again on Wednesdays."

"Including last night?"

"I thought he'd stop by."

"Why?"

"He was in court for driving while over the limit." Artie shakes his head ruefully. "Said he had friends in high places who would see him right, but he knew he was going to lose his licence. That was going to dent his love life on Wednesdays."

"Is that what he told you?" I ask.

"He told me about the court case when I gave him a ride into Tombstone last week."

"You don't start till 10 o'clock, do you?"

"That's right. What of it?"

"Someone told me Collins didn't rise till 10," I reply, wondering what else Artie might know. "Would you give me a lift to his house?"

"Don't you have a car?"

"Gemma's always wanted to ride on the train."

When he glances at her she nods, though I get the feeling she's not happy.

"I'm only supposed to take people who've paid the entrance fee." He gets to his feet and joins us on the platform. "But, if you're going to his house, you could pick up a Marilyn Monroe box set I lent Syd. He never gave it back to me."

"I would if I had a key, Artie."

He takes the black bag from me and says, "There's one under a plant pot by the front door."

While he checks the remaining carriages I consider the idea of an autobiography. It sounds far-fetched, but what if it contains secrets Birchill would rather keep quiet? If he tries to have me thrown off the case, I could do with something to bargain with.

"We need to find the girlfriend," I tell Gemma.

"If he only saw her on Wednesdays she could be married," she says. "She might not go to the inquest."

I pull her back as a surge of children flood across the platform. For a moment, I'm distracted by her perfume. "I think she visited him last night."

"Why?" she asks. Then she snaps her fingers. "The flat tyres on the land Rover?"

I nod, pleased she's on my wavelength.

Parents and children pile into the carriages, fighting for the best places. Artie checks the carriage doors are secure. In a moment he'll be on his way.

"Look, there's no need for both of us to check Collins' house," I say. "I'll go with Artie, which gives you time to collect the paperwork for the tractor service from Tollingdon Agricultural. You could also check with the magistrates about the drunk driving appearance and meet me back here."

"While I'm at the Magistrates Court, why don't I get you a warrant to enter the house?"

"I don't need one," I reply, ignoring her sarcasm. "My powers under the Health and Safety at Work Act allow me to do what I need to do as part of the investigation. There may be valuable evidence in the house."

"Of course. In his autobiography, Collins explains how he removed the guard so he could have a fatal accident."

There are times when I could slap Gemma, but Artie's climbing into his cab. "What if we find the missing guard?" I ask.

"You think he took it home? You'll have to do better than that, Kent."

"Gemma, I really need the maintenance records."

"Sure, but what do I tell Danni when she asks me about today?"

I stop and glance at Artie, who taps his watch. "Do what I do and tell her only what she needs to know."

"And when she asks what you did, Kent?"

I edge towards the train. "Tell her we split up for an hour."

She's shaking her head. "You know Danni has to sign off everything for my learning and development portfolio. I'm not going to lie."

When Artie toots the whistle, I just have time to dash across and jump on board. "You won't have to if we split up."

"I'm sure if you talk to Danni—"

"For God's sake, Gemma, I don't need her permission!"

"Then why are you standing here? Why aren't you on the train?"

I watch Artie pull away, wondering if I've missed my chance to find vital evidence before Birchill removes it. I thought Gemma would understand that. Obviously, I was wrong.

"Lucy would never have questioned my judgement," I tell her.

"In case you hadn't noticed, Kent, I'm not Lucy."

"No, and you're not a team player either."

She smirks. "I'm just following your example, Kent."

I set off for the exit before I say something I'll regret. I wonder if Danni sent Gemma to report on me. Even if this isn't the case, I'm not sure how I can work with someone who won't trust me.

Neither of us speaks as we walk back to Main Street, where the cooking aromas remind me I missed breakfast. My friend, Mike Turner, who makes the best bacon sandwiches in the county, has a mobile café in a layby about a mile away. Before I can suggest this, Danni rings, skipping the formalities as usual.

"How's Gemma doing?" she asks.

"She's fine."

"Excellent. Are you making progress?"

"We are."

"Excellent. I look forward to hearing your full report when we brief the Chief Executive and Councillor Rathbone at one o'clock."

"You want me to leave Tombstone in the middle of the investigation?"

"You can return later," she replies as if I'm a spoilt child. "When Mr. Birchill visits the office at two with his solicitor, we interview him and turn it to our advantage."

So, Birchill intends to take control by offering to help our investigation. No doubt he'll arrive with documents that lay the blame for the accident with Collins. Birchill will have a written statement to show what a model employer he is.

That's what I intend to tell my boss, but it doesn't quite come out that way. "I'll interview Birchill when I'm ready. Not when you say."

"You'll interview Mr. Birchill today. Be here at one."

She ends the call, leaving me to congratulate myself on how well I handled it. At least Birchill can't nose around Collins' house while he's in the council offices. If I can find someone else to interview him, I'll be free to snoop.

Gemma looks at me. "What was that about?"

"We've been recalled to the office. Let's grab something to eat on the way."

"You can eat after what you've seen this morning?"

A bacon sandwich always stimulates my creative juices. "My friend, Mike, runs a mobile café on the bypass."

"Mike's Mighty Munch? Mike Turner's your friend?"

I nod. "Is there a problem?"

"I visited him on Monday to investigate a complaint about poor hygiene." She sighs and looks down. "I'm sorry, Kent, but the place is a mess. You can't let him get away with poor standards."

The van's an old ambulance Mike gutted and refitted for catering a couple of years ago. It's cluttered and untidy, but that doesn't make it unhygienic. Difficult to keep clean, I accept, but not impossible. He's not the neatest caterer I've met, but he passed his food hygiene training, and he has the best management system in the district, thanks to my knowledge and experience.

"It's not fair on other food businesses," she says, growing in confidence. "Imagine what the papers would say if they found out."

She thinks I inspect Mike's food business. "Are you saying you should carry out the hygiene inspections?"

"I wasn't, but... yes, I could do them."

"In that case, I'll clear it with Nigel when we get back to the office."

"Why do you need to clear it with Nigel?"

"He inspects Mike, not me. Didn't you check the file before you visited?"

It was mean of me to lead her on. I should apologise, but I won't. After all, she assumed I'd let a friend break the law. She also needs to learn to check the file before visiting a business.

"Mike can't wait to see you again," I say. "You left quite an impression."

"You knew I visited him?" For a moment it looks like she's going to slap me. "You bastard! You set me up."

"You'll live," I say, leading the way. "You can even show Mike your charming side."

Her cheeks flush. "Why can't we eat here?"

"Mike was a Scenes of Crime Officer before he took up catering. I want to tap into his forensic mind."

"You can't discuss a case with an outsider."

"There you go again, making assumptions, challenging what I do. I'd trust Mike with my life, Gemma, which is more than I can say for you at the moment."

"I've experienced your trust, Kent. Never again, thanks."

Her sneer cuts me down. I deserved that, but I can't change the mistakes I made. I have to look forward, and that means dodging the interview with Birchill. It won't be easy, but I'll think of something. I'm still looking for inspiration when we reach Mike a little after midday. From the number of vans and cars in the layby business looks brisk.

Like most mobile caterers, Mike's customers are mainly plumbers, electricians, builders, plasterers and delivery drivers, topped up by many of his former colleagues in Sussex Police. Mike gives me a nod as I climb out of the Volvo and then serves a mighty burger to a man in a boiler suit. He tips four spoons of sugar into a mug of tea and passes it across.

"Gross," Gemma says. "He's wearing the same white coat as last time."

At a little over six feet, Mike fills the converted ambulance, looking down on customers like a giant. His white coat, smeared with grease and ketchup, gapes to reveal a string vest, stretched like an onion bag over his stomach. His face is just as rounded, sagging into a double chin and fleshy neck that give his voice a booming quality. Everything about him is large, especially his generosity and sense of humour. He needed those as one of the few black coppers in the local force during the 70s.

He gives Gemma a grin that reveals teeth tarnished by too many cigarettes. "Well, if it isn't the Ice Queen. She leaves me cold," he says with a wink.

"I see you haven't done anything about your white coat. It's gross."

He gives it a tug to close the gape. "It shrunk in last night's boil wash."

"I meant it's filthy."

"I know what you meant. In my defence, Your Honour, I've been here since six, cooking hearty meals for hungry travellers." He points to a sign on the wall. "That's one of my slogans, by the way. It's been full on. Try one of my Mighty Burgers and you'll understand why."

"Don't you have a spare coat?"

He turns the burgers on the griddle. "Not since I put it on this morning."

"That's enough," I say. "I came here for lunch and a word with my friend."

"How about the word 'hygiene'?" she asks.

"You should concentrate on the positives like Kent," he says. "He works with people to improve their business, getting them on his side."

"I didn't notice that at Tombstone," she says, giving me a smile.

"Kent hates Birchill." Mike places a couple of mugs on the counter. "I have decaffeinated tea or coffee, as Kent treats his body like a temple. Mine's more of a ruin, so I drink the real thing. Are you planning to refuse a drink again?"

"Unless you can give me a smaller cup."

"Small would take the Mighty out Mike's Mighty Munch. I'm larger than life—portion size, menu choices, the mugs and plates. I'm big on value, big on taste—"

"Big on modesty?"

"I like that. So, what's with the shirt, Kent? Are you wearing it for a bet?" He pulls a pack of bacon from the fridge beneath the counter and turns to Gemma. "Tea or coffee?"

"Mineral water."

"Fresh from the tap every morning. And to eat?"

"It's too early, thanks."

He washes his hands in a small basin, making a show of his antibacterial soap, and then places some rashers on the griddle using tongs. He's not a bad cook for a Scenes of Crime Officer. When he retired three years ago his cooking was as dire as his DIY skills. For someone who could piece together a crime scene from fragments and minute traces, he couldn't assemble a cupboard from a flat pack. The fitter he employed took a shine to his wife and ran off with her.

He took it philosophically. "If I fell into a barrel of boobs I'd come out sucking my thumb."

His marital troubles, coupled with staff shortages and long hours, led him to quit the job. I helped him finish the kitchen in time to sell the house as part of the divorce settlement. He combined his share with the lump sum from his retirement and bought a bungalow on the beach at Pevensey Bay. In the garage he found an old ambulance beneath a tarpaulin. A week in the workshop, a coat of paint, and some second hand catering equipment, and Mike's Mighty Munch was born.

"Stop sniping at Mike," I tell Gemma. "He's on our side."

She watches every move he makes. Like many people new to the job, she expects perfection. In time she'll learn the law's a minimum standard, not a maximum. Most businesses go beyond the minimum, but Mike's broke.

"Honest grub for honest customers," he says with pride.

He wipes his temperature probe and checks the cooking temperature of a sausage. The probe reads 90°C, enough to kill bugs almost instantly. "Are you happy with that?" he asks her.

"You didn't sterilise the probe."

"He leaves it dipped in antibacterial washing up liquid and wipes it with a paper towel before use," I say, aware of the chill in the air. "Check his records and you'll see he also calibrates the probe weekly so it's accurate. Didn't you check all this on Monday?"

Her sigh suggests not. "But it all looks such a mess."

"You don't catch food poisoning from clutter."

Mike serves another customer with a sausage and egg roll before making my bacon sandwich. The aroma's almost unbearable as he takes his time smearing brown sauce over buttered granary bread.

"Are you sure I can't tempt you, Miss Dean?"

When she shakes her head, he turns to me. "On the basis you're not after fashion tips, do I assume you've just come from Tombstone?"

"Bad news travels fast."

He layers three rashers of bacon before encasing them with another slice of granary. "Detective Inspector Briggs stopped by for breakfast. He left it to the Coroner's Officer."

"That's right," I say. "Carolyn Montague. You must have met her."

He shakes his head. "The only Carolyn Montague I remember was fast tracked to a detective inspector in Brighton some years ago. I don't know how she wound up a Coroner's Officer—if it's the same person, of course."

He slices my sandwich diagonally and puts the halves on a paper plate. "I'm guessing it's your case as it's a work accident. I hope you remember what I taught you about examining a crime scene."

I nod, too busy savouring the sweet taste of bacon to talk.

"Miles Birchill turned up," Gemma says, filling the silence.

Mike fills two mugs from a large metal teapot. "So, Collins bought it, did he? There's a happy ending."

"No one deserves to die like that, Mike. It was horrific."

"Collins got what he deserved, if you ask me." He hands me a mug of tea. "You can start your own Sanity Gallery now."

"What's that?" Gemma asks.

"We pinned photographs from our investigations on a wall in the office," he replies. "Then we added captions like 'Norman has no head for business.' That went to a shopkeeper who blew his brains out with a shotgun."

"The humour was blacker than pitch," I say.

"Sounds sick to me," she says.

"It helped us cope." He takes the second mug of tea and heads down the steps at the back of his van. "What do you want to know, pal?"

"Everything you can tell me about Collins."

He taps his fingers on his lips as he thinks.

"We need Hetty. That's former Detective Inspector Harold Wainthropp." He turns to Gemma. "We called him Hetty after the TV series."

She gives him a blank look, too young to remember the pensioner turned detective.

"Hetty spent most of his career trying to nick Collins and Birchill," Mike continues. "He's in a nursing home now. I'll give him a call, if you like."

"Thanks, I need all the help I can get."

"Why are you so interested in Collins?" Gemma asks, sounding frustrated. "You're supposed to be investigating his death, not his life."

"Kent's big on conspiracy," Mike replies, raising a finger to his lips. "He's certain the Royal Family plotted to kill Lady Diana. And don't mention the moon landings; they were mocked up in a warehouse."

"I like the idea there may be alternative explanations and different ways of looking at things," I say. "It's good to speculate and challenge."

"You spent too much time reading books instead of playing football," he says. "How can you grow up in Manchester and not like football?"

Gemma looks surprised. "You grew up in Manchester?"

"Listen to his accent. It's half northern, half southern and half German."

I drain my tea and push the mug into his hand. "Let me know about Hetty."

74

"We could have a bite to eat down at the Bells. Or are you running?"

"I'll let you know."

We're well on the way to Tollingdon before Gemma asks, "What did he mean—you're half German?"

When my mother left Germany she worked in a hospital in Manchester. She never told me how she met my father or came to be in Sussex, and I never thought to ask. We didn't have that kind of relationship.

"My mother comes from Bavaria," I reply.

"How did you end up in Manchester? It's a long way from Downland."

"She went back there when she left my father."

My mother had friends there—not that she ever saw any of them, as far as I could tell.

"I'll bet your father liked that."

"I wasn't keen on the place myself," I say, recalling the move.

I was six or seven at the time and used to open fields and the Downs, not row upon row of sooty houses where people spoke with strange accents that made them sound foreign. The children at school mocked me because I sounded posh. I wanted to go home, but my mother told me my father was dead and we'd been thrown out of the house because she was German. So we lived in a damp basement flat in a road where people played music all night and threw up in our yard.

"Is that why you came back to Sussex?"

"More or less."

When I was 17, my father arrived on the doorstep one evening. My mother was out playing bingo as usual, so we had time to talk, once I'd recovered from the shock. As well as being alive, he was an MP in the House of Commons and a member of several important committees. He couldn't believe we lived in such a dump with all the maintenance he paid my mother. He asked me if I wanted to return home. I packed a rucksack, wrote a note for my mother, and headed south that night.

I haven't heard from or spoken to my mother in the 24 years since that day.

I don't expect to.

CHAPTER SEVEN

Downland is a market town that prides itself on its café culture, art galleries and antique shops. While you're unlikely to find artists and writers sipping peppermint tea or decaffeinated skinny lattes, there are plenty of women sporting artistic fingernails and tattoos.

While the High Street has preserved its Georgian and Victorian brick buildings, the influx of charity shops, takeaways, and nail salons has changed the ambience. The council has tucked away its social housing between the railway line and the sewage works, but they can't stem the influx of teenage mums into the town. According to the *Tollingdon Tribune*, they fill the pavements with their buggies, blocking access to antique shops while they chat and text. Cigarette ends and empty alcopop bottles fill the gutters, while antisocial behaviour turns the town centre into a no-go area on Friday and Saturday nights.

I watch this assault on traditional values from our office in the High Street. We're on the top floor of a three-story red brick building that has all the lavish touches of the Victorians, including ornate windows framed in stone. Majestic chimneys, embellished with intricate corbelling that will cost a fortune to restore rise out of grey slate roofs. The grand oak doors lead into a tiled foyer that has a sweeping staircase, perfect for weddings.

Wood panelling and parquet floors reflect the historic wealth of the area. They also highlight the problems Downland's councillors have in adjusting to the modern world. The council has a building filled with small offices. It can't create the larger open plan spaces it needs for mobile working and hot desks, which would help to cut costs. The old heating system, with its clanking cast iron radiators, needs updating to something greener and more sustainable. Until all these issues can be addressed, the Public Protection Team I manage retains its cosy office. The downside is that Danni is next door, along with the thermostat. Her PA, Kelly, sits outside in a small reception area that boasts unbroken views of the main corridor in each direction. No one sneaks up on us.

Long before I reach Kelly, she's grinning. She struts over in her stilettos and appraises my electric blue shirt. "You look like one of those 1980s porn stars. All you need is a moustache and a mullet."

"You can talk," I say, looking at her short, tight skirt, figure-hugging top and big earrings. "And I bought this shirt in the nineties, not the eighties."

"Geez, Kent, don't you throw anything away—apart from your career prospects?" She points down the corridor. "They're waiting for you in the conference room. When you stroll in, looking like you stepped out of a nightclub, you know what Danni's going to say."

"'You never get a second chance to make a first impression'," we say in unison.

"I need someone like you at home to improve my wardrobe," I say when we stop laughing.

"You'll find it's cheaper to buy new clothes. Now, don't keep Danni and the Chief Executive waiting."

"You haven't asked me about the investigation."

"I don't need to. If Miles Birchill is on his way, you must be making an impression."

Kelly's the smartest person I know. She hides her wit and intelligence by looking, dressing and talking like a barmaid in a rugby club. She flirts with the male directors and managers, who fall over themselves to impress her. Many of the women in the council like the way she manipulates the men by playing dumb. I just love her sense of humour and free spirit.

"Could you tell Danni I'm stuck in heavy traffic and running late?" I ask.

"I could, but she won't believe me. Twinkle Toes is already there."

It takes me a couple of seconds to realise she's referring to Gemma and her diamante sandals. "In that case, tell Danni you haven't seen me. I'll be in Legal if you need me."

"With the dashing Doug or the pliable Philippa?"

"Doug never believes anything I say."

"Then you should stop lying to him, shouldn't you?"

In her office, I explain my dilemma to Philippa Fry, who makes notes between mouthfuls of hummus, forcing me to stop mid-sentence from time to time while she catches up. "I need to interview Miles Birchill," I say, "but he has a restraining order against me. In a moment of madness, I emptied slurry into his car."

She nods as if it's an everyday occurrence. "Yes, I can see how Mr. Birchill might question your impartiality."

"That's why I want you with me in the interview. If he's bringing his best lawyer, then I need our best to balance the odds."

A smile sneaks across her mouth. "I'd be happy to help you, Kent."

I sigh. "Then I realised we shouldn't be balancing the odds."

"No?"

"No. We should tip them in our favour, Philippa. Birchill's coming here, expecting to win because he can rubbish me." I look around the small room and lean closer. "But he can't if someone else interviews him."

She polishes off the last of the hummus. "You mean Lucy, don't you?"

"She's not intimidated by Birchill," I say, as if thinking aloud. "But he won't want to talk to someone from the shop floor, will he?"

"No, those Doc Marten boots don't help, do they?" She pushes her spectacles back up her nose with a forefinger and then smiles. "He'd respect Danni, though."

"Philippa, you're a star. Why didn't I think of Danni?"

"You're too close, Kent."

"Sorry, I'll give you some air," I say, shuffling the chair back.

She giggles. "I mean you're too close to Danni to see her as anything but a manager."

"And you're too smart to waste your time on leases and tenancy agreements. You and Danni are more than a match for Miles Birchill and his overpaid monkeys."

"Then let's get things moving."

Philippa enters the Conference Room with a confidence I haven't seen before. The heels of her sensible shoes beat an assertive rhythm as strides across the parquet floor. She stops and places her folder on the large, mahogany table, surrounded by matching wooden chairs inlaid with velvet.

Danni and the Chief Executive sit at the opposite end with various folders and papers, spread out before them. Gemma, who's chatting to my boss, falls silent when we enter.

The grand room with its oak-panelled walls and intricate plaster ceiling imposes an air of authority and history that can seem daunting when you're holding a team briefing or food hygiene training course. But the grandeur sits uncomfortably with the screen and projector, top of the range sound system, and huge smartboard that only IT knows how to operate.

We sit opposite my boss. "Philippa's had a great idea."

The Chief Executive peers over the top of his glasses. "Why have you brought the Council's Solicitor to this meeting?"

She puts a hand on my arm and rises, as if making an objection in court. "Kent came to me with a problem that could compromise the success of his investigation. Miles Birchill has a restraining order against him."

Danni and Frank glance at each other. "Is this true?" she asks.

"It was five years ago," I reply. "I thought it lapsed when the park was completed. I'm sure my powers of entry override it."

"If Miles Birchill accuses Kent of holding a grudge, it could undermine the investigation," Philippa says.

Danni parts the curtains of brown hair and tucks each side behind her ears. "You never thought to mention this when we spoke earlier?"

"I didn't appreciate how Birchill could use our feud to his advantage."

Danni shakes her head, releasing her hair back into its bob. "You withheld important information that could embarrass the council."

"If someone more senior and respected were to take charge of proceedings," Philippa says, "Mr. Birchill would have no cause to complain."

Frank raises a hand to forestall Danni. "Who do you have in mind?" he asks.

"Danni. She'll show Mr. Birchill we take him seriously."

"I need to keep a healthy distance to remain objective," Danni says, her voice quivering. "I can't take over the investigation."

"You only need to do the interview this afternoon," Philippa says. "I'll be there in case you need legal advice."

"The only advice I need is how to deal with Kent's failure to disclose information that could compromise the council."

"Hang on," I say, meeting Danni's angry stare. "You told me to get the hell out to Tombstone. You never gave me a chance to tell you."

"You could have rung back."

"I was already late. The Coroner's Officer said she'd been waiting for an hour after speaking to you."

"That's my fault," Frank says. "Daniella rang me and I wanted to make sure we covered every base." That's management speak for not knowing what to do. "So," he says, replacing the cap on his fountain pen, "either we cancel the interview, or you and Philippa take charge."

Danni throws another glare at me before turning to Frank. "We'll interview Mr. Birchill when we're ready, not before. I'm happy to take his statement, though."

Frank glances at Philippa, who nods. "I can live with that."

"Good. It shouldn't take too long, either."

Birchill could be in and out of Tollingdon in less than an hour. I'll have hardly any time to nose around Collins' house.

"If he brings any supporting documents, would you check they're genuine?" I ask Philippa.

"I'll make him sit and watch me," she replies. "It could take some time."

I head for the door, barely believing I got what I wanted. Danni intercepts me with surprising speed. "My office in two minutes," she says, striding past.

Gemma falls in beside me. "She won't let you get away with that."

"Get away with what?"

"You stitched her up good and proper. So, how come she got the the top job?"

"I never applied for it. Now, tell me why you rushed off the minute we got here."

"Uncle Frank wanted to know how I got on."

Or Danni wanted to know what I was doing, more like.

I return to the office in silence. Lucy and Nigel scurry over, wanting to know everything. In reality, Lucy wants to know why she's not assisting me, but she can't bring herself to ask outright.

"Gemma can fill you in on the details," I say. "I have to see Danni."

I'm halfway to the door when Kelly waves me over. "I've got Ms. Montague on the phone about the accident."

"Put her through," I say, glad of the distraction.

I return to my desk and search beneath the files and paperwork for a message pad. My "In" tray has enough letters, memos and messages to show I'm behind with my work, mainly food hygiene inspections, complaints and planning consultations. That's in addition to the management meetings, performance monitoring, appraisal reviews and time management training.

The phone rings and I settle back. "Carolyn, how can I help?"

"Back in the office, Kent? Have you wrapped up the case?"

"We're doing okay," I reply, aware that Gemma is taking an interest.

"I'm going to Collins' place in the morning to see if I can find details of any relatives, that kind of thing. Want to tag along?"

I swivel my chair so Gemma can hear me better. "Tell me what time and I'll meet you there."

"10 o'clock. See you then."

She puts the phone down, but I pretend we're still talking. "Two o'clock this afternoon? That's short notice, Carolyn. Yes, I know you're busy, but... okay, I'll see you there."

I hope Gemma caught all that, but just to make sure, I give her the gist as I pass her desk.

Danni's office is an austere room that's functional rather than welcoming. Like the suits she wears, the furniture is grey and modern. The off-white walls are bare, apart from her large Motivational Pinboard, where she places positive and inspiring messages and quotations. The messages vary from week to week, depending on which pithy quotes she culls from her desk calendar.

'A glass that's half full can never be empty' is her current favourite. It distracts me whenever I'm in here because I can't stop wondering what happens if you knock the glass over.

She's standing on a chair, trying to rehang a vertical window blind that's come off its hook. If she strains much further, she'll overbalance. I offer to help, but she tells me to sit.

Danni looks old before her time with her dull bobbed hair, frilly blouse and buckled shoes. Wrapped in a plain grey jacket she can't quite button up and a matching skirt that hangs just below the knee, she only needs glasses to become my old history teacher. We called her Michelin Woman because her blouse bulged into several bands when she sat. She never wore makeup, rarely smiled, and preferred to live in the past, which I suppose you would if you taught history.

"Excellent." Danni jumps to the ground to admire her repair. She hauls the chair back to the table. "'Champions keep playing until they get it right'," she says, determined to turn anything into a learning experience. "Billie Jean King," she adds, nodding at her pinboard.

She sits opposite, back straight and arms on the table, and regards me with pale green eyes. She goes through this ritual every time we meet. I don't know whether she's composing herself, planning her questions, or reminding herself she's a service head at the age of 31. Luckily, she's not at her desk, or I'd have to endure the ritual of her straightening pens, pads, keyboard, mouse and phone.

"How dare you undermine me in front of the Chief Executive?" she growls. "How dare you discuss a case with legal before talking to me? And don't you dare blame me for not knowing you had a grudge against Miles Birchill."

I'm tempted to remind her she arranged an interview with Birchill without consulting me. Two wrongs don't make a right, though, according to the pinboard.

"And why are you wearing such an inappropriate shirt? How many times have I told you—you never get a second chance to make a first impression?"

"My appearance has no bearing on my professional competence."

Her fingers are drumming on table top now. "Are you going to disagree with everything I say and do?"

"I'm not against you, Danni."

"If insubordination were an Olympic sport, Kent, you'd be world champion."

"Don't you mean Olympic champion?"

She grimaces. "You can't stop yourself, can you?"

"I'm not the one demanding three quotes before I seize machinery."

"That was Gemma's role. She was there to help you, not carry the Grab Bag all morning. And before you interrupt," she says, leaning forward, "three quotes would have prevented you selecting the company that services Tombstone's tractors."

"And how else could I prove Tombstone serviced the tractor that killed Collins?"

She folds her arms. "If you have proof, why are you wasting so much time on the victim?"

So, Gemma has reported back.

"I want to know why he was out there so early."

"How does that affect the safety of the machinery or Tombstone's management of the risk?" she asks, relaxing back into her chair. "This is a work accident not a vendetta. Bring me the evidence that proves Tombstone failed in their duty of care."

"I know how to do my job."

"Are you sure?" Her question suggests I've missed something, putting doubt in my mind. "If you've proved Tombstone serviced the machinery, Kent, why won't you confront Miles Birchill?"

I shift in the seat. "I don't have the documents yet."

"Then go and get them. If I have to watch Philippa scrutinise every bit of paper Mr. Birchill produces, then I want to know you're photocopying documents too."

As I reach the door, she calls me back. "I want regular reports on your progress. Understood?"

"How regular?"

"Daily, starting tomorrow morning. I will update everyone on my meeting with Miles Birchill and you can bring the evidence you're collecting this afternoon."

"When you say everyone, who are we talking about?"

She counts them on her fingers. "The Portfolio Holder, Councillor Rathbone, the Chief Executive, Gemma, me and you. I suppose I'll have to include Philippa. Geoff Lamb, our Communications Officer, will attend too. Kelly will take minutes and record action points for us."

Action points is management speak for the instructions Danni intends to give me. "If we prosecute, any minutes will have to be disclosed to Birchill."

"Then be careful what you say. I'll see you at 9.30 tomorrow morning in the Conference Room."

I'm outside the office before I realise she's suckered me. How can I meet Carolyn tomorrow morning if I have to be here?

"What's up?" Kelly asks, pushing an open bag of wine gums toward me.

"Danni's just beaten me at my own game."

CHAPTER EIGHT

My plan to travel to Collins' house by train soon hits the buffers.

My plan was quite simple. We'd ride in the cab with Artie and quiz him about Collins' girlfriend. Artie has other ideas.

"You can't ride in the cab. Health and safety," he says with relish.

Gemma gives him a hurt look. "But I've always wanted to toot the whistle. You'll hardly know I'm there."

With her looks and smile that's highly unlikely. He mops his forehead with a rag. Artie wavers. "I'd like to, but...."

"What if I ride in the carriage?" I ask, taking a seat.

He helps her into the cab and whispers something in her ear. She giggles and watches him trot across the platform to the barrier. He drops his arm and she toots the whistle twice. The noise is almost as big as her grin.

The maelstrom of children swirls across the platform. They pile into the carriage, rocking it in every direction as they push and shove their way to the best seats. It seems like a long time before everyone's seated and ready to go. Artie has his hand next to Gemma's as they toot the whistle to leave. With a jolt, we're on our way across Tombstone's wild plains, as the brochure describes them. With the children churning around me, it's wild enough in the carriage, thank you.

Once we leave the town, the train rumbles through fields and pastures occupied by buffalo, ostrich, llama, and horses. They gather in the shade of the trees, indifferent to our passing. The children on either side of me, however, can't sit still. Not content with trying to clamber over and around me while shooting their toy pistols at each other, they make enough noise to give me tinnitus. Gemma encourages them by pointing her finger at them like a pretend gun.

A few minutes later, the line crosses the road from the barn to the town. We're soon running along the fringe of the woods. The train slows at the end of a chestnut grove and it's time to exit.

"That was awesome," Gemma says, waving to the kids as the train pulls away. "Artie's a real sweetie. You really upset him this morning."

"Yeah, I noticed him crying as he left the station. Did you ask him about Collins' girlfriend?"

"No, but I discovered that Collins and Birchill fell out over Tombstone. Collins assumed he would run Tombstone, but Ben Foley got the job. His father's a Downland district councillor." She raises her eyebrows to signify the obvious. "Birchill wanted Collins to run the maintenance side of things, giving him the house, the barn and all the machinery, but Collins refused the job."

"That's why the machinery in the barn has never been used. Birchill must have been furious after all the money he spent."

She nods. "Collins decided to make fence posts and sell them to Tombstone, but the tractor broke down after a few months. He gave up and spent most of his time in the pub, Artie reckons."

I think about this while we plod through the long grass, disturbing the crickets and grasshoppers that sing to each other. Butterflies fold open their wings to the sun when they settle on the many wild flowers that drift across the grass. Overhead, a kestrel hovers on the thermals, looking for a naïve field mouse or vole. Gemma, coated in factor 50, discovers her sandals offer no protection against stinging nettles. When we reach the woods, her ankle and toes are itchy red. She stops and gently massages the affected areas, her face twisted into a mixture of pain and ecstasy.

"So, what changed?" I ask, resting against a tree trunk. "Why did Collins get the tractor fixed and start work at six this morning?"

"Maybe he was sharpening a stake to drive through Birchill's heart," she says.

We laugh and set off again, stepping over twisted roots and squeezing between banks of nettles stretching to reach the light. The shade feels invigorating, full of an energy that charges the air. I run my hand over the rough bark, sensing the flow of sap beneath as it fuels these mighty trees to oxygenate the planet. No wonder people want to hug them.

"Do you think there's an autobiography?" Gemma asks.

I hope so. If nothing else, it might give me something useful to use against Birchill. "Maybe it's hidden with the missing guard."

"Or a suicide note." She turns, her face full of excitement. "Why not, if he had cancer?" she asks, answering my frown. "What if he couldn't take the pain anymore? If he commits suicide, the insurance won't pay, so he fakes an accident."

And I thought *I* had a vivid imagination. "Who collects the insurance?"

"His family, I guess." She follows her half-hearted reply with a long sigh and rubs at her itching ankle. "I know it sounds nuts, but suicide explains why he was there early and why he was wearing a tie. The empty vodka bottle means he got drunk to numb any pain."

"Why not drive your car into a wall or off Beachy Head?"

She smiles smugly. "The tyres on his Range Rover were flat."

"Good point. Say, did you check if Collins was in court?"

"I went straight to see Uncle Frank and Danni in the Conference Room. I'll ring when we get back to the office."

"Did you tell them about your adventures this morning?"

"I told Danni not to eat at Mike's Mighty Munch."

"You did what?"

"Joke!" she cries, holding up her hands. "I told her we interviewed Cheung, Foley and Artie. Obviously, she wanted to know what they'd told us."

"And who they were," I say, recalling Danni's instruction to focus on the accident, not Collins.

Gemma sighs. "She wanted to know why we interviewed a train driver. I said you wanted to know more about Collins."

"I want to know what Danni said when she rang you this morning."

We walk a few paces before Gemma replies. "I had to ring her, actually. She rang three times before half seven, so I knew it was serious."

That might explain why Danni took 30 minutes to phone me after taking the call from Carolyn. It doesn't explain why my boss rang Gemma first.

"She told me to get the Grab Bag from the office and meet you on site," she continues.

"Did you wonder why she'd asked you to assist me?"

She shakes her head. "Danni said you'd requested me. She said she was surprised, but assumed you knew what you were doing." She pauses, looking confused. "Hang on. You said you asked for Lucy. What's going on?"

That's what I'd like to know. "When Danni rang me, she'd already spoken to you."

"What do you mean? I don't understand."

"Danni rang you first. Why would she do that?"

"I don't know," she says, becoming agitated. "Don't look at me like that."

"Like what?"

"Like I've betrayed you or something. I never asked to come on this case, you know. Danni sent me."

"But why?" I ask. "Why did she pick you? You've said she wants you to report back each day."

She shields the sun from her eyes as she stares at me. A few moments pass before she understands what I'm suggesting. After the initial surprise, which looks genuine enough, she gives me a look of such contempt I almost feel guilty.

"Do you remember when you inspected La Floret?" she asks, struggling to keep her voice calm.

How could I ever forget?

"You told me to follow my dreams. All I had to do was believe in myself. Nothing's impossible, you said, if you want it bad enough."

"Did I say that?"

"Yeah, the night before the morning you snuck out. When I knew you'd dumped me, I went to London to make a fresh start. For five or six years I had a great time, but it wasn't what I wanted. I wanted to make a difference, just like you. So I spoke to Uncle Frank," she says, lowering her head. "I wanted advice. I never thought he'd get me a job in your team."

"You wanted to empty bins, did you?"

"I might have known you wouldn't believe me." She glares at me and turns away. "Well, don't flatter yourself that I came back because of you. I'm not the awestruck virgin you seduced."

She stumbles through the grass and nettles in her haste to get away. I watch, remembering how I had been the nervous one, surprised at how confident and self-assured this young waitress was. Not that it makes any difference now. She's engaged to Richard now, a respectable, trustworthy solicitor who has money and status. Like most solicitors I've met, he operates slowly. She doesn't have a ring on her finger yet.

I set off after her, catching up with her as she breaks out of the woodland onto the grass path that leads to Collins' house. I knock on the front door hard enough to wake the dead. When no one answers, I peer through the adjacent window. I shield my eyes from the sun, but I still can't make out anything inside.

"Carolyn should be here," I say, checking my watch. "Maybe she's parked around the back."

I pretend to search for a few minutes before returning. "She just rang to say she's been called out. She'll be here as soon as she can. Apparently, there's a key under a pot by the front door if we want to make a start in the meantime."

Gemma selects the large variegated hosta nearest the door and heaves the pot back. She pulls out a key on a piece of twine. "How did she know about the key?"

"Artie told us, remember?"

"Yeah, but how did Carolyn know?"

That was a careless slip. "Maybe Cheung told her."

93

She hands me the key and says, "I'm not going in there. It's like we're invading Collins' privacy."

"He's dead. He's hardly going to protest."

I turn the key in the lock and open the door. "Watch out for the rats," I say, pointing to the flattened grass where the foxes run along the base of the wall. "You don't normally see them during the day unless they're hungry."

She steps back, staring at the run and looking along the wall. "Rats? Here?"

"Imagine how big you look to them, Gemma. They'll probably scatter in all directions if they see you. I'll close the door so they don't run into the house."

I walk into the homogenous cream hall, which looks like it's never been used. I run my fingers along the top of the dresser, but there's no dust. The carpet is dirt and stain free. There are no shoes or umbrellas, no hats or coats on the hooks. I feel a warm breeze on the back of my neck, followed by the sound of the door slamming.

"I heard rustling in the grass," Gemma says, glancing over her shoulder. "I didn't wait to see what it was."

"Okay, now you're here, tell me what's missing."

She walks up and down the hall, glancing at the floor, walls and ceiling. "Character," she says without hesitation. "It looks antiseptic."

I open the first door on my left into a living room. "The place should reek of cigarette smoke."

"Not if he smoked outside. There were cigarettes in the Land Rover, right?"

Lieutenant Columbo wouldn't accept that. He'd check every little detail, looking for anything out of place as he unpicked perfect murders. I'm not Columbo, and this isn't a murder, but there are too many details that don't make sense.

I look around the lounge, furnished in the same colour and style as the hall. Maybe Collins landed a job lot of ex-display furniture from a showroom. The money he saved paid for the enormous flat screen TV on the wall. Underneath, in a cabinet, I find a collection of DVDs, all in neat lines on the shelves.

"What are we looking for?" Gemma asks, opening a drawer.

"Address books, diaries, bank statements, photographs." The films are mainly musicals from the 1950s and 60s. Fred Astaire, Doris Day and Elvis feature prominently. "Anything that could identify friends or family."

I slide out the Marilyn Monroe box set. While I've never seen any of her films, I can see why she attracted so much interest. While there's no disputing her beauty, she has a vulnerability that makes her irresistible. I can imagine her surprise if someone told her she looked stunning.

"She's not your type," Gemma says, looking over my shoulder. "You prefer the lean, toned look, judging by the way you watch female runners—and waitresses."

I place the box set on the arm of the sofa, wondering if I'm so easy to read. "Anything else you've noticed about me?"

She runs her finger along the spines of the DVDs. "Collins organises his collection alphabetically by its stars, but you choose genre, followed by the titles in alphabetical order. You rearranged my meagre collection. I didn't notice until you'd gone and it made me madder than ever. It was like you were taking over, imposing your tastes on me."

"I wanted to make it easier for you to find your films."

"You do the same when you inspect kitchens. You scan the room and then home in on the detail. So," she says, looking pleased, "what do you think of this room?"

I look around, wishing there was a photograph or some art on the walls. "It's all lazy," I say, wishing I could pinpoint what troubles me. "He's bought a show house, but he doesn't live in it. Does that make sense?"

"Sure." She's on her knees, looking at the lowest shelf of films. She holds up *Star Wars—A New Hope.* "You went gaga over Carrie Fisher, didn't you?"

Carrie Fisher filled my adolescent fantasies. She was my perfect woman with dark, mischievous eyes, a feisty temperament, and a wry sense of humour. As we shared the same surname, I used to pretend we were married.

"How do you know about that?" I ask, making a note to watch the films again.

"You said I reminded you of her."

I said many things, all of them now safely locked away in a mental cabinet.

The cream theme spills into the dining room, filled with a table and four chairs. A brief search of the sideboard reveals some Blenheim Palace coasters and place mats in one of the drawers. Gemma pulls out a chair and drops into it.

"This is pointless, Kent. Collins filled his house with expensive new furniture and never used it."

I nod, making a connection. "There's a barn full of new equipment that's never been used. Now we have a house full of furniture that's never been used."

"So?"

I shrug. "It's an interesting echo, don't you think?"

"I think we should hurry up and get out of here," she replies. "I feel like an intruder, poking around like this. What if someone catches us?"

"We're in the middle of nowhere."

While she watches through the lounge window for visitors, I go into a modern kitchen extension that's lined with glossy white cupboards, set against black tiled walls. I find nothing out of the ordinary in the cupboards and drawers and join Gemma at the foot of the stairs.

"Maybe we'll get lucky upstairs," I say.

"You wish," she says, sauntering ahead. "I'm not that kind of girl."

On the way up, the smell of stale cigarettes grows until it pervades the landing. I open a window and look out, wondering if Collins walked to the Game Cock or drove. I'm sure the pub isn't far along the lane, but I'll need to check. First, I need to deal with the reek of cigarette smoke that escapes from the rear bedroom.

"Close the door, will you?"

She ignores me and dives into the room, emerging a few moments later. She shuts the door behind her and breathes out in relief. Wafting fresher air into her lungs with her hand, she joins me by the open window. I step back, the acrid smell already burning at the back of my throat.

"I've opened the window," she says, "but it'll take hours to clear the smell. At least we know where he smoked."

"Thanks," I say, keen to put as much distance as possible between me and the room.

The front bedroom continues the Art Deco theme, expanding it to include curtains, pillowcases and duvet, all enhanced with a floral pattern. It's a large room, spanning the width of the house. While Gemma dives into the wardrobes, I peel back the net curtain and look out at the woodland. To my right, the trees give way to grassland. Beyond, there seems to be a road, leading to a gate in the stone wall, but I can't be sure.

"No suits, shirts or ties," she calls, closing the door. "Collins was a denim and tee shirt guy, with a fondness for suede shoes." She crosses the room and opens the other wardrobe. "This one's empty, apart from a spare duvet and pillows."

I fold back the duvet on the bed to reveal a wrinkled sheet beneath, but only on one side. "Damn!" I curse, lifting the pillow. "The revolver's missing."

She rushes over. "What revolver?"

"How would I know? It's missing."

She snatches the pillow from my hand and stares at the sheet beneath. "Not funny," she says, striking me with the pillow. "Can we go now?"

I've no intention of leaving yet. "Why do I get the feeling someone's cleaned this place from top to bottom?" I ask, heading for a waste bin in the corner.

"You wouldn't say that if you saw the office. What are you doing?"

In detective films, the waste bin always contains a clue of some kind. On this occasion, it's the foil and plastic packaging from a condom, nestled among some crumpled tissues.

"What do you make of this?" I ask.

She peers inside and sniffs. "Scented tissues. Unless Collins has a feminine side, he had company last night. Artie said he saw her Wednesdays."

"They had sex, yet she didn't stay." I return to the bed and raise the other side of the duvet to reveal a smooth sheet. "Did she leave last night or this morning?"

"What difference does it make?"

I shrug, interested in anything I can't explain. "When we find her, imagine what she can tell us about Collins. In the meantime, his house will have to do the talking."

The bathroom faces the back bedroom across the landing. It's modest but modern, dominated by a large bath with air jets to aerate the water. As I open the cabinet, I catch a glimpse of my face in the mirror. Some mornings I look and feel like I'm 50. The blue shirt doesn't help, making my complexion look darker.

The cabinet contains the usual toiletries, plus a box of nicotine patches tucked underneath a pack of band-aids at the back. "Maximum strength," I say, showing them to Gemma.

She laughs. "They didn't work, judging by the smell from the office."

I return the patches, knowing I have to face the smell. While I'd sooner avoid it, this last room could be the one that reveals something about Collins.

"No sign of Carolyn," I remark, peering out of the landing window as we pass.

Cigarette smoke has impregnated every surface in the room like an invisible poison. Unlike the rest of the house, this room is a tip. The woodchip wallpaper, once white, has turned yellow and has started to peel at the junction with the ceiling. The carpet feels sticky beneath my feet, having surrendered whatever colour it had to dirt and grease. The net curtain on the window is stained brown, especially along the top where the casement opens. The sticky film on the surface of the glass makes my stomach turn. I hate fat and grease in all its forms, but this film feels particularly nasty. Realising it must be tar from the cigarettes I hurriedly wipe my finger on my handkerchief.

Gemma peers through the window. "Collins could see everyone who passed by while he sat at his desk."

The beech-effect, self-assembly desk, purchased from a DIY store, matches the bookcases that line the side wall. There's a cupboard over the stairwell, and some metal racking, containing rows of cardboard boxes, similar to the ones we use at work to archive documents. Unlike the other rooms, dust is not only tolerated but allowed to flourish, coating most surfaces. I drop into the leather executive chair, which is protected by a polythene wrapper, and swivel from side to side.

"Bit of a contrast to the rest of the place," I say, switching on the tower computer. "Why don't you check the bookcases and cupboards while I see what I can find on his computer?"

She nods, but seems reluctant to move away from the window. I glance about the room, noticing two black and white photographs of Winston Churchill. For Collins, who struggled to read and write, Churchill's wit and mastery of words must have been inspiring. My father would have agreed with that.

Gemma plunges into an archive box. "Pirate DVDs," she says, holding one aloft. "And CDs. Does the printer take CDs?"

I pull down the flap and take a closer look. "Yes, you can print CDs on this. So, that's how he made a living, selling dodgy discs at car boot fairs. I wonder if trading standards knew about him."

The computer continues to boot, and thankfully, it's not password protected. While the hard drive continues to work overtime, I walk over to the cupboard above the stairwell. Inside, the shelves are crammed with duty free cigarettes, purchased on the continent. There are a few packs of tobacco, one with a couple of pouches missing. Maybe

Collins sold them to Cheung. At least I know how Collins made the money to buy his show house furniture.

"I wonder how Birchill would react if he knew about this?"

I return to the desk. I pull a concertina folder full of utility bills from a small drawer to my right. They date back several years. But where are the bank and credit card statements, the calculator, notebooks, calendar and all the other bits and pieces most people have? There's no paper for him to print on. Mind you, if he doesn't write, he won't need to print. At least the PC has booted. In Explorer, I check the folder tree. The 'Documents' folder contains 20 files, labelled Chap 1 to Chap 20 consecutively.

"At last," I say to myself, double clicking Chap 1. To my surprise and frustration, a password window opens. This repeats for the next ten chapters I double click. With a sigh, I fall back in the chair and push the mouse away.

"What's the problem?" Gemma walks up behind me, places her hands on my shoulders, and bends to look at the screen. "Is this the autobiography Artie mentioned?"

"I'll let you know when I crack the password."

She gives me a worried look. "How long's that going to take?"

I glance at my watch. We've been here over an hour. "I'll do it at home."

I remove the memory stick I keep on my key ring. It takes a while for the computer to install the stick, but once completed, I copy the files across. Mike will have friends in the police who can crack the password.

"I'll check his emails," I call, launching Outlook Express. "Then we'll go."

"I hope so," she says, back at the window. "This place gives me the creeps."

"Why?" I ask, looking at a long list of emails in the Inbox. Though tempted to read some, I export them to the memory stick. I can view them at home later without any interruption. "Because Collins is dead?"

She flattens herself against the wall. "Someone's coming!"

CHAPTER NINE

I know it's not Carolyn, but Gemma doesn't.

"It's probably Carolyn," I say, strolling over. "What did you see?"

"Someone in the lane. I saw them through the bushes."

"Man or woman?"

She shrugs. "I only caught a glimpse."

"Could it have been a rambler? Lots of people walk around here."

She shakes her head. "Someone ducked out of sight behind the bushes." She turns those dark brown eyes on me. "Let's go, Kent. If someone finds us here...."

If Birchill's returned from the interview, why would he park in the lane and sneak around? In fact, why would anyone sneak around? No one would be expecting us to be here. Then I realise the window is open.

"Okay, we'll go." I return to the computer, eject the memory stick and pocket it. Gemma's already on her way down the stairs. I still have to shut down the computer. While I wait, I spot her notebook on a bookshelf.

"Come on!" she calls from below.

I set the computer to close. After a final glance out of the window, I head down the stairs to join her. She grabs my arm and hurries me towards the front door. "I don't want to lose my job."

"You're not going to lose your job."

"I don't have your father to protect me."

I wrestle my arm free. "He doesn't protect me."

"You wouldn't get away with half the things you do if you if he wasn't MP."

"While your uncle, the Chief Executive, got you the job, so he won't want you to lose it."

The sound of keys in the back door sends her rushing for the front door. She wrenches it open and stumbles out. I want to wait and find out who's coming in, but Danni will make my life hell if she finds out. I leave quietly, and then as an afterthought, slam the door behind me.

I hurry across the clearing, joining her behind a spotted laurel bush. I lower a branch and watch, certain the visitor will come to the door. There's movement behind the net curtain in the front room, but the reflection off the glass makes it impossible to see who's inside.

"You left the Marilyn Monroe DVDs out," she says, her voice a harsh whisper.

"They won't point to us. Now, had I left the memory stick or my notebook, then I'd be worried."

She looks down at her empty hands and mutters an expletive. "Danni will go ballistic. I told you I didn't want to go in there."

"Look on the plus side. If someone hands in your notebook, we'll know who the visitor is."

She looks ready to strangle me. "All my notes about the investigation are in the notebook."

"Then I guess I'd better check them for accuracy." I pull my hand from behind my back and open her notebook. "You've misspelt 'apology'."

"You bastard!" She snatches the notebook and turns away, so relieved she forgets to thank me.

I'm already ringing Kelly at the office. "Has Birchill left?"

"About half an hour ago," she replies. "Do you want a word with Danni?"

"No. Can you let the duty officer know we're safe? I'll see you tomorrow."

"You haven't forgotten Danni's briefing, have you?"

"How could I forget something so important?" I end the call, wondering how I can get out of the briefing to meet Carolyn at ten. Then again, do I need to go around Collins' house tomorrow?

"Let's go back," I tell Gemma. "We can pretend we were walking past and saw something."

"No way" she says. "I've had enough for one day."

"Don't you want to know who's in there?"

"Not if it means losing my job."

"Where's your sense of adventure?"

"What if there's an intruder in there?"

"They don't carry back door keys, Gemma."

"I'm just saying you could get hurt."

I almost do when I step out from the bush and collide with Cheung. I'm not sure who's more surprised, but I react first, blocking his way. He's wearing the same jogging pants and Nirvana tee shirt he wore this morning.

"I thought you were working," I say.

He pulls out the earphones. "They let me have the rest of the day off. I fancied a pint at the Cock."

"It's not open in the afternoon."

"Pubs are open all day. Haven't you heard?"

"Why don't we all go? We can write up your witness statement."

He shifts uneasily. "I thought you couldn't drink on duty."

"I'm allowed orange juice and lemonade."

He looks about him as if he's expecting someone to walk up. Then he offers to make tea at his hovel. "I don't want to talk about the accident in public."

Without waiting for our agreement, he pushes his earphones in and turns. We follow a few paces behind. Gemma tells me the witness statement forms are in her Volvo back in the main park, but I'm hardly listening. Cheung was on his way to meet the visitor in Collins' house, I'm sure of it. Cheung's appearance on the path is no coincidence.

"Get the number for the Game Cock," I tell Gemma. "Find out if they're open all day."

"Will we have time to visit?" she asks.

If I meet Carolyn in the morning, I can go to the Game Cock after.

We follow Cheung in silence and soon emerge from the trees. At the back of the hovel, the garden's a scramble of weeds, grasses and shrubs that must be a haven for the local foxes. A wooden shed slumps at the end of the patio, propped up on one side by two rusting refrigerators. A tall wooden fence keeps the woodland at bay.

A single glazed lean-to spans the back of the house. The polycarbonate roof panels, streaked green and black with algae, keep out the sun. Not that it's warm inside. The damp walls, stained where the flashings have failed, give the air a cool, musty feel that's as unpleasant as the greasy flagstones under my feet.

I'm surprised to see a fridge and chest freezer. Both plug into an extension block, which hangs from a cable that slips through a small window into the kitchen.

"Why do you have a fridge and freezer out here?" I ask.

He pulls a ring of keys from his pocket. "When you see inside you'll understand."

The musty smell of mould and damp fill the air, oozing from perished and crumbling plaster. Black mould creeps out from the corners like a shadow, sidling down the walls and along the ceiling. The furniture fares no better, with old plywood wall cupboards and base units barely clinging to the walls. Doors slump on aluminium hinges. Shelves sag and groan under the weight of dented and rusty tins. A glance into the stone sink reveals a bowl filled with dark, slimy water.

"You could have some undiscovered strains of salmonella here," I say.

"That's why I keep my food out there," Cheung says.

"How can you live like this?" Gemma asks. "It's unhealthy."

He laughs. "You could speak to my landlord, but he's dead."

My shoes stick to the vinyl floor tiles as I follow Cheung. "Collins owned this place?"

"Sure." He lifts an old metal kettle from one of the rings on the old cooker. "Would you like a cup of tea?"

The burned-on grease on the cooker makes my stomach turn. I hate fat in all its guises, especially when it gets under my fingernails. I strip the skin from chicken, refuse to eat most pork joints and lamb. But, as my stepmother frequently points out, I have no problem with cakes and pastry.

Gemma declines, but I accept. "I can see why you call it a hovel, David."

"It's close to work," he says, pulling two mugs from a cupboard. "I can't afford a place in town, and I'd need a car to get here, so this is fine."

"Why don't you get another job?" Gemma asks.

"Doing what?" He fills the kettle and places it back on the cooker. When he turns on the ring, I half expect a fuse to blow. "I left school at 16 with no qualifications. I'd been in trouble with the law, so no one wanted to employ me. Syd got me the job here. It's crap, I know, but I have somewhere to live."

"It must be freezing in winter," she says.

He dips into a box of teabags. "I only came here in March, so I don't know."

"You said Collins got you the job," I say, trying not to touch anything. "How do you know each other?"

"I guess he got my name from the Job Centre."

"But why did he choose you, David? You got a job and a house. Haven't you ever wondered?"

He laughs. "You've never had a criminal record. I was so desperate I didn't care. He asked me to come and see him and here I am."

Collins had found Cheung, who then returned the compliment. Only Collins was dead.

"What was he like when you first started here?" I ask.

"He liked to talk about his 'special arrangement' with Mr. B." Cheung frames the special arrangement in finger quotes. He steps outside and returns with a carton of milk. He gives the spout a sniff, considers for a moment, sniffs again, and decides it's usable. Gemma looks relieved that she declined tea.

"He said they hooked up during the property slump in the early 90s," Cheung says. "They converted old houses into flats, that kind of thing. He promised to do this place up."

"What went wrong?" I ask.

"He was either drunk or asleep."

He makes the tea and suggests we go into the front room. "I've got chairs in there."

They turn out to be deck chairs, taken from Eastbourne seafront. Three of them form an arc around one side of a small table. Another small table beneath the window provides a base for an old TV with an internal aerial on top. A mattress and quilt lay on the bare boards at the back of the room, suggesting he doesn't use upstairs, except for the bathroom maybe. I look up through missing plaster and floorboards to the roof. It must be freezing in winter, even with a coal fire in the grate.

"My colleagues in Housing could get this place sorted for you," I say.

"And Mr. B will throw me out."

"He can't do that."

"Who's going to stop him? Anyway, I won't be here much longer." He lowers himself into a deck chair and settles. "Why do you need a statement? I've told you all I know."

"It's a proper record, signed by you."

"You can't make me give a statement. I know my rights."

I lower myself into the deck chair at the other end of the arc, forcing Gemma to take the middle one. I almost spill my tea as I come to rest with my backside lower than my knees. There's no quick escape from these.

"David, the accident could have been prevented."

"I know. If Syd hadn't removed the power takeoff guard, he would be alive."

"Tombstone has a legal duty to provide safe machinery. It wasn't safe. They're responsible for his death. Don't you think they should be punished?"

"People die all the time and nobody cares," he says, his voice filled with bitterness. "That's how it is."

"Did you lose someone close?" I ask, sensing an opportunity.

"What do you care? You had a rich daddy to get you anything you wanted. I never knew who my dad was. I grew up in a basement flat with just my mum. We didn't have any money or friends. You should try living like that."

I say nothing about my childhood.

I struggle out of the deck chair and walk over to the window. "What about your father?" I ask. "David? Does your mother know who he is?"

"She's dead." He cradles his mug of tea, lost in thought. "She said it was better if I didn't know."

Gemma puts her hand on his arm. "You must have been devastated."

He drains the rest of his tea. "Shit happens."

I recall how I felt, believing my father was dead. It didn't affect me until I started senior school and mixed with the middle classes. Until then, poverty was a natural state. I didn't know it made me different until others judged me because I was poor. I learned to keep quiet about the free uniform and school meals. I learned not to invite other children home. I hated denying who I was. I hated school and the kids who wouldn't accept me for who I was. And I hated my father for dying and dumping all this on me.

Now I hate my mother.

"You're right," I say, placing the cup on the table. "Shit happens. I'm not going to bother about a statement, but I want you to answer me one question. Was there anything unusual about this morning? Some little detail you've remembered? You see, I don't understand why Collins went to the clearing this morning."

Cheung shakes his head. "Me neither."

He stares into his cup and I signal to Gemma. She extends a hand and I haul her out of the deck chair. As we're about to step into the lean to, Cheung calls out.

"I heard a car."

I head back to the front room. "What car? When?"

"After I turned off the tractor. I thought I heard a car."

"You were certain a moment ago."

"Hey, I'd just found Syd. I freaked, man. I had to phone for an ambulance."

"Okay, I understand. Where was the car?"

"I'm not sure I heard one, but if I did, it could have been on the service road. It comes out near Syd's house."

"Which way was the car going—towards the park or away from it?"

"I don't know, man. My head's scrambled."

"Do you believe him?" Gemma asks when we're clear of the house.

"About the car? I don't know."

"I think he wants to help, but he's afraid of Birchill."

"Like everyone else."

"But not you, Kent."

I wish I could say he didn't frighten me, but he could have me thrown off the investigation or cost me my job.

"We have laws to uphold, Gemma. If we let others intimidate us, we're useless. Now, let's find this service road."

"Why?"

111

"When we pass Collins' house we can check if our visitor's still around."

"No way! I don't want to go anywhere near Collins' house."

We return to the barn to collect my car. When we reach the road junction south of the barn, I head north. A few minutes later, we reach the farm gate I'd spotted from Collins' bedroom.

"Is it locked at night?" I ask, rattling the huge padlock and thick chain hanging to the side of the gate. "Was it locked this morning?"

I drive back to the park, pulling over by the burnt out office. We walk over to the jail. The noise and bustle from earlier has waned to leave the sounds of chairs being stacked, doors closing, and people dumping trash into bins. The smell of cigarette smoke is everywhere as half the caterers step outside for a quick smoke.

"Look at the amount of litter," I say. "Cheung's got a lot of catching up to do."

I knock on the door to the jail and go inside. Rebecca seems surprised to see us, probably because it's almost five-thirty. "I thought you'd left," she says in that irresistible Scouse accent.

"I couldn't keep away," I say, giving her my best smile. "Is Foley in?"

She fetches him from the cells. He stifles a yawn as he approaches. "How can I help?"

"What can you tell me about the service road that exits the park close to Collins' house?"

"Our deliveries come that way. It helps us keep them separate from the public—health and safety and all that."

I perch on the edge of Rebecca's desk. "Take me through a typical day."

"The first delivery arrives about half eight," he replies, glancing at Rebecca for confirmation.

"Does every delivery driver have a key?"

"We have the only key." He points to some hooks on the wall. "We lock the gate on our way home. Then, in the morning, we unlock it."

"Is that what you did this morning?"

He shakes his head. "I got a call from the police and went around the park to the front entrance to meet them. I've got it on CCTV if you want to look."

"Did you unlock the service gate later?"

He shifts from one foot to the other. "I never thought about it until I spotted the delivery vehicles. Someone else unlocked the gate."

"Who?"

"The keys are over there. Anyone could borrow them."

"Anyone?"

"You'd have to know they were here," he says, his voice rising. "Look, what are you suggesting?"

I'm wondering if Cheung heard a car. If he did, was it leaving or entering Tombstone? And why? "Who locks and unlocks the gate when you're on holiday?"

"My deputy, John."

"Did he do it this morning?"

"He's on holiday this week. Look, why are you suddenly interested in this gate? Have you been talking to Cheung? What's he been saying?"

I'm interested to know why they suspect Cheung, so I say nothing, letting the silence invite him to say more. Rebecca cracks first. "A couple of weeks ago, the keys went missing."

"They were returned the same afternoon," he says. "Cheung found them in a rubbish bin. He brought them here and spent the rest of the day cleaning them."

I'm now starting to believe Cheung. It looks like someone could have made copies of the keys to unlock the service gate. The only question is, why would someone do that?

"Who knows the keys are here?" I ask.

"Most people," Rebecca replies. "The office is never locked."

"Maybe it should be," I say.

Gemma and I walk back to the car in silence. While I feel I've made some progress, she clearly doesn't share my optimism.

"What was all that about?" she asks.

"I wanted to test whether Cheung could have heard a car."

"What's it got to do with Collins' accident?"

I smile. "If I knew that, I wouldn't be asking questions, would I?"

CHAPTER TEN

I reach home shortly after six, desperate to swap my sweaty shirt and chinos for something casual. Home is an old barn in a remote corner of the Fisher ancestral estate. My father sold the manor house and grounds five years ago when he could no longer afford the upkeep. This means my 50 acres of low-grade pasture and woodland are all that remain of an estate occupied by the family since the Norman Conquest. While I've no interest in history, I want to safeguard this small plot and maintain the Fisher link to the area.

The land nestles at the foot of the majestic South Downs, which always fill me with wonder, no matter what time of day or year. These gentle hills rise from the patchwork of fields in the valley below to flow across the skyline in waves of green. For thousands of years, mellow breezes from the sea have risen over the chalk cliffs of the Seven Sisters to mould the soft green curves of these hills. The stiffer winds from the west have combed back the trees and the shrubs, spreading seed to colonise the grasslands.

The sun's setting now, stretching the shadows, contrasting the light with the dark. The light softens in the evening, giving the land a contented glow as the animals and birds of the night emerge.

My animal sanctuary, known privately as Fisher's Folly because it devours money, occupies the land. Frances helps me run the place, and we take in donkeys, ponies, horses, goats, pigs and occasionally dogs, which we try to rehome. We rescue any animal that needs help but pass most to those who know how best to deal with them. In spring, we have an influx of orphaned fox cubs and badgers, which we put back into the wild as soon as we can.

All my spare cash goes into this place to supplement the donations and sponsorship we generate. My father makes good the shortfall each month, even though we never meet his targets to reduce the deficit. I can't see how we will ever become self-sufficient unless we charge entry and open a café or restaurant. It means we will need to offer more than a few animals that are getting better or living out a deserved retirement in peace and comfort.

I will also have to pay Frances a reasonable wage. She lives in a small caravan behind the barn. During the cold winter months, she moves into the flat I created across the first floor of the barn. Below are the dog kennels, an isolation room for sick animals, and a store full of second hand catering equipment. Mike and I buy equipment from pubs and restaurants that are closing down. We clean and refurbish the gear and sell it to new and existing businesses. All the profits go to the sanctuary.

Before I change clothes I need to help Frances. With her long, dark dreadlocks, interwoven with beads and ribbons, it's easy to see why people imagine she's new age. Her combat fatigues and Doc Marten boots do little to shift that image, but she's softer than cotton wool if Bambi comes on TV. Her blunt attitude toward men, especially those who wear suits, suggests problems in her past, and the fact she prefers animals to people bonds us together. Like me, she loves lost causes, but she's far too serious for a girl of 20.

"You shot off early this morning."

"Someone died at Tombstone Adventure Park."

"Miles Birchill?"

The grin transforms her brooding features, revealing the beauty beneath the hard image. Her blue eyes, sublime beneath long lashes, gleam at the prospect of Birchill's demise.

"No, one of his workers." I help her set out the stainless steel bowls for the dogs. The noise sets them off, whining and pawing at the walls of their kennels.

"Is it his fault?"

"Birchill? I hope so. It's time his lies caught up with him."

"Just make sure yours don't."

"Me?" I query, pretending to look hurt. "I'm whiter than white."

"Unlike your shirt." She smirks, almost spilling the dried food as she pours it into a bowl. "You said you put it in the charity bag."

"We've had some good times, me and this shirt."

"I know," she says, wafting her hand in front of her nose.

We portion out food for the Lurcher cross, the three mongrels, and the West Highland White Terrier. I found him in a small outhouse behind a pub that had closed. Thin and dehydrated, he was in an appalling state, but after treatment by the vet, a good bath and a groom, he made a remarkable recovery. We should have no trouble rehoming him, judging by the number of enquiries we've had.

"I know he reminds you of you," Frances says, nudging me as I watch him devour his food, "but you can't keep him."

She knows me too well—and she's right, of course.

While the dogs eat, Frances and I chat about the works needed to improve the sanctuary. Like all our previous conversations, we reach the same point fairly quickly.

"We can't do anything until you get the money your father owes you."

I look away. I don't like taking his handouts, especially when I have to ask for them each month. It feels like begging, and they keep him in control of my destiny. "I'm working on it," I say, maybe a little too sharply. "He has got his hands full with this fracking protest at the moment."

"He's missed two payments, and he's a week behind this month. We have bills to pay and we're running short on feed."

"We'll manage," I say, hoping there's enough left on my credit card.

"He made a fortune selling Downland Manor." She pushes the dog food into the store and slams the door, prompting the Westie to bark. "Yet he expects you to protect the woodland on a pittance. Tell me how that's fair."

If he hadn't sold the estate, I wouldn't have a sanctuary and a home I love. She wouldn't have a job she loves. We couldn't save the animals and birds we rescue every year. "Frances, I'll phone him."

As if our conversation conjured him up, my father swerves his Jaguar into the small space behind my Ford and lurches to a halt. He climbs out in his usual languid way. Tall and slim, he seems to flow rather than walk. Everything from his lopsided smile to the sweep of his sandy hair across his forehead looks effortless. His sharp blue eyes contrast his dull skin, which looks as dry and tough as leather. His boyish looks defy the punishment years of cigars and brandy have inflicted. For a man of 67, he looks in his 50s.

118

"Will," he says, rolling an obese cigar between his fingers. "It appears we have a diplomatic incident."

Diplomatic incident means I've been a naughty boy. Like all politicians, he likes the sound of his voice and the words he uses. Naturally, I refuse to play his games.

Only one thing would make him steam down the A22 from Westminster. "You heard about my meeting with Birchill, right?"

He raises his lighter to the cigar, looking about him. "Is Debbie Dreadlocks around, waiting to pounce if I light up?"

"You know her name's Frances. And don't call me Will."

"My father called me Junior. Imagine that!"

The last six or seven generations have named the first-born male William Kenneth Fisher. Apart from bulk buying gravestones, I can't think why. In Manchester, life was hard enough being a William Kenneth. Originally, I dropped the middle name, but that resulted in the kids calling me Willie Fisher. Naturally, I doubled with laughter at this. Kenny Fisher was hardly better, so I contracted Kenneth to Kent. I rather liked the loose association with Superman, and it gave me a neat explanation for the name.

"It's where I was born," I tell people. They usually tell me I'm lucky my mother didn't go into labour in Bognor or Chipping Sodbury.

"Her name doesn't matter," my father's saying. "It's her appearance. It puts off visitors who could become sponsors."

"It's her way with children that keeps them coming back."

"Children don't pay," he says, jabbing his cigar at me.

"No one pays. We ask for a donation."

He pushes the lighter back into his pocket. "Why don't you show me around? I know you've taken in more horses. Ironic, considering you were scared stiff of them at the Manor."

119

"In the beginning." I direct him towards the stores. "You might as well earn your keep. A stile needs repairing, so we can fix that along the way."

I pull on my leather tool belt, grab some nails, and hand my father several pieces of timber I've fashioned for the repairs. We tuck the wood under our arms and walk along the path to the pond. The water has a silver sheen in the fading light, reflecting the trees and the Downs beyond. Another hour will pass before darkness swamps the land, but I can sense the insects and animals getting ready to explore.

My father grew up on this land. He knows all its secrets, from the routes used by smugglers to the secret rooms in the Manor where they hid the contraband. I'd explored a few, revelling in the stories and the atmosphere of these dusty passages. One led to my father's study, overlooking the gardens. When he was in London, I couldn't resist snooping. Having perfected my skills in Manchester, his old desk and filing cabinets were no challenge. It felt strange, reading about people I knew, but I sensed the power he held in his folders. There's no substitute for knowledge and information.

He lights his cigar on the way to the paddock, filling the air with a foul stench. Thankfully, it goes out again before we reach the damaged stile. He drops the wood in the long grass and I remove my claw hammer.

"Someone wants to buy me out," I say, extracting the protruding nails. "The company that owns the Manor has made me a generous offer."

"I'm not surprised," he says. "Without this land there's no access to the holiday village they want to build in the woods. Why do you think I gave you this land?"

"You promised to support the sanctuary."

"You promised to make it self-sufficient."

"I'm doing the best I can." I remove the rotted timber and align the replacement piece to check it's a good fit before nailing it in place. The thud of the hammer feels good. "All my spare cash goes into this place."

"Where's the urgency when you expect me to bail you out, Will? You need to attract investment and generate income."

I grab the handrail and wiggle it. A sharp tug and it comes away from the supporting posts. "If you stop paying I'll have to sell."

"I'm telling you to focus." He hands me the replacement handrail and holds it in place. "Stop fighting battles you can't win. Concentrate on what you can achieve."

The battles he refers to are my opposition to fracking, GM crops, the destruction of habitats, and my ongoing war with wealthy landowners. As the son of a Cabinet Minister, the media love to exaggerate stories about my exploits, hoping to embarrass him.

I pound the nails into the wood. "You're telling me to put my energy into the sanctuary and stop defending the environment."

He reaches into his pocket and withdraws a banker's draft. He could transfer money electronically, but he likes to make a show of things. He unfolds it and takes a closer look, whistling with surprise. "This will help you make a difference here."

The draft will clear debts and pay for repairs to the Land Rover. "You could have posted it," I say.

He gives me that innocent look he does so well. "Can't a father visit his son from time to time?"

"On the day I investigate a death at Tombstone Adventure Park?"

121

His smile fades. He stares at me while he lights his cigar again, blowing out clouds of dark smoke. "What's more important, Will—this place or the accident investigation?"

"It's not a question of choice."

He shakes his head. "You always have a choice. Every morning when you get out of bed and look into the mirror, you have a choice. Make it the right one."

The draft is from an account I don't recognise. "You're not going to release the money unless I drop the investigation, are you?"

"As I said, you have a choice."

I tear the draft in two. I hand the pieces to my father and walk away.

CHAPTER ELEVEN

He calls after me. "You're making a big mistake, Will."

"Me? I'm not the one trying to protect Birchill. Why don't you want me going after him?"

He says nothing, leaving me to guess, as I've had to on many occasions. Never betray your emotions in public. Remain cool, claim the moral high ground, and act with honour and integrity. These are the rules he lives by. These are the rules that led to the *Daily Mail* naming him the most anonymous Cabinet Minister ever.

To me, his rules mean sit on the fence, don't tell anyone what you think. If you're forced to, play the intellectual and claim you cocked up trying to do your best for everyone.

I don't know why he hates Birchill. I suspect it has something to do with him thieving when he worked in Downland Manor stables. His dodgy property dealings, which made him a rich man, wouldn't have helped either. Yet despite this hatred, my father never publicly condemned the plans to build Tombstone Adventure Park. He told me he had to represent everyone and couldn't take sides on a planning appeal, referred to his department for a decision.

Many saw his refusal to speak out as support for the development.

"Why are you protecting Birchill?" I ask, refusing to let him fob me off with silence.

"I'm protecting you, not him."

"I don't need protecting. The law protects me."

He gives me his most intellectual sneer. "Will it protect you from public humiliation when Birchill sets his dogs on you?"

"What dogs?" I demand, my voice rising.

He remains calm. "You've harassed his employees. Carry on like that and you'll make him look like the victim."

"Come on, Dad! If I don't badger them, they won't tell me anything."

"Collins was self-employed. He has nothing to do with Tombstone, and they're not responsible for his machinery."

"You're well informed," I say, collecting the old timber from the ground. "Has Birchill complained about me?"

His impassive expression betrays nothing yet tells me everything. "He already has an injunction against you, Kent. You're making it too easy for him."

"If you're telling me to back off, I can't do that. I have evidence that proves Tombstone employed Tollingdon Agricultural to service the tractor."

"Aren't you overlooking the most important point? Syd Collins removed the guard, contributing to his own death."

"Who told you that? Birchill?"

"Can you prove Collins didn't remove the guard?"

Of course I can't, and he knows it. "I'll find a way," I say, ignoring the odds against me. "That's why I need to find out what Collins was like."

"Maybe you should consult a medium," he says with a smirk. "Though I don't think evidence obtained from a séance is admissible in court."

He's so funny I want to nominate him for a comedy award. I turn towards the barn, adjust the old timber under my arm, and start walking. "I'll stick to evidence from this world, thank you. Collins doesn't wear ties."

"So why was he wearing one this morning?"

I'm starting to wonder if my father planted a listening device on me. It looks like Danni has supplied him with the details of my investigation, but she doesn't know everything.

I stop and face him. "I checked Collins' place. Not a tie to be found."

"You were in his house?" He stares at me in disbelief. "Are you mad or just plain stupid?"

"I'm doing my job."

"You can't just walk into people's houses, you idiot!" For once, his legendary cool has deserted him. His face grows redder as he becomes more animated. "Are you determined to throw away your career?"

"We had a quick nose around, that's all. Under health and safety law I can search for the missing guard."

"Did you find it?"

I shake my head.

He pushes back his hair with a sweep of his hand. "You said 'we had a quick nose around.' Who's 'we'?"

I'm annoyed with myself for that little slip. "Gemma Dean," I reply.

"You took your Chief Executive's niece into an empty house in the middle of nowhere without a warrant?" His voice rises with each word. "Have you any idea what the newspapers will say?"

I break into a smile. He's worried my behaviour will reflect badly on him. "Let me guess," I say. "Son of Government Minister has sex romp in dead man's house?"

He grabs my arm to stop me in my tracks. He's in my face, his breath reeking of cigar. "You've absolutely no idea how much trouble you're in, have you?"

"I'm doing my job."

"Wake up and smell the coffee, Will! You won't have a job when Birchill's finished with you. Drop the investigation or you'll lose everything."

The foul stench of cigar makes me nauseous. "I think Danni might notice if I suddenly drop the case."

"Hasn't she told you?"

I tense. "Told me what?"

"Birchill gave Collins the machinery, the barn and the two houses. Daniella Frost has copies of all the legal documents, signed and properly witnessed by his solicitor. Your case is against Collins, not Birchill."

I might have known Birchill would pull a stunt like that, but I didn't expect my father to play games with me. He could have mentioned this when he arrived, but he wanted to see if I would take his money and drop the investigation.

"The documents are fakes," I say.

He looks at me as if I'm beyond redemption. "And you wonder why you're in so much trouble. You're so prejudiced you have no credibility. You should never have set foot in Tombstone. Be thankful I'm baling you out." He reaches into his jacket and pulls out a second banker's draft, which he presses into my hand. "Think of the animals you can save."

"I'm thinking about the animal that's getting away."

"The case is closed," he says, pointing a warning finger. "If you go anywhere near Tombstone or continue in any way, you'll lose this place."

"You mean you'll stop helping me out?"

"You know what I mean. You can't run this place on what I give you."

"Then give me a chance. You made enough money from the sale of Downland Manor."

He's in my face again and breathing fast. "I'm lucky to have a roof over my head, you ungrateful sod! I gave up everything that was dear to me so you could have this place. Have you any idea how much this small strip of land is worth?"

I nod, refusing to back off.

"Then you know how much I sacrificed to keep this small piece of Downland in our name. Stop playing the hero and make this sanctuary work, because if you don't, everything I did will be for nothing."

He strides towards the barn. I look down at the draft, which allows me to pay some bills. In a month's time, I'll need another. Will that come with conditions too?

I know I should be grateful, but I can't help feeling he's bought me off. My job is to help people who want to comply with the law and punish those who don't. Without enforcement, there's no justice. Without justice, the cheats and the bullies win. People like Birchill can do what they want with impunity. How can that be fair to all the hardworking people who try to do things right?

I follow him back to the barn and dump the waste wood and my tool belt. I hate being boxed into a corner almost as much as I hate being wrong. Not that I think I'm wrong about Birchill—I just can't do anything about it.

My father's watching the dogs in the kennels. They press their noses to the door, hoping for a treat. That's how I feel. Only I have to earn mine by betraying the principles I hold dear. I want to tear the draft into tiny pieces and show him I can't be bought, but I have to consider Frances and the animals. This isn't their fight. They've done nothing wrong.

"So, will Danni close the case, or is that my job?" I ask.

"You're the investigating officer, Will. When you officially close the case, you'll get your money."

"Don't you trust me?"

He laughs and walks outside. "Use the money to smarten the place up. You need to encourage more visitors, not frighten them off."

He freezes as the sound of tyres squealing on the tarmac precedes Gemma's Volvo, which swings into the site, narrowly missing his Jaguar. She swerves past it and slides to a halt in a cloud of dust. She's changed into a pale blue cropped top that reveals her flat, tanned stomach. Her denim shorts, frayed along the hem just about cover her rear, leaving little to the imagination.

As she approaches, my father straightens his shirt and runs his hands over his hair. "At least you've grown out of dating teenagers, Will."

"That's my colleague, Gemma Dean."

He laughs. "Does she make a habit of bringing you supper?"

She saunters up, two boxes cradled in her arm. He looks her over, grins, and nods at the pizzas. "I'm hot and spicy," he says. "You?"

"I'm a meat treat," she replies. "But Kent prefers pepperoni, so we're both out of luck."

"I'm William Kenneth Fisher, MP," he says, looking more clumsy than casual as he pushes his hands into his pockets. "Give my regards to your uncle, Gemma."

She looks at me, then him. "You're Kent's dad? Cool. You're younger than I expected."

"You're prettier than I expected."

"I can see why you have a big majority, Mr. Fisher." She turns to me. "I'll put these in the oven before they go cold. That way to the kitchen?"

I watch her skip up the stairs, wondering why she called around unexpectedly.

"Ring me tomorrow," my father says, heading towards his Jaguar.

"The Coroner's Officer expects a report for the inquest. I need to write up my notes and put them on the computer. Then there's the report for my boss, explaining why the investigation is over. The Chief Executive will want to see me. Then the portfolio holder—"

"My territory," he says, getting in the car. "You inform Miles Birchill."

"Don't worry," I say under my breath, "I'll tell him."

I head up to the flat. Gemma's already switched on the oven and found some garlic bread in the freezer. Now she's searching for some oven trays.

"Do you often walk into people's homes and rummage around?" I ask.

She grins. "Just following your example. Nice kitchen, by the way. I love the blue units."

I retrieve my bottle of chilled water from the fridge. "They were part of a showroom display. I got everything for nothing, including the spotlights and trims."

"And you put it all together?"

I fitted everything but the vinyl flooring and propane stove. "Most of it," I reply.

"I'm impressed. So, where do you keep the oven trays?"

I find them for her. As soon as the pizzas are in the oven, she's heading for the open plan lounge, which runs across the front of the barn. Two Velux windows in the roof and three small casements that overlook the yard provide natural lighting.

"It's huge," she says, scanning the room. "And so organised. You'll make someone a lovely wife."

I've zoned the room. The TV area has an ex-display corner unit sofa that was heading for the dump, a hi fi stack that's borderline antique, and enough CDs to open a shop. The office area has bookcases I salvaged from a shop that closed, a small desk and filing cabinet a showroom was throwing away, and the notice board where I post all my reminders. The gym area has a multifunction machine, bar bells, and a treadmill for those winter days when I can't be bothered to run in the cold and wet.

Gemma wanders around, looking unimpressed. "It's like an operating theatre, Kent. Don't you have any photographs or paintings to liven things up?"

I point to my DVD collection, which includes box sets of Inspector Morse, Columbo and Miss Marple. I have a Sony PlayStation 2. It's out of date, but I'm not dextrous or patient enough to play modern games. I can't keep track of the information on the busy screens. That's not an issue with Space Invaders.

"We like it," I say, picking up one of the games consoles. "Frances and I often battle it out for control of the galaxy on cold winter evenings."

"You never told me you lived with someone."

I should point out that Frances only visits to eat, play games, watch films, and sleep in the spare room during cold winters.

"Let's get back to the kitchen. I think the pizzas are ready."

The aroma of tomato, onion and pepperoni competes with garlic for my attention when I enter the kitchen. Moments later, Frances comes in from the stairs. She stops when she spots Gemma. They regard each other, their expressions giving nothing away. I break the uncomfortable silence with introductions.

"Gemma's brought pizza."

"I only brought two," Gemma says. "I didn't know you lived here."

I raise a finger to my lips as Frances looks ready to explain. "You work with Kent," she says. "Me too."

"Frances runs the sanctuary," I explain.

"And there's plenty to do," she says, moving towards the door.

Gemma peers into the oven. "Please join us. There's enough for three. You can tell me how you do your hair like that. It's awesome."

Frances blushes and moves closer to the door. Normally, she's unconcerned with what others think, but she looks self-conscious. Her fingers fiddle with her braids.

"I've got something for you," I say, realising why she popped in. "Gemma, we'll just be a moment."

I beckon Frances into the lounge and close the door. I pull the banker's draft from my pocket and hand it to her. She looks at it and sighs with relief. Then to my surprise throws her arms around my neck and hugs me. She has the earthy smell of dogs and horses about her. Her cheek's hot against mine.

"Sorry," she says, blushing again as she retreats. "I thought he was going to get rid of me."

"That's my decision, not his, Frances. I can't manage without you here. This money will keep us solvent for another month or two."

"He's changed banks," she says, studying the draft before she hands it back. "I hope it doesn't bounce."

It can't bounce if I tear it in two, but that's a decision for the morning. "Is that it?" I ask when she doesn't move.

"Did you tell her I lived here?"

I shake my head. "She assumed."

"Are you trying to make her jealous?"

I'm not sure what I'm trying to do. "Stay for tea," I say. "You'll like Gemma."

Frances fiddles with her braids again. "She's very pretty, isn't she?"

"And so are you."

She shakes her head. "I can't wear clothes like that. You know how clumsy I get in heels, and I'm useless at makeup."

"Let's just eat. I'm sure Gemma wants to get back to her fiancé."

Frances looks up. "She's engaged? I didn't notice a ring."

"There isn't one."

Gemma's divided the pizza onto three plates. She's standing with her hands on her hips, staring into the fridge. "Do you have anything alcoholic?" she asks, pulling out a bottle of Beck's Blue. "This is neutered."

I'm about to offer it to Frances when she scoots out of the door. "I really need to check the kennels," she calls over her shoulder.

"Is she all right?" Gemma asks, replacing the bottle.

"You intimidate her."

"How? I haven't done anything."

Of course not, I think, looking at her shorts and cropped top. "Can you close the fridge before it reaches room temperature?"

"You must be a laugh a minute to live with," she says, closing the door with a thud. She sits at the table and helps herself to the largest slice of pizza. She tears a chunk off with her teeth, smothering the corners of her mouth with tomato. "Frances is stunning," she says, a sneering undercurrent to her voice.

"Why did you call round?" I ask.

"I thought we could look at the files from Collins' computer." She devours the rest of the slice with vigour. I don't know how she can eat like a horse and not put on an ounce.

I'd planned to check the files and emails after I'd written up my notes for today. But, if we look now, I can get rid of her sooner. "Let's do it now," I say, rising. "I'm meeting Mike in the Bells later."

"Even though you don't drink?"

"Pubs serve fruit juice and coffee these days."

I grab two of the plates and beckon her to follow. My computer lives in an alcove in my bedroom. It used to be in the lounge, but I found the TV distracting.

"Your father's not how I imagined," she says, glancing around the even more minimalist bedroom. "He's quite different from you."

"I've never given it any thought."

"It must be interesting being the son of an MP," she says, sitting on the bed.

I sit in front of the PC and switch it on. "He's a dad like any other."

"Rubbish! Uncle Frank's scared shitless of him. Danni too. That's why you can swan around leading a charmed life."

"He would never interfere in internal matters." I pause, realising what I've said.

She grabs more pizza. "Then why did he drop into the office to see Danni this afternoon? Nigel told me he didn't look best pleased."

Why didn't my father say he'd popped into the office? It's obvious now, but at the time it would have helped. "Tommy Logan at the *Tribune* wanted a quote," I lie, "so dad popped in for an update first."

"Why didn't he come to see you?"

I type in my password, glad to have a moment to think about my response. "We were at Tombstone, weren't we? That's why he popped by this evening."

She doesn't look convinced, but why should I care? She's hardly telling me everything, is she? Neither is my father. Maybe it's time I adopted this approach.

What if I continue my investigation for another day? If I switch off my phone and stay away from Gemma and the office, no one can contact me. They don't know I'm meeting Carolyn Montague at Collins' house first thing tomorrow. From there, I could go to the Game Cock and see if I can uncover anything of interest about Collins. If I learn nothing of value, I can say I was thorough before closing the investigation.

If I learn something useful, I'm on a collision course with everyone.

I slip the memory stick into a USB port on the computer. I can't open the autobiography files, but I can check the emails. Gemma polishes off the remaining pizza while I launch Outlook and import the files.

Collins' deletes most of the emails without reading them. He has the standard folders and one named 'Adele', which contains ten messages. I'm about to double click on the oldest when I spot my father's email username, 'wilkenfish'. Twice.

Why is he emailing Collins?

Gemma leans closer when I double click the newer message, dated only a couple of weeks ago. It's brief.

'Syd, the world has changed. You're on your own this time. William.'

I scroll to the original message, which reads, *'Billy Boy, I could lose my driving licence. Do your stuff. Syd.'*

Billy Boy? What's going on here? It doesn't sound like a constituent, seeking help from his MP. Constituents send my father all manner of requests, as if he has some divine power, but this is different. He tells Collins he's on his own this time. That means there was a previous time. With a growing sense of dread, I open the older email from over nine years ago.

'Syd, equilibrium restored. William.'

That's Fisherspeak for problem sorted and no loose ends. I scroll to the original message. *'Billy Boy, cops on my back over assault, fix it!'*

Gemma whistles. "They're from you father, right?"

While I don't know what the problem was or how it was resolved, my father intervened. He may even have perverted the course of justice. Now he's doing the same for Birchill.

I pull the banker's draft out of my pocket and stare at it.

FRIDAY

CHAPTER TWELVE

"I'm not worried about upsetting my father," I say, settling on the floor. "I have a degree in the subject. We come from the same gene pool, but we're worlds apart."

It's Friday morning, I've had a good night's sleep, and I know what I have to do. I knew before I went to bed last night. I knew before I ate breakfast. So why am I hesitating? I'm concerned about Frances.

"She was so excited when I showed her the banker's draft. What's she going to say when I turn down the money?"

The Westie tilts his head from side to side as I talk, taking in every word. Like a good listener, he never interrupts or passes judgement, and if I've done something bad, he never condemns me.

"She's already earmarked the money. And what about those ideas she told me over breakfast?" I lean forward and ruffle the dog's fur behind his ears. "I'll have to rob a bank to replace my father's money. No, I didn't think it was a good idea either."

The Westie shifts a little, but remains seated before me, aware of the treats in my pocket. It's terrible, having to bribe someone to listen, but I'm afraid to talk to the people who really matter. I should confront my father. He's the one who's protecting a villain.

I push my hand into my pocket and grip the chew. "So, we're agreed: I continue my investigation. If I turn up anything, I'll continue over the weekend. How does that sound?"

The Westie barks and paws at my leg. I hold out the chew and he takes it gently. He trots to the back of the kennel, lies down and begins to attack it.

"Were you talking to your dog again?"

I look up and see Frances watching me. I scramble to my feet. "How long have you been there?"

"Long enough."

There's no disappointment or resentment in her eyes, no hostility lurking beneath the surface.

"If I'm smart," I say, "I'll finish the job and keep the money."

"Some things are more important than money." She looks down at the Westie. "You talk to him more than you talk to me, to anyone. He loves you to bits, so why won't you take him off the rehoming list?"

"You know I'm out too much. It wouldn't be fair."

"I'm here—unless you're planning to change that."

I place my hands on her shoulders. "Without you, Frances, this place wouldn't exist. If we go down, we go down together."

"No, we go down fighting."

"We won't go down," I say. "Our little friend here would be homeless."

"I can't believe you haven't given him a name, Kent. Or have you?"

I look away, feeling a little self-conscious. "Columbo."

"As in the scruffy detective you make me watch?" she asks, frowning.

I nod. "Small, tenacious and determined."

Frances drops to her knees. "Columbo," she calls. "Here!"

The Westie swallows the last mouthful of chew. When she calls his name again, he rises and strolls over, managing a brief wag of his tail.

"What if someone offers £500 for him?" she asks, stroking his back.

"Like you, Frances, he's priceless."

I leave her before her cheeks redden any further. Taking on Columbo when we have no money isn't one of my smarter moves, but it makes me feel good. I need to feel good if I'm going to make any progress today.

Back in the flat, I shower and shave before ironing a white short-sleeved shirt that's seen better days. I text Danni to say the Coroner's Officer wants to meet me urgently at Tombstone. Then I turn off my phone. At 9.45, I approach Collins' cottage from the lane at the rear. I'm the first to arrive and pull in behind his Land Rover.

Out in the lane, I try to work out how our visitor approached the cottage yesterday. Keeping the back bedroom window in view, I turn left and realise anyone could park unnoticed within 10 yards of the drive. However, you can't see the house or the bedroom until you enter the drive. In the other direction, you have to park at least 30 yards away or your car would be visible. Walking to the drive you could be seen at least 50 per cent of the way.

It doesn't explain why the visitor didn't pull into the rear garden. I'm guessing he approached from the direction of the Game Cock, looked up and saw Gemma at the window. He then pulled in beyond the drive and came back for a closer look.

Had he come from the woods on the other side of the house, he would have used the front door. I hesitate to remind myself the visitor could be a woman, even though my money's on Birchill. He left the council offices with just enough time to get back here. He has plenty to lose if Collins' autobiography surfaces.

At the front of the house, the key has gone from under the potted hosta. The visitor doesn't want me to return. Had I left my visit until this morning I might never have found Collins' emails.

I smile to myself. It will be interesting to see whether anything inside has changed or gone missing since yesterday.

Carolyn arrives with 10 minutes to spare, swinging her Peugeot alongside my Ford. She shrugs off her seatbelt and jumps out of the car the moment it stops. Smart in a black pinstripe jacket and trousers, she strides like an executive, flight bag in a firm grip. She's pulled her hair into a ponytail and replaced her cheap perfume with something more subtle.

"Hi," she says. "Is Downland's most wanted here yet?"

"Miles Birchill? Did you invite him?"

"He insisted on helping and I couldn't think of a reason to refuse."

"Apart from investigating a suspicious death?"

"We're here to see if there are any family and friends. Birchill knew Collins better than anyone."

"What if Birchill's responsible for Collins' death?" I ask.

"Is he?"

"I'm working on it."

She laughs. "That makes two of us who can't touch him. I hate the scumbag more than you can imagine, Kent, but we have to play by the rules."

"He doesn't," I reply. "We're letting him control our investigations."

"Yes, I heard he paid you a visit yesterday."

She unlocks the back door and the picks up her bag. "Before I forget, the post mortem yesterday afternoon showed Collins had cancer—lungs, secondary growths in his kidneys and colon. He was on borrowed time. It also looks like he drank heavily."

That could explain the empty vodka bottle by the barn. "Was he drunk when he died?"

"Possibly. We'll have to wait for the results. But the cirrhosis of his liver shows he drank heavily."

I follow her into the kitchen, where she doesn't waste a moment in starting her search. She begins with a cursory sweep of the cupboards and drawers, occasionally pausing to look under some papers or a cutlery tray. She's quick and thorough, working her way round with nimble fingers.

"I'm looking for bank statements, his national insurance card, passport," she says, squatting to look beneath the sink. "Then there are letters, Christmas cards, gifts that suggest a close friend or relative. Let me know if you find anything."

"If Collins was drunk and in pain," I say, peering inside the bread bin, "he did well to walk to the clearing."

"The alcohol probably numbed the pain." She's on her feet, smoothing her trousers over her knees. "Mind you, he could have doubled up in agony and caught his tie in the power takeoff."

It doesn't explain why Collins was in the clearing at six in the morning.

"Ah, here's our guest, come to watch over us." She points to the back garden before striding to the dining room in those short, determined steps.

While she works through the dresser, I drop to my knees and look underneath.

I imagine a scenario leading up to Collins' death. He drank vodka and had sex, but not necessarily in that order. Despite being a man who slept until 10 in the morning, he rose at dawn, pulled on a shirt, and a tie he didn't normally wear, and went to the clearing. Or he never went to sleep. That's more likely. Tiredness could have contributed to his accident, though that won't explain the tie. I can think of no reason why he would start up the tractor, either.

Maybe he wanted to show off to his lover.

I crawl under the table. If he was trying to impress his lover, why did she run off? Why didn't she ring for an ambulance? Maybe Cheung disturbed her. If she's married and doesn't want her husband to know, she might run, even if it's heartless.

It looks like a verdict of misadventure.

"Is everything okay?" Carolyn asks, peering down at me. "You seem distracted."

"I'm fine."

I look behind me, wondering what's happened to Birchill, before following her into the living room. The Marilyn Monroe box set I left on the sofa yesterday has disappeared. I follow Carolyn around the cupboards to see if the box set is back on a shelf. I can't see the films anywhere.

"How's your investigation going?" Her face glows as she hauls herself off her knees. "Collins was dying, so I'm not sure I'll find much here."

"I think someone should pay for removing the guard."

"Someone did," Birchill says.

He's in the doorway, dressed in a black leather jacket, matching shirt and jeans. "Syd removed the guard and paid with his life."

Carolyn marches over, causing the furniture to vibrate as she passes. "Thanks for coming, Mr. Birchill. I know you're busy so I'll crack on. Any help you can give me will be great."

"You won't find anything here," he says. "Syd was all veneer and no substance. What he has will be upstairs in his study."

"I like to be thorough. People keep things in the strangest places.

While she peers behind sofa cushions, I turn to Birchill, surprised he hasn't passed comment on my presence. "How was the meeting yesterday?"

"Don't you and your manager communicate?"

"It's something we need to discuss." When his expression remains neutral, I say, "She's busy."

This seems to satisfy him. "I proved that Tombstone is not responsible for Syd or his machinery."

"Did she agree with you?"

"Do you?"

If Danni didn't commit herself, the investigation is still open. "I'd like to check the barn before I draw any conclusions," I say. "Do you have a key?"

"Why do you want to go into the barn?"

"I might find a missing guard there."

He pulls out his mobile phone and leaves the room. I join Carolyn as she stretches on tiptoes to look behind the wall-mounted TV. She taps the mantelpiece below and nods in appreciation. "This is real wood, you know."

As opposed to unreal wood, I'm tempted to say. Birchill peers around the door. "Foley can meet you at one thirty. He's busy with an audit this morning."

"If he's busy he could let me have the key."

"You might have a right of entry, Fisher, but that doesn't mean you can wander round on your own."

I stroll over to the window to look at the laurel bush I hid behind yesterday. Our visitor might have seen us hiding, but I doubt it. "Did Collins have any family?" I ask.

Birchill strolls up beside me. "I think he was abandoned at birth and grew up in a home. He's never mentioned any brothers or sisters."

"No wife or children?"

"Collins liked fast women and his freedom."

"So he could have an illegitimate child somewhere?"

"He could have a football team, but I don't know who or where they are. Why are you so interested? Have you found something?"

"Only an unprotected power takeoff," I reply with a smile.

"Nothing here," Carolyn says. "Shall we move upstairs?"

She marches out of the room, forcing Birchill to step aside. He extends his arm to let me go next, but I decline. His calm but smug confidence is a million miles from yesterday's agitated animosity. He's happy with the way things are going, which probably means bad news for me.

While she searches the bathroom, I wait on the landing, staring out of the window. In the lane, a navy blue VW Golf slows down as it draws level with the garden, and then speeds away. I wonder if it's a reporter. The media is bound to descend sooner or later. I'd rather they waited until I'm out of sight.

In the front bedroom, yesterday's visitor straightened the duvet so the bed looks unused. While Carolyn checks inside the wardrobe, I nip behind the door.

"Whoops!" I say, knocking the bin over with my foot. I bend and peer inside. The condom packaging has gone. Collins' lover doesn't want us to know she was here. Having seen his horrendous death, she left him and maybe drove away. Was that the car Cheung thought he heard? Did she drive Collins to the barn in the first place?

I have to stop myself nodding and put the bin down. She came back to the house in the afternoon to remove any traces of her presence. What kind of person could do that?

"Looking for something?" Birchill asks, peering into the bin.

"I thought there might be a scrap of notepaper," I reply. "Or a discarded letter or postcard."

Carolyn calls. "Can someone help me lift the mattress?"

While Birchill and I manhandle the heavy mattress, I think about some of the other questions I've yet to answer. With his cancer and heavy drinking, could Collins manage sex?

Inside the dressing table, she discovers a plain brown envelope. Her excitement is palpable as she tears it open. Birchill tries to mask his interest with indifference, but fails.

"Aftercare for the mattress," she says, throwing the envelope down.

Like Birchill, she pays no attention to the smell of cigarettes when she enters Collins' office. A laptop has replaced the PC and monitor on the desk, otherwise it looks the same as yesterday.

"Do you think Collins wrote his autobiography here?" I ask.

"Autobiography?" Birchill stares at me as if I'm bonkers. "Syd could just about write a shopping list. He used Skype mainly, and Facebook."

"He was dying," I say. "Maybe he wanted to set the record straight."

"What record? Look at the place," he says, making a grand sweep with his arm. "It's pirate DVDs and porn movies. He spoke, he watched, but he didn't write."

"You have to type to use the Internet and send emails."

Birchill sighs. "Basic stuff, but an autobiography?"

Carolyn, who's had her head inside the cupboard over the stairs, turns to us. "Who told you he was writing an autobiography?"

"There is no autobiography," Birchill says, his voice rising. "Don't believe anything Barry Stilton tells you. He's the landlord of the Game Cock, by the way. He has a tent flap for a mouth. That's why Syd wound him up."

It sounds like I need to talk to Barry Stilton.

Carolyn resumes her search, but she's going through the motions. Unlike films, where there's a loaded pistol in a drawer, Collins filled his with envelopes and stationery. While she looks through the desk, I sidle over to the cupboard. The cigarettes have gone.

"Are you taking the laptop?" Birchill asks her.

She considers the question. "Are you certain he's illiterate?"

"Start the laptop and see for yourself," he replies, walking over to the window.

She lifts the lid and switches it on. We wait until a password screen appears. "Do you know his password, Mr. Birchill?"

He glances at the photo of Winston Churchill for a split second. "No idea. Looks like we need his personal documents, national insurance number, that kind of thing."

"If they're here, they're well hidden," she says. "You must have some idea where he kept them."

"I've been here twice, maybe three times. I gave this house to Syd, along with the land, when I built Tombstone. I'm away most of the time, so I hardly saw him."

"What's going to happen to the place now he's dead?" I ask.

"It reverts back to Tombstone."

Carolyn smirks. "To you, you mean."

"Do you have a problem with that?"

She seems to enjoy his flash of temper. "I don't care, Mr. Birchill. I'm looking for next of kin and they seem to be in short supply."

Yeah, just like the truth.

CHAPTER THIRTEEN

I'm not sure what intrigues me most—the absence of anything personal in Collins' house, or Carolyn and Birchill's indifference to this. Collins seems to have lived his life without a bank account, a passport, or any insurance policies. Not easy to do in the modern world. Where are the photographs, the personal possessions we all keep? Why was there no food in the fridge? All we have are the driving licence and credit card in the wallet recovered from his body.

Am I the only person who finds this odd?

"Don't forget your meeting with Ben Foley at one-thirty," Birchill says as he walks to his Mercedes.

His helpful manner troubles me. Yesterday, he did his best to remove me from the site and the investigation. Now, he's encouraging me. Either I've woken in a parallel universe or he has a nasty surprise waiting for me.

"He's up to something." Carolyn stops beside me, her bag thudding against the back of my leg. "Be careful, Kent."

I rub my calf, wishing she would follow her own advice. "What did you make of the house?"

"What do you mean?"

"What did it tell you about Collins?" I ask.

She taps her fingers against her chin while she considers her answer. "Apart from his office, the place was about as characterless as a show home. He was obsessive about cleanliness, I'd say. What did it tell you?"

"Much the same. Should we check his Land Rover?"

"Why?"

"We don't want to miss anything."

Her frown almost connects her eyebrows. "What are you looking for?"

"Answers."

"That's right—fence posts and the cigarette that didn't match the others." She leans closer as if she's going to reveal a secret. "Tell me, how will the answers to those questions move your investigation forward?"

Her tone becomes maternal, as if she's giving me a lesson about life. "Let the facts and evidence guide you, Kent. I'm no EHO, but the missing takeoff guard is central to your investigation, isn't it?"

She's right, but I can't let the questions go.

"Without a witness, Kent, we'll never know what Collins intended. We're left with the facts we report to the Coroner. I don't suppose you've had to write a report like this before."

"I'm sure I'll manage."

She raises her hands. "I'm only asking you to keep it factual. The Coroner establishes the cause of death, not who's to blame, so we avoid speculation. Collins was at work early and he died because he was careless. Those are the facts, plain and simple."

"Saying he was careless is an opinion," I point out. "You said he was drunk. He might have collapsed."

"That's speculation," she says with a grin.

She's still grinning when she drives away, cutting across a blue VW Golf in the lane. The squeal of brakes pierces the air. The Golf lurches to a stop and the driver falls back into her seat. I rush over to make sure she's all right.

She has a thin face with prominent cheeks and nose, a complexion that suggests at least one Asian parent, and short black hair that makes her look younger than I suspect she is. I base this on the sharpness of her blouse and business jacket, which suggest designer labels. Her dark eyes regard me for a moment, and then she accelerates away, almost running over my toes.

Despite the shade, the heat inside my car could roast potatoes. Without air conditioning that works, I'm going to slow cook in the car, so I walk to the Game Cock. This gives me time to think about who obliterated Collins' presence from the house. A married lover would want to keep their affair secret, but why take his possessions too?

I turn my attentions to the leafy surroundings where large, expensive houses shelter out of sight, protected by security gates and high walls. Every resident objected to the planning application to build Tombstone. Assisted by an environmental consultant, they had enough firepower to sink a battleship.

Yet Birchill won.

We protested, chaining ourselves to trees, digging tunnels, and generally disrupting everything we could. Then a gang of hooligans gate-crashed the protest, costing us public support. The media filmed their clashes with the police and made claims about anarchy in England's green and pleasant land. We tried to prove that Birchill hired them, but we failed. Within months, the protest ran out of steam as people drifted away to fight the building of a nuclear power station.

Before I know it, I've reached the Game Cock. At some point in the past, someone had knocked together two brick cottages. From the state of the peeling paintwork on the sash windows, and the perished and missing gutters, I doubt if anyone's spent any money on the place since. Even the spritely cockerel on the creaking sign has faded. The sign promoting sports on a wide screen TV tells me all I need to know.

Will the landlord help a council official? He might, with a bit of persuasion.

I switch on my Blackberry to check the pub's National Food Hygiene Rating on the Internet. A low hygiene rating might give me some leverage. Before I check, I glance at the messages left for me. Mike reminds me we have catering equipment to deliver at seven this evening. A text message from Danni says she'll meet with me later to review progress.

The Game Cock has a national food hygiene rating of 2, meaning the standard of hygiene was below the legal minimum when it was last inspected. Unable to suppress a smile, I stroll in.

On first glance, the polished floorboards, low beams, and brick fireplace with horse brasses make the Game Cock look like many other country pubs. The real attraction goes over my head, where customers have plastered the ceiling with bank notes from around the world. Postcards on a large notice board near the pool table reveal the holiday destinations favoured by the locals. Majorca, Venice, America, Thailand, the Caribbean, and Australia seem to be the most popular, with South Africa on the periphery.

"You interested in joining our holiday club?"

The London accent belongs to an overweight forty-something with comb-over hair, a deep tan, and teeth that would look good in a horse's mouth. He's tall, wears tight jeans and an open-necked shirt. He takes a glass from the shelf and helps himself to a whisky.

"I'm Barry Stilton, the owner of this establishment," he says, resting his elbows on the bar. He gestures to my notebook. "Are you a reporter?"

Now there's a thought. Mr. Stilton might want to see his name in the paper. "Dale Wensley," I say, holding out my hand. "Has someone beaten me to the story?"

His sweaty hand grips mine. "If you're talking about Syd Collins, someone was in here looking for him not half an hour ago. Can I get you a drink?"

"Still mineral water. Was it a reporter?"

"Search me, Dale. She marches in like she owns the place and wants to know if I've seen Mr. Collins. I tell her I don't think I'll be seeing him again unless he comes back to haunt me."

He groans as he drops to his knees to rattle around in the refrigerated display cabinet. "She says, 'Are you trying to be funny?'—all self-important like. I tell her I'm not laughing because he owes me £300. I won't repeat what she said."

Back on his feet, he plants a bottle of mineral water on the bar and removes the cap. "She marches off, slamming the door behind her, and that's that. I've no idea who she was or what she wanted. How do you like it, Dale?"

For a moment, I'm not sure what he's talking about. Then he holds up the bottle. "Neat," I reply, taking it from him. "This woman who called in, did she have short black hair, a thin face with a foreign complexion?"

"She had nice boobs."

"That narrows it down."

"You'll get used to Barry Stilton's cheesy sense of humour. Yes, that could be her. You know her?"

"It's a small world," I reply.

He nods. "I thought she were a reporter. Bit fond of herself, you know? Liked to sweep her hair back in a dramatic way and pout like those stick insect models you see on TV. I got the feeling she'd arranged to meet him. She didn't know he was dead, that much I can tell you. She wasn't best pleased about that."

"You're very astute, Mr. Stilton."

"That's what they say. And call me Baz. Everyone else does. Who do you work for, Dale? One of the dailies?"

"The one that pays me the most," I reply without hesitation. "Remember the sports physiotherapist who slept with half the England football team?"

He pretends to doff his cap in respect. "You wrote that? Blimey, I should have offered you something stronger."

"I'm fine," I say, settling on the nearest stool and placing my notebook in a space between the beer towels and copper trays for catching spilt beer. The pumps gleam despite the dim lighting, and the shelves behind boast a colourful array of spirits and liqueurs. The local parish newsletter, produced on someone's home computer, catches my eye.

"Is Tombstone losing money?" I ask.

Barry shakes his head. "Miles Birchill knows what he's doing."

That contradicts the opinion of the chairman of the parish council. Like most elected officials, he believes his opinion counts. I push the newsletter aside. "Tell me about Syd Collins. You must have known him better than most."

"Indeed," he says, pushing out his chest. "He dropped enough money in my gaming machines to take me, Amanda and her kid to Florida in March. She's my barmaid, see, and her kid loves Mickey Mouse."

"Syd liked to gamble, did he?"

"He dropped a couple of hundred every week. Sometimes Lady Luck gave him a jackpot, but it went straight back. He'd buy a pint and head straight to the machines. He only stopped when he ran out of money or beer."

"Did he have any family? I might want to talk to them."

"We were his family, until he met some woman in an Internet chat room." He leans closer. "The lads wound him up, saying he'd been watching too much porn on TV. Then, the next Wednesday evening, he turns up in a suit, smelling like an aftershave factory. He buys a bottle of red wine and we never see him again on Wednesday evenings. The lads snuck round to his house, thinking he was watching porn, but he was always out in his Land Rover."

"He doesn't sound like the type to wear a suit."

"It was one of those cheap, shiny suits from the charity shop."

"Did he wear a tie?"

Barry frowns. "Are you a fashion reporter or something?"

"I'm trying to build a picture. Has anyone seen this woman?"

He shakes his head. "We don't know if she exists, to tell you the truth. Old Ted Johnson reckons she's a fantasy. I mean, Syd comes in here every night and hardly says two words to anyone. Then he spends half the night chatting to strangers on the Internet? Don't make sense, do it?"

I consider it for a moment. He only lived in one room. "Maybe he was lonely."

"When he came in here every evening?" Barry drains his whisky and helps himself to another. "The lads kept pushing him to give us a name or show us a photo, but he wouldn't. Then, a few months ago, he promised to reveal everything when his book was published."

"He wrote a book?"

"He said he'd written his life story, warts and all. He was going to reveal secrets about Miles Birchill and the people he'd corrupted over the years. Syd said some influential people would be quaking in their boots when his story came out."

It's obvious from Barry's tone and expression what he thinks about the autobiography. I'm sure most people would think the same, but I've seen the chapters. Well, I've seen the files. If I could work out the password to access them, Dale Wensley could burst onto the tabloid scene with a scoop.

"Did he mention any of these people?"

"What do you think? Old Ted Johnson might know if you buy him a pint."

"Is he due in later?"

"No, he's right behind you."

An older man shuffles between the tables on his way to the bar. His purple corduroy jacket hangs loose over his gaunt and frail body. A lavender shirt and mauve tie, brown corduroy trousers and Hush Puppies complete the ensemble. At the bar, he removes his flat cap to reveal thin white hair, swept forward to hide the receding areas on his crown. His laboured breathing suggests a heavy smoker before the reek of pipe tobacco confirms it. While his face and chins can no longer defy gravity, there's something proud and stoical in his demeanour.

He looks me over with the piercing eyes of a wolf. "I was once a sprinter," he says in a cultured voice that would grace any TV documentary. Warm, confident and knowledgeable, his voice commands attention. Slowly and painfully, he lifts himself onto a barstool. "Now I pace myself. Are you friend or foe?" he asks, glancing at my notebook.

"He's a reporter, Ted. Dale Wensley. He's interested in Syd Collins."

"Never met a reporter who drank water," Ted says. "You want to buy us both a pint of best? Then you can tell me why you're interested in Collins."

Barry's already filling a pint glass with Harvey's Best Bitter.

"He worked for Miles Birchill," I say.

"So do lots of people."

"They didn't die yesterday."

Ted takes his pint, studies it with relish, and then drinks half of it. He licks his lips for a good ten seconds before speaking. "I won't speak ill of the dead, but he was the most miserable, antisocial person on God's earth. He thought he was something special because he worked for Miles Birchill."

Barry offers me a pint, but I decline and hand over a fiver.

Ted glares at me. "You going to write anything down or am I wasting my time?"

"I will when you tell me something I don't know," I reply.

He stares at me for a moment and then laughs. "With the cost of ale these days, you deserve more than hearsay. Are you aware of Syd's gambling? Without it this fleapit would have closed years ago."

Barry's head jerks up at the insult, but he doesn't complain.

"Collins didn't work, so where did he get his money?" I ask.

"He sold cigarettes and tobacco, smuggled from abroad," Ted replies, pulling out a pipe.

Barry wags a warning finger. "Smoking's banned, Ted, as you well know."

The old man grimaces and pushes the pipe back inside his jacket. "It won't be long before we'll need a permit to fart indoors."

Before the conversation veers into the Nanny State, I ask about Collins' autobiography. "Apparently, he intended to reveal all Birchill's dark secrets."

"You don't bite the hand that feeds you," Ted replies after another few mouthfuls of beer. "Without Miles Birchill, Syd was nothing. Why would he rise up against his benefactor?"

"He didn't have long to live."

"Clear his conscience with a deathbed confession?" Ted drains the glass and smacks his lips together. "How do you know he didn't have long to live?"

"He told you, didn't he?" I reply, taking a chance.

Ted nods. "I bought a lot of cheap tobacco. What did you do?"

This man is good. He knows how to manipulate a conversation. He also knows more about Collins, I'm sure, but he doesn't trust me. Why would he?

"He offered me a couple of chapters. He wanted me to serialise it."

"You work for a newspaper with a big circulation, Mr. Wensley?"

"I'm freelance. I've written about Miles Birchill in the past. That's how Collins found me."

"Well, Mr. Wensley, I hate to rain on your parade, but you've overlooked one small detail. Syd Collins was illiterate. He could write the names of horses on betting slips and leave notes for the milkman, but he couldn't write a sentence, let alone a chapter."

"He didn't need to. His girlfriend did."

It's a punt in the dark, but logical. It winds up Barry, who glares at me. "You knew about this internet woman all along."

Ted looks impressed and suspicious at the same time. "Maybe you'd like to share her identity with us, Mr. Wensley. None of us believe she exists."

"You don't expect me to reveal my sources, surely?"

"Then this fishing trip is at an end."

I notice a photograph of Prince Charles on the wall. "I've never met her," I say, "but she calls herself Camilla. I don't know if that's her real name, but she emailed me the chapters. Two I can read, the rest are protected by password and now Collins is dead."

Ted's smile evolves into a laugh that degenerates into a fit of coughing. Barry rushes over to help, but is waved away with a flailing arm. Ted brings the cough under control eventually and then turns to me. "You're not interested in Syd Collins," he says, pointing at me. "You came here to discover his password."

"Did Collins have a friend or confidant he turned to for help?"

"He might have."

While I'm wondering what Ted's price will be for the information, the door bursts open. In strides Gemma, angry eyes scanning the room until she spots me. I've clearly upset her, so I need to act fast. I step past Ted and intercept her in the middle of the room.

"Gemma, before you say anything, let me explain."

Her mouth narrows to a cold line. Her hands go to her hips. Then she smiles and slaps my face.

CHAPTER FOURTEEN

I can think of only one way to stop Gemma exposing my true identity. Well two, but I've never slapped a woman in my life. Or I could...

The kiss catches her off guard. It's less aggressive than propelling her out of the building and much more exciting. Her soft, moist lips, and the swell of her breasts against my chest, send my brain plummeting into my trousers. Sensing the start of a struggle, I break the kiss.

"I'm Dale Wensley," I whisper. "I know it's cheesy, but please play along. I'll explain later."

She pulls back, her eyes defiant. "You sexually assaulted me."

"You physically assaulted your manager."

"Dale Wensley isn't my manager. He's a reporter."

"He's a fictitious creation, so he can't have assaulted you."

"So, that was an imaginary erection, was it?" She grins and straightens her powder blue blouse. In a loud voice, she says, "You owe me an explanation, Dale."

Though I'm pleased she's playing along, she could take the conversation anywhere, landing me in even more trouble.

"Darling, how many times do I have to tell you? I'm not having an affair with the barmaid. I'm interviewing these gentlemen about Syd Collins. That's what reporters do."

"Dale," she says, making it sound like I've been naughty again, "we both know you can't keep Little Wensley in your pants." She strides over to the bar and peers behind. Hands on hips, she confronts Barry. "Okay, where have you hidden the little tart?"

Barry glares at me. "Are you messing with my Amanda?"

I'd forgotten about their Florida holiday. "Barry, this is the first time I've been to your pub. I don't know Amanda."

"I've read the steamy texts they send each other," Gemma says. "They arranged to meet in Tombstone."

Encouraged by her words, he emerges from behind the bar, looking for a fight. While I can easily defend myself against an overweight, out of shape publican, she's making me look like the bad guy.

"She's right," I say, raising my hands to stop him. "There was someone else, but it's over. It wasn't your Amanda. It was a young waitress in a restaurant in Tollingdon. She was slim, elegant, and easily the most attractive woman I'd ever met. Despite the age difference, I fell for her the moment I saw her. I couldn't help myself."

Gemma's eyes tell me she remembers the moment as clearly as I do. "Were you in love with her?" she asks.

Of course I was in love with her. Only I was too scared to admit it. For a week, I came up with excuses. I was overreacting. I was infatuated. It was lust, plain and simple. Then I imagined how her parents would react if she brought home someone nearer their age then hers. Her friends would mock her for going out with an old fart like me. One morning she would wake up and see an old fart lying next to her.

All I have to do is say I'm in love with her, but she's engaged now. She's in love with someone else. I'm not going to come between them. And even if she still holds some feelings for me, they have to be quashed now. But I can't look into her eyes as I answer.

"She meant nothing to me."

"And it took you a week to decide that?" Gemma turns and marches out of the room, her sensible shoes squeaking on the bare boards. The door swings shut behind her, the thud echoing through the room.

Maybe now, I can move on.

"'Oh, what a tangled web we weave when first we practice to deceive'," Old Ted reprimands me with a shake of his head. "You don't deserve her, Mr. Dale Wensley."

He knows I'm an imposter. I can see it in his eyes. He's not going to tell me anything more about Collins, so I head out of the door and up the steps to the beer garden that overlooks the road. Gemma's perched on the edge of a bench, hands clasped, head bowed, staring at the road below.

"Barry Stilton assumed I was a reporter," I say. "I played along because I thought he would tell me about Collins."

"It's just a game to you, isn't it?"

"Are you referring to my investigation?"

She looks at me with something akin to disgust. "At last I know why you disappeared without a word."

"I never meant to hurt you."

Her eyebrows rise. "What, you expected me to get back to normal and forget we spent a week together? I was sixteen, Kent! I didn't deserve that."

There's nothing I can say to atone for my cowardly actions. The truth now would send the wrong signals, even if she was willing to believe me. I can't change the past, no matter how much I'd like to.

"Why did you slap me, Gemma?"

"Why did you kiss me?"

"To stop you revealing my name, obviously. What are you doing here?"

"I'm here because you couldn't be bothered to come to the meeting with Danni this morning. You knew they were going to close the case, so you stayed away, didn't you? You left me to face the questions. I had to lie for you, you bastard!"

I slide my Blackberry from its holster. "I sent a text to Danni first thing this morning to say I was meeting the Coroner's Officer at Collins' house."

"Even though you arranged to meet her there yesterday? Don't you ever stop lying, Kent?"

When my Blackberry finishes booting, three text messages arrive. Two are from Mike Turner and the oldest is from Danni. It says, 'OK, will cancel.'

I show Gemma. "Danni said the meeting would go ahead because I'd been with you all the time," she says. "Then she wanted to know all about yesterday afternoon."

"What did you tell her?"

"I could hardly tell her we were in Collins' house, could I? I said we were interviewing staff and checking policies at Tombstone. She didn't push the point, but I don't think she believed me. What's going on, Kent? Did Artie tell Birchill?"

He might have.

"She asked me what I'd learned," she says, "what I thought of their paperwork. I said I didn't understand half of it. Then she insisted on checking my notebook. I hadn't written anything for the afternoon, so I said you took the notes."

I guess I deserved that.

"She wants to check your notebook, Kent. I hope you've written something."

While I can understand that she didn't like being questioned, does that explain her actions?

"So, why did you slap me?" I ask.

She walks to the parapet wall and stares down the lane as if she needs to gather her thoughts. "I'm sick of being treated like an intruder."

I say nothing, sensing there's plenty more to come.

"From the moment I joined your team, you made it clear you didn't want me around. Oh, you let me tag along from time to time, but you don't teach me anything. I've learned how to carry a heavy bag or collect a cockroach trap. I get to hang around like an idiot while you do the job."

"Is that what you think?"

"You wanted Lucy on this investigation, didn't you?"

"She's an experienced officer."

"She must have had a first time once. Why shouldn't I? Danni was happy to send me. She thought I would learn something."

"You slapped me out of frustration, did you?"

She shakes her head. "I heard you through the window, talking to the older man and Barry Stilton. I defended your actions to Danni, and you were playing games, telling lies for England, as you like to put it. You think you're immune to the rules the rest of us have to follow, don't you?" She sighs as if she's wasting her time. "That's why I slapped you."

"I wasn't playing games. I was at Collins' house with Carolyn."

"You lied about yesterday afternoon's appointment, didn't you?"

"If I hadn't checked out the house yesterday, I would never have known what was missing this morning. That's right, our visitor yesterday cleaned out Collins' house. His computer's gone, the condom wrapper too."

"Did you record it in your notebook?"

Shit! I left my notebook behind. I race back to the bar, where Barry's polishing glasses. I spot my notebook next to an ice bucket.

"You're not welcome," he says, without looking up.

I slide the notebook off the bar and out of sight. "I wanted to tell you I've never met Amanda. I'm sure she wouldn't dream of cheating on you."

"She doesn't know how I feel about her, does she?"

"Then maybe you should tell her," I say, being an expert in these matters.

As I leave, Ted shuffles out of the toilets, adjusting his crotch. Luckily, he's in no mood to shake my hand. He blocks my path. "You're no reporter, Mr. Wensley. Who are you?"

"I'm the only person who cares how Syd Collins died."

"Then you'll want to know who Syd turned to for help. It was your father, William Fisher," he says with a sly glance at my notebook. "You don't seem surprised, Mr. Fisher."

I'm good at hiding my emotions. "What sort of help did Collins want?"

"The kind that requires influence, I imagine." He shuffles around me and back to the bar.

Outside, Gemma's waiting by her car. "Did Danni tell you anything about the meeting with Birchill?" I ask.

She shakes her head.

"Did you ask her?"

Her eyes avert for a moment. "I just wanted to get away."

I want to believe her, I really do. "There's a new pizzeria in town, if you fancy lunch," I say. "My treat."

"I'm not in the mood."

"Don't you want to know what I've uncovered?"

"What's the point, if the case is closed?"

"It isn't closed. I have to find out why my father helped Collins."

She considers this and nods. "And why his house was cleaned out. You can tell me on the way to the pizzeria."

"I'll get my car from Collins' house and meet you there. I have things to do this afternoon."

As soon as she's on her way, I pull out my phone and ring Kelly.

"Where were you?" she asks, her voice full of intrigue.

"Did Danni go ahead with the meeting this morning?"

"Yes."

"Did Gemma attend?"

"She was summoned after the Chief Executive left. She was only in there a few minutes and came out looking like she'd sucked a lemon." Kelly lowers her voice. "What's going on, Kent? There's an unpleasant whiff around here."

"And here. Have you any idea how it went with Birchill yesterday?"

"He left a wodge of documents for me to scan. I haven't read the detail, but it looks like Birchill had nothing to do with Collins. Do you want a copy?"

"You're a star, Kelly. Say, do you know what time he left?"

"Before three. He was here about 50 minutes, so definitely before three."

Birchill could have made it to Collins' house. While the lover was the more likely, Birchill would want to make sure the autobiography never reached the papers.

A familiar blue VW Golf flies past in the direction of Collins' house. I end the call and trot down the lane until I'm level with Collins' garden. The Golf's parked next to my car. I take a photograph in case I want to check the registration number later. She's locked the doors and taken the keys. I peer through the window at the sumptuous leather seats. An air freshener, shaped like a pine tree, dangles from the rear view mirror. A bottle of Lucozade energy drink sits erect in the driver door bucket. A navy jacket, with sunglasses peeping out of the front pocket, hangs in the back.

Do they belong to the elusive lover?

I try the kitchen door. It's locked. I walk around side of the house, past the Land Rover. It's also locked. When I reach the corner of the house, I pause and peer round. The woman I saw earlier stands with her back against the front door, her face tilted to the sun. She reminds me of Olive Oil in the Popeye cartoons—thin, with drumstick legs and spindly arms.

I step out into the sunlight and clear my throat.

She regards me with eyes as black as her hair. The cheek below her left eye looks a little puffy. There's something cold, almost insolent, about the way she watches my elegant footwork as I weave between the potted plants.

"Is everything all right?" I ask.

"I saw you earlier with the woman who cut me up. You don't look like a policeman."

"You don't look like a double glazing salesman. Maybe you could tell me who you are and what you're doing on private property."

She jerks to attention and salutes. "Adele Havelock. I came here to meet my father, Syd Collins."

CHAPTER FIFTEEN

"Your father's dead."

"They must miss your tact and diplomacy at the United Nations," Adele Havelock says. She's not the emotional type. She might be thin and weigh about 50 kilos, but there's a fighter in her eyes. I can't help feeling she's scrapped for everything she has, challenging authority, the system, and anyone who tells her she can't.

"I know he's dead," she says. "I didn't know that when I left Croydon this morning. That should answer your second question, but feel free to surprise me with your third."

"Do you fancy a bite to eat?"

"There's no such thing as a free lunch, is there?"

"I'm not offering to pay for yours, but talk is free."

"That assumes I have something to say." She raises a hand to shade the sun from her eyes as she looks at me. "My mother told me never to talk to strangers."

"If you don't want to know how your father died," I say, turning, "that's fine with me."

"He died from cancer."

I keep walking, certain curiosity will get the better of her.

166

I take my time, sauntering along the front and down the side of the house. In the back garden, I open the driver's door to let the heat out of the car. Minutes later, she walks up to her car and climbs inside. She slams the door. She waits 30 seconds before starting the engine. She reverses a yard or so. Then she stops, opening the passenger window.

"Are you saying my father didn't die from cancer?"

"He didn't."

"So, you're a policeman."

"I'm an environmental health officer."

She seems confused. "Don't you guys inspect restaurants?"

"That's why we know the best places for lunch."

She leans across and opens the door. "Jump in, Mr. Environmental Health Officer. I've sanitised the interior."

With pine air freshener, it seems. Its intense but sickly scent overwhelms everything. When I climb into the passenger seat, I almost trample on her high heel shoes, discarded in the footwell. Her small feet, tainted by scarlet toenails, don't look strong enough to depress the pedals.

"Nicotine chewing gum," she says, pushing a piece out of the blister pack. "I went smoke-free last week. I'm hoping it'll improve my chest."

Either she's flirting or fishing for a compliment. I refuse the bait and settle back. "Turn left here and then next left about 100 yards down the road. It's a service road, approached through a farm gate."

We reach the gate in seconds. I jump out and open it to let her through. I look around, but there's no CCTV. Back in the car, I settle in the seat as she speeds away. There's no tension in her face or her hands and no aggression in her driving as she speeds through the fields and paddocks.

"Do you have a name?" she asks as we reach the service areas.

"Kent Fisher."

"Kent? Either you think you're Superman or it's where you were born."

"How about you?" I ask.

"My parents originally come from Cockermouth so I suppose I'm lucky." She giggles for a few seconds and then apologises. "Kent suits you. Now tell me how my father died, and why you're involved."

"Work accident. I enforce health and safety at work. You're welcome to surprise me with a third question."

She slows as we pass the burnt out portacabin. "I don't do surprises. Tell me what happened."

"Your father cut fence posts, using a circular saw."

The car lurches to a halt. "Is this going to be gory?"

"I'm afraid so. He died instantly, if that's any comfort."

"I don't do comfort or tears." She slumps back in her seat, nibbling at a fingernail. "Can I see where he died?"

"There's nothing to see. I've impounded the tractor."

She looks at me with those big eyes, now full of emotion. "Is it far?"

"Why don't we eat first and you can tell me about him."

"You'll be lucky," she says, pulling away from the kerb. "Until six months ago, I didn't know Sydney Collins existed."

I direct her into one of the service yards at the rear of Main Street. She winces and wrinkles her nose at the smell from the overflowing bins.

"Can't you make them keep it clean?" she asks.

"Before the Government decided that local authorities were a drain on public finances, we had the officers and the time to look at bin areas. We have neither now."

She follows me down the passageway to the front of the jail. I pause, hoping Rebecca might be close, but she's nowhere to be seen. Unlike yesterday, when the crowds gathered five deep to watch the gunfight, it's more sedate. That will change when the next gunfight starts in 45 minutes.

Adele pulls out her phone and takes a couple of photos. "It's much better than I expected. You know it cost an absolute fortune to create."

"I heard it was losing money."

"Miles Birchill grew up watching John Wayne. He won't let this place go."

"Then why did he join the outlaws?"

"I don't think he saw it that way." She points across the street. "Mexican okay with you?"

We cross the dusty street and head for The Cactus Grill. It's a modest cantina with small rectangular tables covered in red and white check plastic cloths. Large prints on the walls show scenes from Spaghetti westerns to accompany the soundtrack, blasted out from speakers. Adjacent the small bar, two doors lead in and out of the kitchen. A man in tight black trousers and a flamenco shirt bursts through like a matador.

"If he cries, 'Ole', we're leaving," she says.

We sit by the window, which offers a good view of the street. The laminated menu is wedged into a wooden holder that also contains the wine and spirit list, offers for children, and customer feedback cards that look like they've taken a dip in guacamole. I skim through the usual range of fajitas, enchiladas, burritos and nachos, along with a few dishes I don't recognise, looking for lighter choices. When I can't find any, I signal to the waiter.

"Do you have a lunch menu?"

"The children's menu has smaller portions," he replies in a broad Scottish accent. "Can I get you anything to drink?"

He's middle aged, sloppy and unshaven. There are food stains on his shirt, and a greasy black residue lines his fingernails, as if he's been changing the oil in his car. His harassed, aggressive look suggests problems behind the scenes. I wonder if he's helping out in the kitchen as well as waiting tables.

"I see you have the top food hygiene rating of 5," I say, pointing to the image on the menu. "Why aren't you displaying the sticker in the window to let customers know?"

The waiter shrugs. "Do you want to order food with your drinks?"

"I'll have the chicken salad," Adele replies. "And a mineral water."

"Same for me," I say. When he's out of earshot, I ask Adele if she has the food hygiene app on her phone. "You can download it and find out what the rating is."

"I thought it was a 5?"

"Humour me."

"I might write a piece on this place," she says while the app downloads. "I'm a lifestyle reporter at the *Croydon Guardian*. Before you ask, I write the occasional restaurant review. 'Prickly waiter at the Cactus Grill', sounds good."

Collins had contacted his daughter to promote his autobiography. If I'd checked the emails in the 'Adele' folder, I might have learned more about her. Instead, I'd let the emails between my father and Collins distract me. I still can't believe my father would do a favour for a lowlife like him. When I'm through with the investigation, I'll check it out.

"You said you didn't know your father existed six months ago."

She nods but doesn't elaborate.

"Why did he get in touch?"

"He was dying and he wanted to put things right," she says, not looking up. "Well, that's what he said in the email."

"He told you he was your father in an email?"

"Life's a bitch." There's no sign of anger or bitterness in her eyes or voice. "What do you want to know about him?"

It's a good question. "Everything you know."

"Why? You know how he died, don't you?"

I nod. "The Coroner's Officer needs to establish state of mind. I said I'd help."

"You think he committed suicide?"

I say nothing, keen to see how she reacts. If she thinks her father killed himself, she might reveal more. She closes her eyes and says, "'If you ever wondered who I was, today's your lucky day.' That was first line of his email," she says, opening her eyes. "He assumed I thought about him."

"He assumed you'd be pleased."

"That's why I didn't reply. I wanted to see if he would follow up."

"Did he?"

"He sent a second email with a document attached. It outlined my date of birth, all the major events in my life, and contained a couple of photos of my graduation. It was like he'd stalked me, except nothing he produced was that hard to find. Most of it's on Facebook. The apps ready to go," she says, holding up her phone.

"If he was dying, why didn't he ask to meet you?"

"I don't know." She taps the screen of her phone a couple of times and then smiles. "I've got the rating. It's 2, not 5. 'Improvement necessary'."

Just in time—the prickly waiter's arrived with our water.

I get to my feet. "We're not staying. You're misleading customers and your rating is below legal standards."

"We have a top rating," he says, pointing to the menu.

Adele shows him her phone. "You don't. You should inform the owner."

"I am the owner."

"Then you need to reprint your menus." I pick one up and slip it into my pocket. "Evidence for Trading Standards."

Out on the boardwalk, she turns to her phone. "I can search all the eateries around here."

We settle for baguettes and bottled water from a sandwich bar and take them to the corral, where we grab the last free table in the small picnic area. We chat about hygiene ratings, dirty kitchens I've inspected, food business I've prosecuted, and anything other than Collins. After my last mouthful of baguette, it's time to correct that.

"You didn't sound too upset by the email Collins sent."

She finishes chewing. "I never thought he was my father. He had all the facts, but my mother didn't remember him. I told him that, and his next email contained details of an intimate birth mark she had." She pauses to take a mouthful of water. "That's when she admitted working at a casino in Brighton."

"The Ace of Hearts?"

"You know it?"

It's where my father met Collins, I guess. "I've heard of it, that's all."

"My mother wouldn't tell me much. She said she was young, taking drugs, and entertaining rich clients. Collins could be my father. So could lots of other men."

Her sardonic laugh says everything. "I asked to meet him and he refused. Then, a few weeks later, he emails me again with another document."

I settle back, waiting for her to continue after another mouthful of water.

"I got his life story in bullet points. His life with Miles Birchill, to be more accurate. Secrets, deals, violence, bribes, and the people they screwed. Oh, it was all going to be there, ready to be serialised by the dailies, and he was giving it to his only daughter.

"I remember a couple of incidents. One concerned a detective inspector they set up with a young prostitute. A honey trap, I think they call it. Another involved an Arab sheikh they fleeced. Collins talked about corruption, but when I asked for evidence, he would only say they had an MP in their pocket."

"No name?"

She shakes her head. "Then he went silent again, until last week. He asked me to visit him today. When I arrived, I found you and a woman in the house. I called in at the pub and the publican told me he was dead."

"So why were you standing outside the front door?"

"Someone took the key from under the plant pot." She smiles. "He told me it was there in case he was out when I called."

I open a bag of prawn cocktail flavoured crisps while I consider what she's told me. It sounds plausible, but for one small detail.

"What would you say if I told you Collins was illiterate?"

Without missing a beat, she says, "Someone wrote them for him. A friend?"

I shrug. "I haven't seen them."

She seems disappointed. "Wasn't there a computer in the house?"

"It's protected."

She leans closer and looks straight into my eyes. "Did you find anything you're allowed to tell me about?"

"Like a manuscript, for example?"

"You found it?" She gasps and rubs her hands together.

"We found nothing—no manuscript, no diary, no address book. Did he mention any friends?"

Adele shakes her head. "I came here to prove he was a con man, but I'll never know now, will I?"

That's two of us disappointed, but it makes no difference to my investigation. "Do you still want to see the accident scene, Adele?"

We walk back to the car in silence. The only sound comes from her chewing gum as we head out of Tombstone. At the junction, I guide her right to the barn. It's nearly one twenty and Foley hasn't arrived yet.

"It's around the corner," I say, stepping out into the heat. "I'd stick with barefoot, as it's grassy."

She pulls on a pair of trainers she keeps in the boot and follows me around the corner. She stops when she sees the bench saw. To the side, patches of bare earth reveal where the tractor once stood. There seems to be much less blood on the grass than earlier, suggesting the crows have done their best to tidy up.

"The saw had nothing to do with the accident," I say, leading her down the slope. From a couple of yards away, it's easy to see the blood. I go to the barn wall to shelter from the sun and let her wander around with her thoughts and questions. When I was a teenager, I often wondered about the father I didn't have—what he was like, what he did,

174

where he would take me. The reality turned out to be less exciting than my imagination, but at least he was alive.

"Are of any these new?" she asks, running her fingers over a fence post in the enclosure.

I shake my head.

"If he didn't make any posts, why's the ground covered with cigarette ends?"

It's a good point. If Collins didn't use the tractor, why stand by the saw to smoke? Why not smoke in the cab or in the barn kitchen? If Collins didn't smoke here, then someone else, like Cheung, did. Or someone emptied an ashtray, but why would anyone do that here?

"Beats me," I reply. Noticing movement out of the corner of my eye, I turn to see Foley.

"I've opened the barn if you want to check it out, Mr. Fisher."

When we join him by the open sliding doors, he nods to Adele. "Are you another of Mr. Fisher's assistants?"

"I'm a fresh pair of eyes," she says, strolling into the cavernous interior, which smells of petrol and dust.

I should tell her to leave, but she's right. To me, it's a gloomy, cluttered barn, filled with machinery, tools and workbenches that look unused. Light forces its way through dirty skylights to highlight the dust and cobwebs that cover the surfaces and the corners. From the small JCB to the mowers and spreaders, the barn contains everything needed to maintain Tombstone Adventure Park. Shelves, crammed with containers of screws, nails, bolts and a range of hand tools, line the walls.

"You've got too much petrol," I tell Foley, pointing to the Gerry cans. "One spark and this place would burn to the ground."

"I've never been in here before," he says, stepping back. "This is Mr. Collins' domain."

I stroll over to a mower blade sharpener, wishing I had one. "With all this equipment and facilities, why contract maintenance to Tollingdon Agricultural Services?"

"You should ask Mr. B that."

I wander around the barn, weaving in and out of the machinery, pausing to check under benches or inside cupboards. Wherever I look, everything is pristine. While I don't recognise many of the names, quality leaps out from every corner. Inside one metal cabinet I find protective clothing, including full body suits, gloves, wellingtons and face masks with air filters. One shelf contains orange hard hats with built in ear defenders. Unopened packets of neoprene gloves, dust masks and goggles fill the last shelf.

Adele, who has taken the opposite direction to me, joins me and peers inside. "Everything looks new," she says, her brows dipping over her nose. "Am I missing something?"

"Mr. B expected Syd to do all the grounds maintenance, I heard, but Syd refused." Foley glances over his shoulder as if he expects Birchill to walk in at any moment. "They argued and Syd made fence posts for a while. Mr. B refused to buy them for Tombstone. When the tractor packed up—that was that."

"Miles Birchill did nothing?" Adele asks.

Foley shrugs. He doesn't care. Why should he? He drifts back to the entrance for a cigarette while I wander a little more. While rummaging around a mobile tool rack, I spot the missing guard, tucked at the back of a cupboard. I reach in and retrieve it, turning the guard in my hands to look for any flaws or defects. It looks fine to me. I hold it up to show Adele, who realises what it is almost immediately.

"Would that have prevented Syd's death?" Foley asks, strolling over.

"Yes."

"Then why did he take it off? He must have been mad."

"We don't know that he did," I say.

"Then who did?"

"You need to take that outside," I say, pointing to the cigarette between his fingers. "Apart from breaking the law, you're surrounded by petrol and oils. And don't stub it out on the floor!"

He heads back to the entrance and goes out of sight, thankfully.

I put the guard on a bench and head for a door with a small viewing panel. It looks in on the kitchen I saw with Cheung yesterday. The door's locked, so I reach up and run my fingers along the dirty architrave, where I find a key. I unlock the door and push it open, pleased people are so predictable.

"After you, Adele."

The door opens into a kitchen area, fitted with domestic style cupboards, a sink and drainer, microwave oven, and fridge. The wooden table and chairs have a neglected quality that matches the stained and chipped mugs in the cupboard. Forgotten packets of tea bags and jars of solidified coffee suggest no one's used the kitchen for some time. The ashtray on the table, coated with a film of ash, but no cigarette butts, supports this. The milk in the fridge has separated.

A corridor at the back of the kitchen leads to a small wet room and toilet. White tiles cover the walls from floor to ceiling, leaving space only for a small casement window. A bench runs along the far wall like the ones at school, and I imagine Birchill anticipated a small gang of ground staff waiting to shower.

I try the pull cord and the light comes on, followed by the extract fan a second later. At the washbasin, I'm about to turn on the taps when I pause. I glance at the basin and then the bench. "Adele, run your finger along the bench, will you?"

She does as I ask and holds up a finger. "Dusty."

"Do the same along the top of the shower cubicle."

More dust. The top of the cistern above the toilet is also dusty, yet the basin and taps are clean. So is the flush handle of the toilet, and the inside of the bowl. I look a little closer, spotting a lime scale watermark. The water level has dropped lower in the past, probably from evaporation. It means someone has used the toilet recently.

"The shower screen's polished to a shine," Adele says, peering in. She bends to examine the plug. "There are a few hairs in the plughole."

Water runs from the basin taps, confirming that everything works. I find myself smiling, aware that Cheung's assertions are meaningless. Having seen the state of his house, I wonder if he uses the facilities here to keep clean.

"Who uses the place?" she asks. "My father?"

It makes sense. Whatever my reservations, he's the most likely person to have removed the guard and put it in the barn. Had the kitchen reeked of cigarette smoke I would have felt happier.

"Let's get out of here," I say.

After returning the key to its hiding place above the door, we weave our way between the mowers and tractors until we reach the entrance. I shield my eyes against the sunlight that streams through the doorway and step outside.

Then I spot Danni.

CHAPTER SIXTEEN

By the look of contempt frozen on Danni's face, she hasn't come to award me Accident Investigator of the Year. The buttons on her jacket strain, especially when she slides a white envelope into an inside pocket.

"Danni," I say, knowing I have to take the offensive. "Just the person I wanted to see. You'll never guess what I found."

"Unless it's a miracle, Kent, I'd stop right there."

Her fingers tug at the hem of her jacket. It could be a nervous reaction, but I doubt it. Her appearance here is no accident. She knew where I would be. That narrows down the list of people who could have told her to Birchill or Foley. I'm relieved it's not Gemma, who's standing a few paces behind. She looks like she wants to be anywhere but here.

"I found the missing guard," I say, aware of Adele joining me. "And this is Mr. Collins' daughter, Adele Havelock. She came to meet her father, unaware of his tragic accident. Naturally, she's a little upset at the moment."

It's a lame attempt at emotional blackmail, but it's all I can muster.

My boss straightens her jacket and steps forward. "Daniella Frost, Head of Environmental Health and Waste.

Please accept my sympathies on your loss." The handshake is brief and perfunctory. "I hope you don't mind me asking, but why were you in the barn just now?"

"Kent kindly showed me where my father died. It's just around the back of the barn. Have you seen it?"

"You haven't answered my question," Danni replies, walking into the barn. She stops just inside the door and prods the nearest jerry can with her toe. "With all this petrol and machinery, it's not the safest place to be."

"I wanted to see where my father worked," Adele says. "Kent kindly offered to show me."

Danni turns to face us, almost smiling now. "He's good at helping women in distress. I can't imagine how you feel at the moment. It must be quite overwhelming."

"It's devastating."

"Devastating enough to spoil your lunch in The Cactus Grill? That explains why you left so quickly."

Credit where credit's due, Danni has well and truly stitched me up. "Believe it or not, we left because the restaurant had a poor hygiene rating," I say.

Danni laughs. "You're full of surprises, Kent. You disobey instructions, ignore procedures and break the rules, but you won't eat in a poorly rated restaurant."

"It depends on who sets the standards."

"Oh, I think it's more a case of who enforces them, don't you?" Danni's smug grin tells me I'll be lucky to keep my job.

"Leave us, Miss Havelock. This is an official investigation and we have confidential matters to discuss."

Adele crosses her arms. "Are you taking over the investigation, Miss Frost?"

"Operational matters are not your concern."

"You're a manager, not an inspector. I'd like to know what experience you have to ensure my father's accident is properly investigated. I'm sure my readers will want to know too. They expect me to hold public officials to account."

Danni tugs at the base of her jacket. "Which newspaper do you work for?

"The *Croydon Guardian.*"

"I doubt if your readers in Croydon have heard of Downland."

"They've heard of Miles Birchill."

"Then let your readers know the investigation has concluded."

As usual, my mouth ignores my brain. "It's not your investigation to conclude. I'm the inspector."

"Are you now?" Danni's eyes are as cold as her voice. She strides past, directing me to follow with her finger. "We'll consider that back at the office."

"No, we'll discuss it now."

She stops and turns, tugging her unruly jacket down once more. "You know we don't discuss confidential matters with or in the presence of reporters."

If she's about to discipline me, I'd like a witness—one with a loyal readership, I hope. I take my ID out of my back pocket. "Is this what you want, boss?"

"Are you resigning?"

Gemma finally looks at me, her eyes pleading with me.

"No," I reply. "I want to know if you're going to take my authority away."

She starts walking. "Then we continue this discussion in the office."

"If you wanted to talk in the office, why did you bring that letter with you? The one in your jacket pocket," I add when she pauses. "Are you going to suspend me?"

She turns, clearly struggling to keep her calm. "Why would I suspend you when I can dismiss you?"

Full marks again. I wasn't expecting that. Unable to come up with a suitable response, I have no choice but to go after her. I push past Gemma and catch my boss as she reaches her Vauxhall Tigra.

"If you're going to dismiss me, then do it now, Danni. I'm not returning to the office."

She brushes my hand off her forearm. If looks could kill, I'd be joining Collins. At least I could ask him what really happened yesterday morning.

"Do you want to add insubordination to your list of misdemeanours?" she asks, her voice even and restrained.

"You mean it isn't already included?"

"Have it your way." She plucks the letter from inside her jacket and slaps it into my palm. "Kent Fisher, you're suspended from duty with immediate effect. You withheld crucial information about your dealings with Miles Birchill. These cast doubt on your impartiality and suitability to investigate the accident."

She holds up a second finger. "You ignored departmental procedures for impounding machinery, making your own private arrangements. You bullied staff at Tombstone Adventure Park to obtain information, which led to your final misdemeanour." She extends a fourth finger. "You entered the victim's house illegally."

Even Gemma seems surprised by this final point. With only the slightest shake of her head, she indicates she did not tell Danni. That means either Artie or Ben Foley informed Birchill. No wonder he was keen for me to inspect the barn—

he was setting me up. He must have enjoyed telling Danni about my activities.

"Now I find you co-opting members of the press into your investigation. No, don't say anything," she says, raising a hand. "Save it for the meeting on Monday morning. As it's part of the formal disciplinary procedure, you can bring someone with you.

"I'd strongly advise you not to say anything to her," she says, glancing at Adele, "but you've never taken my advice before, so ...." Her voice fades. She seems tired, or is she relieved the formalities are over? "Can I have your ID?"

I hand her the card. "Take good care of it, because I intend to get it back."

"Please stop the macho posturing, Kent. This isn't an adventure story. You've put us both in an impossible situation. Just give me your written authority, your notebook, and any documents you have relating to the investigation."

"They're in my car."

She looks about her. "And where is it?"

"At Collins' house."

"Gemma, go with Kent and collect everything. And forget the charm, Kent. I'm sure Gemma can now see you for what you are."

"And what's that?"

She doesn't rise to the provocation. "You will stay away from Tombstone Adventure Park and any of its employees. Is that clear?"

She slides into her car, fires up the engine, and leaves an angry cloud of dust in her wake. Foley locks the barn doors and slides away.

I push the letter into my pocket. "Come on, Gemma. Let's get this over with. I'm sure you'd rather be anywhere but here."

"This isn't just about you, Kent. I've had a warning too."

I raise a hand in apology. "I'm not allowed to talk to you," I tell Adele as she falls in beside me, "but could you confirm whether you overheard me being suspended from duty and banned from Tombstone?"

She nods. "Of course you mustn't talk to the media. They might confuse things by putting their own slant on events. If they believe Miles Birchill is flaunting health and safety laws in the name of profit, who knows what they might infer?"

While I need all the friends I can muster, I have to deal with Birchill on my own.

We fall into silence on the walk across the clearing. Adele walks beside me, lost in her own thoughts, while Gemma hangs back a few paces. In some ways it might have been easier if she had betrayed me. Maybe then I could put aside my feelings and move on. But one look into those dark brown eyes and my resistance wavers. I don't want to lose my job, but it would help me put some distance between us.

We soon emerge from the woods at Cheung's hovel. "A bit of care and attention and this could be a great place," Adele says, looking it over.

"David Cheung, the man who found your father, lives here," I say.

"I'd like to thank him, if you don't mind. It couldn't have been pleasant."

I head down the front path and rap on the door. "He's probably working, but you never know. We can check around the back."

"I'll leave a card," she says, following.

The glass lean-to looks cool in the shade at the rear. The door slides open with a shudder and we step inside. The whiff of mould and decay is obvious. I rap on the door and peer through the window, but there's no sign of life.

Adele reaches into her bag for a card and a pen. She rests the card on the lid of the chest freezer and scribbles a few words. "What's Cheung like?"

"Disillusioned," I reply. "No, that's unfair. I'm sure the accident upset him more than he admits. He's like a lot of teenagers—he's no idea how to get what he wants."

"You don't have to be a teenager to suffer from that," Gemma remarks.

"Simply a man," Adele says. "Are we far from my father's?"

"About five minutes," Gemma replies.

"Then Cheung knew him."

"Your father spent a lot of time in the pub," I say. "You'll learn more about him there."

"Then we should go there."

I ignore Gemma's smirk as we leave. My Blackberry rings, giving me a few more moments to think of a good reason to avoid returning to the Game Cock. Maybe my friend, Mike, will give me that reason.

"Everything's set for tonight," he says after the pleasantries. "Once we've delivered the equipment we can visit Hetty at the nursing home. He's going to search his archives for us and see what he can find."

I should tell Mike I'm suspended, but I agree to meet him at seven. As we reach Collins' house, I wonder if DI Wainthropp can identify Collins' lover. If he can, I might discover the whereabouts of the autobiography.

I'm tempted to hand the case to Dale Wensley now that Kent Fisher's suspended. "I've always fancied journalism," I tell Adele as we head down the side of the house to the rear. "I reckon I have an eye for a good story."

"Or a nose," she says with a smile.

She opens her Golf and sits inside while I collect my notebook and written authority from my car. I hand them to Gemma, who still looks troubled.

"Is there something else?" I ask.

"I had no idea Danni was going to suspend you. She rang and told me to meet her at the barn. As you didn't show for lunch, I guessed you might be there." Her voice drops to a whisper and she gestures at Adele. "I wasn't expecting you to be with her."

"The moment Birchill found me on site, my days were numbered."

"That's not what I meant, Kent."

"Gemma, I knew the risks when I entered Tombstone. What's happened since makes no difference to the outcome. I took a chance and got found out. I'm only sorry you got dragged into this. I'll tell Danni you were following my instructions."

She sighs. "I want to know who told her about yesterday afternoon."

"What exactly does she know?"

"She knows we took the train. She knows we were there without permission or a warrant. The person who interrupted us at the house must have told her."

While I still think Birchill tipped off Danni, I'm confident Collins' lover was the one who interrupted Gemma and me. The lover removed the computer and all evidence of her presence in the house. Why would she draw attention to herself by ringing the Council to say we'd been nosing about the house? Why not contact Birchill so he could do the job for her?

"We'll never know for sure," I say.

"Doesn't that depend on what we find on the memory stick? Danni doesn't know about that because I told her nothing."

There's something smug and triumphal in Gemma's expression as she turns away. With her nose in the air and a smile on her lips, she saunters away. Adele watches her go. "Is there something going on with you two?" she asks.

I shake my head. "She'll make a good officer if she listens to her heart."

"She might wind up suspended like you. The head has to prevail, Kent." She regards me as if she expects me to argue, or maybe agree. "And mine wants to know about this memory stick."

"Do you have a laptop?"

"I never leave home without it."

"Does it contain the emails your father sent you?"

"Do you have the password for the chapters?"

"No, I was hoping you did."

She folds her arms, looking thoughtful. "What's on the memory stick?"

"I'll let you know when I check it."

Her chuckle confirms she doesn't believe me. "Well, if you happen to come across some emails with attachments that aren't blocked by passwords, maybe you'll let me know."

"I might want to sell the story myself."

"So, your attachments are password blocked. I thought so." She laughs and slips a business card into my hand. "Credit me with some intelligence, Kent. If you had my father's story, you wouldn't be asking if I had a laptop. With my intelligence and your determination, we might crack this one. What do you say? There could be a fat pay cheque if Birchill's laundry is really dirty."

It's a tempting offer, especially if I lose my job, but I want Birchill to go to trial if he's responsible for Collins' death. "I don't do trial by media," I say.

"Think about it," she says. "I'm not going back to Croydon till tomorrow. I'm booked into Birchill's swanky hotel. I'm hoping he'll tell me about my father. So, if you have a change of heart, come on over and have a drink."

"Thanks, but I don't fancy driving over to Brighton."

"Brighton? What are you talking about? You must have inspected Downland Manor Hotel near Tollingdon."

CHAPTER SEVENTEEN

I feel sick. How could my father sell Downland Manor to Birchill? Why would he sell it to a man he hated? Was I asleep when all this happened?

The questions run on a loop in my mind while I drive to Smugglers' Rest, my father's new home near Herstmonceux. He loathes Birchill and everything he represents. My father condemned the development of Tombstone Adventure Park. He opposed the relaxation of gambling laws that allowed Birchill's casinos to lead people into debt and despair. My father accused Birchill of 'getting rich on the debts of the poor.'

Yet I can't dispel the doubts raised by the emails Collins exchanged with my father.

I think back to the sale of Downland Manor, five years ago. One minute we lived there, the next we didn't. Even my stepmother, Niamh, seemed surprised when he announced the deal over breakfast. No warning, no estate agents, no delays. While the house was crumbling and derelict in many places, it had stood for centuries, the last in a long line of settlements that dated back to the Magna Carta. Downland

Manor and the Fishers were as much a part of the land as the South Downs.

I didn't care at the time. The sale gave me 50 acres of meagre pasture on the eastern edge of the estate. The overgrown fields stretched from the A27 to woodland at the foot of the South Downs. I cleared the land, added paddocks, and upgraded the barn to create a home and my animal sanctuary. I didn't appreciate the importance of the narrow dirt track that connected the centre to the main road until the hotel owners sought planning permission to build a holiday village in the woods that adjoin mine. The woods couldn't be accessed from the hotel. The development needed my track and land for access.

I've turned down ridiculous amounts of money for my land. Had I known Miles Birchill was the man offering the money, I might not have rushed into Tombstone. The prospect of prosecuting him blinded me. Now I know why he offered only a token resistance to my investigation. When he let me inspect the barn, I should have known he was softening me up.

If I lose my job, I lose my sanctuary.

When I arrive at Smugglers' Rest, I'm relieved my father's Jaguar isn't on the drive. I don't need him telling me how stupid I've been.

The house overlooks the mist-covered marshes, once crossed by smugglers heading inland from the south coast. When the wind whips up in autumn and winter, it's wonderfully bleak. I can almost hear the calls of ghostly smugglers as they tread a careful path between life and death, their lanterns flickering in the mist.

Though designed to look like a timber framed Tudor mansion, the house was built long after the smugglers faded into history. It's a faithful homage to the period, built with second hand bricks and tiles, but it's let down by double glazed leaded windows and decorative oak beams across the ceilings. The rooms are too square and the floors too even. The chimneys that bookend the roof lack the ornate brickwork and pots of the period.

It's the kind of deception Birchill approves of.

As Frances likes to remind me, my father made millions out of the sale of Downland Manor and bought a modest replacement. I don't fancy moving here if I lose the sanctuary, but at least it has central heating.

I stride past a sprawling bed of lazy fuchsias, across an unkempt lawn pretending to be a wild flower garden, and slip around to the back of the house. In the doorway, Niamh waits, an apron tied around her slender waist and flour dusting her cheeks. She smells of hot scones, smothered in melting butter, when I embrace her. Her thick black hair, carelessly gathered into a loose knot, comes loose as I kiss her cheek. She sweeps it back with white fingers, leaving streaks of flour.

"I've forgotten what you look like," she says, looking me over with blue-green eyes that glint with humour and mischief. "Why didn't you ring to say you were paying a surprise visit?"

"It wouldn't be a surprise if I told you, would it?"

"Oh, it would be a surprise to be told." She pulls back and notices the flour on my shirt. When she tries to brush it off with her hands, my shirt grows whiter. "For here am I, wondering whether it's me you're interested in or my buns."

I sniff the aroma that's wafting down the hall. "I crave your muffins, but it's your wheaten bread that makes me go weak."

Her father ran a small confectionery shop in Moy, near Dungannon in Northern Ireland. He taught his only daughter to bake cakes and bread at an early age. At 17, she came to London to work in a patisserie. When the company supplied cakes and pastries for a tea party in Downing Street, she met my father. It was love at first bite, by all accounts.

"Walk this way," she says, swinging her hips as she heads down the hall in her leggings and slipper socks. She leads me past her watercolour paintings of the Seven Sisters, Beachy Head and Alfriston High Street, but her studies of Downland Manor are not on display. To my left, the utility and laundry rooms overlook the back garden. To my right, the doors lead to the living and dining rooms, filled with antique furniture from Downland Manor. None of it looks comfortable with the fake beams, but then again, neither does my father.

She veers left into the kitchen. "William won't be home until late."

"No problem. I came to see you."

The vast kitchen combines contemporary beech fronted cupboards and cabinets, topped with black composite worktops, with a traditional farmhouse table and chairs. A chaos of food mixers, bowls, oven trays and bags of flour and sugar form a procession to the deep Belfast sink. Despite the AA rated dishwasher in the adjoining utility room, there's no substitute for washing up by hand.

"And why would you be wanting to see me?" she asks, pressing a finger gently on a dark fruit cake.

"Your muffins look wonderful," I remark, nodding to the wire racks on the table. She's baked muffins, scones and shortbread. The wheaten bread is in the Aga by the smell of things.

Her hands go to her hips. "If you're going to prevaricate, I might as well freshen up. Call me when you're ready."

"No, wait."

I pick up a tea towel and go to the draining board to dry a couple of mugs. I'm not sure what to say about the sale of Downland Manor. Does she know Birchill bought the place? My father never told me, so, did he lie to her? If I blurt out what I know, she might react badly.

"Did my father mention I was investigating a work accident at Tombstone Adventure Park?"

"In passing," she replies. She stretches to take a Japanese-looking tea caddy from a wall cupboard. When she puts the caddy down on the worktop, her blouse gapes where a button has come undone, revealing a flash of lilac bra. She notices where I'm looking and sighs. "You looked at me like that when you first arrived at Downland," she says, fastening the button. "You were 17. You don't seem to have matured in the intervening years."

She's seven years older than me, but she looks much younger. We get on well, sharing similar tastes in music and books, though our politics are miles apart. We can laugh and joke in a way I can never manage with my father.

I point to the cuddly toy on the windowsill. "Scooby Doo's mature, isn't he?"

"You're only jealous," she says in a singsong voice. "So, what brings you here?"

I fill the kettle with water while I consider my response. "A man named Syd Collins died yesterday morning in the accident." I pause, studying her reaction. Her eyes widen for a moment at the mention of the name. "He worked for Miles Birchill. He also knew my father."

She squeezes past me and opens the Aga to check the bread. The smell is amazing. "Your father knows more people than the Pope," she says. "It's his job to represent the people of Downland."

"Collins asked my father for help."

"That's what they do—all of them. Sometimes at the strangest hours."

"Why would a handyman, working for Birchill, want my father's help?"

She places the tray on top of the Aga. "Are you asking because he's a handyman, or because he works for Miles Birchill?"

"Both. He's not the type to seek help."

"We all need help, even you, Kent Fisher. What kind of help was Collins wanting?"

"He wanted my father to use his influence."

She bends and studies the loaves. "And did he?"

"No, he refused."

"Then why are you here?"

The smile and the humour in her eyes do little to dull the sharpness in her voice. For someone who likes to appear a little naïve, she'd make a better politician than my father.

I drop a tea bag into each mug while I wait for the kettle to boil. "I didn't expect my father to deal with Birchill's hired muscle," I say.

"They're all constituents."

"But he hates Birchill."

"Miles is an influential person and a generous donor. He owns property and employs lots of people. William has to deal with him."

"He didn't have to sell Downland Manor to him, did he?"

The uneasy silence stretches out until the kettle boils. Niamh stares at the floor, winding a tea towel tight around her finger, like she's staunching a bleed. Finally, she looks up.

"He didn't tell you, did he?"

I shake my head.

"And you never guessed, obviously." She forces some rebellious hair behind her ear. The tension in her face transfers to her voice. "What can I say? We needed a quick sale."

She looks at me and sighs. "Don't be angry. We owed so much money."

I'm not sure if I'm angry with my father for what he did, or for not telling me. He gave me the land for a sanctuary and made it a noble cause. While I occupy the only Fisher land left, the woodlands beyond are safe.

"I owe money, Niamh."

She wraps her hands around mine. "We'll support you. You know that."

"Only if I drop the accident investigation. Or didn't he tell you that?"

"You shouldn't have started it, Kent."

I pull my hand away, sensing I'm not going to get any sympathy. As far as she's concerned, I got some land while she lost everything. If I make a loss, she has to cover it. If that makes me an ungrateful, selfish stepson, there's not much I can do about it.

I pour water into the mugs and mash the tea bags. "Had I known Birchill was my next door neighbour, maybe I would have left it alone."

"Would you?" Niamh brings some milk from the fridge. Her hands tremble as she slops too much milk into the tea, splashing it over the worktop. Cursing, she grabs the tea towel. "You have to drop the investigation," she says, dabbing the spill. "For all our sakes."

"Too late. He's already complained about me."

Niamh tosses the tea towel aside and stares at me as if I'm the world's most difficult teenager. With a shake of the head, she takes the milk and thuds the bottle back into the fridge. "Your father will sort it out," she says, but her voice lacks conviction. "He still has influence."

I take one of the mugs and select the biggest muffin on the cake rack. It's still warm and soft, like the buttered toast on the day my father told me about the land he'd given me. I had so many dreams, so many plans, I barely heard him when he said he'd sold Downland Manor.

"Why didn't he tell me he'd sold to Birchill?" I ask.

"The estate thrived under previous generations and he'd let them down. All that history, all those lives and struggles, all for nothing." She pauses as I bite into the muffin, waiting to see my reaction before continuing. "He was also selling your inheritance. He felt embarrassed."

I don't believe her, but it's my father I need to confront. That means I need information. I need to go into his study and find out what kind of relationship he had with Birchill and Collins. As the last mouthful of muffin disappears down my throat, I have an idea.

"I've been less than honest about why I called," I say. "Birchill's claiming he bought my land with the rest of the estate. He says he was misled and intends to challenge the contract."

"Our solicitors excluded your land, Kent. If Miles and his solicitors forgot to check, that's his outlook."

"I'd feel happier if I could take a quick look at the deeds and contract. Dad keeps them in his study."

"We'll both look," she says to my dismay. "It'll be quicker, for sure."

I find a smile from somewhere when what I really need is an excuse to search alone. As if by magic, the phone rings in the hall. It's her mother in Northern Ireland. That should mean lots of gossip. Her accent grows stronger by the second, especially when she learns one of her nieces has given birth to a baby girl.

The study is nothing like the one in Downland Manor, which had oak panels, ornate cornices and a fresco ceiling. Everything was handmade, including the floor to ceiling bookcases that hid a secret passage. The smell of wood and beeswax, the unbroken rows of old books, and the reverential atmosphere suggested a place of great knowledge and understanding. It was a place where people made decisions of great importance and effect. Cabinet ministers, lords and military figures had all gathered there at various times throughout history.

I can't quite imagine such a gathering in this room of self-assembly furniture.

The old volumes and tomes that smelt of antiquity have given way to paperback collections of Dick Francis and box sets of series like *The West Wing*. I leave the door open an inch before heading to the beech laminate desk. Though tempted to boot up the PC, I don't want Niamh to catch me checking his emails. I shouldn't know his password, of course, but the prints of Winston Churchill that line the walls mean anyone could hazard a reasonable guess. Only my father's favourite photograph with Margaret Thatcher could tempt someone to guess the wrong password.

I drop into the leather swivel chair and check the three drawer pedestal to my right. The top one contains the usual chaos of stationery—scissors, envelopes, staples, pens and rulers, business cards, and notebooks. The cheque book tells me he's changed banks, and the loyalty card for Costa Coffee speaks for itself. The middle drawer contains screen wipes, bubble jet inks for the printer, a box of staples, paper clips and plenty of those clear plastic wallets that people buy and seldom use.

The creak of a floorboard in the hall has me padding to the door. It's silent and empty in the hall. Straining, I hear Niamh giggle. She's retreated to the kitchen. Relieved, I return to the desk. The bottom drawer contains various telephone directories.

Wondering where he keeps personal belongings, I head over to the bookcases. While I like Dick Francis and Ruth Rendell, I wish he'd brought the books from Downland—especially the Sherlock Holmes collection that started my interest in detective fiction and crime stories. I remove a Shakespeare or two, a Thomas Hardy, and several box sets, hoping to find a letter tucked away, but there's nothing. Back in the leather chair, I stare out of the window, wondering if I've missed something. Where has he put the filing cabinets that contained family papers and heirlooms, historical diaries and documents?

More out of boredom than desperation, I open the top drawer once more. I remove most of the stationery and check the corners of the drawer. As I return a cellophane pack of envelopes, they spill out and cascade to the floor. With a sigh, I drop to my knees. As I scoop them up, a faded business card falls out. It belongs to Mandy Cheung, Hospitality Manager at the Ace of Hearts Club in Brighton. The font and typeface suggest the card is old. The lack of an email address confirms this. The big red heart behind the address is more singles club than casino.

Did the card snag between envelopes or was it hidden there?

I turn the card. The handwriting's feminine and confident —neat and flowing, with flamboyant loops and swirls.

'Take a chance with me,' it says. 'I'm worth the risk.'

CHAPTER EIGHTEEN

I drive straight home, my thoughts going round in circles.

I keep returning to the same question. Would my father have an affair when he had a beautiful young wife who doted on him? For all I know, Mandy Cheung could have given her card to another man, who slid it inside some envelopes that were later given to my father.

But I know I'm making excuses. The envelopes are his. That's the most likely conclusion. It means Mandy Cheung gave him her card. He kept it because she meant something to him. What other conclusion is there?

On the rare occasions my mother spoke about him, she claimed he had several affairs after she became pregnant with me. Normally, I would dismiss anything she told me as a malicious lie, but what if she was right on this occasion? What if my father had an affair with Mandy? What if there's a link between the affair and the sale of Downland Manor?

There's certainly a link between my father and Collins. Their emails show they were more than MP and constituent. From Collins it's only a step to Birchill, who owned the Ace of Hearts. Before long, he could own my sanctuary too.

No wonder Mike teases me about conspiracy theories.

I keep running through this loop, determined to find the flaws in the logic, but all I do is strengthen the feeling in my gut that I don't know my father at all.

When I arrive home a little before four, I stop in the lane to take stock of what I could lose. The merciless sun may be pounding the roof of the barn and desiccating the timber in the paddock fences, but they remain defiant. The gentle South Downs are still cloaked in grass despite the lack of moisture. They have withstood the worst of nature for millions of years, buckling only to the sea that undermines the cliffs.

I have to save my sanctuary and the animals it shelters. Where would Frances go if I close the place? Where would I find someone who cares so much but asks for so little?

As I draw to a halt, she emerges from the kennels with Columbo at her heels. He pauses for a moment, tilts his head, and then wags his tail so fast he could generate electricity for the national grid. He bounds over to me and paws my legs, demanding attention. I sink to my knees to fuss him.

"Has he been with you all day?"

She nods. "You're early."

Most days I'm not home until at least six, thanks to the backlog of work I never seem to clear. Frances is still working. It bothers me, but not enough to make me come home earlier, I'm ashamed to say.

"We made good progress," I say.

"You and Gemma."

There's no emotion in her face or her voice, but I sense friction. "And my boss."

"Has Birchill broken the law?" Frances asks after an awkward silence.

"He pulled out his usual box of tricks to convince Danni he wasn't responsible. Has my father phoned?"

She shakes her head.

He hasn't heard about my suspension yet. "Is everything okay here?"

"The same as when you left this morning."

Though she smiles to temper her sarcasm, I can't help feeling she doesn't believe me. When did I last return home early? What if my father has called and told her what happened? She'll know I'm lying, making my situation worse.

My flat's the same as it was this morning. A week's worth of dust covers everything. For someone who spends his working life advising businesses to be clean and hygienic, this is embarrassing. But I've more important things to do than clean. Who's going to notice anyway? Who comes here other than Frances?

Gemma visited the previous evening. Mike will be along later.

With a sigh, I retrieve the cereal bowls and cups that poke through the murky water and place them in the dishwasher. Then I attack every visible surface with antibacterial cleaner. Columbo, who follows me everywhere, pounces on the cloth when it falls to the floor. Then he tastes the cleaner and spits it out in disgust, but it doesn't dampen his enthusiasm. He tails me to the bathroom, where I spend half an hour removing lime scale and smears from the shower cubicle. I won't say what I cleared out of the plug hole.

I had hoped cleaning would distract me, but I can't stop thinking about my father's deceptions and the troubles I'm facing. I need to clear my mind. The best way to find a solution is to stop thinking about the problem. Let the subconscious work on it in the background and release the answer when it's ready.

I need a long run over the Downs to start the process.

Once I put the cloth and cleaning fluids away, I change into shorts and vest. Though it's hot, I pull on compression socks before slipping into my Mizuno trainers. While I fill a bottle with chilled water from the fridge, my BlackBerry rings.

"Good afternoon, Mr. Fisher. How are we today?"

The unmistakable drawl of Thomas Hardy Logan, editor of the *Tollingdon Tribune*, masks his excitement at the prospect of some meaty news. In his late fifties, he's a frustrated hack, sensationalising local news. His rambling style and dry wit are more suited to a parish magazine, but he seems to find at least one scandal a week to interest people. Birchill and my father often feature, but the son of the local MP offers far more possibilities.

"A little bird tells me you have more free time on your hands than usual."

"I thought you ran a newspaper, not an aviary," I say.

"You missed your true vocation, Mr. Fisher. You could have had them rolling in the aisles with your wit. Instead, you claim to protect our residents by closing down food businesses that lack paperwork."

He's never forgiven me for downgrading his favourite takeaway and restaurant. When spotted dining there, a rival reporter vilified him as a hypocrite. From that day, he changed his tune about the hygiene ratings and claimed it was an unfair burden on business.

"Had you closed down Tombstone, you would have saved Sydney Collins."

"It's down to Birchill to comply with the law," I say.

"Can I quote you on that, Mr. Fisher, Environmental Health Manager?"

"I'm simply telling you the employer is responsible for complying with the law, not the inspector. You could quote that, but I can't comment at the moment."

"Is that because you're no longer investigating the death?"

"No, Tommy, it's because my manager, Danni, deals with the media."

"Daniella Frost, the Ice Maiden," he says in a tone that suggests he'd like to melt her. "As she won't return my calls, I could resort to the reporter's stock in trade response of speculating. However, you could ensure I don't misrepresent you in the town's favourite read."

"You'll write whatever you want whether I speak to you or not."

His laugh lacks humour, but he's enjoying himself. "Then permit me to speculate, Mr. Fisher. If you are investigating a work death that involves our favourite entrepreneur, why are you at home?" When I don't respond, he says, "The normally charming Kelly was unusually offhand earlier. My nose is twitching."

"You mean your beak, surely, with all the little birds you mix with."

He sighs as though he's done his best to save me. "My next call will be to Ben Foley at Tombstone. He has no qualms about talking to me, bless him."

For all I know, he spoke to Foley before he rang me. "Tommy, what if I said there might be a better story next week?"

"I'm all ears, dear boy."

I clear my throat to give me a few more seconds to put my thoughts in order. "You know Birchill owns Downland

Manor Hotel. Have you ever wondered how he could afford to buy my father's estate, renovate the manor and build Tombstone in the same year? We're talking millions."

Tommy purrs like a contented cat. "Are you going to tell me?"

"I'm asking you how he did it."

"I'm surprised you haven't spoken to your old flame, Tara McNamara. She was running the estate at the time. And," he says, his voice drooling, "she opened her own hotel, didn't she?"

I can't believe I never thought of Tara. What's wrong with me?

"You'll be the first to know, Tommy. Early next week, I promise."

"Don't leave me waiting," he says. "I want to know why you were suspended."

He ends the call, leaving me with a smile. As much as I want to dislike the man, I enjoy bantering with him. To be fair, he's treated me well over the years, taking my side when Birchill won his injunction against me. That was a few months after he started Tombstone. He helped Tara buy her hotel, if I'm reading Tommy's hints correctly. Does that mean she helped him buy Downland Manor?

Columbo nudges my leg the moment I put the phone down. I lift him so he can look through the windows. His ears prick as he studies the scene below. After a minute, I put him down and make a cup of tea before ringing Kelly. Her voice changes to a whisper when I introduce myself.

"She's hovering. Can you ring back?"

Among the background chatter, Danni's voice is clear and confident as she directs the team.

"Kelly, I need the name of the food business operator, and the phone number for the Brigadier public house near Mayfield."

I can hear the tap of her keyboard and the click of her mouse as she speaks. "Yes, you'll need to register the business," she says. "You can download the form from our website and... oh, you don't have the internet, Mr. Townsend. Okay, I'll call you Peter. You're the new owner of the Brigadier Public House, Mayfield."

She rattles off the postcode and, most importantly, the phone number, and says, "I'll post the registration form to you."

"Thanks, Kelly, you're a star."

"You know where I am if you need me," she whispers.

A few moments later, I'm talking to Peter Townsend. He's one of those people who know everything because he's run so many businesses over the years. Most of them failed, disputing the adage that you learn from your mistakes.

"I don't know if you remember, Mr. Townsend, but I visited you at the White Horse Hotel near Alfriston before it closed down. Kent Fisher."

He clicks his tongue against his teeth. "Yeah, I remember you. You came barging in when we had that food poisoning outbreak at a wedding reception. No one proved it was my fault, but the bastards tried to sue me, you know. They ruined my reputation so they could screw me for every penny I had." He laughs. "Well, I had the last laugh, didn't I? I closed the business down."

My recollection of events doesn't quite tally with his, but it's irrelevant. "That's right," I say, remembering how it took him two years to sell the place. "You waited a couple of years to sell so they wouldn't find out."

"There's not many health inspectors understand how to run a successful business," he says. "You had another complaint about me?"

"No, I need to get in touch with the woman who bought the place from you. She liked horses, and had a name that rhymed."

"Tara McNamara, wasn't it? Good looking woman, as I recall. Shame she was in a wheelchair or I could have gone for her. Mind you, she was as hard as nails. She haggled me down to just under a million and paid cash."

"Cash?"

"Compensation for her accident, she said, but I didn't care about that, did I? All I wanted was a fair price for a hotel in prime condition and location, but how do you argue with a woman in a wheelchair? It's hardly fair, is it?"

I bite back a response and draw breath. "Isn't it unusual to pay cash in these days of money laundering?"

"She brought the money in a briefcase. Well, the goon she brought along had the briefcase. Military looking chap with close cropped hair and chips on both shoulders. He looked like he wanted to thump me."

"Did you get his name?"

"I didn't ask, and I don't want to know. I did them a favour, and all I got was bellyaching, like I'd let the place go to the dogs."

"Maybe you should have sold it to a vet."

I end the call, confident I know where Tara got £1 million in cash. Birchill's involvement should be simple enough to prove if he's a partner in the business. I'm sure Mike Turner can help me with that.

I rise from the table and head for the door. My Blackberry rings again and it's the Coroner's Officer—brisk, business-like and blunt. "I have the pathologist's preliminary report, if you're interested, Kent. Collins was a dead man walking—advanced lung cancer, cirrhosis of the liver, and failing kidneys. He must have been in pain and struggling to breathe."

So, how did he walk from his house to the tractor?

"I can imagine him doubling up in agony," Carolyn says. "Maybe that explains why he bent over the power takeoff."

"Maybe," I say.

"He'd been drinking too—heavily, we think. No breakfast consumed, either. Did you find anything in the barn?"

"The missing guard," I reply.

"Did Collins remove it?"

"I can't think who else it would be."

"But you considered the possibility, didn't you?"

She's sharp—I'll give her that. "I like to keep an open mind, Carolyn."

"You're not still fretting about why he wore a tie and smoked the wrong cigarettes, are you? Facts and evidence prove the offence, Kent. Remember that."

It sounds like a slogan for Danni's Motivational Pin Board. "I don't have the evidence to take formal action against Birchill."

"Don't you? Why not?"

She'll find out soon enough, but I'm in no mood to talk about my suspension. "I can't prove he's responsible."

"Is everything okay, Kent? You sound—deflated."

"I'm tired, that's all."

She chuckles. "Is your assistant wearing you out?"

"Only with questions."

I put the phone down and consider what I've learned. If I'm right, Collins had sex the night before his death. He may not have slept at all, which explains why he went to the clearing so early. The empty vodka bottle suggests he was drinking, maybe to numb the pain. Exhausted, in pain, and drunk, he lost his balance and....

I could just about accept that, if someone hadn't repaired the tractor.

Back in the bedroom, I place my Garmin on the windowsill. While the GPS satellites locate the watch and tune in, I hunt around for my head torch. With the evenings drawing in, I can either run in Tollingdon under the street lights, or use my head torch on the Downs. I may be back before darkness falls, but it depends how much thinking I do.

When I'm ready, I grab a bottle of water from the fridge and head down the stairs. Columbo races past me. At the bottom, he turns and barks to encourage me. Frances comes over and scoops him up, struggling to hold onto him as he wriggles.

"You have to stay here," she tells him. "I'll put him in the kennels or he'll follow you."

"Thanks."

I set off towards the sleeping hills, darkening beneath the setting sun. My legs feel heavy, my gait uneven, as I dodge the flints that poke through the chalk like spearheads. Once clear of the paddocks, I feel the muscles loosen and lengthen my stride. Within five minutes, my breathing settles into a familiar rhythm. I'm in the zone, my mind free to go where it wants.

No matter which way I approach Collins' death, I can't make everything fit. Add the speculation and hearsay—the autobiography, the lover, the illiteracy, the colourful past— and they show a man determined to tell his story before he died.

The path meanders up the hill between the trees. With every minute, the view expands below me, stretching across the A27 and the Eastbourne to the London railway line towards Arlington Reservoir. Most of the fields have been ploughed for next year's crops, leaving only corn and the pastures, grazed by sheep and cattle.

Moments later, the former Fisher estate comes into view. Where horses once roamed, golfers now reign. A few are finishing on the last of the nine holes as the light fades. In time, the trees will mature to separate the almost intestinal tangle of fairways and greens.

In the silvery light, the Georgian elegance of Downland Manor dominates the gardens and parkland like a stately home. From up on the Downs, I'm struck by the symmetry of the sash windows and the ornate chimneys that thrust through the slate roofs. Even the satellite dishes and the Velux windows that ventilate the staff accommodation in the attic evoke no reaction.

I don't miss the place that never felt like home. Though it's now a luxurious hotel, it remains a crumbling relic in my mind. The empty rooms, bedrooms without ceilings and floorboards, and secret passageways blocked by rubble made it a cold, heartless place, too big and unloved to be a home.

In my first few weeks at Downland Manor, the horses, with their long heads and rows of stained teeth, terrified me. Tara helped me conquer my fear. We rode a lot that first summer, but not always on horseback. Then, just as the sex became something more than thrashing about between the sheets, she married a computer programmer. A few months later, while we were galloping through the woods, she fell from her horse and broke her back. Within weeks the marriage failed. She turned to me for comfort, but it wasn't the same. I couldn't handle her bitterness.

My breathing eases as the path levels out at the top of the Downs. The wind blows strong from the south-west up here, giving the hawthorn and gorse their distinctive quiffs. Rabbits scatter across the grass. Some hikers linger, admiring the orange wisps of cloud as they bleed into red. Between the sky and this undulating green canvas, I'm an insignificant dot.

After another mile, I turn back. The dark swoops in, blotting out the trees and bushes, merging the sky and the ground. My years in Manchester never prepared me for the dense black of the countryside. I switch on my head torch and follow the beam on the ground. I slow my pace and descend, guided by the lights from Downland Manor in the west and Tollingdon to the east. The lights of the sanctuary come into view and it's easy to picture the line of the road Birchill wants to build for his holiday village. It's not so easy to follow the path that will lead me to safety.

Now I know why he let me loose in his theme park. He wanted me to break rules in my quest to prosecute him, and I obliged. Without a thought for the consequences, I snooped around Collins' house. I pressured Ben Foley. At least I took a more sympathetic approach with David Cheung.

A connection sparks in my mind. I stumble to a stop. Is he Mandy Cheung's son?

I must talk to Tara. She knows more about the sale of Downland than I ever imagined.

Back at the sanctuary, I race up the steps. I gulp back half a bottle of chocolate flavoured milk and skip my usual stretching routine. My thoughts focus on how to break down Tara's resistance. Once in the shower, I savour the hot water and let it rush over my head and body. It won't be long before Mike arrives for the delivery of kitchen equipment.

Then we'll visit his retired colleague to find out what he can offer to bring down Birchill.

That's what I have to do to save my job.

Feeling invigorated and ready for the fight, I wrap a towel around my waist and exit the bathroom. The scamper of claws on laminate flooring signals Columbo's arrival. I scoop up the flurry of white fur and let him lick my ear and face while I ruffle his fur. It's a while before I spot Gemma, smiling in amusement.

Her smile widens into a grin when the towel slides off my hips and drops to the floor.

CHAPTER NINETEEN

The last time I stood naked before Gemma, I had only one thing on my mind.

"I don't often see something so cute and hairy," she says, strolling over. She ruffles Columbo's fur, tickling him behind the ears. "Who are you?"

"His name's Columbo."

"Like the scruffy detective? See, I paid attention," she says, bending so he can lick her face. "You're pleased to see me, aren't you?" She picks up the towel from the floor and holds it out to me. "I can see you're not."

I put Columbo down and wrap the towel around my waist. "What are you doing here?"

It looks like she's on her way to a party in fitted black jeans and a matching silk blouse. A small, silver pendant, shaped like a tear, rests at the base of her slender neck, just like the first time I saw her in La Floret.

"I came to see if you're okay. You didn't deserve that." She drops to her knees to play with Columbo, who's demanding more attention. "Look, a Fisher who likes me."

"If you don't mind, I'd like to get dressed."

"You never used to be self-conscious."

"What do you want, Gemma? You didn't dress up to come here, so I'm guessing you're off out with your fiancé."

"Why don't you ever use his name, Kent?"

Because he becomes more real if I do.

"I'm coming with you and Mike," she says when I don't answer. "He said you had some catering equipment to deliver, so you can shift your lazy butt."

I stride over to the window and see the van, backed up to the store. "He's early."

"It's a big delivery."

Apart from a select few, no one knows I run a business on the side. People could easily assume I find problems in kitchens and then offer to supply new equipment from my own stock. I wouldn't do that, but I feel I should justify myself.

"Every penny we make supports this place," I say.

"Mike told me. You're lucky to have a friend like him."

I take a pair of black chinos from the wardrobe. "Unlike Mike, I don't believe you dressed up to help us move cookers. Why are you here?"

She fingers the pendant as she watches me pull a black polo shirt from the dresser. "I thought you might want some company."

"I have all I need here, thank you. Now if you don't mind, I'd like to get dressed."

Without a word, she turns and totters away in her high heels, flicking her glossy hair off her shoulders. A moment ago, I stood naked before the woman I'm in love with, revealing everything but my feelings. Now, I've rejected her.

"It's for the best," I tell my reflection, running a comb through my damp hair.

As I pass through the lounge, I catch sight of her in the yard. She's walking towards the paddocks, Columbo at her heels. Once there, she leans over the fence and encourages the donkeys over. She pats and strokes them before feeding them some chopped carrots, saving a chunk for Columbo. He almost takes her fingers off as he snatches the treat from her.

In the kitchen, Mike's brewing up. "Why did you invite Gemma?" I ask.

"I didn't." He squeezes the tea bag and then tosses it into the bin. "Why didn't you tell me your boss suspended you?"

"I was going to tell you later. Has Gemma just told you?"

He shakes his head, helping himself to milk from the fridge. "She stopped by Mighty Munch as I was packing up. She was well upset, I can tell you."

"So, how does inviting her on a delivery make her feel better?"

"I thought it would make you feel better." He thrusts a mug of tea into my hand. "I've seen the way you look at her."

"I've seen the way *you* look at her."

He smirks. "I'm a dirty old man, but you're potty about her."

"What time are we meeting Hetty?"

The door swings open and Gemma saunters in. "Is he the retired detective you spoke about yesterday?"

I nod, wondering if she's been listening at the door.

"Does he know you call him Hetty?"

"Sure," Mike replies. "He didn't mind. I think he was quite pleased, really. They called *me* Chunky."

Her eyebrows arch. "That's a bit insensitive, isn't it?"

"Why? What's wrong with Chunky Kit Kats?"

I raise a finger to silence her. "Hetty knows all about Birchill and Collins."

"What if Danni finds out?"

"Where's Columbo?" I ask, surprised he hasn't come through the door.

"With Frances. She's taking care of him while we're out."

The van needs a good clean. The seats are grubby and worn, the dashboard covered in dust, and the carpets sticky. Mike pulls out some antiseptic wipes from under the dash and hands them to Gemma. She cleans down the passenger seat and then dries it with a tissue. Satisfied it's safe to sit on, she climbs inside. As I climb in to join her, she picks up a Chunky Kit Kat from the dashboard.

He snatches it from her. "That's my supper."

"You should eat something nutritious."

"I'll have a kebab once we've finished with Hetty."

Mike tells us about Hetty and Birchill as we bounce along the uneven track towards the main road. We sit at the junction with the A27 for what seems like 10 minutes before he floors the accelerator. The van lurches and takes a couple of seconds to pick up speed as we push into the traffic. The noise is deafening.

At Wilmington village, we take a right, heading north. The road narrows and weaves through the countryside, past some lovely old houses with Sussex tiled roofs, terraced gardens, and triple garages for the Mercedes, Audi and Lexus monsters on the drives. Further along the road, many of the houses are modern and out of place, which makes me wonder why we bother with planning laws.

"Government inspectors have a lot to answer for," I say. "Look at Tombstone Adventure Park."

"You know it's about influence and favours, pal."

"Collins knew about that," I say, nodding. "That's why I want to read his emails."

Mike jerks his head round. "What emails?"

215

"Kent copied them from his computer." Gemma makes me sound like a master spy, which I quite like. "We were in his house yesterday."

Mike groans. "No wonder you were suspended."

"Not before Danni caught him in a barn with a woman," she says.

"Collins' daughter, Adele," I say. "We were looking for evidence that would explain his death. She's a journalist. He wanted her to publish his autobiography."

"Autobiography? Syd Collins?" He shakes his head in disbelief. "What's this got to do with his accident?"

"Nothing," she replies. "That's why Danni closed the case."

"Closed? You only just started."

"If I can get my hands on the autobiography, who knows what it might reveal?"

Mike pulls up at a junction and turns right for Upper Dicker. "Collins wouldn't rat on his friend. They'd both go down."

"Collins did—yesterday."

"What are you saying?" he asks.

"Nothing, Mike. I can't open the files. They're password blocked."

"I hope you're not asking me to help," he says, his voice rising. "I'm not taking files to my old friends in IT, especially if they were obtained illegally."

"I wouldn't dream of asking," I lie.

A few minutes later, we arrive at the Downland Arms, once part of the Fisher estate when the family owned everything for miles. Mike reverses the van up to the wooden gate at the rear and toots the horn. We wait until a young chef in dirty whites opens the gate and walks up to Mike.

3 333333

"You're late," he says, pulling out his cigarettes. "Brendan wants a word about that steam cleaner you sold him. It worked once and then died. Hello, darling," he says, giving Gemma a wink. "Are you on special offer?"

"Only to adults," she replies. She gives him such a withering stare, I'm surprised he doesn't turn to dust.

I jump down from the van and head around the back, as I always do, in case anyone recognises me. "Brendan's a tight-fisted bastard," Mike says as we unload the first of four microwaves, "but I'll sort him out."

We stack the microwaves on a small trolley, which he pushes into the yard. I shuffle a couple of deep fat fryers forward.

"What a dump," he says as we lift the first fryer onto the trolley. "Brendan sacked the kitchen porter when takings dropped, so no one's cleaning the place."

Once he's on his way, Gemma says, "You can't do this, Kent. It's unethical. You're a law enforcer."

"Not while I'm suspended."

"If the place is dirty, you can't ignore it."

"I have a sanctuary to save."

I want to tell her that Mike will make an anonymous complaint in the morning, but she might inadvertently blurt something out if she knows. Nigel will investigate and take action if necessary.

After moving the deep fat fryers, Mike's sweating. He makes one final trip with a small refrigerator, taking 15 minutes to return. This time he's boiling.

"Brendan won't pay until we produce electrical safety certificates for the microwaves and the fridge."

"You told him they were less than a year old, right?"

"Of course I told him, but without the invoices, we can't prove it."

"Then let's take the goods back."

"He threatened to report us to Trading Standards for selling unfit appliances. Chef told me he hasn't paid his suppliers for months."

"So, why do they keep supplying him?" Gemma asks.

"Because if they stop they'll never get any money," I reply. "This way, there's a chance."

Mike pounds the van door with his fist. "We can't let him get away with it. On Monday you can close him down. Chef won't be there to remember you."

"I'm suspended, Mike."

"Brendan won't know that."

"We'll think of something," I say.

"Where's Gemma?" he asks, looking down the side of the van. I check the other side and catch a glimpse of her entering the yard. "You have to stop her," he says. "Brendan's a bastard."

I grab his arm. "She can handle herself. I saw her deal with a couple of difficult customers when she was only 16."

"All the same...." He sighs and leans his back against the van. "So, you've known her some time, then. You kept that quiet."

"I'm better acquainted with her mother, Sarah. You know, Sarah Wheeler, the vet."

"She's Sarah's daughter?" He whistles. "So, that's why you're holding back."

"You think I had a relationship with Sarah?"

"You never did 'relationships'," he replies, framing the word with finger quotes. "You spent a lot of time together, though."

"Protesting against Tombstone, that's all."

"Methinks you protest too much, pal." Mike laughs at his own joke and slaps me on the back. "Even though you like them young and naïve, there's no way you'd pass up Sarah Wheeler."

"I would if I'd slept with her daughter."

He stares at me for a moment and then grins. "You slept with Gemma? Not when she was 16, surely? You have no scruples, pal."

"And you make too many assumptions."

"That's because you never tell me anything."

Don't I wish I'd kept my mouth shut. "If you breathe a word, Mike."

He makes a zipping motion across his mouth and we drift into silence, watching the pub. A few minutes pass before Gemma returns and climbs into the van. We jump in beside her. She leans back, sighs, and lets her shoulders relax.

"I never understood the word odious until tonight," she says. "Brendan Farmer's offensive and patronising." She hands me a wad of notes as if they're contaminated. "It cost him another £50."

"He coughed up?" Mike looks at her with a mixture of disbelief and admiration. "How did you manage that?"

"The rat running into the pub routine," she replies. "He told me not to worry my pretty little head, so I got out my phone and rang my uncle, Tommy Logan, at the *Tollingdon Tribune*."

"Tommy's your uncle?"

She shakes her head at Mike. "That's what I told Brendan. I said I'd also tell my uncle he bought knocked off equipment for his kitchen."

"And he paid up?"

"Sure, when I offered to show him the photos of the rats." She smiles, obviously pleased with herself. "He doesn't want any more gear, by the way."

Mike laughs, thumping the dashboard for extra effect. "Well done, Gemma."

She gives me an expectant look.

"Indeed," I say, "but you took a big chance. Things could have got nasty."

"No way. He'd never hit a woman."

"I don't think his ex-wife would agree with you," Mike says, starting up the van. "Let's go see Hetty."

On the way to Willingdon, Mike reveals more about his years with DI Wainthropp. Happy years, Mike calls them, as if modern policing has taken the fun out of the job. While policing may be dogged by paperwork, environmental health is plagued by people with big expectations complaining about small problems. The faintest whiff of smoke and there's a pyromaniac living next door. A dog barks and the neighbour's starting a boarding kennel. No one's prepared to talk to their neighbours unless it involves mediation.

The Prestige Nursing Home looks like a jaded hotel with its stained render and paintwork. We leave the van in the staff car park and head for the entrance porch. Mike buzzes the intercom and announces us and who we're visiting. Moments later, we're inside a carpeted lobby, face to face with a nurse who insists we sign the visitor book. We double the number for the day.

There's something sad and neglected about the lobby. The magnolia walls have seen better days. The scratches and scuff marks on the mahogany table and dresser are mirrored on the skirting boards. The brown carpet is lifeless, flattened by years of people walking to the old-fashioned, high backed chairs that line the walls of the lounge. Two elderly men, with expressions set by years of routine, watch the news on an old TV that fills one corner. The spider plants and chrysanthemums have faded to pale green from a lack of light. Only the photographs of old Eastbourne show any life, but that life passed years ago. No wonder the press and stand-up comedians refer to Eastbourne as God's waiting room.

They should join the clubbers and foreign students on the pier each Saturday night to see the other face of the town.

A faint whiff of stale urine threatens my nose when we push through a set of fire doors and climb three steps into a rear extension. The carpet and furnishings are cheaper here. There are no photographs to distract people from the fact they're here to die.

"This wing houses referrals from the hospital," the nurse remarks, managing to make it sound like the patients are foisted on her. "Most have little hope, I'm afraid. Your friend, Mr. Wainthropp, refuses to quit smoking, even though he's got emphysema and lung cancer."

Why do health professionals insist you give up smoking when you're about to die?

"You allow smoking?" Gemma asks, sounding surprised.

The nurse stops at an open door. "Only in certain parts of the garden. If Mr. Wainthropp asks you to take him outside, don't. He's not got long, so go easy. I'll check on you every five minutes or so to make sure he's all right."

DI Wainthropp looks like a starving refugee, hunched in an armchair that dwarfs him. His face is pale and thin. Every bone is visible beneath the dry, wrinkled skin that covers his angular nose and sunken cheeks. A glistening trail of saliva runs from the corner of his mouth down a groove in his chin. Only his eyes are alive, especially when he spots Gemma.

"Sit." His arid voice rasps through his lips. He reaches for the oxygen mask and takes several slow and painful breaths. "Be lost without this," he says patting the huge cylinder beside the armchair. "Sit opposite me, young lady. If I can look at you I won't need morphine."

Mike shakes his head. "You'll do yourself a mischief, Hetty."

Wainthropp's hands are small and gnarled, withered by arthritis. His jacket's clearly too big for his shrunken frame. His shirt, unbuttoned at the neck, reveals a scrawny neck with folds of skin, scarred from some kind of surgery. If I ever wondered what death looked like, I now know.

"It's been a long time, Chunky. Another week and you'd have to watch them lower me into the ground." He shifts his gaze to Gemma. "I might look like Freddie Kruger, love, but I'm still human. Well, the bits that work are. I don't smell and I don't bite, so there's nothing to be afraid of."

He turns his attention to me. "You're not what I imagined."

"What did you imagine?"

"Your father had breeding and class. You couldn't get into the Ace of Hearts without it. I tried." He pauses to catch his breath. "Your father had it in spades, but it didn't stop him being a cheat."

Wainthropp pulls the oxygen mask over his mouth, shooing Mike away with the other hand. "I'm not gone yet," he says through the mask. A minute later, he pulls it off and slumps back in the armchair. "Not till tomorrow. It's shepherd's pie for lunch."

"How do you know my father cheated?"

"Have you been in a coma? He's cheated all his life." He pauses to regain his breath and then smiles maliciously.

"Gambling. Fraud. Women. Ah," he says, pointing a bony finger at me, "that one you already know about."

"I don't know what you're talking about."

"I think you do, Mr. Fisher." Wainthropp points a shaking finger at a pile of manila folders, bursting with paper. "Try the folder, 'Missing Persons'."

I go over to the small table. The Missing Persons folder is top of the pile. The papers inside smells musty. Some of the sheets are parchment coloured, filled with a shaky, spidery writing. Some pages have women's names at the top. Some have a photo. Some pages start with a list of police officers. I'm guessing they worked with Hetty.

Most of the women listed are from the Far East, brought into the country illegally, destined for the sex trade, it says.

"Who am I looking for?"

Hetty's eyes close and his head rolls back. It looks like he's fallen asleep, or died, until he speaks. His voice is clear. "Mandy Cheung went missing about 20 years ago. Presumed dead."

I find her details, but there's no picture. The notes are clear enough. PC F Pritchard and WPC L Maynard responded to the original report from a colleague at the Ace of Hearts. DI Wainthropp and DC Porter carried out the investigation. Mandy came from the Philippines, entered the country illegally as a teenager, and worked as a prostitute in London. It's not clear how she made her way to Brighton, but Birchill has casinos in both cities.

I look out through the window at the garden. It's difficult to imagine this clandestine world coexisting with the peaceful one I inhabit. In my world, the biggest crime, apart from Tombstone Adventure Park, is to build social housing in villages.

"A couple of the girls said Mandy had an affair with your father," Hetty says, forcing out each syllable. "Before she went missing, some girls said they heard shouting. Some..."

He winces and doubles up. The oxygen mask comes loose. Mike pulls the emergency cord and bends down beside him. He fits the mask back and tries to ease him back in the chair, but it's futile. Hetty's gasping for breath. The colour's draining from his face. The nurse rushes in and takes over.

"You'd better leave," she says, lifting his chin so she can look into his eyes. She presses the oxygen mask to his face. "You don't want to go yet, Mr. Wainthropp. It's shepherd's pie tomorrow. Your favourite."

He mouths something, but it's inaudible. The nurse bends closer and he mouths again. Another nurse rushes in with a medical bag. While she attends to Hetty, the first nurse ushers us out.

"Are you relatives?"

Mike shakes his head. "We're friends and colleagues. He has no one."

"I'll call the doctor, but you should be prepared for the worst. His lungs can't take much more. I'm sorry." She's about to go back inside, but she stops. "I don't know who he's talking about, but he said she's pregnant."

My stomach tightens. "Do you think he meant Mandy Cheung?"

"I imagine so," Mike says, trying to see what's happening in Hetty's room. "He was methodical to the point of obsessive. He had a phenomenal memory and the patience of a saint. He spent years trying to prosecute Birchill, slowly building a case, but he never did, poor sod."

We retrace our steps to the front entrance in silence. Once outside, I turn to Mike. "How did Hetty know who I was looking for?"

"When I rang and mentioned your name, Hetty knew why you wanted to see him. That's why the right folder was on top."

"How would he know?" I ask.

Mike shrugs.

"What are you going to do?" Gemma asks.

"Find the truth," I reply. "It's in short supply in my family."

I need to know what happened all those years ago. My mother lied about what happened. My father never explained what happened. It's time he came clean about Mandy Cheung.

"What if she didn't die?" I ask Mike when we reach the van. "What if Mandy Cheung was pregnant? What if she had the baby?"

"You heard Hetty. She's probably buried in the foundation of some bridge."

I don't go for the gangster movie cliché. "Who do we know who's the right age to be her son?"

He shrugs, more interested in smoking a cigarette.

Gemma gasps. "David Cheung! You could have a stepbrother, Kent."

I could have a lot more than that.

CHAPTER TWENTY

"Mike, I need to talk to Cheung. Take me to Tombstone."

We're not far from the sanctuary. Since we left the nursing home, I've been thinking about the spiky-haired punk, who bears no resemblance to me or my father. I don't believe for a moment that Cheung's my stepbrother. It's a common name, but what are the chances of finding two Cheungs linked to my father, Birchill and the accident investigation?

Mike hits the brake hard. The van lurches to an ungainly stop, plunging us forward. The seatbelt locks. My head continues to roll forward, and then suddenly I'm jerked back. My head thuds into the seat. Feeling out of control, I grab Gemma's hand.

"That hurts!" she cries, wrenching her hand free.

Mike pushes the gear stick into neutral, yanks up the handbrake, and turns to me. "The takeaway's just around the corner. My stomach's shrivelling."

"I have to talk to Cheung."

"To find out if he's your brother?" Gemma asks.

"To confirm he's not my brother," I reply. "If he is, why hasn't he contacted my father? Why didn't he say something to me?"

"He wouldn't just come out with it," she replies, rubbing her fingers. "And he was in shock after finding Collins."

"Maybe he has contacted your father," Mike says, checking the mirror. "Maybe he told Collins. They are neighbours."

It's possible, I guess, but why would Cheung get a job at Tombstone? If he believes he's a Fisher, surely he would contact my father, not Collins. Then I remember the emails they sent each other. Collins worked at the casino when Mandy was there. He would have known about the pregnancy. Maybe he knew about David and arranged a job for him. Maybe Collins sought some gain from the situation.

"What if Collins orchestrated everything?" I ask. "What if he intended to blackmail my father?"

"That's one hell of a leap, pal."

"That's why we go to Tombstone."

Mike's tummy rumbles at this point to emphasise his reluctance. He checks his mirror and pulls out into the road, slowly building up speed until we're on the A27. We soon pass my sanctuary and drive on in silence. I wonder if Cheung thinks I had a privileged upbringing while he went from foster home to foster home.

I would have swapped the damp basement flat in north Manchester for a warm foster home. Cold and damp, it remained mouldy, even in summer. In winter, ice tempered the inside of the windows, while the cold air penetrated the rough blanket I rescued from the airing cupboard. The Calor gas heater couldn't banish the icy draughts. Its heat faded quickly as you moved across the room.

"Your father left us nothing." My mother's German accent hardened her words. "I have nothing. You have nothing. That means you are nothing without me. If you do not take good care of me, you will have nothing."

As she only had lies to offer, nothing turned out to be a better deal.

"What if he is your stepbrother?" Gemma asks, breaking the long silence.

When I returned to Sussex and met my stepmother, I was surprised I didn't have a brother or sister. But being the only child made me the centre of attention at home and in the community. For a while I felt like a celebrity. Everyone wanted to meet me. People kept commenting on how I'd grown. My accent, though not completely northern, attracted a lot of attention. Some people wanted to know if the north was as grim as they'd heard.

The novelty soon wore off when I discovered my father spent most of his time in Westminster. My stepmother, who was nearer my age than his, also had a busy life. I was often alone in a sprawling, crumbling relic of a house. Fortunately, I had Tara to lust after. Several years older than me, and with a wicked sense of humour, she kept me more than occupied.

"He'll want his share of the Fisher millions if he is," Mike says.

Gemma nods. "That will make him popular."

"He'll need to prove it," I say, tuning back into the conversation. "Who's going to take his word against that of a respected politician?"

"If he is your brother, you wouldn't begrudge him his share, would you?" she asks.

"He's not my stepbrother," I say. The prospect of sharing my sanctuary with a stranger is hardly appealing. It probably makes me seem selfish, but I've built the place up from a derelict barn and low grade pasture.

We lapse into another silence that lasts until we draw close to the road to Tombstone. I tell Mike to drive past the main entrance and follow the road around to the back of Collins' house. I rummage through a jumble of receipts and scribbled notes in the glove box.

"Do you still have a Maglite?"

"Watch my accounts," he says, as a small bundle falls into the footwell. "Don't mess them up."

I examine the handwritten receipt for a gas stove we sold over a month ago. "When did you last update the accounts?"

"I have every invoice and receipt," he replies. "They were in order until you messed them up. It's going to take hours to sort them out."

"You were so organised at work, Mike."

"There's nothing like the buzz of a crime scene, pal. When you have to identify murderers and rapists, it focuses the mind. If I do my job well, it's easier for the lads to catch the perpetrator."

"I was so excited when I arrived yesterday morning, I almost wet myself," Gemma says. "Someone was dead because of a faulty machine. Beats complaints about spiders in sandwiches."

He groans. "Don't start on food, please. I get enough grief over what I can and can't eat from Kent. Has he told you they scrape meat off bones to make burgers?"

"I don't eat burgers," she replies.

"Neither do I anymore."

I take the torch from the glove box and feel its weight in my hand. Long, thin, and cased in metal, it casts a strong beam, which I'll need in the woods. I shine it out of the side window as we pass the service road.

"Slow down, Mike. We're there."

"Should we try the Game Cock first?" Gemma asks.

I spot a familiar blue car at the back of the house. The lights in the kitchen and upstairs are on. "Drive past and stop behind the trees, Mike. Adele Havelock's in the house."

He accelerates past and stops 20 yards down the lane. I'm already unbuckling the seatbelt and sliding out of the seat. "You and Gemma check the pub in case Cheung's there, then meet me back here."

"What if she's not alone, pal?"

"You worry too much." I slam the door and stick close to the bushes as I make my way. When I reach the driveway, I pause and peer around the laurel. The landing and back bedroom lights are on and the curtains are drawn. When I'm certain she's not in the kitchen, I sneak across the concrete and duck down behind her car. I hear Mike drive away in the van.

I move along the side of the car, checking the driver's door. It's locked. Once I reach the kitchen extension, I can move along without being spotted. I duck below the window and stop when I reach the door.

If Adele has a key, why didn't she use it earlier? Why was she waiting by the front door? Someone else has a key. Collins' lover, maybe, hoping to sell the autobiography.

I depress the door handle and open the door a fraction, listening for any sound within. I can hear the blood pulsing through my head as I slip inside and close the door behind me. I hold my breath and listen. Finally, the groan of floorboards above confirms her location. While it's difficult to tell, it sounds like she's alone.

I fish her business card from my wallet and dial her mobile number. She must have her phone on vibrate because I don't hear it ring. The sound of her voice makes me jump.

"Hello, Adele Havelock speaking."

I turn away from the door to the hall. "It's Kent Fisher. I wondered if you fancied dinner."

"Now? I'm rather busy."

"Why don't you join me downstairs and we'll walk over to the Game Cock."

There's a sound like a curse, followed by rapid footsteps down the stairs. She pushes open the door and glares at me. She's swapped her suit for a black polar neck jumper that looks baggy on her tiny frame. She complements this burglar chic with leggings, running gloves, and deck shoes, all in black. All she needs is a balaclava.

"What are you doing here?"

I pull out one of the stools. "I could ask you the same question. Don't tell me you were just passing, because it's the back of beyond."

"Then you must be spying on me."

"In case you've forgotten, I'm investigating Collins' death."

"You seem to have forgotten you're suspended."

"You're breaking and entering. Tell me why I shouldn't ring the police."

She saunters over, full of confidence, her dark eyes gleaming. "I have a key. Syd was my father."

"Have you found the autobiography?"

She shakes her head. "He was going to give me the manuscript today."

"But he died."

"There's no need to be glib." She places the phone in her handbag and pulls out a small bottle of mineral water. She takes a sip and leans back against the worktop. Her eyes are reddened and tired. "Have you any idea how it feels to find a father you never knew you had?"

I suppress a smile. "No idea."

"Unreal. That's how it feels. You wake up, have breakfast and do all the mundane stuff. You trot into work for another day, wondering whether today's the day you get your break with a big story. Instead, you get a poorly written email from the father you never knew you had."

She walks across to the window, bottle in hand. "Naturally, you dismiss the email as a sick joke, a cruel hoax. It's a nutter, trying to get your attention. But something in your stomach tells you it's true. This is the father you never knew.

"Then the anger takes root. While he had good health, he didn't care about my mother or me. Then, when he discovers he's dying, he has to crash into our worlds, but only because he wants to publish his life story."

Slowly, she turns to face me, her expression grim. "I'm glad he's dead, but it leaves me with a problem."

I wait for her to continue.

"I don't want anyone to see or read his manuscript, Kent. I don't want anyone to know about my mother or me, but what if it's a good story? What if he reveals secrets about Miles Birchill? What if it's worth thousands?"

"Someone's already read the manuscript though," I say. "They could also sell it, couldn't they?"

She nods. "I need to find this mystery woman, if only to learn more about my father. He can't have been all bad, can he?"

"He only saw her on Wednesday evenings, according to local gossip, so she could be married."

"Does anyone know who she is?"

"It doesn't look like it, but she might email you if she wants to sell the autobiography."

Adele smirks. "Not if she wants to keep her affair secret from her husband. My father might have visited her so she could write up his autobiography."

I'm tempted to mention the condom wrapper I found in the bedroom, but I'm not sure I trust her yet.

"So, Mr. Fisher, you know why I'm here. What about you? As you said, it's the back of beyond."

"I was on my way to the Game Cock when I spotted the lights were on."

She stares out into the darkness. "Where's your car? I didn't hear you drive in. I didn't see any headlights. Are you checking on me?"

"If I was, why would I ring you?"

She breaks into a slow smile. "Why were you going to the Game Cock? Why didn't I see or hear your car?"

"I'm with a friend."

"Your assistant? She looked uncomfortable earlier. Did she know you were going to be suspended?"

I shrug. "Have you looked everywhere?"

"Everywhere but the loft."

Why didn't I think of that? "Is there a loft ladder?" I ask, heading for the stairs.

The hatch sits above the landing, just out reach. There are no chairs in the front bedroom. The chair in the study is on castors and will move or rotate if I stand on it. "I'll have to get a ladder from home."

Adele puts her bag on Collins' desk and sits in his chair. "What would happen if I took this?" she asks, pointing at the laptop.

"You're probably his beneficiary, so I guess it's yours."

She glances at her watch and sighs. "There's nothing more we can do here, so I'll freshen up and we might as well go. Is your offer of dinner still on the table?"

"Maybe."

When she closes the bathroom door, I check my phone. Mike hasn't sent a text to say he's found Cheung, so maybe I should leave. Then Adele's phone vibrates inside her bag. After a quick look down the landing, I open her bag.

Syd Collins is ringing his daughter.

Either he isn't dead or someone took his phone. Without a thought for the consequences, I accept the call, but say nothing. Neither does the caller. Every few seconds I peer out of the study, expecting Adele to return. When the caller hangs up, eleven seconds have elapsed.

I thrust the phone back in Adele's bag. The next time she uses the phone she'll spot the call and work out what happened. But was she expecting the call? Does she know who has the phone? If I had to guess, I'd say it was the lover, mainly because I can't think who else would take Collins' phone.

It looks like the lover has an autobiography to sell.

The sound of the toilet flushing prompts me to leave. With a nifty bit of footwork, I descend the stairs, taking the last two in one leap. I grab Mike's Maglite from the counter and slip out of the back door. Outside, I move to the front of the house and scurry into the bushes.

I don't want to turn on the torch and give my position away, so I feel my way into the woodland. The sound of insects seems louder in the black. Even the brush of my legs against the undergrowth sounds loud. I stub my toe on tree roots, scratch my ankle on some brambles, and bang my head on a couple of branches as I make slow progress into the woods. Finally, I switch on the torch, confident I'm far enough from the house. With it pointed at the ground, I speed up and reach Cheung's hovel in a few minutes. I turn off the torch and remain in the bushes. There are no lights on in his house.

I ring Mike. "Where are you?" he asks.

"Outside Cheung's house. Did you check the Game Cock?"

"No one's seen him for a couple of days."

He could be in the house. "Where are you, Mike?"

"We're parked in the lane behind Collins' place. Hang on, something's happening."

There's a pause and some muffled sounds. Then I hear a car drive past, accelerating away. After some further muffled sounds, Mike's back. "We ducked down. I'm guessing it was Collins' daughter."

"I'm going to check Cheung's place," I say. "If I'm not back in 15 minutes, send the cavalry."

Guided by the torch, I hurry across the clearing and vault the front gate. Once flattened against the front wall, I catch my breath and shuffle along, ducking under the leaded windows. Around the corner, I scamper to the back, dousing the torchlight.

The garden is made up of different shades of impenetrable black. The smell of rotting rubbish hangs in the air, becoming more intense as I edge along the wall. The metallic clatter as I crash into the bin probably wakes half of Sussex. That's me resitting my stealth exams.

I hold my breath and wait. Minutes pass before I'm confident no one's home. Even then, I still try to slide the glass door open without making a noise. Unfortunately, it scrapes along its frame, making a sound similar to fingernails on a blackboard. Finally, I slide it open enough to squeeze through. All I can hear is the hum of the chest freezer. I'm tempted to look inside for an ice cream, but resist.

I try the kitchen door, but it's locked. I shine my torch through the window, but all I can see is a bowl of dirty water in the sink and some cups on the drainer. The living room door is open, but I can't make out anything beyond.

Then a noise in the bushes makes me freeze. Inch by inch, I turn, the Maglite ready to be swung like a truncheon. The sweep of the torch beam forces a rabbit to scamper into the undergrowth, and I start breathing again.

Back at Collins' house, Mike and Gemma are waiting in the van. "I was just about to send the cavalry," he says, looking relieved.

Gemma looks pale and cold. "Why couldn't you wait until tomorrow?"

I get inside and close the door. "Someone used Collins' mobile to ring Adele. I think it's the lover, but as the person didn't speak, who knows?"

"You answered her phone?"

"Wouldn't you if it said Collins was ringing?"

"She doesn't know, I take it."

"She will when she checks the call history. Cheung's not at home."

"Can we get something to eat?" Mike's voice has a pleading quality that suggests he's had enough. He's right.

"Can you drop me home on the way?" I ask.

"We could pick up a pizza and...." His voice fades as he looks at me. Then he grins. "Okay, you two don't need me around. So, what's the plan for tomorrow? Do we come back?"

Not before I visit my old friend and lover, Tara McNamara. I don't think she'll be too pleased to see me when she learns I'm interested in the sale of Downland Manor. Then I need to talk to my father. He's holding his Saturday surgery at the leisure centre, so it will be after lunch before I can see him. As he's used to fending off the likes of Jeremy Paxman and David Dimbleby, I'm not going to pose much of a challenge.

"I don't know," I reply.

For the past two days, I've followed my instincts, trying to understand why Collins changed his habits and routines. That change led to his death. While it looks like carelessness, all my enquiries suggest the death is part of something much bigger and more complex. He's asked for and received help from my father, who probably acted illegally.

Why? I don't know.

Then I discover that my father is acquainted with Birchill's casino, the Ace of Hearts Club. It looks like he had a fling with Mandy Cheung, who worked there. She could be David Cheung's mother. He could be my stepbrother. He's also living five minutes from Collins.

Why? I don't know.

Then my father sells Downland Manor to Birchill.

Why? I don't know.

Underpinning all of these questions is Collins' autobiography, written by a lover no one knows. She was with him on the eve of his death. She may even have been with him when he had his accident. Either way, she didn't hang around. She didn't call the emergency services. Yet it looks like she took his phone and rung his daughter not 30 minutes ago.

Why? I don't know.

When Mike drops us off at the sanctuary twenty minutes later, I'm certain Collins' death was no accident.

SATURDAY

CHAPTER TWENTY-ONE

I was 16 when I first watched Lieutenant Columbo unpick a perfect murder on TV. This seemingly disorganised and absent-minded detective mesmerised me with the way he picked up tiny inconsistencies and turned them into a trail of evidence. Had I not fallen hopelessly in love with Barbara Booth, who stood me up on our first date, I would not have returned home to watch the lieutenant.

From that moment, I wanted to solve a murder.

And now I have one. Only it's too surreal for words. I keep wondering how the police will react. They'll listen without comment, study every movement, every gesture I make, and ask me the questions I asked myself last night.

Then they'll wonder which planet I'm from.

"I need to get some evidence first," I tell Columbo, ruffling his fur.

When Frances taps on the door, he bursts into life. He rushes over, barking and jumping up at the door. I stifle a yawn and get up from the table, still groggy after oversleeping until ten.

"You went to bed late," she says when I let her in.

I gave up trying to guess the password to the autobiography files about three in the morning. "Then you must have been spying on me."

"Well, if you will spend your time in chat rooms." She says it as a joke, but then her cheeks redden. She kneels and fusses Columbo. "I fed him with the other dogs, as you were dead to the world, but you should feed him here."

"Tomorrow," I say.

"I was joking about the chat room," she says, looking up. "It's none of my business what you do."

I won't be doing much now I'm suspended. I should tell her, but I don't want to worry her.

"I'm off to see Tara at the White Horse," I say. "Can you manage?"

She nods and hurries away. After a shower, shave and a bowl of oat granola, I take an extra fish oil capsule to stimulate my brain cells. I need to be sharp and at my best if Tara chooses to be difficult. While I change into a shirt and smart trousers, a text message arrives from Kathryn, Animal Welfare Officer at Eastbourne. She wants to know if I can take a Border Collie for the weekend.

When I end the call, I notice the unusual spelling of her name on my contact list. It reminds me of the way Collins spelt Sydney. Columbo barks and chases after me as I rush to my computer. He leaps on the bed and watches as I pace about, wishing the PC would boot quicker. If I'm right, I could have the evidence I need to convince the police I'm not bonkers.

When the password window appears on the screen, I type Wynston instead of Winston. It fails, so I try Churchyll. There's a pause and then the document opens. I punch the air in delight, almost hitting the monitor. After a calming breath, I reach for the mouse and start scrolling. 'Chapter

One' appears about two-thirds of the way down the page. It's followed by line after line of exclamation marks, which continue for the remaining 20 pages.

This repeats for all chapters. Each time I open one, I tell myself it will be the last, but I can't miss one, just in case. As I come to the end of the 20th chapter, Frances strolls in with a mug of tea.

"I thought you were off to Tara's. What's that?" she asks, joining me.

"Part of Collins' autobiography," I reply, closing the document. "It's nothing but exclamation marks."

She settles on the bed next to Columbo. "Have you checked the file at the bottom called 'Introduction'?"

It's dated 15th March and opens without a password.

If you ever wondered about your father, it's your lucky day. Your mother, Amira, worked at the Ace of Hearts in Brighton where I ran security for Miles Birchill. He owns the casino. We go back a long way, me and Miles, when we was both poor and penniless. With his brains and my gift for persuading, we done well.

Amira left home because her parents wanted her to marry some wealthy cousin in Pakistan. She entertained the best punters—politicians, footballers and celebrities. She made more in tips in one night than I earned in a week, but she saved herself for me.

Then she got pregnant. Sensible women take precautions, don't they?

Miles gave her money for an abortion, so she could get back to entertaining, but we never saw her again. Then, a few months ago, someone sends me your birth certificate and some photographs. If she'd told me about the baby, I

240

could have been there for you. But I can still put things right before I shuffle off this mortal coil.

Cancer will kill me, but I have a story. I'll tell you things about Miles the tabloids will kill for. You'll be rich, my daughter. That's my gift to you.

                    Sydney Collins.

"What do you think?" I ask. "Do you think it's genuine?"

"I don't know. He thinks birth control is for women, and then quotes Shakespeare. Shuffling off this mortal coil," she says when I give her a blank look.

"I think the woman he was seeing wrote it for him."

"Why would any woman write that? It doesn't say much for the man she's with."

I wonder if the lover wanted to make Collins look bad. "When I find her, I'll ask."

It's almost eleven by the time I'm on the road to Alfriston, shadowing the Cuckmere River, which is like a ribbon in the wide valley that runs to the coast. I'm stuck behind a tractor that's trimming the hedgerow with a cutter attached to a power takeoff. It's a wonderful bit of kit that can tackle all kinds of jobs—spraying, cutting, trimming and killing. Whoever killed Collins understood this.

A few minutes later, the White Horse Hotel, named after the chalk carving on the escarpment, comes into view at the northern edge of the village. Like Downland Manor, it has symmetrical rows of sash windows, grand chimneys, and a Grecian entrance. I'm not sure who thought blue render was a good idea, but it's distinctive.

The drive weaves between striped lawns and formal beds, terraced up an embankment to the hotel. Stone balustrades and steps, weathered green with algae, separate the terraces.

The flowerbeds are overgrown with sparse roses thrusting through dense layers of marigolds, petunias and bindweed.

I skip the public car park and head to the rear of the building where I can enter via the kitchen. I park next to a battered Fiat Panda, which has a pair of checkered chef's trousers on the passenger seat. The smell of rancid fat draws me through wooden gates that hide a yard at the back of the kitchen. Beyond the bins, a lake of greasy water spills out from a manhole. Curdled grease and fat coat the concrete like soap. Staff must see this every time they put refuse in the bins.

Why hasn't someone dealt with the blocked drain?

I sidle around the edge of the fat lake and through double doors into a long, dark corridor, which smells of damp and mould. Every windowsill has its own collection of dead flies and cobwebs. The filthy mesh fly screens cut out half the light, helping to disguise the sticky black grouting between the quarry tiles.

The familiar noises of a kitchen increase as I get closer. Someone who hasn't a prayer of hitting the high notes sings along to Bon Jovi. The hum of the extract system harmonises with the drone of refrigerator motors, encouraging someone to beat out a steady rhythm on some pots and pans. I push through the door to find Chef playing air guitar with a broom.

Neglect pervades the kitchen like a virus. Many of the tiles in the suspended ceiling have warped and stained. Every wall has tiles like colanders, punctured with holes where shelves were once fitted. Chipped and cracked quarry floor tiles are obscured by the black grease that's settled on them. Old cookers with faded enamel huddle back-to-back beneath a huge stainless steel canopy, streaked with lines of dark grease. Everything looks grubby, especially the feet of the stainless steel tables. Under some of the cabinets, I spot food waste, including an orange coated in green mould.

If Tara proves stubborn, the poor hygiene might give me leverage.

The tanned kitchen porter with a snake tattoo on his forearm points me out to a young man in whites, nonchalantly breaking eggs into a large bowl. Like many chefs, he has a small, grubby towel, hanging from his waist.

Chef discards the broom and lumbers up, muscles straining the seams of his whites. He's unshaven, apart from his head, and sports several studs in each ear. "Who are you?" he demands, blocking my path.

I hold up my notebook. "Dale Wensley, freelance reporter and mystery shopper. Tara employs me to carry out undercover hygiene checks."

"Then how come I ain't seen you before?"

"There wouldn't be much mystery if you knew me."

This seems to confuse him. "What do you want?"

He's already granted my first wish by stopping his singing. "I'm here to make sure your guests get safe food," I reply, running my finger along the underside of a worktop. I hold up the greasy digit.

"I don't prepare food under there, do I? I ain't poisoned no one, neither."

"You're doing all the right things to change that," I say.

He steps closer. "Are you trying to be funny?"

His young colleague hurries over. The smell of testosterone overpowers the aroma of tomatoes and chillies on the stove. Unimpressed, I point to a pan, boiling over on the stove. "You might want to deal with that."

Chef rushes across and grabs the metal handles, forgetting how hot they are. He curses and drops the pan, spilling more water. The gas flames hiss and struggle. Some of the boiling water cascades onto his trainers, making him jump back. Thankfully, the kitchen porter turns off the gas. Armed with a tea towel, he lifts the pan to an adjoining ring.

I use the distraction to slip into the dining room, which has also seen better days. While clean and pleasant, the walls have faded to the colour of parchment. Silver adhesive tape repairs wounds to the carpet. Old salt and pepper pots prop up tired breakfast menus. I walk the length of the stainless steel server, littered with crispy bacon pieces and dried baked beans.

A waitress with piercing East European eyes intercepts me. She has an athletic build, highlighted by the tightness of her skirt and a blouse stretched over a well-filled bra. Her small, delicate face would improve with a smile, but I'm guessing Olga's paid the minimum wage and bored senseless.

"You want something?" she asks.

"Decaffeinated coffee for two, please."

"You have a friend?"

"Miss McNamara," I reply, glancing up at the security camera. In her suite, Tara has a bank of monitors so she can watch every part of the hotel. She must have spotted me by now.

While Olga's in the kitchen, I stroll over to a table by the window. I part the mouldy net curtains to look out at the half empty car park. A hotel that offers riding holidays for the disabled needs stables, horses, qualified trainers and helpers, and a high occupancy rate to make a profit.

An older man in a suit enters the dining room. He pauses only to straighten his black jacket. "Miss McNamara will see you in her suite, Mr. Fisher. She wishes to know if your visit is social or antisocial."

"I'll tell her myself if you'll bring the coffee."

"I'll have someone do that."

I thought he might. Once he's in the kitchen, I nip down the corridor and take the service lift to the top floor, where the staff quarters nestle in the roof. Tara's suite occupies the southern wing. Like the woman herself, it's functional. White, unadorned walls, a brown, heavy-duty carpet, and industrial steel furniture create a practical but unwelcoming atmosphere. The desk that engulfs the centre of the room contains only a PC, printer and telephone to allow her an unhindered view of the security monitors.

"Look what the cat dragged in."

Tara propels her wheelchair into the room. She's piled on a few kilos since my last visit, but it hasn't softened her face. There's something cold and cynical in the way her pale blue eyes regard me. She's bleached her hair blonde and dragged it into a flimsy ponytail, secured with a red bulldog clip that's as garish as her hastily applied lipstick.

"Do I get a kiss?" she asks. "I haven't seen you for years."

I buzz her cheek and straighten up. She grabs my hand in a firm grip and pulls me back. "That's not a kiss."

"This isn't a social call."

"Is that why you were in my kitchen?"

"Your chef needs singing lessons."

"He needs cooking lessons too."

The laughter's polite, considering how long we've known each other. The fun-loving, vitriolic Tara has given in to weariness and apathy.

"You've let the place go," I say. "That's not like you."

Her voice rises. "Everyone complains these days. The water in the therapy pool's too hot or too cold. The towels are too rough. The shower gel isn't for sensitive skin. The beds are too lumpy. The beds are too soft." She makes a frustrated growling sound. "What the hell do people want?"

"High standards, excellent service, and an experience you'll remember for years to come."

She sticks two fingers up at me as I quote her mission statement. "I'm sure you didn't come here to mock me, Kent. What do you want?"

"As an EHO, I'm duty bound to deal with the contraventions I've witnessed." I stroll around the desk and over to the window to let her think about this. "How I deal with them depends on what you tell me. For instance," I say, turning to face her, "the hotel next door to me wants to buy my land."

She shrugs. "What's that got to do with me?"

"You dealt with them when you were estate manager."

"I didn't."

"What about when my father sold Downland?"

"That was a private sale. Nothing to do with me. I lost my job, remember?"

"That's how you bought this place. You got redundancy. Wow, that was some pay off."

"Here's the coffee," she says, pointing to the monitor. In the corridor outside a young man with tousled black hair and stubble carries a silver tray. He struts into the room like a matador, winking at Tara as he makes a grand sweep through the air with the tray. He sets it on the desk without spilling a drop of coffee or cream.

"Would sir like me to pour?" he asks in a Mediterranean accent.

"I can manage, thank you."

"Then I will pour for the lady," he says, eyeing her with lust. "She likes me to pamper her."

She shakes her head. "Leave us, please."

"Enjoy your coffee, sir," he says, as if he's put poison in it. "I will be back to collect the tray shortly."

Tara grins as she watches him leave. "You're not the only one who can shag waiting staff, you know. He's hung like a donkey."

"And you're making an ass of yourself."

"Bitch!" she says, making a cat scratch in the air.

I take her a black coffee, keen to get the conversation back on track. "So, we'll assume your redundancy payment didn't cover the asking price for the hotel. Who put the balance up?"

"Why the sudden interest? You never cared before."

"I'm wondering how long your backer will allow you to haemorrhage money."

"I'm not losing money."

"The hotel's half empty, Tara. You haven't spent a penny on maintenance for years. Someone's footing the bill. Miles Birchill, maybe?"

She'd make a formidable poker player. Without a hint of emotion, she remains silent, sipping her coffee from time to time. "I didn't get redundancy," she says finally, "whatever your father told you. I had a legacy from my aunt."

"And compensation from your accident, right?"

"What compensation?" She bangs the cup down, sloshing coffee over the desk. "When I broke my back, I wanted to die. Your father promised to look after me. He said I was the daughter he'd never had. He would find the best doctors in the land to repair me. He would make sure I wanted for nothing.

"When the NHS gave up on me, he told me to claim from his insurance company. They would settle out of court, he said. Like a fool, I believed him."

I recall my father going out of his way to help her. He got someone to drive her to physiotherapy twice a week. He employed a nurse in the early stages. Then as the realisation that she would never walk took root, he paid builders to adapt a bungalow near the Manor for wheelchair use.

"The insurance company refused to accept liability, so I got a solicitor," she says, her voice barely containing her anger. "We had enough medical evidence to beat them on every count, but they fought dirty. They got people from the estate to say I was reckless, racing horses through the gardens, jumping them over fences and gates like I was riding the Grand National."

"But you did," I say, remembering it well.

"They didn't have to stitch me up though," she cries. "What difference did it make to them? I was the one whose life was shattered. I lost my mobility, my freedom and my marriage. What did they lose?"

I don't answer. Nothing I can say will change her mind. She's stuck in the past, blaming everyone but herself. I feel saddened, knowing how full of life she had been.

"The judge awarded a substantial sum in compensation," she says, her voice low. "Then he took most of it away for contributory negligence. Have you any idea how devastating that was?"

"Why did you tell me you'd won?"

"Come on, Kent! Why do you think? I told you I loved you once."

"Yeah, the night before your wedding."

"You're so straight, Kent. That's your trouble. If you'd suffered like me, you'd know morals don't pay bills. They don't set you on your feet when your back's broken. They don't buy you a hotel so you can help disabled children."

"So, who did?"

She wheels up to the desk and starts using her computer. After several mouse clicks, she beckons me over. The image on the screen shows her having sex with the waiter who'd just left.

"I've got cameras everywhere," she says. "Miles installed them for me. Like me, he was set up by your father."

I shake my head. "He stole from my father. His fingerprints were on everything. But my father made the police drop the charges."

"Then how did Miles get a suspended sentence? I can show you, if you don't believe me. It's a matter of public record."

"It would have been wiped years ago, Tara. He's misled you too."

I turn away as she double clicks the image and starts playing the video, enlarging it to full screen. It's sad the way bitterness has corrupted her. I don't want to be in the same room with her now.

"I don't have any videos of us," she calls as I head for the door. "Nor your father. He visited me regularly before I became a cripple."

I should keep walking, but how can I? She's planted an unwanted image in my head. How can I look at my father again without seeing an image of him astride Tara?

"Your father's a politician, Kent. Lying, deception and adultery come as standard. He hasn't told you the truth since you returned home."

Her cynical, triumphant smile taunts me. She wants me to get angry and lash out. It takes all my will to resist.

"If you're talking about Mandy Cheung," I say through gritted teeth, "I already know."

"I wasn't," she says, "but he told me about her. Miles sorted it out, of course."

"Like a regular good Samaritan. Then, with your help, he forced my father to sell Downland Manor."

I'm half way down the corridor before she calls out. "Miles didn't buy Downland Manor—your father gave it to him."

CHAPTER TWENTY-TWO

She slams the door as I rush back. "Downland Manor was worth millions. Why would my father give it away?"

"Why don't you ask him?"

I pound the door with my fist. It takes me about five seconds to realise I'll need a battering ram to get through. Made of oak, with simple but elegant panels, the door will be there long after I've shuffled off. In the absence of an axe, I try my shoulder.

"Stop, please!" The waiter steps closer. Though his hands are raised, his eyes tell me he's happy to take me on if I don't stop. "How will it look if you frighten a woman in a wheelchair? Come downstairs and I get you a drink."

I brush past him, keen to speak to my father. If he was blackmailed, he should report it to the police. Birchill won't expect that.

Blackmail? The significance of the word fails to register until I'm back in my car. I can't believe how stupid I've been. "You prize idiot! You let Tara wind you up and you lost all reason. You idiot, Fisher!"

15–20 years separate my father's assault on Mandy Cheung and Birchill acquiring Downland Manor. Would

Birchill wait that long to claim his reward for hushing up the assault? I doubt it. So, why did my father give away his home?

The answer still eludes me when I reach Tollingdon Community Centre at 12:35. Between ten and one, my father holds his monthly surgery for constituents here. Today, he's sharing the venue with an indoor market. After a frustrating 10 minutes looking for a parking space in the town centre, I find one near the cattle market and walk back.

I push through the glass doors of the Community Centre into a melee of shoppers armed with bacon sandwiches and cups of tea. I take the stairs to the first floor and push through the fire doors. The seats outside the committee rooms are empty. Normally, there's a queue of people, waiting to see my father. Inside the anteroom I find my father's agent, Victor Lewis, browsing the Argos website.

"Braziers burn secret documents much better than gas barbecues," I say, studying the screen. "You don't strike me as the outdoor catering type, Victor. I can't imagine you shopping for burgers and chicken drumsticks." I peer into the empty committee room. "Did my father wrap up early, or have you sent him to get the burgers?"

"Your father rushed out of here like Lord Lucan on his way to catch a ferry," he replies, pouting like a drama queen. "I had to send everyone home, of course. Lead balloon barely describes the situation."

"Why did he rush out, Victor?"

"He received a text." He emphasises the last word as if it's the cause of all the world's evils. "Mrs. Christie told me after he left. Her neighbour has a ghastly 30-foot-high Leylandii hedge, you know. Why isn't that a criminal offence?"

"Did my father say anything before he left?"

"It's over."

"What's over?"

"No, that's what he said—it's over. At first, I thought he meant his surgery was finished for the day. Well, it's a logical deduction, but he rushed out in the middle of Mrs. Christie's story. Mind you, she tends to ramble."

Outside, I look for my father's Jaguar and then ring his mobile—twice. On both occasions, the phone goes straight to voicemail. I leave an innocuous message for him to contact me. Back in the car, I ring Niamh.

"Did you text my father earlier?" I ask when she picks up.

"Good afternoon, Kent," she says in her soft Irish lilt. "Yes, I'm fine and dandy, thank you. And you?"

"Niamh, he dashed out in the middle of his surgery after receiving a text."

"What were you doing at William's surgery?"

The question catches me off guard. I can hardly repeat Tara's poisonous views. "I called in to collect money for the sanctuary. We have some overdue bills, so can you ask him to ring me when he gets home?"

"We're off to Glyndebourne this afternoon."

"It's urgent, Niamh."

"It always is."

I put my phone down, puzzled by her abrupt tone. Nothing fazes or upsets her. She breezes through life with a smile and a cheery word, enchanting all who meet her. Today, she wasn't surprised or interested in my father's early departure.

I drum my fingers on the dashboard, sensing I'm way off the pace. Everything's happened so fast. In the space of two days, my father has gone from loathing Miles Birchill to giving him Downland Manor. In the same period, Sydney Collins has gone from accident to murder victim.

Are the two connected?

Only Mike's bullshit detector can tell me if I've lost all reason.

When he doesn't answer his phone, I decide to visit anyway. He could be in the pub, having lunch, or he could be dozing on the sofa. I take the old A27 that runs north of Eastbourne and through Westham village. Usually, it's the quickest route, but road works at Pevensey Castle have generated a long, impatient queue. With windows down and my arm on the sill, I look at the crumbling stone walls that have stood since William the Conqueror invaded England in 1066. The Fishers were already at Downland and managed to retain their land by serving the new king and marrying his barons.

With my small plot, I'm the last in the unbroken occupation of the land.

The overwhelming responsibility sweeps over me, filling me with doubt and apprehension. I need to find my father, and fast.

"The fat lady hasn't sung yet," I remind myself as the traffic inches forward.

It takes another ten minutes of stopping and starting to clear Pevensey and head for the coast. In Pevensey Bay, I turn left and then swing right towards the beach. The Moorings stands high on the shingle, overlooking the sea. The full car park tells me the pub is busy, so I drive down the track towards Mike's. The smell of the sea, driven inland by a steady breeze, reminds me of holidays with my parents before I was taken to Manchester. I recall little from those early years, but they feel like happy times with memories of a burning sun, melting ice creams, and the surge of the waves.

Despite the Indian summer, the beach is deserted. The sparkling sea has retreated to reveal a strip of sand, which stretches along the coast to Sovereign Harbour. I've run along the strip at low tide, hurdling the old wooden groynes that keep the shingle from migrating. The views of Eastbourne and Beachy Head, rising out of the sea to slumber in the sunshine, never fail to rouse me.

I park up next to Mike's Mighty Munch and walk around the bungalow into the garden. Garden is perhaps an exaggeration, as the lawn is more weed than grass, and the flowers in the thin border of soil have long since shrivelled and died. By his own admission, he has brown fingers. The timber workshop, which looks like a rundown alpine ski lodge, is his domain, where he repairs the equipment we buy from failing food businesses.

I'm glad to see him. He's cleaning the interior of a microwave oven propped on a flimsy Formica table, which wobbles as he scrubs. He looks up when I push through the squeaking gate and throws the cleaning cloth into a bucket of murky water.

"Grab a Diet Coke," he says, nodding to a bucket of iced water. "I know it's not cranberry, but it's all I had. Then you can try shifting the grease from this oven."

I peer inside the microwave, which is streaked with greasy marks. "Half fill a jug of water and add a few drops of lemon juice. Two to three minutes on full power and the steam will lift the grease. The oven will smell heavenly, too."

He wipes his forehead on the sleeve of his denim shirt. "How many years have we been sprucing up equipment?"

"About three?"

"Nearer four, pal. So, why have you waited till now to pass on that tip?"

"I normally clean the microwaves."

"Fair point," he says, taking a Budweiser from the bucket. He drops onto an old sofa on the decking that runs across the back of the bungalow. "But you don't normally invite yourself round. What's the problem?"

I pluck a can of Diet Coke from the water and take a few mouthfuls while I consider my words.

"My father's missing," I say.

"When did he go missing?"

"Sometime in the last couple of hours."

"Are you winding me up, pal? He's missing if he doesn't come home tonight."

Mike takes several mouthfuls of beer from the bottle, watching me all the time. I don't know if my face registers surprise or disappointment, but it seems to temper his reaction. "Sorry, I wasn't having a go," he says. "You know how ratty cleaning makes me. Tell me what happened."

"He got a text and rushed out of his surgery, leaving one of his constituents sitting there. He said, 'It's over' on his way out."

He drains the remaining beer and wipes his lips with the back of his hand. "Have you rung him?"

"His phone goes straight to voicemail. I've also rung Niamh."

"What did she say?"

"She didn't seem concerned."

"Then why are you?"

I don't want to explain about my father's sordid past. I would trust Mike with my life, but when he's out drinking with some of his old colleagues, his mouth can grow to the size of a tent flap.

"Maybe I should wait in case he rings," I say. "Any news about Hetty?"

"He died soon after we left." Mike stares into space, his expression sombre. "I'm collecting his files this afternoon, if you want to join me."

"Sure. He may have something that will help."

"I know what will help me," he says, easing himself off the sofa. "And it's not the love of a good woman. I hope you haven't eaten, because there's a steak and ale pie with mash and onion gravy calling my name."

He gets to his feet and rubs his hands together. "Let's grab a bite to eat. And on the way over, you can tell me why you were suspended."

"Who told you—Gemma?"

"She's worried about you, pal."

"What did she tell you?"

"Nothing. That's why I'm asking you."

I suspect he's being diplomatic to protect Gemma. He listens without comment as I give him a brief account of my misdemeanours and misfortunes.

"And before you ask," I say, "I don't fancy Adele Havelock. I never mix business with pleasure."

"Then how do you pick up all those waitresses?" He smirks and play-punches my arm. "Anyway, back to serious matters. I'm not surprised your boss suspended you. What were you thinking, pal? No, don't answer that. Let's just say I can see why you want to speak to your father. He's about the only thing keeping you from the dole queue."

"He ordered me to give up the investigation."

Mike stops and stares at me in disbelief. "Why?"

I shift, wishing I'd kept my mouth shut. "He was trying to protect me from Birchill, but I have to fight fire with fire."

"No," he says, shaking his head. "You fight fire with water and put it out. You have to defeat Birchill with the law."

"Nobody's managed that so far, have they?"

"Kent, you want justice, not revenge. Play the long game."

I know he's right, but it's too late.

Inside the Moorings, the lounge bustles with people, all talking loudly. Most are pensioners, in pairs or quartets, on their way to the conservatory dining area for their 'Three Courses for a Tenner' offer. The waiting staff look harassed as they weave through the tables with a never ending supply of food. I look to the family area on my right, where the tables are further apart to allow for high chairs.

"Looks like we wait," Mike says, scooping a handful of peanuts from a bowl on the bar. "St. Clements?"

"I wouldn't eat those if I were you," I say.

He groans. "If it's another of your food stories, you told me all about the fungus that can kill you."

"I wasn't going to mention aspergillosis, or aflatoxin."

He stares at the peanuts. "Okay, what am I missing?"

"It's not what you're missing, but what you're gaining," I say, moving closer. "When you last went to the loo, did you wash your hands?"

"Of course I did. What's that got to do with anything?"

"Studies show that you're among the 50% of men who wash their hands. As long as the other 50% don't push their hands in that bowl of nuts, tainting it with their urine, or worse, you're safe to eat them."

He stares at the nuts as if they're radioactive. "You're a barrel of laughs with your food stories."

"I'd avoid the crisps too," I say, pointing to another bowl.

"Why don't you stop them putting food on the bar?" he asks, heading for the toilets. "It's your job to protect public health."

The barman walks up. "Is your friend okay?"

"He'll be fine after a pint of bitter. St. Clements for me. Oh, and I'd remove the nuts and crisps from the bar."

"Why's that?"

"My friend just sneezed over them."

While I wait for the drinks, Niamh rings. I head outside where I can hear her.

"I've rung everyone," she says. "No one's seen or heard from him. Where is he, Kent? What's going on?"

"I'm sure he'll be in touch," I say with more confidence than I feel. "He seemed fine when he popped by on Thursday evening."

"He wasn't fine when he got home. Honestly, Kent, I've never seen him so angry. What did you say to him?"

Funny how it's my fault. "We talked about Birchill, Niamh, that's all. Do you want me to come over?"

Fifteen minutes later, I'm driving north through the marshes towards Herstmonceux Castle. The reeds and rushes blur as I swing through the bends. As I bear down on Wartling, the trees block out the light. I don't see the pheasant until the last moment. I brake and swerve to avoid it, almost colliding with cars coming the opposite way. While my lip reading skills are a little rusty, there's no misunderstanding the gestures.

A quick glance in the rear view mirror tells me the pheasant escaped unharmed.

I pick up speed and catch a brief glimpse of the cold, grey dome that conceals a telescope from the former Royal Observatory. Mike once did an astronomy course there and was upset when they didn't award stars for good work. Any minute now, he'll ring me to find out why I left the Moorings.

As I reach the junction with the main road at Windmill Hill, he calls. There's nothing behind me, so I pull over and pick up the call.

"What happened to you, pal?"

"Niamh rang."

"Has your father come home?"

"Not yet. I'll be in touch."

I don't like cutting him off, but I want to get to Niamh. I look right and groan as a tractor-and-trailer of hay bales passes. Had I ignored Mike's call, I would be in front of the tractor, not waiting to join the long tail of traffic in its wake.

When I reach the turn for Flowers Green, I'm still behind the tractor. After another half mile of crawling along, unable to overtake, it turns into a farmyard. I press on and speed to my parents' house, crunching to a halt on the gravel. The place is hardly Downland Manor, but it's worth at least half a million. How could my father afford this house if he gave away the Manor?

It looks like Tara lied to me.

Not for the first time, I suspect.

Niamh's standing in the doorway. She glances both ways before ushering me inside. She looks pale and drawn, the skin puffy around her reddened eyes. Without warning, she hugs me. The tears soon follow.

"Come on," I say, stroking her hair. "He'll be fine. You'll see."

"Something terrible has happened."

She's always so strong and sure, supporting his career and organising him while running the house. She's campaigned by his side in the most atrocious weather and dealt with the most trivial of constituency complaints with a smile and a kind word. When she needs to be the perfect host, she excels. When she needs to be the quiet wife at his side, she can blend into the crowd.

260

Not bad for a 'gold-digging marriage wrecker' as Tommy Logan painted her in a column for the *Tollingdon Tribune*.

"He sent me a text." She peels away to retrieve her mobile phone from a nearby table. The text reads, 'Emergency at the ranch. Might be some time.'

"The Prime Minister's probably summoned him," I say.

She shakes her head. "William never texts. He rings if he's going to be late."

I read the text again. "By ranch, he means the office, right?"

"I guess so. I don't know." She directs me to the suitcase behind the door. "I just want to get out of here."

"What if he rings you here?"

"He'll call my mobile, won't he?"

I hand back the phone, certain she would remain if she thought he would come home. "What aren't you telling me, Niamh?"

She looks down. "Can we just go?"

Had she not broken eye contact, I would have picked up the suitcase and followed her out. "Not until you tell me what's happened," I say, planting myself between her and the door.

She fiddles with the collar of her jacket as she speaks in a low, hesitant voice. "He had an affair. Well, several affairs. None of them meant anything," she says, more to protect her image than his, I suspect. "This one was different. It lasted for over a year. I thought he was going to leave me."

She swallows and closes her eyes, clearly trying to hold back her emotions. "A few weeks ago, she emailed him. She wanted to meet."

"Who is she?" I ask, certain I know.

"She claimed he was the father of her child."

"Are you talking about Mandy Cheung?"

Her head jerks up. "Don't tell me you know as well? Who told you, Kent? I need to know."

I put my hands on her shoulders and look into her eyes. "Her name came up during my investigation into Collins' death."

"What's she got to do with that?"

"Her son, David Cheung, found Collins. He lives and works at Tombstone. I only discovered the connection yesterday evening." I pause, interrupted by an uninvited thought. "Is that why my father came round on Thursday evening?"

"No. He had to stop your investigation."

"In case I found out he had a son?"

"You don't have a stepbrother. You never had and you never will."

The pleading look in her eyes begs me to drop the subject, but I can't. "What makes you so sure?"

She hangs her head and won't look at me. "William shoots blanks. That's the expression, isn't it? He's sterile. He can't have fathered Mandy Cheung's child."

Or me.

"Come on," I say.

CHAPTER TWENTY-THREE

I feel strange, subdued even. It's like I knew he wasn't my father, though I can't say why I suspected. It wasn't just the difference in politics or outlook, or my years of poverty in Manchester. The difference was more innate and fundamental.

He didn't feel like my father.

I'd put his distance down to a stuffy upbringing where tradition dictated his role. When he spoke to me in his vast study, he was like a headmaster, quick to expose my faults and weaknesses as if they were diseases he had to cure. But it was the lack of physical contact that set us apart. I had blamed my time in Manchester, mixing with boys who didn't show emotion. But the sight of me, each day, was a reminder that he couldn't have children.

My thoughts turn to the sanctuary. Will I lose it, as I'm not a Fisher?

If I lose my job on Monday, I'll probably lose the place anyway, but that's not the point. I should be the last in a long line of Fishers, but I'm not. William Kenneth Fisher carries that burden. The Fisher name will die with him. Maybe that's why he gave Downland Manor away.

So... whose son am I?

I pull into a layby near Hellingly village and turn to Niamh. "Who is my father?"

"You need to ask your mother."

I haven't spoken to my mother since I returned to Sussex. That's not going to change. "Is that why she took off to Manchester?"

"William loves you so much," Niamh says. "I know he finds it difficult to show his emotions, but that's his upbringing. He's a fine man. If I can live with his condition almost all our married life, then you ...."

Her voice fails, swamped by tears. I hug her, realising how tough it must be for her, knowing she can never have children with the man she loves. I wonder if she's ever come to terms with that, no matter how well she hides it.

"I want you to make an effort, Kent." She stares into my eyes, piling on the pressure. "Is that too much to ask?"

"I won't live a lie, Niamh. He could have told me when he brought me back, but he pretended to be my father. He chose to be an impostor and a fraud."

"He treated you like a son, you ungrateful eejit. He found you a job. He embraced you as his own. That wasn't easy, you know, with you protesting about everything and getting into trouble."

"Why are you blaming me? What did I do wrong?"

The anger in my voice silences her. She looks helpless, exhausted even, as if the strain of the lies has caught up with her. "I knew this would happen," she says quietly. "I knew you wouldn't understand."

"Then stop blaming me!"

"He came for you, didn't he? Well, didn't he? Isn't that enough?"

"I was stuck in a strange city, dependent on a spiteful mother who told me he was dead. I hated school because I was an outsider, but I hated her even more for robbing me of my father. She never had a good word to say about him, about anything. Where was he *then*?"

Niamh shrinks back in the seat, her eyes wide with fear. "He couldn't come for you. Ingrid's solicitor wrote a letter, accusing William of the vilest physical and psychological abuse. It was all lies," she says with a shudder, "but she threatened to go to the newspapers if he came anywhere near you."

My mother never missed a chance to accuse my father of beating her, especially when he came home drunk. She was never good enough for his upper class friends, who laughed at her accent and made rude remarks because she didn't understand English humour. Being German, she couldn't read or write English, though she understood social security benefits. At the age of ten, I wrote to the Inland Revenue, challenging their tax assessment, demanding a rebate. I wrote sick notes to my PE teacher to excuse me from swimming because I'd almost drowned as a child. I even wrote letters to companies, complaining about bad service or damaged clothes so she could claim compensation.

"She would have destroyed his political career," Niamh says.

"That's all right then," I say, making no effort to hide the sarcasm and bitterness. "I'm glad he put his career first."

Niamh glares at me, her eyes wild with rage. "You've no idea how he felt. He couldn't father children. A light inside him went out. Then, when he realised Ingrid had slept with someone else, he was a broken man. The life went out of him."

Yeah, he was so broken he had to sleep around to cope with his troubles.

Though I keep this to myself, I'm sure she can read my thoughts. "He's given you a good life in Downland," she says. "You've never wanted for anything."

Apart from the truth, a few words of encouragement and a little intimacy.

I sigh, realising I'm in danger of being like my mother. With a determined effort, I try to draw up a mental list of all the things William Kenneth Fisher gave me. His wisdom and wit inspired me. He allowed me the freedom to be who I wanted to be, even if it embarrassed him. He found me a good job with prospects, where I had to work hard to earn the respect of colleagues.

His status allows me to get away with far more than I should.

Well, it did until yesterday.

I start driving again, wondering what will happen to me. Two days ago I had a routine job that paid well and an exciting sanctuary that didn't. Now I could lose both. I'll add them to my other losses, like my judgement, my warrant card, and Gemma's respect. All I need to do is lose hope and I'll have nothing. I'll never prove Collins was murdered and Birchill will own everything that once belonged to the Fishers.

At the Boship Roundabout I weave into the traffic heading south towards Eastbourne. Angry with myself, I accelerate down the dual carriageway as if it will somehow prove I'm not a complete loss. I don't register the turn for Tollingdon Agricultural Services until it's almost too late. I slam on the brakes and swerve across two lanes of traffic, overshooting the turn by a couple of yards. Niamh's face is white and frozen with fear as she stares ahead.

I start the car, check the mirror, and reverse off the central reservation onto the road. Then I turn across the other carriageway and drive down Dogwood Lane, wondering why I risked our lives with such a reckless manoeuvre.

"I want a quick word with Tom Gibson," I say, answering the question in her eyes. I'm hoping he can give me the evidence and paperwork to show Tombstone ordered the tractor service. I'm also hoping to find something that will prove Collins was murdered.

We pass old bungalows and houses set back from the road and a farm, ironically called 'World's End'. From here the road becomes a track for half a mile before entering a farm, now converted into industrial units. Tollingdon Agricultural Services occupies the furthest, and biggest, unit, overlooking fields and woodland, hemmed in by the River Cuckmere.

The busy yard is filled with trucks, tractors, diggers and trailers. The old cowshed houses a service area, complete with hydraulic ramps, trolleys of tools, blade-sharpening machines and all the spare parts needed to maintain farm machinery. The office and reception area occupy the adjacent barn, which overlooks a small compound, surrounded by a mesh fence. I pull up alongside the locked gate and stare at the Massey Ferguson tractor.

"Is that it?" Niamh asks. "I was expecting something bigger and newer."

It looks old and tired in solitary confinement. Without the rusty bench saw, the corrosion and neglect in the tractor are more noticeable. The rear wheel arch has a dent I hadn't noticed before. The sides of the vinyl cab flap in the breeze. The power takeoff hangs limply from the rear, looking harmless.

Tom's striding across the yard, his bushy eyebrows knitted into a deep, unwelcoming frown. His demeanour changes when Niamh climbs out of the passenger seat. He diverts to her side of the car, gives her a broad smile, and holds out a hand. The roughness of his skin and blackened fingernails contradict the clean lines of his suit. He's muscular and strong, with hands that can perform the most intricate tasks with ease. He might own and run the company, but he can't stop tinkering with machinery.

"It's always a pleasure to see you, Mrs. Fisher." His voice deepens, as does the colour in his cheeks, when she smiles. "I don't believe you came here to buy a tractor, did you now?"

"Would you believe me if I told you I learned to drive one in Donegal?"

"Of course I would." When he turns to me his smiling charm evaporates. "If you're expecting a report, I have paying customers to attend to."

"I'll settle for your first impressions," I say.

"I could do a passable David Beckham if you close your eyes," he tells Niamh. "And everyone does Michael Caine, don't they?"

"I get the impression you're stalling, Tom. So, let me focus your mind. You remember the muck spreader I used to fill Birchill's Mercedes?"

"Of course."

"How do you think he'll react when I tell him you loaned it to me?"

Niamh stares at me in disbelief. "Kent, that's blackmail!"

"You get used to it, Mrs. Fisher." Tom punches the code into the lock and opens the gate. When we reach the tractor, he runs a hand along the body, patting the engine cover. "Someone removed the guard we fitted. There's no sign of any abuse or damage, no wear and tear. That's all I can tell you."

While it's what I expected, I'm still disappointed. I take a closer look, hoping I'll spot something, but I'm not sure what to look for. Not that it matters, since the case was closed.

"You must know something about this tractor," I say, straightening. "You know every tractor for miles."

He smiles. "I helped Gerry Maynard restore her after he bought her at auction. About thirty years ago," he says, anticipating my question. "She was a rusting wreck, but we brought her back to life. Then, when Gerry died in the fire, Collins claimed it. He wrecked her within three months and left her to rust."

"Why did Gerry sell the farm?" I ask.

"He needed the money for Martha."

Niamh nods. "Martha had dementia."

"Some days she recognised you, others she was like an empty shell," he says. "She got confused all the time. She swore blind their daughter, Lynne, had returned home and told her not to sell the farm."

"I didn't know they had a daughter," Niamh says.

"She ran away when she was 16. Gerry never spoke about it. She was adopted and wanted to find her real parents or something like that."

"Did she?" I ask Tom.

He shrugs.

"Did anyone try to find her? She's entitled to her parents' estate."

"Not if they sold to Birchill," he points out.

We follow him out of the compound and wait while he locks the gate. "It's always a pleasure to see you, Mrs.

Fisher," he says, bowing his head. "I was sorry to see you leave Downland Manor. Your roses were spectacular."

She blushes slightly. "We have to go, Tom. Thank you for your time."

He opens the passenger door for her and helps her in. Then he walks around and joins me. "I don't understand why Tombstone ordered a service," he says in a low voice. "The tractor hadn't worked for the best part of three years."

"Who requested the service?" I ask.

"Ben Foley's secretary, I imagine. He couldn't organise the proverbial in a brewery. She leaves him notes to remind him when it's his birthday or his wedding anniversary."

"I didn't know they were married."

"They're not. He has a wife and two kids, but he wants everyone to think he's having an affair with Rebecca. She doesn't have a car, so he gives her a lift to work and back." Tom grins. "She's a good looking lass, as I'm sure you've noticed."

"She remembers when I went to her school to talk about my work."

He laughs. "That put you in your place. So, when can I expect someone to check the tractor over?"

I'm about to tell him the investigation's closed when my Blackberry rings. I walk away from the car and he heads towards his office. "I didn't know you worked Saturdays, Carolyn."

"People die all week," she replies in a humourless voice. "Want to tell me why you were suspended?"

"You must stop beating about the bush and get to the point," I reply, caught off guard by her directness. "Someone didn't approve of my methods."

"Birchill always fights dirty. Look, if you need someone to back you up, give me a shout."

"Thanks."

"Who's taking over?"

"No one—the case is closed."

"You're joking. Why?"

"I'll tell you another time, Carolyn. I'm busy at the moment."

"I'll still need a report for the Coroner. No frills, no waffle. Tell it as it was, Kent. My investigation's still open in case there's anything you want to tell me."

I can't imagine her putting murder in her report, but her police colleagues are more likely to listen to her than a suspended EHO. But will she listen to me? There's only one way to find out.

"What if I said I had doubts about Collins' accident?"

"What kind of doubts?"

"It's complicated. Collins wrote an autobiography." I pause, expecting her to interrupt, but she remains silent. "Only he didn't, because he was illiterate. Someone else wrote it, or so I thought. I copied all 20 chapters from his computer, but they contain nothing but exclamation marks."

"Slow down, Kent. You said you copied the chapters from Collins' computer. Do you mean the knackered laptop on his desk?"

"There was a working PC on the desk the day before. I copied the files onto a memory stick. We had to get out then as someone came to the house."

"We?"

"Gemma and me. We—"

"You went into the house on Thursday? Why didn't you tell me yesterday? Why did you go round with me if you'd already seen the house?"

"I wanted to see if the killer had removed or changed anything. And he'd swapped the PC for an old laptop."

"Did you say killer?"

I draw a breath. "I think Collins was murdered."

"With a power takeoff?"

She sounds incredulous. I can picture her making gestures to her colleagues to say she has a nutcase on the phone.

"I know it sounds crazy, but it's a clever way to disguise a murder."

"I must be crazy to even ask this, but do you have any evidence?"

"Murder's the only answer to all the questions. If we could persuade the police to send a SOCO team to the clearing, they might be able to unearth something."

"Oh, I get it," she says. "You want me to put your theory to my colleagues. Nice try, Kent, but you're on your own with this one."

"They'll never believe me."

"Can you blame them? I mean, what sort of twisted mind would think of killing someone like that? You'd have to know all about power takeoff shafts. Then there's the blood. And how would you get the victim over the shaft? He'd have to be drugged or something."

"You said Collins was drunk."

"I didn't quite say that, but...." She pauses for a few moments and then sighs. "I must be going soft in the head. Why don't we meet at the clearing at six? Bring the memory stick and I'll hear you out."

I return to the car, feeling relieved and excited in equal measures. I have a chance to convince Carolyn I'm right. It won't be easy, but then few things are, in my experience. I just need to get everything together and give a killer presentation.

"You seem pleased," Niamh says as I climb into the car. "Was that Gemma on the phone?"

"No."

"I've seen the way you look at her," she says. "And when you talk about her, there's a twinkle in your eyes."

"Niamh, she's engaged."

"And you'll start chasing after someone else within a few weeks. That's your trouble, Kent. You won't settle down and make a go of things."

I drive away and head for the dual carriageway, barely listening as she tells me to set down roots and build a proper house at the sanctuary.

"I'd love to," I say, seizing the chance to change the subject. "Do you think my fath—William would help me? You must have made quite a bit when you sold Downland Manor. Do you miss the place?"

She shakes her head. "William pretends he's fine, but I see him looking across to the Downs. He regrets moving, even though he couldn't afford to maintain the relic. I never thought he'd sell it, mind."

"What if didn't sell it?" I ask, accelerating into a gap in the traffic.

"What do you mean?"

"Tara told me he *gave* it to Birchill."

"Why would he do that? The place was worth a fortune, even if it ate money. And how would she know, anyway?"

I swing around the roundabout and head for Tollingdon, wishing I'd kept my big mouth shut. "I don't know what happened, but it was all so sudden, don't you think? No estate agents, no solicitors, no explanation."

She withdraws into herself as we speed south, only speaking when I draw up at the lights. "He sold so many paintings and heirlooms over the years to pay for repairs, but he was paying off gambling debts, wasn't he?"

I'm not sure what to say. "He hated gambling in all forms."

"He couldn't stop himself," she says bitterly. "I know he visited casinos, but I've no idea how much he lost over the years. I thought he had an endless supply of money until he started selling the antiques." She closes her eyes over the tears. "He gambled our home away, didn't he?"

I can't believe he racked up the kind of debts that would cost him Downland Manor. Then again, he only had to use it as security for a loan and default.

"And now he's run off," Niamh says. "I'm sick with dread, wondering where he is and what he's done. I don't want to lose another house."

I don't want to lose the sanctuary. I accelerate away from the lights, hoping there isn't a bailiff waiting for me at home.

CHAPTER TWENTY-FOUR

"What's she doing here?"

Niamh frowns at Gemma, who's sitting on the top step by the kitchen door. She looks amazing in a pastel yellow blouse and leg-hugging jeans. If she had worn heels or diamante flip-flops I would have assumed she was going out, but she's wearing trainers. I need to get rid of her so I can settle Niamh in the spare room. Then I can track down William Fisher.

I jog up the stairs, looking around for Frances or Columbo. I had hoped he would rush over to welcome me. When I reach the next to the top step, Gemma looks up. She's swept her glossy hair to one side, holding it in place with a clasp that matches her blouse. She raises her Audrey Hepburn glasses.

"You're not pleased to see me, Kent."

"It's not a good time, Gemma. Can't it wait?"

"I have something you need to look at," she says, getting to her feet. She leans closer and whispers. "Niamh mustn't see it."

She steps aside to reveal a cardboard box, similar to the ones we use at work to archive files. She scoops it into her arms and waits for me to unlock the door. I push it open and gesture her inside, following close behind.

"Did Mike ask you to collect Hetty's files from the nursing home?" I ask.

"Good call, Sherlock. How did you work that out?"

"Elementary, my dear, Watson. It says DCI Wainthropp on the box."

She puts the box on the table and turns, giving Niamh a big smile. "Hello, Mrs. Fisher. You look well."

"That blouse brings out your tan, Gemma." Niamh drops her holdall inside the door and rubs her numb fingers. "I'm afraid to spend that long in the sun. You hear so many stories about cancer."

"That's why I keep fit and healthy, Mrs. Fisher, but I haven't seen you at Pilates for weeks. Is there a problem?"

"I've found a more advanced course that suits me better."

Gemma nods. "Yes, you can plateau when you do something too long."

There's an undercurrent beneath the warm tones and smiles. I'm not sure they like each other, so why do they pretend to?

And people wonder why I prefer animals.

Right on cue, Columbo barks and leaps through the door. He stops to look at us in turn and makes for Niamh, sniffing her legs. The moment she bends to stroke him, he scurries to Gemma. She pulls a chew from her pocket and drops to one knee. Columbo grabs the chew and disappears under the table.

Niamh takes charge of the kettle. "Tea, anyone?"

"Not for me," I reply, picking up the holdall. "Let's pop your stuff in the spare room and settle you in."

She shakes her head. "If you two have plans, I'd hate to get in the way. I have this gorgeous Westie for company, and I can find the bathroom when I need it."

I take the holdall to the spare room, which Frances uses in winter. She removes her clothes from the wardrobe and dresser in spring, takes her books and disconnects the X-Box from the TV. Only the life-size poster of a musclebound man in budgie smugglers remains.

"Envy's a terrible thing," Gemma says, cradling the archive box. "You won't look cool in yellow Speedos, trust me. Where do you want this?"

"Put it by the computer in my room," I reply, placing the holdall on the bed. "I'll take a look later."

"Are you off to meet Adele Havelock?"

I squeeze past her. "You can have the poster, as you seem to like it."

"Danni will go ape if she finds out you're with Adele Havelock again."

"It's nothing to do with you."

"I thought we were a team, Kent."

"You mean you're miffed because I took her into the barn."

"No, I'm angry, Kent. You're a law enforcer, but you're always breaking the rules. You say you want to do what's right, but you do things the wrong way. You tell me we're a team and then you ignore me."

"That's unfair," I say, wishing I could tell her how much she means to me. I hate the way she looks at me as if I've let her down.

"Is it? I waited in the restaurant for you yesterday. When you didn't show, I thought you'd had an accident or something. I should have known you'd be with another woman." She pauses, her chest rising and falling as she regains her breath. "If you'd taken me into the barn, you wouldn't be suspended now."

"Sometimes you have to take a chance."

"You didn't take a chance, Kent. You broke the rules."

"Birchill plays dirty. How else am I going to get him?"

"Get him for what, exactly?"

I can hardly tell her he's a killer. She'd never believe me.

"See," she says, her voice rising. "You don't know and you don't care." She thrusts the archive box into my stomach. "You never think you've done anything wrong."

She's not referring to my recent behaviour, that's for sure. "I have to find William Fisher," I say, preferring to look forward. It's three forty and I'm running out of day. "He's disappeared."

"Disappeared?"

"It's linked to Collins' death, but I don't know how. Maybe Hetty can shed some light."

"So that's why Niamh's here." Gemma takes the archive box from me and puts it on the bed. "She mustn't read the files. If she finds out your father's involved with Birchill ...."

"I already know," Niamh says, stepping into the bedroom. "Most months I don't know whether the bailiffs will call. I don't know if he's sitting in the House of Commons or lying with another woman."

The uncertainty and pain are etched into her features. Suddenly, she seems hesitant. "Put me out of my misery—tell me about Adele Havelock and Hetty."

"Hetty is DCI Wainthropp. These are his memoirs," I say, patting the box. "He was writing a book, but he died yesterday."

"Are you looking for something you can use against Miles?"

"I haven't had time to look."

"Don't!" she says, coming closer. "You've already seen what Miles can do. Destroy the files, Kent, for all our sakes."

"Not until I've uncovered the truth. William Fisher has some serious explaining to do when I find him."

"If you find him."

Her heels thud across the wooden floor. She casts a furtive glance at the archive box as she heads out of the room and towards the kitchen. She wants to read Hetty's files as much as I do. Maybe she wants to know how her husband could lead a double life without her knowing. I want to know how he could look me in the eye and tell me integrity mattered.

"How can she defend him when he's lied, cheated and gambled everything away?" I ask.

"That's what people do when they love someone."

If that were true, then the divorce rate would drop.

I want to understand the man who was my father until an hour ago. I can imagine how being the last Fisher would have weighed heavy. History would be ready to record him as the Fisher who failed to produce an heir. Yes, he would feel a failure. It could explain his affair with Mandy Cheung. It could explain why he gambled his estate away. The Fisher dynasty would die with him. What did he have to lose?

I need to find him, and fast.

"I have an errant husband to find," I say. "Look after Niamh, will you? She's not holding up well."

Gemma takes the top file from the box. "I could, but what if let it slip that you've been suspended?"

"Don't you think she has enough to worry about?"

"You're not being honest with her, Kent. Just like your father."

"I want you to leave." My voice is calm and even, but I'm struggling to contain the anger. How dare she invite herself round and criticise me? "I didn't ask you to come round here."

"No, Mike did," she says, refusing to move. "He thought you might need some help. That's what friends are for, isn't it? Or don't you consider me a friend?"

Just when I think my feelings can't hurt me, she unleashes them with effortless ease. What makes me think she'd consider me as more than a colleague or a friend? How can I be so dumb?

"You'll never get into Tombstone without this." She pulls her ID from the back pocket of her jeans. "You no longer have one."

If I go to Tombstone, I'm not using the main entrance. "William Fisher has nothing to do with you or work," I tell her.

She pats the folder. "You should read Hetty's notes. It's all there—the gambling, the assault on Mandy Cheung and the birth of her child. He interviewed a Government inspector who says your father persuaded him to grant planning permission to Tombstone. Even the fire at Maynard's Farm looks suspicious."

"You're not suggesting he had something to do with the fire, surely?"

"No, that one's down to Birchill, if Hetty's right. It's all in here."

Finally, I usher her into the corridor and close the bedroom door. "Another time, Gemma. I have a missing Cabinet Minister to find."

"What if he's not at Tombstone?"

I pause, unable to repel the doubt she's put in my mind. In truth, I have no idea where to look or start. "He must be," I say, knowing I don't sound convincing.

She gives me a smug smile and wanders into the lounge. "I know where he is."

"He's at Tombstone. That's what his text said. Emergency at the ranch. The ranch is Tombstone. It was a coded clue."

"So why didn't you go straight there?"

I've only just thought of it, and she knows it. I don't want to take her with me in case it's dangerous, but if she's worked out where he is from Hetty's notes, I have no choice. At least she can't accuse me of not working as a team.

"Okay, lead the way," I say.

In the kitchen, I say something well intended but inane to Niamh about not worrying. I fuss Columbo for a moment, reminded of his namesake's dogged determination to get to the truth. I could do with some of that. Once in the car, I turn to Gemma, who gives me a quizzical look.

"Where do we go?" I ask.

"To the main road and turn left."

She opens the file to read as we bounce along the uneven track. "Hetty believed the fire was started deliberately to kill the Maynards," she says. "He never believed the inquest verdict of accidental death. Neither did many of his colleagues, including Carolyn Montague."

"The Coroner's Officer?"

"She was a police officer at the time. She arrived at the scene with the fire crew. She told Hetty the fire looked suspicious. Hetty believes Birchill got Mr. Maynard drunk, lit a cigarette, and pushed it down the side of the sofa while he slept."

It's the same kind of speculation I've indulged in. All it lacks is proof.

At the junction with the A27, I wait for the traffic to rush past. It's just gone four o'clock and in a couple of hours the light will fade. My chances of finding William Fisher will also fade.

"Birchill wanted the farm so he could build Tombstone," I say, inching forward. "If the Maynards refused...."

"The Maynards wanted to sell," Gemma says. "It was the daughter who didn't. She ran away when she was 15. No one had seen her for 20 years, and then she shows up as if nothing happened. Two days later, a fire breaks out, but she's nowhere to be found."

"Tom Gibson mentioned a daughter. She was adopted or fostered, I think."

"She hears about Birchill's interest, comes home and persuades her parents not to sell. Birchill's livid and burns the place down." Gemma chuckles. "You've got me at it now, coming up with crazy conspiracy theories."

"Like someone killing Collins?"

"Exactly. You'd have to be nuts to believe that."

"So, what happened to the daughter? Why didn't she report Birchill to the police?"

"She disappeared, according to Hetty. What if Birchill killed her?"

Finally, there's a gap in the traffic and I accelerate away. "I'm meeting Carolyn later. I'll ask her."

"Turn here," Gemma says, pointing to the entrance to Downland Manor Hotel.

"Here?"

"When people say back at the ranch, they mean work or home. Your father grew up here. He feels safe here, especially with Birchill to protect him."

I swing between the two stone pillars that support an ornate black metal arch, bearing the name of the hotel in gold letters. The Fisher crest has given way to a gold outline of the hotel. Gold is Birchill's brand. He loves it when the media compare him to Midas. I think of him as Auric Goldfinger, destined for an unsavoury end.

Gemma steadies herself with a hand on the dashboard as I speed through the bends that weave between ash, oak and sycamore. "Take it easy," she says. "I'd like to stay alive long enough to see your old house."

We emerge from the woodland for our first glimpse of the Edwardian manor. It looks the same as when I first arrived here, aged 17. Three storeys of red brick, trimmed with stone on each corner and around the windows, rise out of a flagstone terrace like a mansion from a period drama. Any moment now, women in long dresses, pinched at the waist, will promenade onto the clipped lawns that swirl around ornate borders of roses and ponds of koi carp. They'll linger on the stone bridges to gaze at the South Downs, rising out of flower meadows to bask in the sun.

"It's awesome!"

For once, she's right. There's something stately about the tall windows. They're so lofty the people inside must be giants. They were, I recall. They had stature and a quiet confidence I'd never seen before. They didn't need to talk about their wealth. It was part of them—in their rich voices, their elegant clothes and the large glasses of cognac they sipped from.

"It must have been amazing to live here," she says.

After a damp basement flat in Manchester, Downland Manor was a palace. But the grand façade hid an empty interior, rotting and perishing from neglect. The basement, which contained the kitchen, wine cellar and secret passages used by smugglers, was a great place to explore. Only one tunnel survived, connecting the dry store behind the kitchen with my father's study in the south-eastern corner. It emerged through a bookcase that opened out into the room. I loved snooping around, reading files on people I'd seen on TV, business leaders and all manner of dubious characters, singled out for attention.

"I loved the attic," I say, remembering how I occupied a new room every month to introduce some variety into an otherwise dull routine. "Many of the floorboards and stairs were rotten, so I could walk on the joists like an acrobat."

A familiar blue VW speeds out of the car park, cutting across us on its way out. Adele's sunglasses can't mask her grim expression. Whatever she was doing at the hotel, it was not successful.

"Must have been hell being in charge of all the staff," Gemma says.

I never felt comfortable having others serve me lunch. I retreated to the stables where Tara had her office. I hung about there most of the first summer, losing my fear of horses until I could ride into the woods and hills, where I lost my virginity. When my father found me a job with Downland District Council and sent me to university to study environmental health, I lost the freedom I'd enjoyed that first summer.

I drive past the main car park, tucked away among mature trees at the side of the hotel, and head for a large cobbled courtyard at the back of the hotel. Birchill has converted the stable block into a health club with a gymnasium, pool, and sauna.

"People leave here with wallets slimmer than their waists," I say, pulling into the health club manager's parking bay. It's directly beneath the only security camera. "Stay close to me and we won't be seen."

"Why are we sneaking around the back? What's wrong with reception?"

I'm assuming that Birchill has taken the study as his office. If he hasn't, my surprise will fall flat.

"Act casual," I say, pointing to a chef, who steps out of the kitchen opposite. His white coat exhibits most of the lunch menu. With a cigarette pinched between his fingers, he leans against the wall and checks his mobile phone. No doubt he's texting instructions to the second chef on how to cook aubergine, as most young people seem unable to communicate verbally.

At the corner, we turn down a shaded lane that runs alongside the hotel. To our left, the dense woodland screens old agricultural buildings. These contain the workshops and machinery stores that serve the 9-hole golf course Birchill built after Downland Golf Club rejected his membership application for the third time.

"There's Birchill's Mercedes," Gemma says, pointing.

The black Mercedes waits in the shade alongside the study. When we draw level, I stop and raise my hand. I flatten myself against the wall, sidle along and peer through the window. Birchill's sitting at a vast desk that occupies almost all of a Persian rug. He has his back to me, which means I should make it to the French doors at the front without being spotted. The doors are wide open, so there's nothing to stop me bursting in.

"I can see Birchill, but no one else," I whisper. "I'm going in. If anything goes wrong, get out of here and ring Mike."

She groans. "If only I'd asked Q for the reality meter. It would have sent us to reception."

"I want to surprise Birchill and catch him out," I say.

"You want to play James Bond."

"I'd look pretty stupid, bursting into the study without a gun. I could point my finger, I guess, or challenge him to a game of stone, scissors, paper."

I'd settle for a witty one-liner in the 30 seconds it takes to creep to the front. I pause, taking a deep breath as I step into view. I'm so focused I don't notice Birchill beside the doors.

"Welcome, Mr. Fisher. Unlike me, you haven't mastered the secret of surprise. Come inside. Your faithful poodle will be with us shortly."

Gemma soon follows, propelled by a shaven-headed man with a flattened nose and tattoos on either side of his neck. I've no idea what the Chinese symbols mean, but they should warn of the dangers of squeezing into a tight suit if you're built like a brick outhouse.

"As you can see, I watched your progress," he says, nodding toward the flat screen TV on the wall.

With nothing witty to say, I stroll to the bookcase. The weighty tomes that smelt of leather and dust have given way to modern hardbacks and paperbacks, which seem to shrink to the back of the grand shelves. "I see you like Dick Francis."

"I like success." He walks over and opens the small fridge. "Can I get you a drink? Sparkling mineral water might help, as you look a little flat."

Not only does he have the advantage of surprise, he's ahead in the wisecracking stakes. Wondering if he found the secret passageway while renovating the building, I try to remember where the hidden catch was located as I walk along, looking at the books. He has an interest in the natural world, which his developments smother with concrete. Biographies about Napoleon, Caesar, Wellington and Lord Mountbatten, among others, reveal leaders he wishes to emulate, I imagine.

"As you can see, my interests are diverse," Birchill says. "I imagine you like Ian Fleming. You see yourself as James Bond, no doubt."

"More Dirty Harry," I say.

He smirks as if the idea is ludicrous. "You should study the great leaders who shaped our world with their courage, foresight and bravery." He takes a bottle of water back to the desk and drops into his leather chair. "What are you doing here?"

"I'm looking for William Fisher."

"What makes you think he's here?"

"This was his home."

"Mine too." The bottle hisses as he unscrews the cap a little. "I slept above the stables—something we have in common, Fisher. Now, sit down. Marcus will think you intend to escape if you keep walking about."

When Muscles steps forward, Gemma pulls me back to the sofa. "He'll flatten you, Kent."

"Is William Fisher here?" I ask, shrugging off her hand.

"Why would he return after gambling the estate away?" Birchill watches me closely and then grins. "You know about his gambling, I see."

Gemma gives me a surprised look. "I thought your father sold it."

"No, Miss Dean, he offered it as security against a substantial loan. He wanted to win back the money he'd lost. I advised him against it."

"Yeah, I'll bet you did."

Birchill turns his chair through a sweeping arc. "He didn't care about the money. He didn't care for this place. A thousand years of history and expectation weighed him down. He wanted to be free of his high-maintenance wife.

She had dreams of becoming Lady Fisher. He had dreams about Mandy Cheung. I see you know about that too," he says with a smile.

"Yeah, you put paid to that."

He raises his hands in innocence. "The gentry think they can have anything they want. Without me, he'd be another disgraced MP, paying the price for keeping his brain in his trousers. Instead, he's a respected politician."

"A politician who got you planning permission for Tombstone."

"He enjoyed opposing it in public, while pushing it through in private. His only regret was that he couldn't tell anyone."

I get to my feet, staring at Muscles to goad him. "He didn't tell you he'd hived off a strip of land for me. I'll bet you were livid when you found out he'd duped you. I wish I'd seen your face at the time."

His laugh never reaches his eyes. With only the slightest of head movements, he unleashes Muscles, who pulls my arms behind my back, immobilising me. Birchill walks round the desk and punches me in the solar plexus. The second punch makes my legs buckle. I collapse to my knees, gasping for breath. Adrenaline has numbed the pain for the moment, but not the effect. I'm aware of Gemma attacking Muscles, but he soon flings her onto the sofa.

As I try to stand, he plants his foot behind my knee and forces me back to the floor. He grabs my hair, yanking my head back. I look up at Birchill and say, "Serves you right for not checking before you grabbed Downland."

I brace myself for the punch to the face or the kick in the guts. Instead, he pulls some papers from the desk. "I've offered you twice the market value of your land," he says. "All you need to do is sign this contract and build a proper sanctuary somewhere more suitable."

"I'd rather expose you and your pet politician."

He pulls a hand back, ready to slap my face. "You need to show your father some respect, Fisher."

I can't help laughing. "It's not your day, Birchill. He's not my father," I say, enjoying his look of surprise.

He gives Muscles a sign, and I'm hauled to my feet. Birchill takes my Blackberry from its holster. "Yours too, Miss Dean," he says, going over to her.

She looks dazed, but hands over her phone. "Top it up for me, will you?" she says.

He walks to the French doors and nods. Muscles propels me across the room. I crash into the desk. While the pain in my thighs registers in my brain, my face plunges towards the desk. Just in time, I turn my head. It thuds into the wood. My jaw feels like it's dislocated. Half stunned, I pull myself upright. Birchill and Muscles are outside. Muscles smashes the phones with a rock from the garden and then hurls them into the woodland.

"You're welcome to stay," Birchill says. "You have books to read, water in the fridge and security cameras to watch over you."

"Where are you going?"

He shakes his head. "Marcus will keep you company."

"I'll call the police, Birchill."

"And throw your stepmother out onto the street? I don't think so."

"What are you talking about?"

"Who do you think owns their house in Herstmonceux?"

CHAPTER TWENTY-FIVE

Gemma steps in front of me and studies my face. "You're going to look like the Elephant Man unless you stop pacing about and let me put some ice on that."

"I'm not pacing. I'm looking for a way out."

"No change there then," she says with a sneer. "Okay, play the hero, but at least tell me about your father not being your father."

"We need to get out of here and go after Birchill."

She doesn't budge, her mouth set to stubborn. "And go where? We're trapped, in case you hadn't noticed."

I wish she could look after me and sooth my battered face and aching stomach, but not now. "I only found out about my father a couple of hours ago," I say.

"Niamh told you?" Gemma's voice is pure disbelief. "Why now? Because her husband is missing? What's going on, Kent?"

I push past her to resume my examination of the bookcase. I follow it to the back of the room and try the handle on the door again, in case some unseen force has intervened to help me. It's still locked, of course. Our only hope of escape lies with the passage behind the bookcase.

I've no idea if the passage still exists, or whether the hidden lever is still in place and working.

All I need to do is find out without Muscles seeing me.

"Talk to me, Kent. This is massive."

She means well, but I can't deal with this now. "I'm not bothered who my father is," I say. "What difference does it make? Will it help us get out of here?

"You're not who you thought you were."

I stride over to the mirror on the wall. "I'm a little bruised and battered," I say, surprised at how swollen and fiery my cheek is, "but still Kent Fisher."

"This morning you woke as the son of William Fisher, now you're..." She flaps her hands, trying to dislodge the words from the air, "... not."

"I'll have to ring the BBC and book you a place on Mastermind. Specialist subject—stating the blatantly obvious."

"Better than denial, Kent. You're not who you thought you were."

"Really? So, my past has suddenly changed, has it? My childhood and adolescence no longer cast a shadow over me. I never lived in this place, so I won't know how to get out of here."

I move along the bookcase as I speak, pretending to look for a book. When I reach the section where the lever should be, I stop. I place myself between the books and Muscles and pretend to read. My left hand feels along the smooth wood. I hope the bookcase won't spring open—if it opens at all after so many years.

"Don't you want to know who your real father is?" She plucks a book from the shelf and saunters over to the sofa.

I can't help noticing the way Muscles watches Gemma. There's something sinuous and effortless about the way she lowers herself. She has a strong core, as the runner in me would say, and beautifully toned muscles. She's as near to perfect as I can imagine.

"Do you think your mother will tell you?" she asks, giving Muscles a wave.

"No. And I'm not talking to her either."

"You don't know who your father is. You want nothing to do with your mother. And there's no one special in your life. I find that sad."

I wish I could find the lever.

"You don't look like William," Gemma says. "He's fair with blue eyes and you're dark with brown eyes."

"You don't think my mother had something to do with that?"

"Why do you hate her, Kent?"

I stroll to the next section of bookcase. It's nearly five o'clock, and I'm trapped with someone who wants my life history. I pull Sue Grafton's *A is for Alibi* from the shelf, surprised Birchill likes the Alphabet Series.

"What did she do to you?"

When I left Manchester, I pushed all memories of my mother into a safe corner of my mind as if she never existed. Now, for the first time in 23 tears, I can hear her harsh voice, coloured with that flat, Germanic tone and clipped sentences.

"Nothing I did was ever right, or good enough," I reply. "She lied about everything and never had a good word to say about my father." I stop, floored by a thought. "She knew William Fisher wasn't my father, didn't she?"

"Maybe that's why she took you away from here."

I'm in danger of re-evaluating the mother who spent more time waging war on dust than she spent with me. "No, she resented everything and everyone. Men were only after one thing. Governments penalised poor divorced mothers. God made it rain when she hung out the washing." I pause, remembering the constant drone of complaints and negative words. "William Fisher took the blame for everything that was wrong with her life."

"No one's all bad, Kent."

Frustrated at not finding the lever, I ram the book back and stride to the desk. "She was clean and fastidious around the flat, I guess. She spent most of her life with a duster in her hand, or ant powder."

"Ant powder?"

"She could stand for hours at the back door, poised to wage war on ants. All the joints between the flagstones were picked out in white powder. If a cat strayed into the garden, she would chuck water over it. She collected any poo they left and lobbed it back over the fence into next door's garden."

"Maybe that's why you love animals," Gemma remarks.

I perch on the desk, recalling the moment when I felt like the cruellest person on the planet. "When I was 15 or 16, I discovered a mouse nesting in some compost in the shed. There was a mother and three baby mice. The mother was too quick and scurried away, leaving the babies. They were so small. I collected them in a plastic tub, knowing they wouldn't survive without their mother."

I pause, remembering how I agonised. If I turned the babies outside, they would die. If I left them in the nest, my mother would kill them.

"I took them down to the river and set them free in the grass, hoping they'd survive. But they had no chance. I'd killed them. I felt rotten for months, imagining how scared and cold they must have felt."

I close my eyes, trying to hide the memory. "I vowed then I would never hurt another animal. Everything has a right to live."

Gemma's in front of me when I reopen my eyes. "You did what you thought was right," she says, her voice and expression sympathetic.

"I could have left the nest undisturbed. My mother might not have found them."

"And if she had?"

I run my finger across the base of my neck. "She hated everything."

She sighs. "Have you ever considered how alone and vulnerable she felt, leaving this grand house and her husband? She lost everything."

"Maybe he threw her out for the affair."

"Then she lost her lover too, didn't she?"

I don't want to listen or understand. Whatever the reasons, my mother didn't have to take out her problems on me. What had I done to upset her? If she didn't like or want me, why did she take me?

"She wanted to spite William Fisher," I say. "That's why she took me."

Gemma looks appalled. "Come on, it couldn't have been easy, bringing you up on her own. Why don't you ring her? You've got the perfect opportunity. You can ask her who your real father is."

I slam my fist on the desk. "Will you just leave it?"

Like Gemma, the mouse jumps. The computer's hard drive whirs and the picture returns to the monitor. The Google search page offers results on 'Fire at Maynard's Farm, Uckfield'. Birchill was on Page Two of his search when we interrupted him.

I move around to the chair and take a seat. Gemma's right behind, resting her chin on my shoulder as I go back to the first page. He's viewed items from the *Tollingdon Tribune* and *Eastbourne Herald*. He's viewed every entry bar the blog from 'Gyro the Enviro'.

Unlike the newspapers, the blog bemoans the loss of ancient woodland habitats, criticising Miles Birchill, The Concrete Cowboy. The blog pokes fun at Tombstone's shallow appeal, comparing it to the 'blonde bimbos' he likes to be seen with. It's all cosmetic and fakery, Gyro rants, repeating himself. I'm about to leave the page when Gemma puts her hand over mine on the mouse.

"There," she says, guiding the pointer to a thumbnail photo. I double click and an image loads, showing a burnt out farm, courtesy of East Sussex Fire and Rescue. Most of the building has gone, reduced to charred timber beams and a mess of damp, black debris. The resolution of the photo is poor and I can't make out the fine detail, but the metal springs of a bed are visible. The charred remnants of appliances show where the kitchen was located.

Gyro wonders if The Concrete Cowboy's burning ambition to build Tombstone had anything to do with the fire.

"Look at the date of the photograph," she says, pointing.

Today is the fifth anniversary of the fire.

"You and Birchill talked about a killer," she says as if it's an everyday topic of conversation. "Do you think Collins was murdered because he started the fire?"

It's an intriguing thought. Birchill was checking this out when we arrived. Like me, he wasn't convinced Collins died in a work accident. So why didn't Birchill say something to me? Why didn't he compare notes? Why did he get me thrown off the case and suspended?

Then everything tumbles into place so fast my mouth can't keep pace.

"He's the real target, Gemma. Birchill, I mean." She backs away as I stand, fired by the thoughts coursing from my brain to my mouth. "He gained the most from the farm burning down, didn't he? William Fisher helped him get planning permission. He's a target too. That's why he's missing."

I'm over at the bookcase in a couple of strides. "That's what he meant in his text, Gemma. Emergency at the ranch. He meant Tombstone."

"Slow down, Kent. You're making me dizzy."

I turn and put my hands on her shoulders, looking into those lovely eyes. "This is about revenge. Collins was the first. He probably started the fire. Now she's moving on to Birchill, who wanted the farm flattened. And for good measure, she's going to kill William Fisher because he got them the planning approval."

"Who are you talking about, Kent?"

"The Maynards' daughter. She's avenging the death of her parents."

Gemma thinks about this for a few moments. Her eyebrows dip and rise a few times before she gasps. "We have to get out of here and call the police."

She runs across to the French door and thumps on the glass, calling to Muscles. She makes a phone sign with her thumb and little finger, shouts some abuse, thumps on the door again, and freezes. Her arms drop. Her shoulders sag. With more resignation then defiance, she gives him a middle finger salute.

When he laughs, she picks up a small wooden table and hurls it at him. The table thuds against the glass and bounces off, clattering to the floor.

Muscles applauds.

"Cool it, Gemma. The fire started about nine in the evening. Birchill will be there long before that."

"Why doesn't he ring the police?"

"That's not his way."

"What if he fails?"

She's right. We need to get out. I'm out of the chair and heading for the bookcase. "Distract Muscles."

"How? He ignored me a moment ago."

"Appeal to the brain in his trousers?"

"You want me to whip out my tits?"

"As tempting as that is, I need to find the lever to open the bookcase. No, go over there and let Muscles think that's what you're going to do." I look across to the French doors, then back to the bookcase, trying to work out times. "Stay by the door and be ready to close the curtains. We'll only have a few seconds after that."

She nods. "I get it. We go into the passage and close the bookcase. He rushes in and thinks we've vanished, right?"

"No, we close the curtains and you hide behind the sofa."

"Why?"

"Trust me."

"You said that once before, remember?"

Will she ever let me forget? "I'm not going to leave you this time," I say. "Now, go and do your stuff."

She saunters across the room, swinging her hips in a sinuous rhythm. When she's in position, she beckons him closer with her finger. I can't see what she's doing, but he's transfixed. It takes me a few moments to realise I'm no better. With a sigh I turn to the bookcase, sliding my hand to the back. I start at the underside of the top shelf and slide my fingers down to the shelf below. I repeat the process on the next two shelves with no success.

"How long are you going to be?" she calls.

She's turned her back on Muscles, gyrating her bottom at him. She's undone several buttons to reveal more than a hint of cleavage and lacy bra. "I'm running out of buttons."

It takes a lot of willpower to turn back to the bookcase. I shuffle along to the next section and slide my fingers down the back. The texture of polished wood changes to something colder and smoother.

"Got it!" I call, sliding my finger into the small recess. The lever refuses to budge. "It's stiff, Gemma. And so's the lever," I add quickly.

"Muscles too," she says. "If you don't hurry up, he's going to come and drag me away."

Once more, I slide my finger into the recess and try to pull the lever. Once more, it refuses to budge. I glance back, noticing that Muscles has moved to the door to get a closer look. His hand gestures suggest he wants her to get her clothes off.

Then the lever moves a little. Gritting my teeth, I bend my forefinger, straining to free the lever. Finally, it frees and flies open. With a quiet click, the bookcase swings, crashing into my shoulder. A cold, musty draught fans my face.

"Get ready," I call, steadying the bookcase. If it swings open when I join Gemma, we're sunk. "Take the left curtain. I'll take the right."

Without missing a beat, she sidles across to the left and wraps the curtain across her. Muscles looks confused. Then he notices me at her side and frowns. I wink at him and cry, "Pull."

Thankfully, the curtains slide effortlessly on the metal pole. While Gemma rushes for the sofa, I position the wooden table at the foot of the curtains. Muscles thumps on the glass. I rush to the bookcase and pull it open to reveal a veil of dusty cobwebs. Then I hear a key in the lock. I just make it behind the desk as he flings open the door. He grunts as he tangles with the curtains. Then, a few moments later, there's a cry of surprise and a crashing thud that registers on the Richter Scale. After some superlative Anglo Saxon, it sounds like he's back on his feet and crossing the floor. In the silence that follows, I wonder if he'll realise the cobwebs are undisturbed.

I look over the top of the desk. He's gone into the passage.

"Run, Gemma!"

I reach the bookcase in two strides and push it closed with all my strength. I've no idea if the catch engages because I turn and follow Gemma. She leaps through the gap in the curtains. I'm seconds behind. As I turn to close the door, Muscles, who's smeared with cobwebs, bursts out through the bookcase, scattering books.

I slam the door and yank up the handle to engage the locking bolts. My shaking hand reaches for the key he left in his haste. He thuds into the door. His hand reaches for the handle. I turn the key. To my relief the handle holds firm. From the fury ingrained in his face, it won't take him long to wrench the handle off the door.

Delighted that my lip reading skills have improved, I wave goodbye to him, before throwing the key into the bushes. Gemma and I don't stop running till we reach the courtyard. Once in the car, I take a deep breath, grin to myself, and drive off. We're past the hotel and heading for the woodland before either of us speaks.

"That was amazing," she says, glowing from the exertion. "You know how to show a girl a great time, Kent Fisher."

"You might want to button up your blouse."

She looks down and smiles. "I never thought I'd hear you say that."

Me neither.

Within a minute, we reach the main gates and the A27. Without thinking, I swing left and accelerate hard.

"We should go back to your flat and ring the police," she says.

"By the time they send someone out, take a statement and check out Downland Manor, the barn will be burnt to the ground. And that's if they believe me."

"Why wouldn't they?"

"Where do I start?" I ask, glancing at the dash. It's a quarter to six and Tombstone will be closing. Even with a fair wind, it will take us 30 minutes to get there, maybe a little less. If Foley has left, the trade entrance will be locked.

"Let's overlook my feud with Birchill. Let's forget I'm suspended and discredited, okay?" When she nods, I say, "Consider how difficult it must be to murder someone with a power takeoff."

She arches her back into a stretch that threatens to burst open her blouse. Her grimace melts into a sigh as she relaxes. "Go on," she says.

"You need to lift and position Collins over the power takeoff so his tie will snag and become entangled. He'll be heavy, so they have to be quick."

"They?"

"Even Muscles would struggle to hold the dead weight of Collins on his own."

"You're thinking Cheung, right?"

I wasn't, but I nod. "Then, when the tie snags, Collins is wrenched out of their hands. Blood will spurt everywhere. I can't imagine the noise or the smell. The two of them will be covered in blood."

I have to slow as we join the end of a tail of traffic, heading towards Brighton. "They're already at the barn," I say, thinking aloud. "They already have William Fisher. They may now have Birchill. But they won't be expecting me."

"Us, Kent. I'm coming with you."

I should have dropped her at the sanctuary. With Niamh to help, she could have contacted the police. They would listen to Niamh, maybe send a patrol car to Tombstone, even to the barn. While I picture the scene, I'm sure it wouldn't happen that way. The response car would turn up outside the barn with its lights and sirens flashing. By then the damage would be done. The fire would be started. The daughter would be escaping by the trade entrance.

"Us," I agree, settling back to make my own plans.

Gemma sinks into the seat and falls silent. The road dips down towards the Cuckmere River, which is little more than a stream at this point. Moments later, we reach the Alfriston roundabout and take a right towards Berwick Station. It's not the fastest road in the district, but it's the shortest route north to the A22 and Tombstone. I hope we don't encounter any tractors.

"Collins had to be unconscious," she says. "He'd struggle like a caged animal if he wasn't. They'd never hold him still."

"They filled him with vodka until he passed out. When the post mortem reveals he was drunk, his death is ruled to be accidental. Neat, don't you think?"

"Practical," she says. "Someone planned this in great detail."

I nod, hoping Collins was unconscious when they held him over the takeoff. Anything else is too terrible to consider.

As we drive into Berwick Station, the lights flash and the level crossing barriers descend. I draw to a halt and switch off the engine. I turn to face Gemma.

"It must have taken months, maybe years, to plan this. The tractor has to be repaired, especially if you want the blame for the accident on Birchill. Collins slept late. He never wore ties. Someone had to get to know him."

"You mean Wednesday Woman, don't you? She's the daughter." She cringes and turns away. "If she slept with him... it's too horrible for words."

"Then you have to clean up afterwards," I say, hoping to distract her and push the image from my thoughts. "The shower in the barn had been used recently. Cheung must have showered, disposed of the clothes, and then rung the police. No wonder he got his story mixed up. I...."

My voice tails off as I look into Gemma's eyes. I'm not sure what she's thinking, but it's making me go weak. "What?" is all I can say.

"You're amazing," she says. "When did you work this out? You had your doubts on the first morning, didn't you? You knew then."

I shake my head. "No, I knew something wasn't right. We were meant to believe Collins went to make fence posts. There was no space for new posts in the enclosure, no fresh timber to make any. That's what bothered me, though I didn't understand the significance until yesterday evening. I had a hazy picture, which only came together today.

"I thought it was Birchill," I say. "I wanted it to be Birchill because it solved so many problems. But he also knew Collins was killed, so it couldn't be him."

"When you and Birchill started talking about a killer, I thought you'd lost the plot. But you both worked it out, didn't you?"

"Only when you pointed out the anniversary of the fire. Then it had to be the daughter."

"Who is the daughter? Adele Havelock?"

The train rushes through in a blur of noise and lights. The barriers lift and we're away, speeding through the village to make up time.

"It could be," I reply. "She went back to Collins' house yesterday evening. But she got a call from the killer, using Collins' phone."

"Could have been Cheung using the phone."

I nod, glad I have Gemma with me.

With traffic light on the road, we make good time to the A22. Here, we join the steady flow of people returning home from shopping or working in Eastbourne and the surrounding towns. We make good progress through Whitesmith and pick up speed on the East Hoathly bypass. Clouds have rolled in from the west, signalling the end of the hot, dry spell that's kept September so warm. The darkening sky reminds me we may be too late to get into Tombstone.

If only we had a phone.

"What's the plan when we get to Tombstone?" Gemma asks as we slow for the speed camera in Halland. "Round up a posse and save the day?"

There's a nervous undertone to her words. Like me, the reality is dawning. This is not a TV drama or a novel. Collins has already been brutally murdered, and two more deaths are planned. I'm not James Bond or Dirty Harry. I have no idea what I'll do when I get to the barn. I just know I have to do something.

I'm assuming Birchill will fail. He may succeed, especially if he took some of the workers from Tombstone with him.

"We go and see Foley," I reply. "If he's still around."

"You just want to impress Rebecca by playing the hero."

"I want to find out if Birchill saved the day."

"And if he didn't?"

"I'll have to impress Rebecca."

We turn down the entrance road at a quarter past six. The light's fading now, but the gates are still open, allowing a trickle of cars out. Behind, the cortege snakes around the car park. I head straight for the ticket office.

"I'll lead," Gemma says, pulling out her ID. "You're suspended, remember?"

The youth from yesterday remembers us and offers to ring Foley. She beckons the youth closer and whispers something that makes him chuckle. The dreamy look he gives her as we walk past must be similar to mine when I first met her.

"What did you say?" I ask in the gallery of Western stars.

"I said, if anyone was going to interrupt Foley while he bonked his secretary it would be me. He seemed to like that."

"I think he rather likes you."

"Do I detect a hint of jealousy, Kent?"

A few weary parents are still leaving, dragging tired toddlers behind them. Most of the parents look more shattered than their offspring, confirming my belief that children are as bad for your health as they are for your wallet.

Most of the shops and franchises are closed. While those in charge work out their profits, the minions wipe down tables and chairs, or push dirty water in and out of corners with their mops. A small army of staff pick up litter and empty the bins into bulging black sacks. These are tossed onto a trailer, pulled by a quad bike. No one seems to take any notice of us as we hurry to the sheriff's office. The door's locked, but there's a light inside. Gemma raps on the door and steps back, joining me to look at a defaced 'Wanted' poster. Some wag has converted the barrel of a Colt .45 into a penis.

"Does it make you feel inadequate?" she asks.

"No. Mine's real."

The door opens a fraction and Rebecca peers out. "Oh, it's you."

"We need to talk to Mr. Foley," Gemma says. "It's urgent."

Rebecca opens the door and steps aside. As I step through the door, she notices the bruising to my face and makes a sympathetic noise. "That swelling looks painful," she says. "Do you want me to rub something soothing on it?"

Gemma's glare dares me to answer.

"Maybe later," I say, following my colleague inside.

Rebecca's closed everything down. The blue jacket which matches her short skirt lies across the desk, next to a co-ordinating bag with a silver clasp. Even her shoes harmonise. I hope they're not indicative of her mood, as she looks pale and tired. Then I get an unhealthy whiff of vomit and air freshener.

Gemma flaps her hand in front of her nose. "What's that?"

"The reason we're still here. Some brat threw up everywhere." Rebecca opens the door that leads to the cells. "Ben? It's your favourite officials."

A few moments later, Foley appears, also looking jaded. His weary eyes register Gemma and then fix on me. "You were suspended."

"I wasn't," Gemma says, stepping in front of him. "Has Mr. Birchill been through recently?"

Foley and Rebecca look at each other and shake their heads.

Gemma pauses and glances at me.

"Do you know where David Cheung is?" I ask.

"No," he replies. "He didn't show for work again today. No one's seen him since the accident. His mobile goes straight to voicemail. There was no answer when I called at his place this morning."

"He's done a runner," Rebecca says. "Finding the body freaked him out, if you ask me."

It sounds like they've already debated this. "Did you go inside his place?" I ask.

"I went around the back to the conservatory, but I couldn't get in."

"Can we go, please?" Rebecca asks, turning to Gemma. "The smell in here's making my stomach turn. It was bad enough when it was just vomit, but that awful air freshener makes me gag."

"You wanted me to get rid of the smell," Foley says, his voice rising.

"Yes, with disinfectant. If I'd wanted you to mask the smell with the cheapest, nastiest air freshener known to mankind, I would have said."

I'm about to agree with her when my brain makes a connection. One thought leads to another and another until I know who killed Syd Collins.

But I've no idea how to prove it.

CHAPTER TWENTY-SIX

"Do you have security cameras at the main gate?" I ask.

We're outside on the boardwalk. I'm staring at a photographic shop on the opposite side of the street. The owner checks his shop and then pulls down the metal shutter, securing it with a twist of a key. He glances up to the sign above the shutter, adjusts his hat to a jauntier angle and smiles. It's impossible to see, but I'm sure he has a security camera hidden in the sign. Even with Tombstone's security, he still wants to protect his expensive equipment.

"We do," Foley replies, his voice hesitant with suspicion. "But I have to be on my way."

"Do you have the footage from Thursday morning?"

"You can't look at it," he replies, a little too quickly. "You're suspended. And we're closed. You'll have to come back on Monday."

Gemma steps in front of him. "I'm not suspended. And no one's leaving until we've seen the footage."

His sigh tells us how unhappy he is, but Rebecca shows no reticence. "The computer's in a room behind the ticket office. Follow me."

Gladly, I think, watching her negotiate the boardwalk and steps with ease in her stilettos. Her stride has purpose, but there's a relaxed, almost lazy quality I find alluring. She's exaggerating her movements for Foley, I guess, letting him know she's not forgotten him. Unfortunately, he seems more interested in the time. Maybe he's forgotten to record something on TV.

"Why do you want to watch a video?" Gemma asks, her voice low. "Shouldn't we be phoning the police and rescuing Birchill?"

"We don't know if he's here," I reply. "We don't know if there's a woman planning to burn down the barn."

"Don't we? I'm confused now. What's going on?"

"I'm hoping the answer's on video."

Gemma studies me, trying to pierce my defences. "You know something, don't you?"

I don't answer, keeping my gaze firmly on Rebecca's athletic legs.

The room behind the ticket office turns out to be a windowless cupboard with a tiny desk and fold out plastic chair. Foley sits and switches on the large flat screen monitor. He fiddles around for a few minutes until finally he settles on the camera at the main gate. After clicking through a few folders, he calls up Thursday's footage. I wait for him to vacate the chair, but he shows no signs of relinquishing his place.

"We'll take it from here," I say.

He shakes his head. "No way am I leaving you alone, either with or without your assistant."

I want to tell him I can't be alone with an assistant, but this isn't the time for semantics. "Wind back to when the emergency services arrived."

He concentrates on the screen, using a slider to go back in time. He pauses every few seconds to check the image, before winding back further. At last we reach a point where an ambulance is on the road leading to the main gate. It's 6:43 am. He plays the footage, and Gemma and Rebecca push up close on either side of me.

The footage is grainy due to the poor light as dawn breaks. The headlamps from the ambulance shine directly into the camera once or twice, obscuring the image. The ambulance stops at the gate and the minutes tick by. Sensing my mood, he says, "I can fast forward to when I arrive to let them through."

He winds on seven minutes before the ambulance moves again. A patrol car follows it through the gate. Carolyn Montague's Peugeot 206 Convertible is right behind, leaving only Foley's vehicle on the roadside.

"Why didn't you use the service road?" I ask him.

"I didn't want to keep the police waiting."

"So, you drove around the outside of the park to the main gate and unlocked it for the emergency services. Did you stay there?"

"I had to wait for the doctor to arrive. He got here about ten minutes later. He left first about 15 minutes later, followed by the ambulance. Do you want me to check?"

I shake my head. It's half past six and I'm no closer to confirming my suspicions about the killer. "Can you step frame the video?"

He glances at Rebecca, who says, "You can pause and play. That's all."

"Then maybe you'll allow us to take a closer look. I'm sure you want to take Rebecca home." I nudge Gemma and point from me to the screen. She nods and taps him on the shoulder.

"Mr. Foley, we need to study the video in detail. Please leave us."

He takes his time, forcing me to back out of the room so he can leave. Once outside, he stands there, feet firmly planted on the ground. I move to the screen and slide my hand over the mouse. I rewind to the point where the ambulance first appears. I let the video play, pausing and restarting in several places. Once I reach the point where they wait for Foley, I rewind and repeat the procedure.

"We really have to leave," he says.

"No rush," Rebecca says, her head close to mine. She's watching as intently as me, but I doubt if I'm having the same effect on her as she has on me. Gemma's also watching, her hand resting lazily on my shoulder.

"What are you looking for?" she asks.

I'm about to give in when something catches my eye. I stop the video, rewind, and repeat the process. It takes me four attempts to repeat what I saw.

"Did you see it?" I ask Rebecca.

"I think I saw a brief flash of light." She shrugs and looks at Gemma.

"I couldn't see anything," she says.

I wish I could pause on the exact frame to show them. "It was so quick I almost missed it," I say, trying one last time.

"Or you imagined it," Foley says. "How much longer will you be?"

This time I freeze on the right frame. There's a faint glow of light at the back of the ambulance on the right. "There," I say, pointing.

Everyone pushes closer to look. "What is it?" Rebecca asks, her hot skin almost touching mine.

"It's the police car behind." Gemma sounds disappointed.

"It's not. Watch."

I rewind again until the police car's headlights can be clearly seen behind the ambulance. As they draw closer to the gate, the police car moves closer and disappears from view. Then I freeze the footage a few moments later.

"This is roughly where you see the glow. It's Carolyn Montague. Can we zoom in?" I call to Foley.

"I wouldn't bother. The image pixelates."

"It's definitely her," I say, rising. "We'll want a copy of the footage, Mr. Foley."

He looks alarmed. "Now?"

"Later."

"Later!" He almost shrieks. "I've had enough of this. I want you to leave this minute."

"Shut up!" Rebecca says. She turns to me. "What's this all about?"

"Don't look at me," Gemma says.

"Okay," I say, realising they're blocking my escape from the cupboard. "Do you know how far down the road the vehicles were when I paused the video? No? Remember the layby where we turned around on Thursday, Gemma?"

"When we left the park and came back? Sure. But how do you know you've got the right place on the video? It's too dark."

"There was a dip in the surface, remember?"

After a moment's thought, she nods.

"If you had your headlamps on, and the front of your car rose up as it came out of the dip...."

Rebecca and Gemma nod at the same time.

"The headlamps shone into the camera for a split second. Then they were gone, hidden behind the ambulance and police car."

"So Carolyn Montague pulled out of the layby," Gemma says. "So what?"

"She was there before the emergency services arrived."

"I had worked that out, thanks. So?"

I glance at my watch. "We need to go," I say. "Could I borrow your mobile for half an hour, Rebecca?"

She purses her lips and then breaks into a sly smile. "Tell me why this car in the layby is so important."

"How did the Coroner's Officer get here before the ambulance? The emergency call doesn't go to the Coroner."

She pulls her phone out of her bag. "Half an hour," she says, placing it in my hand. "And no reading my messages."

"Why didn't you just ask her out?" Gemma calls as she chases after me. "She has no idea what you're talking about. She doesn't know there's a murder."

"No, but she understands my point. The phone's for you," I say once we're in the car. I speed off, heading for the service road. "You might need it. So, why did Carolyn beat the ambulance to Tombstone?"

"She lives closer, obviously."

"She was close, all right. She was showering in the barn when Cheung called the emergency services."

Her mouth falls open. "She killed Collins? Why?"

"Think about it, Gemma. She's the daughter. She was first on the scene when her parents' house was burnt down."

She shakes her head. "How could she murder Collins and then roll up to investigate as if nothing had happened? She can't have any feelings."

We leave the main town behind and head into the countryside. My headlamps pick out the road and the animals that stand close by in the paddocks. Within minutes we're approaching the fork in the road that leads to the barn. I continue along the service road.

"Carolyn arranged to meet me by the barn," I say. "I think she's already lured William Fisher and Birchill there. Now she's waiting for me. Well, I hope she is."

Gemma picks up the phone. "I'll ring the police."

"Not yet. We have time. We also have surprise. Before we do anything, let's make sure she can't escape."

Right on cue, we reach the service gate. It's closed, but the padlock has walked. "When Carolyn's burnt us all in the barn, she comes out this way and goes to meet the emergency services again. Only this time she can't. Open the gate, Gemma, and I'll park on the other side."

"Why not this side?"

"If you're on the other side, you can drive off if you need to."

"You can't go after her, Kent. She's dangerous. And I'm not hanging around here in the dark."

Despite her arguments, she opens the gate, closing it behind me after I drive through. It takes a few moments to manoeuvre the car so it's parallel with the gate and blocking the exit. I take my Maglite from the trunk and hand it to Gemma. Then I retrieve my head torch and slip it on. The LED beam lights up a circle of grass like a spotlight.

"You won't surprise anyone with that beam," she says.

I switch it off. "Carolyn will be in the barn."

"And Cheung?"

"With her."

"I'm calling the police, Kent."

I grab her forearm as she raises the phone. "If Carolyn hears or sees the police, who knows what she might do? Give

313

me 15 minutes. That's enough time for me to confirm they're here and come back. Then we ring the police."

"What if she surprises you, Kent? She could kill you."

I shake my head, looking into those dark eyes. The thought of not seeing her again sweeps through me like a deep dread. It can't end here. It can't.

"I'll be back," I say, placing my hands on her shoulders. "I have to come back. I'm hopelessly in love with you."

I kiss the tip of my forefinger and press it to her lips. "15 minutes," I call over my shoulder as I run towards Collins' house.

"You can't do this! You can't run away from me again!"

There's just enough light to make out the grass beneath my feet. When I draw level with Collins' house, I stop. What if Carolyn parked her car at the back, not at the barn?

I hurry down the side of the house. If her car is here, I'll have to go back and get mine to block her in. Or I can let the tyres down. When I emerge from behind Collins' Land Rover and see the car, I groan. It's Adele's car. For a moment, I wonder if she's still searching for the manuscript, but the house is in darkness. The rear door's locked. She's not here. So, where is she?

As I retrace my steps, I wonder if she's working with Carolyn.

Back at the front of the house, I head into the chestnut grove. The varicose roots and covering of autumn leaves force me to slow down. All around me the sounds of scampering and calls from owls play on my senses. I stop for a moment and listen, certain someone's nearby. Something brushes past my face. I just manage to stop myself crying out. But my heart thumps like crazy. I switch on the torch, which illuminates the chestnut leaf in front of my face.

The darkness seeps into the woods like ink, closing around me. My light shines a bright beam about 5 yards ahead of me. Beyond, the darkness lets nothing escape. A few minutes later, after a couple of close scrapes with branches, I reach the clearing in front of Cheung's hovel. I stop and switch my torch to the lower setting while I wait for my breathing to slow.

Then a woman screams.

I sprint across the clearing and leap over the gate. When I reach the back, I stop, turn off the light, and listen. I peer around the corner into an impenetrable black fog. Seconds seem like minutes as I wait, listening for the slightest sound. Finally, I edge along the wall of the lean-to. The humming of the chest freezer grows louder as I approach the door.

I switch on my head torch and spot Adele's feet, clad in navy blue court shoes. The trousers lead to a loose jacket, open to reveal a pale blouse. Adele's skin is warm, her pulse steady. There a soft swelling on her temple where the skin is red. Did she trip and bang her head? It's impossible to say. I ease her into the recovery position.

Then I realise that the lid of the chest freezer isn't fully closed. The hinges groan as I raise the lid. I stare at the rust coloured spikes of hair, now frozen white. David Cheung's head rests at an unnatural angle, wedged into the corner. He's cold and frozen. It looks like he's been in the freezer since Thursday afternoon.

I'm about to close the lid when I spot something glinting at the bottom of the freezer. I slide my hand past the body and retrieve a set of keys. They must have fallen from his pocket as he was bundled in. I count off the front and back door keys to the hovel, which leaves one unaccounted for. Does it open the back door of the barn? If I sneak in that way I can surprise Carolyn.

"Stay chilled," I tell him, slipping the keys in my pocket.

At least I know why he didn't report for work. He must have been on his way to meet Carolyn at Collins' house when Gemma and I bumped into him. Unaware of where we'd come from, he took us back to the hovel so we wouldn't stumble on Carolyn. She must have killed him to stop him talking.

But what brought Adele here?

I check her pockets for a mobile phone, but find only tissues. Her bag's missing too. Women don't go anywhere without their bags, in my experience, even if they sneak around at night. Then the familiar smell of cheap perfume reaches my nose. The hairs on my neck tingle.

"Carolyn," I say, keeping my back to her as I rise. "Sorry I'm late. I was on my way to the barn when I found Cheung, stuffed in the freezer."

"I'd given up on you, Kent. Then I saw your head torch in the woods."

So much for the element of surprise. I'm not sure what to do now. If I can keep her talking, hopefully Gemma will call the police. With any luck, she's already called them.

"I was watching a security video of Thursday morning," I say, still not turning. "You got here fast, I must say."

"I live quite close, Kent. Did you see the killer?"

"Killer? What are you talking about?"

"The killer you told me about. I checked the video before I came here and you'll never guess what I found. Collins' killer left Tombstone about half an hour before we arrived. Can you believe it? Talk about cool."

"Who was it?"

"Birchill. Who else? Luckily, I lured him here under a pretext and now he's trussed like a chicken in the barn. Shall we join him?" Something hard pushes between my shoulder blades. "Switch off your head torch. Good, now turn slowly. Any tricks and I'll blow your head off."

Carolyn also has a head torch, which almost blinds me when I turn. As my eyes adjust, I stare into the barrels of the shotgun. I'm reminded of Mike's sanity gallery and the photo of the man with the back of his head missing. 'Michael wanted to get ahead' the caption said. If I'm not careful, mine will say, 'Kent lost his head'.

"Black suits you," I say, looking her over. While I can't see her eyes, I'm confident she's not about to shoot me. She wants to tell me how clever she is first. "We also share similar tastes in headwear."

"Put your hands on your head and interlock your fingers." Her voice is cold and mechanical, like a robot. Maybe she'll warm up when she sets fire to the barn.

I do as she says. "Aren't you going to kill Adele before we leave?"

"Do you ever stop talking?"

Naturally, I remain silent.

She backs away and gestures me out of the lean to. "Get moving!"

She falls in behind me nudging me along with the shotgun. I stop at the front gate. "I can't call you Carolyn Montague now I know you're a Maynard."

"You're smarter than you look, Kent, but I became Carolyn Montague a long time ago. Now, let's head for the barn."

"It must have been devastating, finding the farm burnt down and your parents dead."

"Not at all," she says. "I started the fire."

CHAPTER TWENTY-SEVEN

"You killed your parents?"

I can't keep the surprise and disbelief from my voice. She speaks as if it's an everyday event. I can remember wanting to kill my mother on numerous occasions, but I never got past planning it in my head. That helped me deal with the anger, frustration and the sheer helplessness of my situation.

"What else could I do?" she asks. "They sold the farm to Miles Birchill. My father said he'd rather die than let a dyke squander his money. So, I filled him full of vodka and granted his wish."

She prods me with the shotgun. "You like to think you're hot stuff, Kent. I can grant your wish too. And don't get any bright ideas," she says, prodding me with more venom. "Cheung had an attack of conscience before he chilled out."

If she cracks any more puns, I might have to make a dash for it.

Not that I can escape into the woods without using my head torch. The clouds have all but extinguished the light. That leaves me a couple of choices. I can disarm her if a chance presents itself, but I need her to stumble on a tree

318

root or bang her head on a branch. Or I wait till we reach the barn.

In the meantime, she's walking in silence behind me, completely in control.

"I'm guessing your father didn't approve of your sexual preferences," I say, wondering if I can get her talking. "That must have been tough."

She doesn't answer for a good 30 seconds. "My parents were strict Catholics. Not in the going to church sense, as they only went Christmas and Easter, but they believed the doctrine. Homosexuality was a worse sin than murder."

When she pauses, I'm tempted to say something, but I remain silent, wishing I didn't have to rely on the beam from her head torch. I'm casting a shadow on the ground in front of me and I've stubbed my toe twice already.

"My father called me an abomination," she says. There's no resentment or anger in her tone. If anything, she finds it amusing. "I was 16 when he walked in on me doing it with my biology teacher, Evelyn Farmer. She freaked, worried she would lose her job, but he didn't care about that. No, he fetched some tools from the shed and made us dismantle his double bed. We took it down to the garden piece by piece. Then he tossed our clothes on top and set fire to the lot."

She chuckles at the memory. "He left us naked in the garden in the middle of November and told me never to return."

I can't believe a father could do that to his daughter. I don't know what to say. I'm not sure there's anything to say, but I need to keep the conversation going. "Just think how different your life would have been if your father hadn't found you."

"But I wanted him to find us," she says.

For someone who intended to use surprise to his advantage, I've failed dismally today. I'm already reeling from several unwelcome surprises without Carolyn's masterclass. In fact, my only success so far was to tell Gemma I was hopelessly in love with her. And I'm not sure which of us was more surprised.

"I tried to tell him several times," Carolyn is saying, "but I dried up when he looked at me. That made me angry at how feeble I was. So I started making plans. I was rather good at them," she adds, nudging me with the shotgun. "I seduced Evelyn and set her up. I couldn't believe how simple it was once I had a plan.

"Stop!" She pushes the gun into my back. "Did you hear that?"

The ground goes dark as she turns to scan the woodland. I follow the beam, but it doesn't travel far enough to penetrate the trees. I listen, but there's only the background whisper of invisible insects and small mammals in the undergrowth.

While she's scanning, I'm tempted to spin and knock the shotgun from her hands. Only I'm not sure if I need to jump around or swivel from the waist. No, I have to jump and spin in one movement, I decide, picturing the action in my mind. Had I joined a karate club as a teenager instead of writing poetry and situation comedies in my bedroom, I'd know exactly what to do. Now, all I can do is record it in my blog if I survive.

She turns off the head torch.

I stand there, listening, wondering what's spooked her. I look from side to side, but I can't see anything. I lean back slowly. The shotgun isn't in my back.

"Stay where you are!" Her voice is no more than a whisper, but it's close. "I grew up in these woods. I know my way around them blindfolded."

"I have a handkerchief in my pocket if you wish to try."

"What's it like, being a smartass? When you sauntered into the clearing on Thursday morning, you thought you were better than me. So, Lord Snooty, tell me which one of us has the gun."

I turn to face her. "A gun doesn't make you superior. You must be deluded if you think you can get away with this. The police are already closing in on you."

She switches on the head torch, blinding me. As I recoil, she thrusts the shotgun under my nose, forcing my head back. Too late, I realise my chance to disarm her came when she took one hand off the gun to switch on her head torch.

"Now who's deluded," she says, pushing me back. "You're not even a Fisher. Your father shoots blanks, but this shotgun's for real."

My heels catch on some roots and I'm falling. I land among some brambles and finish prostrate, staring up at Carolyn. She adjusts her aim and points the shotgun at my groin. If she's hoping to intimidate me, she's succeeding. Only my sweat glands seem to be working.

"I could sterilise you too," she says. "Then you'd understand why William hit Mandy Cheung so hard when she told him she was pregnant."

"I guess you got all this from Collins."

"Yes, he thought I was writing his autobiography. Now, get up and let's get to the barn."

I disengage myself from the brambles and get to my feet. "It was a clever diversion, Carolyn. It had me fooled for a while."

"You've been duped from the start," she says with contempt. "Now get moving."

"What do you mean, I was duped?"

"I told your boss I wanted you to investigate because you were the only one who could stand up to Birchill."

"You set me up?"

"You should be flattered, Kent. Without you, my plan could have gone off the rails. I spent a long time putting it together."

"You mean I've just ruined five years' work?"

"Hey, I had a career," she says, her tone sharp. "While you were setting up your sanctuary, I went from constable to detective sergeant in three years. I would have made detective inspector too, but...."

"But what?"

"I burnt out," she replies, her tone defiant.

"You had a breakdown, you mean. That's why they moved you into scenes of crime and then to the Coroner's office. You couldn't handle the pressure."

I tense, half expecting her to either shoot or beat me with the shotgun.

"You won't be so cocky when the flames are all around you," she says. "Just think, no one will know you solved Collins' murder. So, what gave me away?"

"The cheap perfume you wore on Thursday morning. You had to mask the shower you took after killing Collins."

"I wore it to mask the smell of cigarettes."

"Why hide the fact you smoke?"

"What did you find on the ground? Cigarette stubs. The one you put into a specimen bag was mine. I nearly died when you picked it up."

"But the other cigarettes were roll ups," I say.

"Collins and I spent hours here, smoking roll ups, talking about his fence post business. That's how I got the idea for a work accident. If the police had investigated as the protocol demands, they would have crawled all over the scene."

"And found cigarettes with your DNA on them."

"Fortunately, DI Briggs is an idle sod. He couldn't wait to pass the case to you. But all your hard work has been for nothing, I'm afraid. In a few minutes, you'll be toast. You know too much."

"I know you'll struggle to explain Cheung's death."

"I'll think of something," she says, sounding bored.

I almost walk into the bench saw as we head up the slope. I detour around it and continue to the top, where light streams out of the open barn doors. On the far side, tucked in the shadows, I make out William Fisher's Jaguar and Birchill's Mercedes.

I turn to face her. "Birchill worked it out. I bet you weren't expecting that."

She sighs. "How can you be so smart, yet so dumb? Birchill came to buy the autobiography for an obscene amount of money."

"The autobiography that doesn't exist."

"I wanted to humiliate him before I killed him. I can do the same for you."

She raises the shotgun to her shoulder. She pulls back the hammer on both barrels and slides her finger over the trigger.

"If you want me to beg, forget it."

"Credit me with more finesse than that," she says. "You visited Birchill earlier. Why do you think he locked you in?"

"Amaze me."

"To protect you," she replies. "For someone who can solve a murder based on a whiff of perfume, you're so dense. Think of all the hassle and grief you've given Birchill over the years. Think about the money you've cost him. Didn't you ever wonder why he never sued you for damages?"

I have wondered this from time to time, but I never found an answer. "He took out an injunction against me."

"Do I have to spell it out?" she asks, losing her temper. "William's sterile. He throws you and your mother out of Downland Manor. Why? Because she had an affair with a groom."

This can't be true. She's goading me out of spite. Yet despite my denials, I know she's not making it up. I go numb with disbelief. Then the nausea kicks in. Of all the people who could be my father, why is it him? The thought sickens me.

"Isn't it just the most delicious irony? The person you hate most in the world turns out to be your father." Carolyn smirks. "You couldn't write this stuff. But thanks to me, you'll die together. So, don't keep daddy waiting. In you go."

Just when I don't think things can get worse, I spot movement behind Carolyn. Gemma emerges from the shadows, carrying the Maglite. While she's come to save me, she's no match for Carolyn.

"You'll have to shoot me," I say, stepping forward to distract her.

"Or the lovely Gemma," she says, turning. She points the gun and beckons her over. "Drop the flashlight and come where I can see you."

Gemma does as instructed. "Sorry," she says.

"Oh it wasn't entirely your fault. Kent has an expressive face. And you made enough noise following us. Still, Kent's less likely to be heroic now that he knows I can hurt you."

Carolyn grins at me as she points the gun at Gemma's chest. "In you go, Kent."

If I go into the barn, I may never see Gemma again. If I don't, Carolyn might kill her.

The light from the barn blinds me at first. I turn away. "At least let her join me."

"I have plans for this little beauty."

Squinting until my eyes adjust, I walk into the barn. Birchill's perched on a jerry can of petrol, his hands tied together above his head. The rope goes over a beam and back to a tractor behind him. He looks tired and defeated. We might have the same colour hair and eyes, but otherwise we're from different planets. I spot William Fisher, slumped on the concrete floor near the door to the kitchen.

"His heart gave out." Birchill's voice is low and tense. "I'd check his pulse, but my hands are tied."

It appears we also share the same sense of humour.

"That's fine." Carolyn bends, never taking her eyes off me as she unscrews the cap from one of the jerry cans by the door. "Gemma, darling, be a sport and take off your blouse."

Gemma's trembling fingers struggle with the buttons, but one by one she undoes them. She looks beaten as she slowly removes the blouse.

"Good girl. Now tear off the sleeve and dip it in the can."

While Gemma follows instructions, I notice an axe on a workbench a few feet away. With great care, I inch towards it.

Carolyn takes the sleeve and tells Gemma to slide the door across. It's a struggle to get it moving, but once she does, the door slides smoothly. Carolyn kicks over the jerry can. Petrol pulses out and seeps across the concrete floor like a creeping stain. She lights the sleeve and swings it around her head as she backs up to the door.

For a moment, time freezes. The burning sleeve flies through the air. The petrol vapour catches fire. Flames rise up and roll across the floor towards us. The sliding door slams shut.

"Legs up!" I tell Birchill. I grab the jerry can and drag it out of the way of the advancing petrol.

"Cut me down!" he cries as he dangles, legs kicking the air.

The flames are already curling up the sides of the barn. They ignite anything flammable in their path, swooping over lawn mowers, surrounding the remaining fuel cans on the floor. The heat is so intense, the whole building seems to be melting.

It takes three blows from the axe to sever the rope. Birchill drops, staggering when he hits the floor. Fortunately, his momentum takes him away from the flames. I grab his arm and pull him across the room. We hurry to the back of the barn, ducking as rogue flames roll along the underside of the roof. In a couple of minutes, the smoke will overwhelm us.

Crouching low, we hurry along the back of the building to William. I feel for a pulse, but I can't find one. "Nothing," I call above the roar of the fire.

Birchill tugs at my sleeve. "Leave him! We can't do anything for him."

I fish Cheung's keys out of my pocket and hand them to Birchill. "There's a key on the ledge above the door. This one should open the door to the outside."

While he heads into the kitchen, I turn William so his back faces the door. With my hands under his arms, I take the strain and drag him across the floor. It seems to take forever, but once inside I slam the door. Immediately, smoke creeps under the door and around the edges. Feeling a draught, I notice the door to the outside is open. Birchill has bolted.

Once more, I slide my hands under William's arms and pull. He seems to have doubled in weight. All around me, smoke is pouring in. Gloss paint swells and blisters. Another explosion shakes the walls. Ceiling plaster tumbles around me.

"Wrap this around your face."

Birchill rushes out from the shower room and throws a wet towel to me. He wraps another around his face and goes to William's feet. We lift him off the ground. Half staggering and half walking, we bundle him out of the door.

"Keep going!" Birchill cries.

Flames burst through the roof, lighting up the trees. Burning debris falls out of the sky as we stagger through the undergrowth. William becomes heavier with each step. Another explosion sends more flames and debris into the sky. With a creak and a groan, the roof collapses, crashing to the ground. A ball of flame shoots through the doorway like a bullet. Birchill and I are already falling as the heat and flames surround us. Then they're gone.

As I catch my breath, I hear a car start and accelerate away. Its headlights cut through the darkness.

"I have to stop her. She's got Gemma."

Birchill fumbles in his pocket for his car keys. "Take the Merc. I'll call the police and stay with William."

I switch my head torch onto full brightness. I know where she's heading.

The flames should be visible for miles, so it won't be long before the fire brigade arrive. I pass Cheung's hovel, my breathing growing ragged as I twist, jump and dodge the tree roots. In the chestnut grove, my tired feet fail to clear a root and I'm tumbling. I don't even have the strength to cry out as

I hit the ground. Pain shoots through my stomach and pelvis as I scramble to my feet.

When I emerge onto the grass path, I see Carolyn's headlights, racing towards the gate. It's going to be close. I dim my head torch to the lowest setting and hope she's too focused on escape to notice me. With burning muscles and ragged breath, I stumble behind a bush a few yards from the gate. I douse the light and wait. The car screeches to a halt. The passenger door opens and Carolyn jumps out, shotgun in one hand, my Maglite in the other, spraying its beam everywhere. She curses as she spots my car.

"Where are the keys?"

"Kent has them." Gemma raises her hands to show she doesn't have any keys. She looks cold and vulnerable without her blouse.

Carolyn rattles the gate and smashes it into the side of my car several times. She knows she can't escape. She stomps up and down, clearly undecided. She puts the Maglite down. Then, without warning, she raises the shotgun and discharges one barrel into the windscreen of my car.

Gemma shrieks and puts her hands in front of her face as Carolyn turns the shotgun on her. "Walk!"

"Where are we going?"

"Adele's parked behind Syd's house. We'll use her car."

They walk towards me, Gemma in front, Carolyn a couple of yards behind with the Maglite. As they draw closer, I know I'll only get one chance.

Gemma passes. With a roar, I rush out.

Everything slows. Carolyn drops the Maglite. She raises the shotgun as I charge at her. I crash into her. The second shot discharges as she thuds to the ground. I land on top, knocking the wind out of her.

I'm on my feet in seconds, getting my bearings. I hear the butt of the shotgun before it whacks me on the back of my neck and head. I stagger forward, barely aware of the pain, determined to stay on my feet. Somehow, I dodge the second swing of the gun, grabbing the butt as it whistles past. I wrench the gun from her and toss it into the bushes. As Carolyn rises, fingers curled into claws, I punch her in the face.

She crumples like a rag doll.

Aware that Gemma's on the ground, I call her name. She doesn't move. It's only when I bend down beside her that I notice the blood.

SUNDAY

CHAPTER TWENTY-EIGHT

I thought I'd be safe at the back of the café, hiding behind the *Sunday Times*. The sudden death of the Rt. Honourable William Fisher, MP, was shoe-horned onto Page Two before the printers rolled. In the days to come, the coverage will increase, especially when journalists link his death to the arrest of Carolyn Montague. Whether his indiscretions die with him remains to be seen.

Thomas Hardy Logan, looking more like a vagrant than an editor in a faded tweed jacket and corduroy trousers, hopes to impress the daily newspapers with his local knowledge. He slides into the chair next to me and places a skinny latte on the table to replace the cold one I'm nursing.

"A little bird told me you were in the thick of it," he says, pulling a fountain pen from inside his jacket. He studies my face for a moment and tuts. "You look like shit, Kent."

"And you want a scoop."

"I'm always willing to plumb the depths of misfortune, you know that. And yours promises to be deeper than most." He removes his trilby and places it on the table. "How did you acquire the black eye and bruised cheek? Birchill only picked up cuts and bruises."

"He's an expert at dodging the knockout blow. You know that, Tommy."

"Another little bird told me you spent four hours in the interrogation suite. Birchill was in and out within an hour."

"He has an expensive lawyer," I say, refusing to be drawn.

"Who offered to represent you, I hear." He leans forward and smiles. "Now, that's interesting, wouldn't you say?"

While he knows most of the events, he's fishing for the details he can't get from his sources in the police. "You know I'll speculate if you don't tell me," he says. "Then there's Adele Havelock. I'm sure she'll pool resources with me."

"Are you aware she slept through the evening's events?"

"After she found a body in a freezer," he says, tapping the side of his generous nose. "Now that's what I call a cold case."

A clamour by the entrance distracts us. With the help of hospital security, Birchill eludes several reporters and enters the café. He's dressed in a black shirt and trousers, minus the ornate cowboy belt buckle and his knuckleduster of gold rings.

"The plot thickens," Tommy says, rising. "Well, if it isn't Downland's most infamous entrepreneur. Taking a rest from wealth generation, are we?"

Birchill's cold stare could freeze the surface of a lake, but Tommy just laughs. "If it was me in that burning building, I'd have left you in there. So, why didn't you, Kent?"

Birchill lifts the trilby off the table and pats it onto Tommy's head. "Push off and peddle your perjury somewhere else."

"I never had you down as alliterate," Tommy says, rising. He looks at each of us in turn and taps the tip of his nose. "I can smell intrigue, so I'll keep sniffing."

I wonder whether Birchill will tell the world he's my father before someone guesses or finds out. I'll dispute the claim, of course. I should demand a DNA test to prove he's not my father, but what if it reveals the opposite?

Without a test, there's always doubt. And hope.

Once Tommy has left, Birchill sits. He unzips a leather pouch with a gold monogram and extracts a legal document, which he slides across the table. "The deeds to your land," he says.

"I already have a copy."

A slight smile twitches the corner of his mouth. "You don't think I'd acquire the Downland estate and leave out a small, strategic part, do you?"

I shouldn't be surprised after everything I've discovered these past three days, but I am. "Are you going to evict me?"

He fiddles with the zipper on the pouch, in no hurry to answer. When he looks up, his eyes seem apprehensive, nervous even. "I'm going to develop my holiday village in the woodland," he says. "I want you to be part of it."

"I'll be there, fighting it all the way."

"Even if it's a sustainable, carbon neutral village packed full of the latest green technology? From design to construction to occupation, it will be revolutionary."

"A rotating holiday village?"

"Grow up, Kent. If you're going to run the project, I'll expect a little more professionalism."

"What about my sanctuary?"

"It looks homemade," he replies. "We need a visitor centre with a coffee shop, toilets, and activities to inspire children and adults alike. Once we've achieved that, we need to improve the adoption and rehoming programmes. Then I'd like to link it to the holiday village in some way."

While it sounds promising, he's only doing this because he wants to be my father.

"What if I'd rather be an environmental health officer?" I ask.

He considers this for a moment and then shrugs. "I'm not expecting us to become father and son, but you need to accept you're not a Fisher. You never were, Kent. The land you occupy was never yours."

He rises and buttons his jacket. "I want you to be free to do what makes you happy."

"If I'm so free, why did you lock me in the study?"

"What father wouldn't try to stop his son getting killed?"

He looks down and I'm sure his cheeks redden, though it's difficult to tell with his tan.

"And thank you for saving my life," he says quickly. "Now let me save yours."

He leaves me with a pouch full of possibilities and a conflict I can't possibly resolve.

A few minutes later, my trainers are squeaking on the polished floor as I make my way to the stairwell at the back of the hospital. Once upstairs, I follow the signs for the surgical wards. At the nurses' station, I ask for directions and they point me to a private room at the end of the ward.

"She already has a visitor," the nurse says. "A charming young man."

When I reach the room, I straighten my shirt and run my hand over my hair. It won't make any difference to my appearance, but it gives me another few seconds to calm my nerves. I was never like this on a date. Then again, I'd never told a woman I was hopelessly in love with her.

Why did I say that?

I'm still caught in indecision when the door opens. A man in a tailored navy blue suit, white shirt and silk tie steps out.

He's my height and much younger than me, with a strong jaw, impossibly white teeth, and puppy eyes, partially obscured by a mop of brown hair. This is the son William Fisher always wanted—smart, privately educated and perfect for dinner parties.

"I'm Richard," the man says. "Gemma's fiancé."

His voice is cultured, his handshake firm. "You must be Kent Fisher. I'm delighted to meet you. I can't thank you enough for saving Gemma's life."

"How is she?"

He glances back through the open door, as if she might be listening. "Sore and bruised. And tired. She barely reacted when I showed her the engagement ring I bought this morning. I don't suppose she'll be her old self for some weeks."

She'll never be her old self after what she went through.

"I came this close to losing her," he says, his thumb and forefinger a inch apart. "That's when I knew how much I loved her. That's why I can't thank you enough for saving her, Mr. Fisher. You must come to the wedding—as our guest of honour, naturally."

At this moment, I can't think of anything I'd like to do less.

"Congratulations," I say through a dry mouth and throat. Inside, it feels like I've had the hope sucked out of me. "I'm sure you'll be very happy together."

He shakes my hand once more, almost wrenching my arm from my shoulder. "Why don't you talk to her? I'm sure she'd love to see you."

Somehow, I doubt it. If I hadn't charged out from the bushes, she wouldn't be lying in hospital. The surgeons might have removed the shot, but they can do little for the pain in her eyes. Pale and exhausted, she's propped up by pillows. She slides the engagement ring up and down her finger.

No matter how I feel, I can't come between them. Richard doesn't need to be scared witless to tell her he loves her. He has prospects, not a sanctuary that devours money. He's everything I'm not—kind, charming and reliable.

Hearing the click of heels, I look up. Rebecca from Tombstone Adventure Park is heading towards me. She looks amazing in a tight blue dress that reveals almost all of her slim, athletic legs. Without the heavy makeup, mascara and hair extensions, she looks more natural and so much prettier.

"What brings you here?" I ask.

"I've come for my phone." She studies my bruised face for a moment and then brushes her fingers over my cheek. "That's an impressive swelling. I think it might need attention."

The smile rises from my groin to my mouth. "Well, I am in a hospital."

"Oh, I think it needs personal attention," she says. "Don't you?"

THE END

About the Author

Robert Crouch

Rob Crouch lives and works in East Sussex, England, in the shadow of the beautiful South Downs. During his career as an environmental health officer, he's focused on improving hygiene standards in food businesses. This has led to him editing and writing for a respected food hygiene manual for caterers. He has also specialised in workplace health and safety in the leisure and service sectors, investigating several fatal work accidents.

But secretly, he's always wanted to solve a murder.

It started when he watched TV's Lieutenant Columbo unpick perfect murders with an affable but dogged pursuit of incongruous details. A healthy diet of crime fiction and drama followed, including Sherlock Holmes, Inspector Morse, and Miss Marple. When he became an avid fan of Sue Grafton's Kinsey Millhone, he realised he wanted to create a different kind of private detective to solve his murders.

Set beneath the rolling hills of the South Downs, *No Accident* is Rob's first novel featuring Kent Fisher, an environmental health officer with more baggage than an airport carousel. Within minutes of arriving at the scene of a fatal work accident, he uncovers details that don't quite make sense. Like his hero, Columbo, Kent digs deeper and deeper, disregarding procedure, until work and his personal life collide with devastating consequences.

http://robertcrouch.co.uk

If You Enjoyed This Book
Please write a review.
This is important to the author and helps to get the
word out to others
Visit

PENMORE PRESS
www.penmorepress.com

All Penmore Press books are available directly through our website, amazon.com, Barnes and Noble and Nook, Sony Reader, Apple iTunes, Kobo books and via leading bookshops across the United States, Canada, the UK, Australia and Europe.

ÆGIR'S CURSE

BY
LEAH DEVLIN

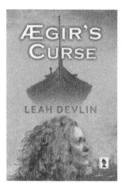

A thousand years ago, the Viking colony of Vinland was ravaged by a swift-moving plague ... a curse inflicted by the sea god Ægir. The last surviving Norseman set the encampment and his longboat ablaze to ensure that the disease would die with him and his brethren.

In present-day Norway, a distinguished professor is found murdered, his priceless map of Vinland missing. The ensuing investigation leads to the reclusive world of Lindsey Nolan, a scientist and recovering alcoholic who has been sober for five years. Lindsey reluctantly agrees to help the detective who's hunting the murderer, but she has a bigger problem on her hands: a mysterious disease that's spreading like wildfire through the population of Woods Hole. As she races against a rising body count to discover the source of the plague, disturbing events threaten her hard-won sobriety—and her life. Will Lindsey be the next victim of Ægir's curse?

Leah Devlin is rapidly establishing herself as a writer of modern day mystery-thrillers. This story is as tight as a piano wire. Life at a seaside town in New England is full of treacherous undercurrents and peril, as residents are threatened by a menace from a thousand years ago. Murder, romance and deceit are a potent mix in this gripping novel, which I didn't want to put down.—James Boschert, author of the Talon Series and *Force 12 in German Bight*

PENMORE PRESS
www.penmorepress.com

Force 12 in German Bight

by
James Boschert

Considering that oil and gas have been flowing from under the North Sea for the best part of half a century, it is perhaps surprising that more writers have not taken the uncompromising conditions that are experienced in this area – which extends from the north of Scotland to the coasts of Norway and Germany – for the setting of a novel. James Boschert's latest redresses the balance.

The book takes its title from the name of an area regularly referred to in the legendary BBC Shipping Forecast, one which experiences some of the worst weather conditions around the British Isles. It is a fast-paced story which smacks of authenticity in every line. A world of hard men, hard liquor, hard drugs and cold-blooded murder. The reality of the setting and the characters, ex-military men from both sides of the Atlantic, crooked wheeler-dealers, and Danish detectives, male and female, are all in on the action.

This is not story telling akin to a latter day Bulldog Drummond, nor a James Bond, but simply a snortingly good yarn which will jangle the nerve ends, fill your nose with the smell of salt and diesel oil, your ears with the deafening sound of machinery aboard a monster pipe-dredging ship and, above all, make you remember never to underestimate the power of the sea.

–Roger Paine, former Commander, Royal Navy .

PENMORE PRESS
www.penmorepress.com

Penmore Press

Challenging, Intriguing, Adventurous, Historical and Imaginative

www.penmorepress.com

Lightning Source UK Ltd.
Milton Keynes UK
UKOW06f2040140916

283015UK00020B/416/P